Across the
Blood-Red Skies

Across the Blood-Red Skies

Robert Radcliffe

Little, Brown

LITTLE, BROWN

First published in Great Britain in 2010 by Little, Brown

Copyright © 2010 Standing Bear Ltd

The moral right of the author has been asserted.

'If You Were the Only Girl in the World' Words by Clifford Grey/Music by Nat Ayer – © 1916
Remick Music Corp. and Chappell & Co. Inc – Redwood Music Ltd (Carlin) London NW1 8BD for
the Commonwealth of Nations, Germany, Austria, Switzerland, South Africa and Spain in respect of
the 50% interest in the Estate of Clifford Grey. All rights reserved – used by permission.

A CIP catalogue record for this book
is available from the British Library.

ISBN 978-1-4087-0185-0

Typeset in Perpetua by M Rules
Printed and bound in Great Britain by
Clays Ltd, St Ives plc

Papers used by Little, Brown are natural, renewable and
recyclable products sourced from well-managed forests and certified in
accordance with the rules of the Forest Stewardship Council.

 Mixed Sources
Product group from well-managed
forests and other controlled sources
www.fsc.org Cert no. SGS-COC-004081
FSC © 1996 Forest Stewardship Council

Little, Brown
An imprint of
Little, Brown Book Group
100 Victoria Embankment
London EC4Y 0DY

An Hachette UK Company
www.hachette.co.uk

www.littlebrown.co.uk

Author's Note

There was a 13 and a 166 Squadron operating in the First World War. They have no connection with the 13 and 166 Squadrons in this story.

Introduction

A History of Air Combat in World War One
by George M. Duckwell

Nobody had a clue what to do with aeroplanes at the outbreak of the First World War. The age of powered flight was only a decade old and aeroplanes were regarded as a daft idea with no imaginable function. Then, early in the conflict, a British army captain pottering about in an Avro saw German troops encircling the British near Loos. Hurriedly he reported the sighting to High Command who immediately ordered a withdrawal, thus saving a hundred thousand British lives. Suddenly aeroplanes had a use – spotting – and for much of the next year that's what they did. Quite often German and British pilots found themselves spotting the same patch of turf, whereupon they waved, doffed their caps and shouted, 'No no, dear fellow, after you.' Then someone (history doesn't relate who) thought it might be fun to toss out a rope to tangle the other chap's propeller, thus forcing him to land. Appalled by this ungentlemanly behaviour, the next day somebody threw a brick, the day after that a grenade, then a blunderbuss appeared, then pistols and shotguns, and suddenly it was open season. The first fixed armament on an aeroplane consisted of a sawn-off Lee Enfield rifle screwed to the upper wing of a biplane. To fire it the pilot had to stand up, load it, sit down, point the aeroplane at his target and tug on a piece of string. But a firing rate of one bullet every five minutes proved inefficient and it wasn't long before machine-guns were being borrowed from chums in the trenches. Machine-guns were marvellous but had one drawback: they shot your propeller to pieces when you fired them forward. The British solution to this was to spruce up all their old pusher aeroplanes which had engines in the back, and hand the machine-gun to an observer who sat in front blasting away to his heart's content. The German solution meanwhile was to devise a mechanism that allowed a machine-gun to fire through a propeller without damaging it. This proved a thorny problem and for a while our solution seemed superior. But then Fokker came up with a working synchronising system, we eventually followed suit, and the era of modern aerial combat was upon us. The End.

Prologue

I seem possessed by threes. Three people, three events, three score years, and so on. It's three in the morning. Normally I sleep soundly, but this is the third successive night insomnia has dragged me from bed to desk. Upon its scuffed leather surface sits a tumbler containing three fingers of Scotch, and the three pieces of paper responsible for my restiveness. I've been avoiding them like the flu since they flopped on to my mat three days ago. But I can't go on ignoring them; their triumviral presence compels attention. So, buttressed by whisky, I'm studying them now.

The first is from Her Majesty's Inland Revenue and is a particularly ill-timed tax demand for, you guessed it, £3000. The second is a letter from my publisher reminding me that my oft-promised manuscript *Blue Yonder − Memoirs of a Great War Pilot* is now about three decades overdue. The third, a clipping from the obituaries page of the *New York Times*, is both the root cause of my dilemma (tri-lemma?) and also, ironically, its solution. In theory its simple message, that Senator Daniel Frith has died at the age of eighty-four, cancels out the other two, freeing me to start the memoir which will easily earn an advance sufficient to cover the tax demand. Thus killing the three birds with one stone, so to speak.

But it's not quite as simple as that. I first seriously attempted this book around the time of the abdication in 1936, then again in 1953 in honour of the Queen's coronation. Both attempts covered the facts well enough, but omitted important details and thus lacked honesty. Now Frith's dead any such barrier to objectivity is removed; yet although his passing allows me to start writing, it also lifts the lid on a witch's cauldron of memories I've spent half a century trying to forget. That's the first problem. The second is that to tell the story of my war is to tell the story of three people's war, for the one is inextricably bound up with the other. That complicates matters. The third problem is that for the narrative to make any sense I must begin, perversely, in the middle. On Saturday 21 April 1917, to be exact. A day that started badly, quickly deteriorated, and, despite a providential denouement, was without doubt the worst of my life.

Third time lucky, then.

Chapter 1

Saturday 21 April 1917 began before dawn with the persistent shaking of my shoulder by Corporal Larkin's bony hand.

'Sir? Lieutenant Duckwell, sir. You've got to get up, you're on dawn patrol.'

'No, I'm not. I'm on holiday. Go away.'

'No, sir, you're flying. Don't you remember? Briefing's in ten minutes.'

'Larkin, if you don't leave me alone I will have to shoot you.'

'Sir, for God's sake, Major Strickley's waiting, you must get up.'

It went on like that, Larkin shaking and nagging, me cursing and groaning. Eventually I struggled to awareness. Larkin was right, I was not tucked up in a warm bunk on a luxury ship bound for England, as I had dreamed, I was sprawled on a hard cot in a freezing hut in France. This was the first shock. The second was that I had absolutely no explanation for this. Having devoted the previous evening to an alcohol-fuelled celebration of historic proportions my memory was largely blank. Yet a twinge of unease nagged, like a half-forgotten toothache. Clearly something had gone awry with the plan which, as far as I could recall, merely required me to get drunk, catch a lorry to Calais, and be home in Blighty by morning.

Larkin was still shaking, me still cursing. Resentfully my eyes swam open. The hut, in darkness save for the glow of an oil lamp, was damp and cold, and stank of drink and sick and cigarettes. Or maybe that was me. The Arras morning hate was underway, a pre-dawn artillery barrage that had gone on for weeks. Even though it was ten miles away, my bedside table still wobbled with each hefty crump. As did the egg upon it. The hard-boiled egg that said it all. The egg the cooks boiled the night before for those on dawn patrol, so you didn't have to fly on an empty stomach and they didn't have to get up to cook you breakfast. You got breakfast when you got back. If you got back. So if you woke to an egg wobbling at your bedside, that was it, dawn patrol and no question.

Suddenly my head was spinning. Larkin dragged me upright, dutifully holding an enamel bowl while I vomited into it. 'That's the spirit, sir,' he encouraged. 'Soon feel better.'

'Oh God,' I groaned, in accordance with custom. 'Oh Lord, oh Christ.' Cursing into the enamel bowl was another staple of the dawn patrol routine. Morning prayers, the orderlies called it. 'Lieutenant so-and-so'll be along in a minute, sir,' they'd say. 'He's just finishing morning prayers.' That or yodelling practice.

A shadowy figure stirred on another cot. 'Are you going up?' it enquired meekly. The cot used to belong to Rogers, before that Hartfield, before that someone else. But Rogers, Hartfield and the others were all gone, and this new man arrived only yesterday and would doubtless be gone tomorrow, so I didn't know him and didn't want to.

'No I'm bloody well not. I'm on leave. This is just some stupid cock-up.'

Five minutes later, yodelling duly practised, I presented myself before Major Strickley.

'Ah, Duckwell, there you are.' He frowned. 'Why aren't you in flying togs?'

This was rich. His wispy hair was uncombed, his face creased from sleep, and pyjamas poked from beneath his uniform trousers. In other words the moment he'd dispatched his gallant charges to certain death, he was going straight back to bed. Still dazed, groggy and nauseous – still drunk, truth be known – I stood my ground. 'Sir, I'm not supposed to be flying.' I produced a crumpled chit. 'I'm on leave, you see. As of yesterday midnight. Here's my authoris—'

'Yes, yes, George, we know all that. But you missed your transport, remember? Got sozzled and couldn't be found, so the tender went without you. It had to, three other chaps were waiting.'

Now I remembered. Drunken voices baying my name in the moonlight like hounds after a hare. 'Duckwell! Hey, Ducky, where've you got to, you silly ass!' It was a joke, I'd thought, a game. So I'd hidden in one of the barns, giggling like a schoolgirl. Then must have passed out.

'Sir,' I tried again, pausing while his window rattled to a

salvo. 'Sir, that may be so, but I'm still technically on leave. I shouldn't have to fly today and, well, I can simply catch the Calais tender tonight, can't I?'

Strickley's frown softened. 'Of course you can, George old thing. But after you missed the bus last night I asked if you'd help C-Flight with this morning's patrol. In fact I asked you to lead it. Don't you remember?'

'No, sir, I don't. Not for a moment.'

'Well, we talked about it, and you agreed. Readily. So it's all arranged.'

Impossible. Not in a million years. And me leading? It was absurd. Overwhelmed by the injustice of it all, my composure quickly crumbled. 'But, sir,' I pleaded, 'it's not fair. I mean, why me?'

He began steering me for the door, a paternal arm at my shoulder. 'Because, George dear boy, this is exactly the sort of selfless devotion to duty I've come to expect from you. And a typically brave and generous way to finish your spell here with 13 Squadron. Rest assured it won't go unmentioned.'

Now I knew he was lying, but with a final friendly shove I was back out in the moonlight.

Numb with disbelief, wretched and tearful, I don't mind admitting, I returned to the hut to dress. There was nothing else I could do. Short of outright refusal, of desertion in effect, I was stuck with it. Strickley, under colossal pressure to mount observation flights and desperately short of pilots to fly them, had seized a God-given opportunity of my own stupid making. Or he lied and tricked me. I'll never know which but it makes no difference: in short, my drunken idiocy had got him out of a hole.

Ten minutes later, bundled up in my quilted Sidcot suit, I was plodding miserably across the frosty grass towards the waiting aeroplanes. An icy wind sighed through the fir trees beyond the perimeter, overhead stars still shone through a ragged overcast, while flashes to the east lit the coming dawn with pink. This is it, I remember thinking, without drama. This is the day I die. I was eighteen years old.

The Royal Aircraft Factory FE2 reconnaissance two-seater was an absurdly outdated aeroplane even by the standards of 1917. Indeed it was one of those ridiculous-looking contraptions that seem old-fashioned even before they leave the drawing-board, like the penny-farthing bicycle. First designed in 1911, barely eight years after the Wright brothers first flew, its appearance owed much to their formative fumblings. A biplane of course, with two fabric-covered wings lashed together with struts and wires, its engine and propeller were mounted behind the pilot, thus pushing the aeroplane along rather than pulling it as in modern aircraft. A sort of rounded open coffer not unlike an oversized baby's pram was stuck on in front to house the pilot and observer. Not so much a cockpit as a coracle, this wood and fabric nacelle was our only cover and protection, and as such completely useless. It did afford a pleasant all-round view though, which together with stable flying characteristics and a leisurely turn of speed is why the FE2 was favoured for observation duties. Like most of the aircraft we flew it had nicknames. 'Dawdling Deathtrap' springs to mind; 'Gothic Horror' was another I recall. The Germans, who loved the FE2 for its stately progress and lumbering inagility, called it the *Kiste prähistorische* or 'Prehistoric

Packing Case'. We in 13 Squadron knew it as the 'Balsa Bathtub'.

Like spindly giant moths, four Bathtubs were lined up outside the canvas marquee serving as our hangar, a gaggle of mechanics in attendance. Cajoling FE2 engines to life in winter was no trivial matter in the days before anti-freeze. You either had to completely drain them at the end of each day then refill them with hot water the next, or you had to house the aeroplanes in heated hangars – an improbable luxury for a lowly observation squadron. Some enterprising mechanics swaddled their engines in blankets and hot-water bottles like arthritic old men; one I knew even tried lighting a little fire beneath his, with predictably heart-warming results. A Bathtub going up in smoke was always a cheery sight. Except when someone was in it.

Nearby the flight crews were also trying to keep warm, seven figures bundled in sheepskins and leathers standing wordlessly around a brazier. I knew not one of them, at least if I did I can't recall a single face or name now. Except one. Raymond Gates, my observer, whom I'd never set eyes on before that frosty dawn, but who would haunt me the rest of my life. The others were just six of the scores of faceless unknowns who processed through our squadron that spring like lonely ghosts. As I neared they visibly stiffened, appalled perhaps at the pasty-faced youth appointed to lead them, or maybe just realising any chance of escape was now gone.

A few words of encouragement seemed called for. 'Well, I suppose we'd better do a group take-off, then form up in finger-four. Don't get too close, and watch your height.' It was all I could think of. 'Any questions?'

'Is there any high cover?' someone asked unhappily.

I gestured towards the end of the field. '166 Squadron will be patrolling at fifteen thousand, so I'm told.' I thought of Mac. My guardian angel. Would he be among them? 'But it's ground-fire you've got to watch. Keep your eyes peeled and don't fly straight or level for more than a few seconds.' I checked my watch. 'Come on, let's get it over with.'

Pep talk over, we made for the aeroplanes. By now the engines were all running, busy making the contented clickety-click noise characteristic of idling Bathtubs. Drawing near our machine I noticed the white leader's pennant fluttering from a wing strut. That shook me. Finally it was dawning I was actually in charge. And more importantly why. At eighteen years old and with just four months' service with the squadron I was the most senior left in my flight. The others were all dead. A familiar quaking started in my knees, nausea rising once more. Four aeroplanes, eight men, me leading – how on earth could this have happened?

In an effort at control I turned to Raymond and started gabbling questions. He was an infantry sergeant from Epping, I quickly learned. He'd never flown operationally before, had only made two practice sorties using a dummy camera, and had transferred to the Flying Corps because he 'fancied a change from the trenches'. Bloody idiot. He also mentioned he was thirty-four and married with one son.

Two mechanics helped us board, their expressions neutral, their eyes studiously avoiding ours as they fiddled with straps and switches. In the old days mechanics used to crack jokes, whistle cheerily and clap us on the back for luck. But they grew tired of sending off young men never to see them again, and soon gave up on the jollity. I preferred it that way: there's nothing worse than being humoured to your death.

A few minutes more and we were ready. Raymond sat in front checking the Lewis gun and sorting plates for his camera, while behind him I tested the flying controls and revved the motor to a hearty roar, listening head-cocked to its indignant labourings. This didn't impress the mechanics clinging to the shuddering wingtips, but I knew it was time well spent. Bathtub engines were notoriously untrustworthy, as I had learned to my cost, so wise pilots quickly attuned their hearing to any sounds of protest amid the chorus of rattles and clanks. An oiled plug, bent rod or sticking valve and we were home free, mission cancelled. But not today, for though I strained to listen, the engine bellowed lustily on, so with no further ado I waved away the mechanics, turned the machine into wind and off we all trundled.

Several bone-shaking bounces later the four Bathtubs attained the breathtaking speed of forty-six miles per hour and rose majestically into the cold morning air. But not for long. We'd only just cleared the perimeter when I detected erratic movement to my right. One of my charges was already in trouble. Peering across, I watched helplessly as it dipped a wing, flopped on to its back and corkscrewed into the ground, there to explode in a ball of orange flame. Too slow on the climb, it had simply stalled and spun in – a basic error of an inexperienced pilot. Thus barely a minute into our mission we had lost a quarter of our force and two men were dead. Not the ideal start, but there you go. Adjusting my goggles, I squirmed lower in my seat and set course for the eastern horizon.

*

By the winter of 1916 the Great War, as it later became known, had settled into the Great Bore, at least as far as the Western Front was concerned. Both sides were well established along opposing lines of trenches stretching from the Belgian coast in the north to the Swiss border in the south. Apart from the odd wiggle, these trench systems, which were often highly complex and sophisticated, hadn't moved in months, and in effect a stalemate had set in. But generals hate stalemates so a French one called Nivelle came up with a Grand Plan. His gallant French troops would mount a massive offensive in the Champagne region to the south, punch through the enemy lines, rout the German army and end the war in forty-eight hours. Seriously, that's what he said, forty-eight hours, although he did concede it might cost a few lives. Only ten thousand though, he estimated. So far so good then, but for his plan to work Nivelle needed a distraction up north, so it was agreed that before his offensive began British troops would launch a diversionary attack in the Arras area, the idea being the Germans would panic and send reinforcements up from the south, thus weakening their defences so Nivelle's mob could charge through and do their stuff.

It didn't work though. Poor communications, contradictory orders and leaky French security meant the Germans knew all about Nivelle's masterplan in plenty of time to thwart it by withdrawing to defensive positions along the so-called Hindenburg Line. Astonishingly this didn't deter Nivelle who insisted everyone press on regardless, so despite serious misgivings the British had no choice but to continue preparations for their Arras offensive, set for April 1917. Softening up began on the 4th with an artillery barrage of truly monstrous proportions. Two and a half million shells were fired into the German positions in one week – that's a million more than the Battle of the Somme and in half the time. Then on the snowy morning of 9 April the main attack began with the British and Australians advancing to the east and south of Arras while the Canadians assaulted the now legendary lump of high ground to the north called Vimy Ridge.

Our job, the observer squadrons of the Royal Flying Corps that is, was to photograph the battle area. All day and every day, from first light to last, shit or bust and never mind the cost. Looking back now it's easy to be facetious, but the fact is, trying to monitor the progress of a battle raging along a twenty-five-mile front in 1917 was phenomenally difficult. These were the days long before backpack radios and walkie-talkies, remember, and field telephones are of limited use to an army on the charge, so apart from runners bearing hastily scrawled messages on scraps of paper the only way the generals could find out what was going on was by direct observation. This meant a constant supply of up-to-the-minute aerial photographs, and if pilots and observers had to be sacrificed in droves to obtain them, so be it.

This interlude would later go down in the annals of RFC history as 'Bloody April'. At the time we simply knew it as a bloody nightmare. Statistics abound regarding the life expectancy of RFC pilots during the Great War; the reality depended on where you were and during what phase of the conflict. But I'm telling you that around Arras that April an observation pilot's life was measured in hours. Eighteen hours to be precise, for that was the average clocked up in their log-books before they died. And about twelve of those were flown in training back in England, so the actual operational hours they were expected to survive was six. Barely worth unpacking for.

The point is, the German generals also knew how vitally important these blasted photos were, so exhorted their troops to stop us at all costs. There were even extra rations doled out for every Tommy airman they killed. And they killed them wholesale. Aerial photography involved dawdling along in our Balsa Bathtubs, nice and straight, while an observer leaned over the side fumbling photographic plates in and out of his camera. Slow, easy targets, every anti-aircraft gun, artillery piece, machine-gun, rifle, pistol and spud-gun the Germans could muster was blasted at us. If that wasn't enough German scout pilots, patrolling high above in their Fokkers and Albatroses, fell upon us like hungry falcons at every opportunity. Surviving a photo-reconnaissance mission that spring without injury or damage to the aircraft was practically unheard of. By the middle of April, surviving one at all was a miracle. That's why I may appear unfeeling about the death of two men I didn't know. So many had come and gone I'd grown inured to it by then. I'd also learned that pondering these things is futile when all you can think about is getting through the next half hour. Their problems were over, in other words, whereas mine were just beginning.

13 Squadron's patch was the Canadian-held area around Vimy itself, less than fifteen minutes' flying time from our airfield at Noyelette. With daylight breaking and a wintry breeze at our backs, we were soon crossing their previously held positions and heading into no-man's land. Below lay a wasteland

dreamscape straight out of Dante. Lifeless, scarred, desecrated, scorched – countless adjectives have been penned to describe Great War battlegrounds, but to appreciate the true scale of such devastation you have to see it from the air. Not a house, not a tree, not an animal, not a vestige of green, just mile after mile of churned-up brown earth stained with grey snow, punctuated with water-filled craters and littered with the detritus of war: abandoned field guns, burned-out tanks, more than a few aeroplane wrecks, and the forsaken corpses of men and horses. Aptly named (for no man would want it), millions would nevertheless die for it. Such is the madness of conflict.

We pressed on, and were soon detecting movement ahead: drifting smoke, grey figures scurrying for cover, the flash of gun muzzles, galloping horses pulling artillery. *Where have the lines settled?* This was the question the generals always wanted answered, in other words who currently occupies what piece of ground and where. With Vimy Ridge itself looming ahead it was time to find out. Waving the other two Bathtubs into echelon left, I leaned forward, tapped Raymond on the shoulder and gestured downward. Get snapping, Sergeant, that meant, and let's make it quick. He turned and nodded, his face a sickly grimace. At the same instant Archie opened up and hell broke loose with a vengeance.

Archie was what we called German anti-aircraft fire. Exploding dirty brown clouds of red-hot shrapnel that tore through men and machines like buckshot through paper. A near miss and a wing was in tatters, a direct hit and all that remained was a smudge in the sky and little pieces of gently falling wreckage. Apart from running away, the only technique for avoiding it was to try to fool the gunners' aims by throwing the aeroplane about the sky like a lunatic. But you can't do that and take photographs, so I had evolved the Duckwell Slew. This involved flying with controls crossed, rudder one way, control stick the other, then reversing every few seconds so the old Bathtub was never actually travelling quite in the direction it was pointing. Pretty it wasn't, but I'm still here, aren't I?

Slewing furiously, we commenced our first photo run, traversing north above the Ridge. Ugly brown Archie clouds filled the sky all around us now, buffeting the aeroplane like a toy. Then a machine-gun found range and before my eyes a neat row of holes stitched its way across one wing before snapping a strut like a toothpick. Hunched as low as I could, I checked on the other two Bathtubs just in time to see the entire tail section break away from one in an Archie burst. Almost in slow motion the doomed aeroplane nosed over and began the long dive for the ground, affording its two occupants plenty of time to contemplate their oncoming demise. Parachutes, though they existed then, were not allowed, incredibly, because they might encourage us to jump unnecessarily and thus be 'bad for morale'. Such was the logic of RFC top brass. Anyway, two down, two remaining, there was nothing I could do except hang on and thank God it wasn't us.

I kept slewing, Raymond kept snapping, somehow we made it to the finish of the first run. But to complete the mission we had to come back again, like the bloody Light Brigade. Signalling the remaining Bathtub, I began the turn. Ten minutes more, I swore to myself, in just ten minutes the job was done and my days as an observer pilot were over for ever. But it might as well have been ten years. By now the Germans had us accurately ranged and were ready, and within seconds of starting the return run we flew into a barrage of such furious intensity as I've never encountered before or since. One second relative calm, the next total insanity, as though on a signal the sky about us had erupted into an exploding hell of bullets and shrapnel, smoke and fire. The air seemed to boil. I could see nothing, do nothing except cling on as the Bathtub bucked and reared in my hands like a dying horse. And the noise, mind-numbing, deafening; even above the howling engine I could hear the crash of exploding Archie, the menacing buzz and whine of flying metal, the splintering of wood and the frenzied flapping of shredded fabric. The assault on the senses was total, beyond processing. Soon events were slowing and contracting into single sounds and images, like in a slide show.

Something tugged at my sleeve. I looked down and saw a bullet-hole appear, missing my elbow by an inch. As I stared another punched a smoking rent in the cuff of my glove. Then a shower of wood-splinters hit my face and a larger piece of wing-strut broke off and went crashing back through the propeller, snapping a blade and setting up a shudder so violent the aeroplane felt as if it would shake apart. Then came a bang and flash to my left. I turned and there was the last Bathtub, enveloped in flames, fuel tank exploded. Fire trailed from it like a comet, then its pilot stood up, engulfed, flailing his arms like a puppet while his observer looked on in horror. I turned away, lost in shock, a tune on my lips suddenly: 'If you were the only girl in the world, and I was the only boy . . .'

My mouth was bone dry, I recall, with a strong metallic

taste; I smelled doped fabric, cordite and hot engine oil. Then I heard something new and the trance broke in an instant. A fractional lessening of the barrage, followed a moment later by the stutter of machine-guns behind. Strings of phosphorous tracer bullets flew by, more woodwork splintered, control wires snapped with a twang. Raymond, still astonishingly hunched over his camera, jerked upright suddenly, turned to me with an expression of surprise, and sagged forward. Then a crimson shadow flashed by ten feet above us, ominous black crosses on each wing. A German Albatros, fast, agile, lethal, had arrived to administer the *coup de grâce*. So much for 166 Squadron and high cover. No escape now, this was the finish.

Ridiculously, as though further terror was futile, I felt calmer, rational even. Though I couldn't see it, I knew the Albatros was already circling round for a final pass. Meanwhile our Bathtub was in its death-throes – controls shot, wings in shreds, engine tearing from its mountings. I had no means of defending myself and no chance of escape; all I had was four months' experience, the Colt pistol Mac had given me, and a card-player's instinct for bluff. So I stopped slewing, put the nose down, throttled the motor back and waited. Seconds later the Albatros made its attack, dropping swiftly down from above and behind like a hawk on to a mouse. Waiting until its guns began chattering once more, I counted to three then dragged back on the stick for all I was worth. As hoped, the slow-moving Bathtub reared into its path like a doomed elephant, forcing the startled pilot to break violently away to avoid collision. The Albatros shot by rolling hard to the right, I loosed off three shots into its belly with the Colt, stuffed the controls fully forward and dived flat out for the ground, slewing for all I was worth.

It worked. At least, it allowed us to reach ground level before he could get back on our tail and shoot us to ribbons. But ground level was as far as we were going, for the old Bathtub was finished. As I hauled gingerly back on its ruined controls, the nose rose reluctantly to the horizon, hesitated, then gave up and sagged earthward. I didn't care, enough was enough. A peaceful pause, with the wind singing softly through the rigging, then came a succession of splintering, bone-jarring, mud-flying crunches, and we ploughed unceremoniously in.

Crash-landing a Bathtub is not like crash-landing a Spitfire, or even a Meteor (survived both, thank you). No, events unfold rather more sedately in those old string-bags, as though you and a scrap-load of packing cases, fruit boxes, deckchairs, telephone wire, bicycle parts and an old lawn mower have fallen off the back of a lorry into a muddy field. You have to take care to avoid the hard bits, especially the engine, which has a tendency to hurtle forward and squash you to pulp, but handled correctly a Bathtub prang is rarely fatal. I should know, for this was my fourth.

I came to my senses sprawled on my back, dazed, winded, but otherwise uninjured. All was blissfully quiet. Not silent, for gunfire still echoed round the plain, but none seemingly in our immediate vicinity. Staring up in wonderment at the grey morning sky, I lay there savouring the sudden stillness and rejoicing in my survival. For precisely ten seconds. Then with a whoosh the Albatros thundered overhead, wings rocking. From my supine position I clearly glimpsed the pilot's face, even his expression, which together with the vigorous shaking of his fist suggested one very angry Hun. This seemed unfair. My rearing elephant stunt hadn't seriously endangered him, nor had taking pot-shots at him with my pistol. They were simply a ruse to throw him off while we dived for the ground. But judging from the determined way he was now banking round for attack, he didn't appreciate being thrown off by a British Bathtub, and having seen the aircraft duly destroyed was now out for its crew.

Galvanised suddenly into motion I scrambled to my knees, casting frantically about for cover. But there was none: we were trapped in no-man's land without so much as a stunted bush to hide behind. In theory, by putting the higher ground to our backs and running for it, we might reach Canadian-held lines and safety. But I knew the Albatros would be upon us before we'd gone twenty yards. Always assuming there was a 'we', that is.

'Gates!' I yelled above the rising engine noise. No answer. I couldn't see him, didn't even know if he was alive. Pieces of Bathtub littered the ground like jetsam on a beach, ten yards away lay a bigger heap of crumpled wings and smashed nacelle. 'Gates, can you hear me?' But then Albatros guns started rattling, and mud was spurting up everywhere, and me standing there shouting for Raymond was no longer sensible. Searching frantically, I spotted a shell-crater beyond the wreckage and set off. Twenty feet wide, half-filled with freezing water and lousy cover from overhead attack, I nevertheless made the shell-hole in seconds and dived gratefully in, rolling myself into a hunched ball just as the Albatros rocketed by, inches from my head.

Then, to my amazement, a second aeroplane rocketed by. A khaki-coloured one this time, with British roundels on its wings. An SE5 to be precise, the RFC's nimble new scout and the envy of every pilot in the Corps. I stared, breath held, scarcely believing my eyes, then spotted the 166 Squadron markings and knew we were saved. Bugles blaring and late as usual, the cavalry had finally arrived. Or put another way, Lieutenant William 'Mac' MacBride, formerly of the 2nd Battalion 1st Canadian Infantry, now of 166 Squadron the Royal Flying Corps, had come, yet again, to my rescue.

I'd like to report that I sat cheering in my shell-hole as Mac valiantly duelled with the Albatros before shooting the bastard down at my feet. But it didn't happen like that. Basically they vanished, the Albatros dodging and weaving, Mac in hot pursuit, until in seconds they were lost from sight. Peace descended once again. I waited a safe interval, nothing happened, so I rose from my shell-hole, brushed myself down and went in search of Raymond.

I found him amid the main wreckage, imprisoned within a tangled mass of struts and wires beneath what was left of the upper wing. Injured, bleeding, but alive.

'Gates. It's me, Lieutenant Duckwell. Can you hear me?'

A pained groan came in response.

I began pulling debris away. 'Gates, speak to me, man. Where are you hurt?'

'Ah . . . I, it's my leg, sir, mainly. Think I stopped a bullet in the thigh.'

'Well you're a lucky chap then, that's a ticket home and no question. Can you move it?'

'I . . . I don't know. Can't feel it. Can't feel anything much.'

22

A sizeable puddle of blood had formed beneath what was left of his seat. His eyes lolled, his face was deathly pale, I suspected he had other injuries. Time was short, fuel trickled from the Bathtub's ruptured tank, the whole area reeked of petrol and red-hot engine, and we were sitting targets an unknown distance from safety. I pulled harder at the wreckage. 'Gates, we've got to get you out. Can you help?'

'Do my best, sir.' He pushed feebly. We worked on in silence, gradually creating a gap in the mess. 'Did the other lads make it, do you think, sir?' he puffed after a while.

'No, Gates, unfortunately I don't. Just us. Now come along, shove against that piece there, that's it.'

Just then something thudded into the woodwork by my knee; a moment later came the crack of a rifle-shot, distant, maybe half a mile, but a shot, and aimed at us without a doubt. It was the final straw. After everything we had endured and impossible though it seemed, we were under attack again. Quite apart from the obvious danger, this was the worst possible news, for if stranded in no-man's land there is but one question of consequence: whose lines am I nearest, theirs or ours? Now I had my answer. In case of any doubt, a second shot hummed by inches from my ear.

Raymond heard it too. 'That's a Mauser,' he declared, ever the infantryman. 'There'll be plenty more where that came from in a jiffy, sir. You should scarper.'

'And leave you here? I don't think so, Sergeant.'

When a third shot whizzed overhead I began tearing at the wreckage with something approaching frenzy, for the need to free him now was extreme. German riflemen, mindful of their orders to kill British aircrew, and of the extra sausage

23

they'd earn doing it, were now squirming along communications trenches, slits and saps, working their way forward into no-man's land, as close as they could, preparatory to picking us off like two pigeons on a perch. If we were lucky we had a couple of minutes.

But luck was in short supply that day. Without warning a machine-gun opened up, much closer and from a different angle, firing short staccato bursts that kicked up mud, tore chunks off the wreckage and bounced off the engine with a ping.

Immediately, and with surprising force, Raymond punched me in the chest. 'Go! That shell-hole! Now!'

So I went. I'm not proud of it, and many, many times over the years I've wondered if given a few seconds more I might not have dragged him free and into the shell-hole with me. But I'll never know because I didn't try, I did precisely as he ordered, partly because he ordered it with such passion and, well, authority, partly because standing there in the open was clearly not going to help either of us, but mostly, let's be honest, because I was scared witless. He in effect gave me permission to run away, and I ran away. So there you have it.

In seconds I was back in the shell-hole I'd just vacated. Silence descended, both the rifle and machine-gun fire having stopped, at least for the moment. Spread-eagled in the mud I waited, listening to my own hoarse breaths and the furious banging of my heart. Still nothing happened, so after a minute or two I raised my head. Ten yards away, exactly as I had left him, sat Raymond, or the visible parts of him, mostly his head and legs, amid the Bathtub's remains.

24

'Gates!' I lifted my head higher, to be met instantly by clods of flying dirt from a machine-gun burst.

'Keep your fucking head down!'

'Right.'

'Sir, that is.'

'Never mind that, Gates. Listen, can you move?'

'Ah, I shouldn't think so. That machine-gunner's directly behind me. Maybe five hundred yards. I've got the engine between me and him, so as long as I stay put he can't hit me. He can see you right enough, though.'

'So I gather.' I eased myself down the crater another inch. 'But you can't stay there. What about that rifle fire?'

I swear the bastard chuckled. 'Been wondering about that myself, sir. Thought maybe if I lay here doggo, you know, play dead like, then they'd lose interest and bugger off out of it.'

'Yes. Right. Good idea.' But I strongly doubted it, not before they'd made sure. And anyway, for how long? Until nightfall? It was still barely seven in the morning, the man was bleeding and had other injuries, he needed medical help. Soon. Not in nine or ten hours.

Silence fell again while we digested this. Then, quietly: 'You still got that little pistol of yours, sir?'

'Pistol? Oh, yes, yes I have. And look, just call me George, all right?'

'George. Right-oh. Got an uncle called George. And I'm Raymond. Keep it handy, then, George, will you?'

'Keep what handy?'

'The pistol. You never know, eh?'

'What? Oh, yes, well all right.'

But an icy chill ran through me then, and not just from the

water seeping through my Sidcot suit. Suddenly I felt exhausted, and wretched, and thirsty, and appallingly hung-over as the dreadful reality of our predicament sank in. And with him stuck out there in the open, me cowering in a hole brandishing a pop-gun, and the whole German army closing in, I admit I also felt resentful. What did he want from me, this man I didn't know? Make a stand? Take them all on? I'd done that already, and survived, and earned my ticket home, and now all I wanted was to divest myself of my Sidcot, scramble from that hole and run for it while there was still a chance. But I couldn't. Because I couldn't leave him.

Although if I'd known what was coming, I definitely would have.

It started about fifteen minutes later. With much to dwell on but little to say, conversation had lapsed somewhat. I lay on my back watching rain clouds assemble, feeling colder by the minute and bemoaning my luck. In the distance echoed more sustained gunfire as battle was joined around Vimy. Every so often a series of loud tearing noises passed high overhead as artillery rounds were fired from our lines into theirs. Apart from that and the rumble of distant Howitzers, all in our immediate neighbourhood was eerily quiet.

Then Raymond's voice drifted over once more: 'Why do you carry it?'

'What's that you say, Raymond?'

'The pistol. I mean it's totally useless against Hun aeroplanes. Anyway you've got the Lewis for that, a proper machine-gun and that. So why on earth carry that little pea-shooter?'

Because some of us older hands just did, that's why.

Because too many times we had watched men burn to death in aeroplanes, and without doubt it's the worst thing imaginable. And because if our aeroplane burst into flames and we had to choose whether to sit there and fry, jump out and plummet, or draw our service-pistols and end it quickly, we knew which we'd prefer. We didn't make a thing of it. Newer pilots thought we carried them because we were madcap Wild West cowboys of the air, nor did we correct them. But sooner or later, assuming they lived long enough, they quietly cottoned on and started carrying their service-pistols with them too.

'Oh, I don't know, Raymond. Silly superstition perhaps. Mine was given me by a friend. It's American, you know.'

'Sort of lucky mascot, then. Like a rabbit's foot.'

'That's the idea. What about you? Do you carry anything?'

'Snapshot of the missus. Few of her letters. Nothing as fancy as—'

A rifle-shot rang out, close, just two or three hundred yards. At the same instant came a sickening thud and a scream of agony from Raymond. 'Jesus fuck!'

'Raymond, what happened? Are you hit?'

'Yes, Jesus! Fucker shot me in the fucking knee. Christ!'

'Stay there, I'm coming.'

Rolling on to my front, I crawled up the lip and stole a look. Raymond was still there exactly as before, but his face was contorted in agony and I could see a bloody gash in one leg. Then, as I stared, his ankle exploded in a mass of flesh and bone as a second bullet struck him. Again he cried out. Instinctively I made to rise, only to be stopped in my tracks by a hail of machine-gun fire. All I could do was dive back into

27

the hole cursing. A momentary lull, a distant shout of German abuse, then another rifle-shot rang out. Again Raymond screamed, again I tried to rise, only to be warned off once more by the machine-gun.

Then I got it. This was the reason for the delay. The fifteen minutes' silence. To set up this cosy little scenario. The riflemen had manoeuvred into position, approaching as close as they dared without exposing themselves to the British lines, then waited while the machine-gunner set up a cross-fire. Now they could enjoy their amusement at leisure, sniping at Raymond's legs, killing him by agonised degrees, while the machine-gun kept me pinned helplessly in my hole. They didn't want to kill me. Not yet anyway. They wanted me to watch.

A fourth bullet thumped home, and Raymond sobbed pitiably. Unable to help, unable even to move, I could do nothing but lie there and listen to his anguish. A fifth bullet struck him, a sixth. I clapped my hands over my ears. Stop, I found myself pleading, for God's sake please stop this madness.

Then, mercifully, they did. A silence gaped suddenly, breathless and expectant. Seconds ticked by; the hiatus grew, and stretched into a lull. Then, as I knew and dreaded it would, Raymond's voice, gasping, weak, but clear, called out to me: 'George . . .'

'No!' By now I was curled in the bottom of the hole, arms clamped over my head. I heard him all right, I understood him, I knew what he wanted. But I couldn't do it.

'George, for pity's sake!'

'No!'

'You must.'

'I can't.'

'For the love of God!'

'No, I can't. I . . . You see, I need to—'

'You don't need fuck! Just do it. Before they start again.'

And as if on cue they started again, two more shots spaced a few seconds apart, as though taking turns. Raymond's cries now were tortured shrieks, animal, sickening beyond description. But what sickened me more was what came next. Drifting on the wind, faint but unmistakable, the sound of laughter. And it was this laughter that finally got through to me.

Raymond, appallingly, was still conscious.

'George,' he groaned. 'Please . . .'

'All right . . . It's . . . Yes, all right, I'm coming.' And before I properly realised it I had fumbled the Colt from my Sidcot and was crawling back up the crater.

He was waiting for me, relief showing in his eyes despite the pain. He nodded, trying to smile, and murmuring encouragement. I raised the Colt and took aim, but my hands were shaking so badly I could barely hold the thing, let alone fire it. Raymond saw this too, and kept smiling and murmuring, trying to calm me. 'Don't miss us,' he seemed to be saying, although by now he was beyond coherent speech. Then yet another shot rang out, ripping flesh and bone from the bloody stump of his leg. Reflexively I too fired, but wasn't ready and missed, hitting wood six inches above his head. Raymond didn't flinch, just kept looking at me and nodding like a bird and mouthing, 'Don't miss us.' And suddenly our gazes met properly and everything became still and calm and clear, the feel of the Colt in my hand steadied me, I took aim again, squeezed the trigger and fired between his eyes. His head jerked back, then sagged slowly forward, one eye still on mine, the other closed, like a wink, and the ghost of a smile on his lips.

Time passed. Hours evidently, I saw from the muddy dial of my watch, although as a concept time had lost all meaning. For a long while I just sat numbly in the bottom of the hole, staring at the Colt and waiting for them to come and get me. But they didn't come, the morning wore on, and I just grew colder and more tired and strangely detached and lethargic. At some point I even folded over and slept, deeply, despite the clamour of battle off to the east. Even a fresh artillery barrage in the afternoon barely penetrated my consciousness. None of it had anything to do with me, I felt. Shock, I suppose it was, shock and exhaustion.

Finally, late in the afternoon, the cold, an excruciating thirst, and a nightmare about Raymond's voice calling my name dragged me to my senses. Sitting slowly upright, I took stock. Snow had fallen, draping the crater with grey; my boots were frozen and mud-caked, the Sidcot soaked through. Cupping a hand, I drank from the filthy water, splashing more on to my face to wake up.

'George.'

I froze, hand midway to mouth. This wasn't possible. Yet nor was it a dream, Raymond really *was* calling me. But how? I'd killed him myself, killed him dead and watched him die. I waited, the hair literally prickling with fear on my neck. Then, to my horror, it came again.

'George, can you hear me?'

The sound was faint, quite far off, and from a different direction. And something about the cadence . . . it was familiar, but different.

'Raymond?' I ventured fearfully.

'For Pete's sake, George, are you there?'

Mac! Impossibly yet unmistakably it was Mac's voice. Splashing across the crater, I scrambled up the opposite lip. 'Mac, is that you?'

'Yes! Am I glad to hear you. Are you OK, are you hurt?'

'No . . . No, I'm not hurt.' I scanned the surrounding area. 'But where are you?'

'Stay down, George, and don't move. I'm in a FOP about a hundred yards back.'

A forward observation post, a tiny listening hole far out in no-man's land.

'Christ. How on earth did you find me?'

'Marked your crash-site, flew back to Noyelette, grabbed a tender and drove. What about your observer? Is he with you?'

'No, he, I had to . . . He was killed.'

'Too bad. Listen, George, we're going to get you out of there, but you have to hold on until dark. Can you do that?'

'Yes, yes, all right. But you're not leaving are you?'

'No, George, I'm not leaving. I'm staying right here. I promise.'

And he stayed, as promised, talking and cajoling, calling out in the silences, bullying me into staying awake, until finally that hateful day's meagre light began to fade at last. At dusk, exhausted and frozen to the bone, I lapsed into stupor, unaware that Mac too had stopped talking. Another half hour crawled by. I became convinced I was floating above my crater, looking down on myself from on high. Then, suddenly, came the sound of heavy running footsteps. I awoke with a start, and three soldiers jumped into the hole beside me. One of them was Mac.

'Say, there you are. Ready to go?'

Speechless with emotion, I could only nod. Strong hands immediately reached under my arms, propelling me up and out of the crater.

'Right. Let's go. Everyone stay close.'

'Wait!'

'Jesus, stop, George, what are you doing?'

'It's Raymond.' I turned for the shadowy remains of the Bathtub. 'I've got to . . . Just wait a moment.'

I stumbled back to the wreck. He was still there, waiting in his seat, his hair dusted with snow, his face white and waxy in the pale light. Fumbling beneath his leathers I reached for the breast pocket of his tunic. *Don't miss us*, he'd been saying, nodding and murmuring, at the end. Shoot straight, in other words, I'd assumed. But I was wrong. It wasn't *don't miss us*, but simply *the missus*, and he'd been nodding at his breast pocket, not me. Quickly my fingers closed on paper, I pulled out the letters and photograph, tugged an identity tag from his neck and hurried from that place for ever.

The next few hours passed in a blur. Safely back in the FOP, a brandy bottle was pressed to my lips, repeatedly, until the shock was numbed, sensation returned, the quaking stopped in my knees, and we were ready to set off rearward. The FOP, a tiny dead-end of a pit, led back to a narrow communications passage which in turn eventually joined a larger fire trench. Twisting and turning, fatigued beyond caring and anaesthetised by the brandy, I soon lost all track, so concentrated on keeping my eyes on Mac's back and putting one mud-caked boot in front of the other. Miles passed, it seemed, and gradually the trenches grew larger, better appointed and more populous. Figures swam by clad in khaki, someone shook my hand, another clapped me on the back, the smell of tobacco-smoke assaulted my nostrils, ribald cursing and Canadian laughter filled my ears. Soon dim lighting began to appear, solid walls, covered roofs, then after what felt an age we mounted stone steps to emerge into a large cleared area of tents and huts. More figures hurried to and fro, many of them officers. Orders were barked, salutes exchanged, papers checked, then with final handshakes and more back-clapping our escorts took their leave and we were alone.

'What now?' I asked Mac in a daze.

'We take the train.'

And so we did. A tiny diesel narrow-gauge with open wagons for relaying troops and ammunition between rear positions and the trenches.

'How on earth did you get to me?' I asked him as we boarded. 'I mean, the clearances and the escort, and finding the route to the right FOP and everything.'

'I may not be one of them,' he replied cryptically, 'but these are still my people.'

The train lurched, then clanked into motion.

'Did you get him?' I asked. 'The Hun that shot us down.'

'Sorry. He was too good, he got away.'

'I saw his face. It was him, wasn't it. Richthofen.'

'I believe so, George. He sure flew like him.'

The little train rocked gently through the night. As the front lines fell behind, so too did the war and its awful desecration. Shadowy crop-fields began to appear, then the first trees, snow-covered firs and dark statuesque poplars; soon lights could be seen in the windows of passing farmhouses; I heard barking dogs and the hoot of an owl. Punch-drunk and drowsy, I felt no strong need to converse, content just to watch the monochrome nightscape unroll before me like an old film. Mac too appeared in reflective mood, as though revisiting the area had stirred up waters better left stilled.

Shoulder to shoulder we rocked along in contemplative silence until twenty minutes later we pulled up at a large depot area with more tents, wooden warehouses and fenced compounds of stores and equipment. Parked to one side stood an assortment of vehicles, an RFC tender among them.

'Say, where do you think you're going with that?' a quartermaster sergeant called out as we approached it.

'Calais,' Mac replied warily. 'This is our vehicle. Why?'

'Well, I need ident—' The sergeant broke off. 'Dan? Dan Burton, is that you?'

'I'm sorry?'

'It's me, Jack Collingwood. D-Company, Sixteen Battalion. Colonel Peck's old outfit. You are Daniel Burton aren't you?'

'No, Sergeant.' I stepped between them. 'He isn't. I think perhaps you have the wrong man.'

'You sure?' The sergeant peered suspiciously.

'Quite sure. You are speaking to officers of the Royal Flying Corps.'

'What? Oh, well, right, yes, sir, sorry, I see that now. My mistake.'

'That's quite all right. Easily made, easily corrected.'

We climbed into the cab, startling a dozing RFC corporal who jumped down to swing the starting-handle.

'Thanks,' Mac breathed.

'Don't mention it. We're going to Calais?'

'Unless you'd rather go back to Noyelette.' His dark eyes looked anxious, yet still gleamed like polished jet.

'Not much. But I don't have so much as a toothbrush with me.'

'Buy a new one when you get to London. I'll lend you the money.'

'You don't have to do all this, Mac. You don't owe me anything.'

'I promised.' He sighed. 'I promised to make sure you caught the tender last night, and failed because my watch doesn't work, I lost track and fell asleep. So today you had to fly an extra patrol and damn near got killed.' His North American tones were slow and measured as always, as though speaking was something he did with care. 'The least I could do is come find you and send you on your way. You still have your leave chit, don't you?'

'Of course. But how will you manage, Mac? I mean, how will you manage the other things?'

'I'll figure it out somehow.'

'That was a close one with that sergeant.'

'Somebody I once knew.'

'Are you sure you're all right? It doesn't feel right, leaving you here.'

'I'll be fine. Anyway there's another reason you should go now. All pilot leave has been cancelled. As of today, until this Arras push is over. Seems they ran out of replacements. So you go back to Noyelette to collect your toothbrush, and Strickley will never let you go.'

'In that case I'll manage without.'

'Good idea.'

'But I want you to keep this.' I unstrapped my watch.

'George, what are you doing, I can't take that.'

'Yes you can. I want you to look after it for me. It'll help you keep track of things.'

'It's too much.' He fingered the watch. 'All right, but I'm giving it back next time we meet.'

'Be sure that you do.'

We set off Calais-wards, lurching and bumping along rutted tracks lit by the beams of the tender's shielded lamps. Soon the tracks improved to proper roads and the motion eased to a soporific rocking. Physically exhausted and emotionally spent, I parked my head on Mac's shoulder and slept the forty-mile journey to the port.

An hour or so later we were pulling up on a crowded quay beside the rust-streaked flanks of a battered troopship. Blearily I took stock. Drizzle fell past hissing floodlights, bathing the area in a damp sheen, smoke from hundreds of cigarettes hung in a hazy pall; above its tang I smelled fuel oil, exhaust fumes and the pungent stench of the docks. Sounds echoed off wet cobblestones, a resonant clamour of revving engines, banging tools, shouted orders, singing squaddies and squawking loudspeakers. People milled about like hens in a pen: dock workers in overalls, civilian labourers, hawkers, hangers-on and servicemen by the hundred, some now in navy blue as well as khaki, and many of them injured. Lines of walking-wounded toiled slowly up gangplanks, the more seriously injured were carried aboard on stretchers. Several had limbs missing, a few cried out in agony, one or two were clearly dead. Among the hundreds of men, that noblest of commodities in war, servicewomen, though not many: a few Red Cross volunteers dispensing tea from a van, some white-clad nurses attending the wounded, two smartly dressed Wrens in a staff car, and a mixed bag of assorted VADs, FANYs and WAACs.

And that's when I saw Emily. Mac and I had climbed down from the tender and were standing about stretching limbs and wondering where to report for my boarding pass when my eye was caught, I make no apology, by a particularly pretty FANY standing beside a Crossley ambulance. Initially it was her slender bearing, delicate features and the way curls peeked cheekily from beneath her cap that captured my attention, but then as I stared, I realised with a lurch that I knew her.

'Jesus. That's Emily Parker.'

'Who? George? Wait! Where are you going?'

I was pushing through the throng in a daze, stupefied, incredulous. After everything that insane day had brought, now this. Emily Parker, in the flesh, beyond all reason or explanation. And as I neared she turned, and saw me, and I knew then I wasn't dreaming, for her expression also went from curious to incredulous, and her hands went to her mouth, and mine were spread in disbelief, and all the commotion and hubbub started spinning about us like a roundabout at the fair, and then we were standing before each other, gawping.

'George?'

'Emily?'

'Is it really you?'

'Yes, it's me. I'm a pilot in the RFC. What on earth are you doing here?'

'I work here. I joined the FANY. Six months ago. I'm an ambulance driver.'

'Six months? But you never wrote. I mean, not that . . . It's just . . . I didn't know.'

'You never wrote either, George. We weren't exactly writing.'

Her voice was different, I realised. The Shropshire burr was gone, now she sounded like a duchess. And looked like one, despite the FANY uniform, daft cap and scruffy belted mackintosh. Her poise, her demeanour, her features . . . she looked, well, so mature, so demure, so assuredly feminine.

'No, well, yes, that's quite true, but . . . My word, Emily, it really is smashing to see you. Wonderful, actually.'

'You too, George.' She laughed. 'I think.'

But her glance was slipping past me, and polite coughs came from behind.

'What? Oh, yes, sorry, Emily, this is my friend and colleague Mac – ah, Lieutenant William MacBride, that is. And Mac, this is my, well, friend, Miss Emily Parker.'

And that's how Mac met Emily.

Chapter 2

The Arras push of spring 1917 achieved practically nothing. True, some ground was gained, but little of importance, and the much-touted mass German withdrawal never materialised. Yet the price was astronomical, casualties on both sides amounting to some three hundred thousand. The only gain of significance was Vimy Ridge itself, hard won by the Canadians at a cost of ten thousand dead and injured. But even securing Vimy and its coalfields ultimately made little difference, and soon both sides were digging in and the situation reverting to stalemate. General Nivelle's drive in the south was a total failure. No useful territorial gains were made, the Germans held their ground, and far from hastening an end to the war the offensive succeeded only in killing and injuring a hundred and ninety thousand French troops, and provoking mutiny among the rest, one division famously arriving for battle blind-drunk and weaponless. Nivelle himself, who spent much of the build-up blabbing about his plan to all and sundry, including journalists, was swiftly removed as chief of the French army and posted to Africa to contemplate his hauteur.

Good riddance. I went home to Greenwich on leave.

High on the banks of the River Severn in the heart of rural Shropshire stands Shrewsbury School, one of England's oldest and most respected public schools for boys. Set in a hundred and fifty acres of manicured grounds, the school prides itself on an enlightened and progressive approach to the curriculum, particularly in the teaching of science and the classics. It is also justifiably proud of its close ties with the town of Shrewsbury, with its many fine pubs, bookies and knocking shops. Many famous men attended Shrewsbury School including Charles Darwin, the writer Samuel Butler, and Judge Jeffreys, he of Bloody Assizes fame. Up until October 1916 one George M. Duckwell was also a pupil – indeed he should still have been in the spring of 1917, diligently swotting up on Horace and Chaucer in preparation for his finals. But he wasn't, he was blundering about the skies over France in a Balsa Bathtub. How had this peculiar turn of events come about? Well, it had something to do with a local garage-owner's daughter called Emily Parker.

Incredible though it seems now, I was still seventeen at the time. Emily was twenty. I was in my final year at Shrewsbury, not diligently swotting up on Horace but relishing the sunshine of an unusually balmy autumn and reaping the long-awaited privileges of the sixth form: a study of my own, hot water in my bath, and the right to smoke a pipe, grow a moustache and wear a fancy waistcoat. Best of all, I was at liberty to walk down into town, there to pick a winner at the bookies, browse the second-hand bookshops, or simply sup on decent food and drink, notwithstanding my meagre allowance and the privations of war.

The war. The war which was by then already two years old and fast establishing itself as an immovable blot on the landscape of the British psyche. The war without precedent in the manner of its conduct, the profligacy of its management, and the sheer industrial scale of its slaughter. The war which had already witnessed the carnage of Gallipoli, Mons, Jutland, Verdun, Ypres and a million casualties at the Somme. The war destined to go down as mankind's most infamous, remembered not for glory and honour but waste and folly. The war I wanted nothing to do with.

Why? Denial, mainly. I was a wily rascal of seventeen, out to embrace life while still I had the time. Yes, I knew about the war, and knew I'd probably participate one day, but unlike my fellow sixth formers I couldn't see the hurry. We had just endured four years of fagging and beatings and freezing baths and the worst food imaginable, now finally we had a few months' freedom and opportunity yet they wanted only to rush to the trenches and get shot. It made no sense. Why, I asked them, puffing on my pipe in bafflement, why are you so desperate to join this war? Are you sure it's a worthwhile war, a just war, even a well-managed war? But they only wagged their heads in pity and went back to their newspapers. Their one qualm, it seemed, was the war might end before they could join it. My qualm was that I might get killed – a concept I understood well enough, but was not ready to confront. As I say, I was in denial.

This non-conformism, together with an obsessive need to challenge everyone at cards, snooker, liar-dice, and anything else one can gamble with, marked me out as a crank. Consequently I passed much time on my own. I wasn't lonely, but did learn self-reliance. And a few like-minded stalwarts remained to make school endurable, profitable even, when the cards fell right. One or two, Bertie Wilkins for example, I counted as friends. Even if he did go on about the war.

'But Ducks old thing,' he would argue, sipping beer, 'far better surely to volunteer now rather than wait to be called up. That way you can write your own ticket, you know, choose your regiment and so on. Otherwise you might end up in the clerical corps, typing reports in Mesopotamia or something ghastly.'

'If you say so, Bertie.'

'Although you're jolly lucky, what with your pater being a colonel in the Fusiliers. You'll probably get straight in on the nod.'

'Probably.' My father was a retired colonel as it happened, and I was indeed expected to join his regiment.

'That's why I'm signing up for the Navy.'

'The Navy? But Bertie, that's madness. I mean, didn't you hear about the Battle of Jutland? The one where we lost fourteen ships and six thousand men?'

'Really? I thought we won the Battle of Jutland.'

'That's just the point. We did!'

A typical exchange of the day, and significant only in that it exemplifies my contrary views. That and for two other reasons. Firstly, it was on one of those beery evenings, at a pub called the Rose and Crown on Swan Hill, that Bertie, who was always dreaming up madcap ideas, first mentioned the Royal Flying Corps. Secondly, it was on the same evening in the same pub that I first beheld Emily.

I knew about girls, or so I thought, for after dreaming up money-making schemes and playing cards, girls were my favourite preoccupation. They came in two varieties, I had learned: town-girls and sisters-of-boys-at-school. Town-girls were delightful rosy-cheeked creatures who spoke with country accents and worked at Woolworth's or on veg stalls at the market. They were giggly and saucy and in exchange for a cider or two would happily kiss and cuddle. Sisters-of-boys-at-school were altogether different. More complicated, harder to understand and far less fun, they were also strangely insubstantial, like wraiths, which made them difficult to get to grips with, both literally and figuratively. Town-girls, I soon concluded, were far better.

Bertie and I were sitting in the saloon bar of the Rose and Crown one September evening when Emily entered with two other women. This in itself was mildly unusual, for in those days respectable young ladies rarely ventured into pubs, and never the public bar, which was why we were in the snug. Bertie, having wisely abandoned plans to enlist in the Navy, was waxing lyrical about his latest scheme to run away and join the RFC. 'It's a doddle, George. Look, they sent me the forms. Apparently they don't check your age, the pay's better, you get to wear that spiffing RFC uniform which the popsies all swoon over, and best of all they teach you to fly aeroplanes!'

'Flying's strictly for the birds, Bertie, everyone knows that. Anyway, why join now? Why not wait until next summer when we graduate? With luck the war'll be over by then.'

Bertie picked at his beer-mat. 'Because I'm not going to graduate, George, as you jolly well know, I'm going to fail the exams. So I won't get into the Guards and pater will be livid and send me to some ghastly crammer in Watford, and my life will be ruined for ever. That's why I have to do something now.'

'It can't be as bad as that, Bertie, we've loads of time before the exams. Anyway, better surely a crammer in Watford than a trench in France, no? I say, who's that wonderful-looking girl in the hat, do you suppose?'

Emily, dark hair tucked up beneath a simple felt cloche, was wearing a long coat above overalls and work-boots. As though she'd covered up in a hurry. She and the second girl were studying pamphlets while the third, an older woman, addressed them in hushed tones.

Bertie glanced round. 'She's from Parkers garage, up the hill. Her family runs it.'

'Really? How do you know?'

'Pater's Tourer broke down at the Salopians cricket match last term. Parkers fixed it in a jiffy.'

No more was said at that juncture, and Bertie lapsed back into lamenting his luck one minute and enthusing about the RFC the next. I nodded and tutted accordingly but was only half listening for my attention was firmly held by Emily who, despite an anxious demeanour, odd garb and oil-stained fingers, was without doubt the most beautiful creature I had ever seen. At one point, unsettled by my staring no doubt, she glanced up, our eyes met, and a nervous smile crossed her lips.

Whereupon I was skewered like a fish on a stick.

Raymond Gates's house was a small terraced affair off Epping High Street, about a mile from the station. Clean-dressed in a new uniform, washed and shaved, I presented myself there five days after my return from Calais. Or rather I paced about on the corner opposite, beset by doubts. Why I needed to make this visit I didn't know; it was ill advised, improperly thought out and likely to fail. But I had no choice. Tormented by the events of that awful day in no-man's land, unable to sleep, or eat, or even think, I was not so much drawn there as driven. Compulsorily. What I was seeking, in my desperation, was release from my nightmares through absolution. By offering comfort, in other words, I hoped also to find it.

The door was opened by a slight, nervous-looking woman of about thirty, with auburn hair heaped in an untidy bun, wearing a house-coat and bedroom slippers. In one hand she clutched a feather duster, in the other a small boy of about four.

'Oh, ah, Mrs Gates? I'm sorry to trouble you. My name is George Duckwell.'

'What is it?' she asked, anxiously scrutinising my uniform. Then she saw the RFC insignia and the colour drained from her face.

'Mrs Gates?' She didn't know. In my stupidity I'd assumed she knew, but she didn't. 'Ah, er, Mrs Gates, perhaps this isn't the best time . . .' But it was too late.

Eyes wide with fear, and with one hand clutching at her

throat as though choking, she let out a strangled sob. 'Oh God, it's Raymond, ain't it!'

'I'm so sorry, Mrs Gates. I take it you haven't heard. From the Ministry, that is.'

'Raymond! Jesus, not my Raymond!' Then she was sinking to her knees, clasping her head in her arms. A single drawn-out wail rose from her, like an approaching siren, while her body, rocking, folded slowly over as though in supplication. 'No, sweet Jesus, please not Raymond.'

I froze. I'd expected sadness and sorrow, but also composure, not this. Beside her the little boy slipped an anxious thumb in his mouth, while out on the street children played football and nosy neighbours craned necks to see. A horse-cart clopped by, birds sang, dogs barked, a tabby cat pushed past my legs, and I just stood there in the April sunshine like a fool, my carefully rehearsed lines undelivered, my agent of absolution sobbing at my feet.

Pity took over and I stooped to her side, raised her gently upright and led her inside. There I sat her, still weeping, by an unlit fireplace in the parlour, gave her my handkerchief and went in search of drink. But there was none, only a bottle of stout which I poured for myself while brewing tea for her. Standing at the sink watching laundry flutter in the yard, I listened as her grief ebbed and flowed like primal song. Small fingers tugged at my tunic. 'Biscuit,' he said, so I ransacked cupboards until I found one. Still she wept, pleading in disbelief as though yet there was hope.

Shakily, I carried in the tea, placed it at her side, rested a clumsy hand on hers. Slowly she grew calmer. A few minutes later we were settled opposite each other, like strangers at a wake, she sniffing into my handkerchief, me staring at her feet. Neither of us spoke, but the settling quiet was a relief.

I sipped beer and took stock. The room was small, the floor bare, the furniture cheap, yet all was clean and tidy and homely. As though in preparation. A flight of plaster ducks ascended one wall, and a clock ticked on the mantelpiece beside a photo of Raymond in uniform. The cat sprang on to my lap, the little boy padded in holding a toy, finally Ann's crying subsided.

'He's a bonny little chap,' I ventured. 'Your Jimmy. How old is he?'

'Four,' she whispered. 'In June. How d'you know his name?'

'Raymond told me.' Not strictly true. I read your letters. Over and over. They're all that's keeping me sane. That's how I know you're Ann, he's Jimmy, and there's another on the way, God help you. Dutifully I produced the envelopes. 'Here. He wanted you to have these.' Handing them over felt like severing a lifeline; predictably it also triggered fresh tears from Ann. So we waited once more, until she was ready.

'When did it happen?' she sighed, at length.

'Last Saturday. In the morning. Quite early.'

She nodded. I waited, breath held this time, for the big one.

'How?'

'Well. We were on a photo-reconnaissance mission, you see. Our job was to fly over the lines and take pictures. But we were attacked, both in the air and from the ground, and the aeroplane was badly damaged. Raymond was hit.'

'What 'appened?'

'We crashed. I was fortunate to be unhurt. But I'm afraid Raymond was mortally wounded. He died soon after.'

'Was you with him?'

47

'Yes, I was close by him throughout.'

She looked at me then, directly, watery eyes searching mine. 'Did 'e, you know . . . Did 'e suffer, at the end?'

'I can honestly say he suffered not at all, at the end. It was over in the twinkling of an eye. Furthermore, Ann . . . it is Ann, isn't it? Furthermore, he was speaking of you as he passed away. I heard him quite clearly.'

By the time I'd walked back to the station, swallowed two brandies at the buffet and taken three trains home to Greenwich, I was late for dinner. Anxious only for the sanctuary of my room, I clicked across the marble hallway as lightly as possible. But the Fusilier's ears were on full alert.

'Is that you, George?' he barked from the dining room. 'Where in God's name have you been? We've been waiting hours!'

They were at the table, cut glass, silver cutlery, starched white napkins, dressed formally as always for dinner, he in black tie and mess jacket, my mother in chiffon and pearls. Instantly, and perhaps for the first time, I was struck by the contrast between their lives – safe, secure, free from anxiety – and the lives of people like Ann Gates, with her bare cupboards, shoeless child and newly dead husband.

'Come and sit down, George.' My mother reached out a hand. 'You look tired.'

Soup, mutton, claret, Stilton. The clink of silver on china and the murmuring of inconsequential small-talk. I went through the motions, mainly for her sake. She was right, I was tired, and edgy, and fretful. So much was happening, so fast. My final mission, Raymond's death, Mac's rescue, meeting Emily again, all in one day and all so starkly fresh in mind.

Eight hours later I was sitting in a drawing room in Greenwich discussing the weather. Today, Ann. Then in two days' time I was due to report to Upavon in Wiltshire, there to be trained to fly scouts, and somehow magically transformed from ham-fisted Bathtub driver into skilled hunter-killer like Mac. It was a posting I'd yearned for, begged for, and ultimately machinated for, but now it was imminent I doubted I had the mettle to see it through, let alone the aptitude. And then what? A return to France, and the war? The prospect made my blood run cold.

'So, young man,' the colonel enquired. 'And where were you today?'

'Visiting someone, father. The widow of a chap in the squadron.'

'Pah!' he scoffed. 'Pointless. We always left that sort of thing to the padre, or the family liaison bods. Otherwise you end up doing more harm than good.'

Glancing up at the framed portrait of my older brother, Hugh, gazing proudly from beneath his uniform cap, I realised that for once my father was right, and hated him all the more for it. Thank you for coming, sir, Ann had said as I took my leave. *Thank you for coming, sir*. An hour earlier she and Jimmy had been two members of a growing family with a hopeful future. I left them widowed and fatherless, adrift in a desolate void.

'Was he a friend?' my mother asked gently.

'No,' I replied. 'Not as such. But he was someone I came to know intimately.'

The great Duckwell debacle of October 1916 was one of Shrewsbury School's darker hours, so dark that for decades no mention of it existed, nor of me, its misunderstood architect. Until the present day, that is, for one of the many peculiarities of the English public school system is that even the most scurrilous rascals eventually become rehabilitated. Take Judge Jeffreys for instance, the meanest, most vengeful and bad-tempered prosecutor in English history, yet I hear the school is considering a rose-garden in his memory. And spare a thought for Charles Darwin, who so detested the place he couldn't wait to leave. Following his rise to fame the school erected a statue of him, so now the poor chap's stuck there in perpetuity. Nor does he look happy about it.

As for this infamous old boy, I never heard a word in thirty years, until one day a book review in *The Times* mentioned I'd been educated there. Within a week a letter of congratulation arrived, together with an invitation to take tea with the current headmaster, which some months later I accepted. Stepping back into his study after all those years was a peculiar sensation, but tea was a success, everyone was charming, and since then I've been bombarded with invitations to dine, lecture, even hand out prizes on speech day. Last month they asked if I'd host a soirée entitled 'Leaving School for the Great War – An Old Boy Remembers'.

But I'm not sure they're ready for that one yet.

What happened was this. I ran a sixth-form book, an entirely innocent piece of fun which slightly infringed the school's no-gambling rule. Every Saturday I'd go from house to house collecting horse-racing bets from boys which I then took down to Ernie Grant's bookmakers in town to place. Everything went swimmingly, boys won and lost, a good time was had by all and no harm done. For a month. Then I got careless. Firstly, unknown to me a few boys ran short and started writing home for subs. *Dear Mater and Pater, Duckwell does betting on the horses which is terrific fun but I've used up all my allowance so please send more.* Next, the school groundsmen learned of my operation and pressed me to take their bets, some of which were hefty. Then, because schoolboys will back a donkey if it has a nice name, I started using their bet-money to back horses I chose. Next, a prefect called Cheeseman threatened to go to the headmaster if I didn't cut him in on profits. Finally, and inevitably, a Saturday came when I didn't take the day's bets down to Ernie. This wasn't as insane as you'd think: the stake-money usually exceeded any winnings so my trips were often needless. But that Saturday half the school backed a nag called Hotspur which strolled home at 33–1 and suddenly I was in the soup. Unperturbed, I stalled everyone at school, took the bet-money down to Ernie's on Monday and placed it all on the 2.30 at Ludlow. And lost. Then I spent the rest of the day attempting to win it back on credit. And lost again. By the close of play I owed twelve guineas to school punters, six to the groundsmen, two to Cheeseman and a whopping twenty to Ernie – a total of forty, which in 1916 was an astronomical sum for an infatuated schoolboy on ten guineas a term.

Yes, infatuated. For if all that wasn't enough, Emily was now much in the frame.

Following that first sighting with Bertie in the Rose and Crown I had resolved to win her heart – no mean feat considering our vastly different lives, the exigencies of school, and my mounting business commitments. Undaunted, I set to work. First step was to engineer a meeting and many hours were spent pacing Swan Hill to this purpose, hours that with hindsight might have been better spent attending to business, or even turning up to lessons. Never mind. Parkers garage, I soon learned, consisted of an open workshop with a yard area in front and house-cum-shop to one side. The family – mother, father, grandfather, little sister – all lived in the house, whereas Emily had a room above the garage itself. She and her father ran the forecourt and mechanical side of the business while her mother and grandfather tended the shop. Emily worked long and hard, and clearly knew her trade, readily rolling up her sleeves to change a wheel, or crawl beneath a van to fix an oil leak. Many people considered such doings disgracefully inappropriate in a girl, but I was both impressed and entranced, gazing in love-struck awe as she leaned over the bonnet of a sports coupé, or swung lustily on a starting-handle. No wonder my commercial interests languished.

Anyway, this was all very well, but as my ardour rose so too did my frustration, for Emily was seldom alone, and if ever she did leave the premises she was invariably accompanied by her mother or sister. I began to despair, and seriously considered abandoning the venture, particularly as other matters were now pressing. Then, on the Thursday before Hotspur Saturday, her father suddenly disappeared into the house leaving a deserted forecourt and Emily alone in the workshop. Throwing caution to the wind, I hurried over.

'Good afternoon. Would this by any chance be the famous Parkers garage?'

Startled, she looked up. 'Beg pardon, sir?'

'Parkers. I hear it's a jolly fine garage around these parts.'

'Yes, sir, this is Parkers. Can I 'elp you?'

The voice was deliciously accented, and at close range she was more ravishing than ever, quite tall and slender, with a delicate round face framed by those dark curls. Her lips were generous, her nose freckled, and her eyes, which were a deep mahogany colour, hinted at both passion and strength. Spellbound, I blundered on.

'Sorry? Oh, yes, well, I'm interested in, what, yes, a motor-car, I should think.'

'We don't sell motor-cars, sir. We mend 'em.'

'You do? Silly me. I say, didn't I see you in the Rose and Crown the other day?'

Instantly the eyes narrowed. 'The Rose . . . No, no, I've never been there.'

'But surely you remember? You were with another girl, and an older woman.'

'No. Must've been someone else. Look, what d'you say you wanted, sir?'

'Nothing.' I shrugged, helplessly. 'Only to talk to you.'

Now she was aghast. 'What did you say?'

'Talk to you, meet with you, be only with you. You see, I'm madly in love!'

'Good 'eavens, sir, you can't be saying things like that, it ain't proper!'

'I can't help it. I'm desperate. What time do you finish tonight?'

'I don't. I 'elp my mum evenings. Listen, you'd best be gone before my dad comes back. He doesn't like me talking to the gentlemen customers.'

'But I must see you. What about Saturday?'

'I work Saturdays. Please, he'll go spare.'

'Sunday?'

'I work up the livery stables in Uffington.'

'I could meet you there! At the stables, that is.'

'No! I mean, if you must, anything, only for 'eaven's sake go!'

And there ended our first assignation, one of only three, and not exactly the love-tryst I'd envisaged, but at least contact had been established.

Flushed with success, I hurried back to school and my creaking business empire. Two days passed, then came Hotspur Saturday which I confidently expected to resolve at Ernie's on Monday. Meanwhile, straight after chapel the following morning I boarded Bertie's borrowed bicycle and pedalled off to Uffington.

After supper on the day I went to see Ann Gates, I excused myself from the table, collected a decanter from the study, and escaped to my room. For a while I sat by the open window, trying to quieten my mind with cool air and warm brandy. Couples strolled, church bells rang, children played on the common – the scene was ordinary and calm, yet time and again my thoughts flew cross-Channel to the skies above Arras and the desperate struggle ongoing there. Recalling its horrors made me shudder, and the notion of a return was impossible to contemplate, yet the sense of kinship I felt for those still there was powerful. As if they were my family. The ground-crews and mechanics I'd got to know over the months, my orderly Len Larkin, Mac of course, whose steady support I missed especially, the countless lost faces of 13 Squadron, even Raymond Gates whom I'd known only hours.

After a while I moved to my desk, took out notepaper and began a long-overdue letter of apology and explanation to Emily. But normally reliable word-play skills deserted me and nothing came but sentimental clichés. Night fell, the room grew chilly, draft after draft ended in a crumpled ball at my feet. In desperation I turned to the book of American poems Mac had given me, speed-leafing through its pages like a bank-clerk. But the platitudes of my pen continued to ring hollow, and even Whitman's words turned to babble, so I gave up, collapsed on the bed and stared at the ceiling.

A while later came the expected knock on the door.

'Hello?' My mother appeared, her face a picture of concern. 'May I come in?'

'Of course. Would you like a brandy?'

'No thank you, dear. I just came to see if you were all right.'

'Fine thanks, mother. Couldn't be better.'

'That's good.'

Cautiously she arranged herself at my side, all rustling silks and wafting lavender, her grey eyes surveying the room as though for the first time. For a while neither of us spoke. The breeze stirred the curtains at my window; far down-river rose the doleful blare of a ship's horn. I waited, for her visits invariably had purpose.

'I noticed you're not wearing your watch,' she began, as eagle-eyed as ever.

Hugh's watch, more accurately, a Breitling, and sorely missed. 'That's right. I'm having it serviced.'

'Ah.' She nodded at the mess on my desk. 'Looks like you've been writing again. One of your stories, is it?'

'No, just a letter. Not much of one at that.'

'It's so nice to have this room occupied again, you know, it is so little used. But these walls do look tired. Shall we have them redecorated for you?'

'As you wish, mother, but please don't go to any bother. In any case it hardly seems worth it.'

'Oh, yes, I'd forgotten, you're leaving again.'

'I'm afraid so. The day after tomorrow.'

'So soon? It's barely been a week. And the house feels so empty without you.' Still her eyes studied the room, her neck erect, hands neatly folded. As though in readiness. 'How long for, this time, do you suppose?'

'That's hard to say, it depends on postings. Could be a few months.'

She nodded again, then said her piece: 'You see, it always feels to me, George, as if you are only passing through. As though the moment you arrive here you can't wait to leave again. Is that true?'

'Good heavens, mother.' I hauled myself upright. 'Of course not, what on earth gives you such an idea?'

A tiny shrug. 'Oh, I don't know. You spend school holidays with friends, you cancel visits home at the last minute, you always have somewhere important to rush off to, and when you are here you stay out all day or lock yourself in your room. It's not a criticism, George, I only hope it isn't because we make you feel unwelcome in any way.'

'Absolutely not. Father and I, well, we have our differences.'

'He loves you, you know. He may never say, but it is true. Yes, he was angry about the business at school, and joining the

56

Flying Corps so suddenly, but that doesn't stop him caring about you. He's desperately concerned for your safety. We both are. We hear such dreadful stories.'

'You shouldn't believe stories, mother. The Corps has been going through a difficult patch, what with equipment problems and crew shortages and so on, but better aircraft are promised any day, together with more experienced pilots, so matters can only improve. As for me, I'm fine, as you can see. In the pink.'

'No. You're not.'

'Really, mother, perhaps a little tired . . .'

She turned to me, grasping my hand tightly in hers. 'You've been gone four months yet I barely recognise you. You look ten years older, you're thin and haggard, you don't eat, you drink too much, you twitch and fidget, and snap at everyone, and you're either wandering the house like a ghost or off on endless walks.'

'It's just fatigue!'

'And you cry out at night. Horribly. Like an animal.'

'Ah.'

'We hear you through the wall.'

'Well, I'm sorry to disturb you. As I say, I'm leaving in a couple of days, so——'

'That's not what I meant.' Her eyes were filling, and round with pleading.

I sensed something heavy, and cold, and long-buried turning over in my stomach. 'What do you mean?'

'I won't lose you, George, I can't. I wouldn't be able to stand it.'

So, the nub.

An awkward silence followed, filled appropriately by the sombre tolling of the church clock. Gently I disentangled my hand from hers and rose to fill my glass, rather unsteadily, from the decanter. Then, because I couldn't think what else to say, I spoke the unspeakable.

'Would you be able to stand it if Hugh hadn't been killed?'

A gasp escaped her lips. 'What did you say?'

'Hugh. He was your favourite. And father's. I've always known. After all, he was the oldest son, the serious one, the studious one. The one who did well at school, whom everyone liked and respected, and who followed father into the regiment.'

'Is that what you think? That this is about Hugh?'

'Isn't it?'

'How can you say such a thing? This is about my love and concern for you!'

And because I desperately wanted to believe it, and because she looked so shocked and forlorn, and because she'd never voiced such feelings before, and because I was just too exhausted to argue, I caved in.

'Mother.' I knelt at her side. 'I'm sorry. Please forgive me.'

A handkerchief quickly appeared. 'It's all right.'

'No, it isn't. You're right about those things. I suppose I did stay away, even before Hugh died. We were so different, he being so much older, and so much more . . . mature, I suppose. I don't know, I felt like an outsider.'

'We made you feel like that?'

'No. It was me, trying to be different. That's why I joined the Flying Corps, partly.'

'I understand.' She sniffed. 'I think.'

'And you're right about those stories, by the way, they're all true. Only worse.'

'I thought so. Your father wouldn't have made them up. But it's all right, George, everything's being fixed, you'll see.'

That stopped me. 'What did you say?'

'Your father. He's sorting it all out.'

'Sorting what out?'

'He knows one of Trenchard's aides. At the Air Ministry. He's arranging to buy you out of the RFC and get you commissioned into the Royal Fusiliers. As a captain on the general staff. It's the best possible news, George, don't you see? You'll be safe.'

Technically speaking, I am not actually expelled from Shrewsbury. I resign.

Hotspur Saturday comes and goes, then Uffington Sunday, a day of calm before the storm and the occasion of the second and most successful rendezvous with Emily. Then Black Monday arrives and by noon I'm banging impatiently on Ernie Grant's door, pockets bulging with schoolboy bet-money. Five hours later I stagger out again, pockets now flapping and forty guineas in hock. Shock sets in and for a while I just wander the streets in a daze.

Sunset finds me in the Rose and Crown drinking porter on tick and desperately reviewing my options, which are few. The boys at school I can stall. Gambling is against the rules, so who can they complain to? Cheeseman can also go hang. But the school groundsmen are not to be messed with, and Ernie has made clear he wants his debt made good within the week, helpfully quipping, 'Get your rich Pop to send it!' But my rich

Pop won't send it. He's army, and old school, and believes if a man gets in trouble he must sort it out himself. Even if the man happens to be his own son. There's mother of course, and many a time have I charmed a pound from her handbag. But forty guineas? I drink some more, racking my brains for alternatives. Loan-sharks. I've heard such creatures exist but have no idea what pools they swim in. A bank, then. Open an account and take out a loan. But secured against what? Anyway it would take weeks. Friends. Bertie has money, and one or two others might help. But how much? Maybe five pounds? What then?

They throw me out of the Rose and Crown at eleven. They say I'm causing an affray which is probably true, but I don't remember. All I do remember is cold night air hitting my face like a damp towel, and the gibbous glow of the moon above. More street-wandering ensues, accompanied by much angry shouting and wolverine howls. The next thing I know I'm standing in bushes beside Parkers garage, propping a ladder to Emily's window. Somehow I make it up without falling, and to her infinite credit she doesn't scream as I unlatch her window and tumble inside. What she does do is crack me over the head with the tyre-iron she keeps handy for such eventualities. When I come to, I'm sitting on a bare floor holding a bloody rag to my brow while she dabs at my skull.

'Never 'eard of such a thing,' she mutters. 'Daft idiot, I could've killed you.'

'Emily?' I croak. A sparsely furnished room emerges. A bed, a chest of drawers, a chair, a bedside table with candle. 'Emily, is it you?'

'Ah, so 'e's alive, more's the pity. And what d'you 'ave to say for yourself?'

'I'm sorry. I . . . I just wanted to see you.'

'In the middle of the night?'

'No, well, yes. Because I've nowhere else to go.'

'Go to school!' she hisses. 'It's where you belong! Don't you get it?'

'But I love you.' And hope you might lend me the running-away money you keep hidden under your bed.

'No!' She brandishes the tyre-iron. 'No, George Duckface, or whatever your name is, you don't love me, and I won't 'ave you coming 'ere saying so, like it's all a little game. Go back to your poncy school, find some poncy girl and play your games with 'er. Now get out that window before my dad comes, and don't never come back.'

'Yes, Emily, I will, but just give me one moment, please.'

She's wearing a simple nightdress with cotton shift beneath. Squatting on one knee beside me, I can see the smooth skin of her thigh, and the outline of her breasts which move as she flexes her arm. I'm feeling faint again, but have one thing more to say.

'You asked me why I'd come to see you. Yesterday, at the stables. Remember?'

'What of it?'

'I know why now. It's the war. I'm scared of it. Scared of it ending my life. Before I've had a chance to live it. And I needed to tell someone, to explain. And you . . . You're the only one I can tell.'

She fixes me with those beautiful eyes, and just for a second I see them soften. 'George bloomin' Duckface.' She breathes. 'What am I going to do with—'

A squeak comes from outside, like a mouse. Or a door-hinge.

'What's that?'

'Jesus! It's my dad! Go, for God's sake, go!'

I make it. Almost. At least I'm half in, half out as the door opens and Parker strides in, sees me, lets out a roar and charges at the window. Dispensing with the ladder I leap into the bushes, struggle to my feet and hare off into the night.

More time passes, mostly on a park bench, then around dawn I gather myself and head back to school. First stop, Bertie's study. He's asleep, a stuffed bear at his side.

'Bertie. Bertie, wake up!'

'George?' He yawns. 'Is that you? But isn't it frightfully early?'

'Yes. Listen, Bertie, this is important.'

'What is? I say, George, you do pong. And is that blood on your shirt?'

'Never mind that. Listen, have you got any money?'

'Loads! I put everything on that horse Hotspur on Saturday. Must have won a fortune. Which reminds me, have you got my winnings?'

'Christ, I'm done for. Do you still have the forms? The ones for the Flying Corps?'

'Yes, right there on my desk. Why?'

'Never mind. Go back to sleep.'

I take the usual fire-escape route up to my own study where I wash, change and pack. Then, because I can't think what else to do, I have breakfast and go to lessons.

The axe falls at ten. I'm in a Latin tutorial, nursing a horrible hangover and the sore head from Emily's tyre-iron, when Cheeseman enters, smirking. 'Begging your pardon, sir,' he simpers, 'but Duckwell is required by the headmaster. Right away.'

I feel ready now, and ignoring his murmured 'You're done for, Duckfart' I stride chin-high from the room for my appointment with destiny. On the way I pass poor Darwin, cemented for ever to his plinth, and reflect at least I won't be sharing his fate.

Arriving at the headmaster's building I plunge straight in, but the first thing I see, sitting cap in hand in the lobby, is the head groundsman. That's a shock. Spotting me he starts to rise, but the head's secretary tells him to wait, and ushers me through.

The head is at his desk, sorting papers. 'Sit,' he growls, not looking up.

Then comes the obligatory wait. I pass it gazing through his window at a huge chestnut tree, heavy with fruit. Tufted clouds drift above; I hear boys at play; from the secretary's office comes the ringing of a telephone and the murmur of voices.

'Well,' the head begins eventually. He lifts a sheet from his desk with thumb and forefinger. 'And what have you to say about this?'

I have no idea. A cautious opening bid is called for. 'Well, sir, if it's about being off school premises last night, then it is true, I admit, and I apologise, but also assure you there were important reasons—'

'I'm not talking about that, you imbecile!'

'No, sir, I was going to add that it is also true I was on licensed premises, contrary to regulations about pubs on weekdays, and may have over-indulged slightly.'

'For God's sake, Duckwell!' He flaps the paper. 'Have you no idea what this is?'

'Actually, sir, no. Sorry.'

'It's your attendance record, you halfwit. And it's an utter disgrace.'

Attendance record. I've been hauled up for skipping a few lessons. I can scarcely believe my luck. Swiftly I change gear. 'Yes, sir, it is poor, I admit, but I've been spending a lot of time in the library, revising hard you see, and—'

A knock comes on the door and the secretary enters, looking harassed. 'Sorry to trouble you, Headmaster, but Sir Reginald Aspinall is on the telephone.'

'Aspinall?' The headmaster scowls. 'Do I know him?'

'Yes, Headmaster. His youngest son, Crispin, is in the third year here.'

'Really? What does he want?'

'I'm not sure, sir, something about a gambling ring his son's become involved in.'

'Good God! Very well, tell him I'll call him back in a few minutes.'

'Yes, sir. Oh, and er, there's something else.'

'What now for pity's sake!'

'There's a man waiting to see you. Another man, that is, apart from the head groundsman. A Mister Parker.'

'Parker? Is he another father?'

'No, Headmaster, he's from the town. He seems very angry about something.'

'Well, put him in the drawing room and give him a glass of sherry. I'll deal with him after everyone else. Now, where was I? Oh, yes, Duckwell.'

But I am already on my feet. 'Sir, it's no good, sir, I must tell the truth!'

'Have you gone mad, boy? Sit down this minute!'

'No, sir, I cannot, for it is my duty, and intention, to leave this place today.'

'Leave? What on earth are you talking about?'

'I am going to enlist in His Majesty's armed services, and fight for my country.'

'Enlist? But . . . But . . .' And the old fool's mouth starts opening and closing like a hooked trout.

I've nearly landed him, but mere seconds remain, for through the door angry voices are being raised. 'Yes, sir. I've thought about it, and as the chaplain said on Sunday, it is our duty to rally to the cause for the sake of our king and kinsmen. So I'm joining the Royal Flying Corps. Indeed I have the papers right with me, and all I need is your signature, here, as a sort of reference, and also here, thank you, sir, and then I can take up the shield of God and fight for freedom and justice! Goodbye, sir, praise be the Lord and amen!'

And that, more or less, swear to God, is how it happened. The head, lip quivering with emotion, signed the forms, shook me manfully by the hand and sent me off to fight the good fight. Half an hour later he was howling for my blood, but by then I'd gathered up Bertie and was in a taxi to Telford, from where we took the train to London and his cousin's flat in Chelsea. The fact that a few weeks later I was wishing I'd stayed at Shrewsbury and taken my punishment like a man is beside the point.

And the unwitting victim of all this mayhem of course was Emily, whom I wasn't to see again until our chance encounter in Calais six months later. I'd stormed uninvited into her life, caused her nothing but trouble, and stormed out again without a word of thanks or apology. That my tomfoolery provided the call to action she'd been waiting for is of no consequence, even if that action would change both our lives for ever. I behaved abominably and regret it to this day.

We'd met, as stated, on the Sunday, at Uffington livery yard. This meeting, the second of the three, was our most successful, a steadying breath of calm before the chaos that was to follow. Emily was a different person away from the garage, relaxed, assured and unruffled by my gaucheness which, sensing time was short perhaps, I tempered in keeping with the mood. Arriving at the yard, I spied her outside the stables and stopped to watch. Dressed in riding clothes beneath a leather apron, her dark hair blowing free in the breeze, she was grooming a thoroughbred, completely absorbed in the task, murmuring softly to the beast as she buffed its gleaming hide. What a beautiful animal, I said, drawing near. It was a hunter, she explained, smiling wryly at my appearance, it belonged to a countess who let her ride it in exchange for grooming duties. But aren't you exhausted, I asked, labouring all week in the garage then working here on your day off? Not at all, she replied, she loved being with horses, they were her passion, and her escape. Escape from what? But she didn't answer, just rested a cheek on the animal's flank, studying me with those brown eyes. What's your name? she asked then, and I told her. And why have you come? Good question, I said, and standing there in my blazer and bicycle-clips I gave it due consideration, watching the wind stir crows in the elms above Upton Magna, and rain-showers brushing Wenlock Edge far to the south.

The war. Everything seemed to come back to the war, and my obsessive need to blot it from existence. Only an hour earlier the school chaplain had tearfully blessed the names of two more old boys killed in the trenches, then in the same breath exhorted us to follow them. Let not their sacrifice be in vain, he'd thundered, put on the armour of God and fight, for right is on your side. But was right really on our side? How did he know? Had anyone thought to tell the Germans? And where did beautiful, unwitting, other-worldly Emily fit into all this? Was she not simply another of my diversions from reality? An innocent accessory to escape, like her horses?

'I'm not sure,' I replied finally. 'Perhaps I shouldn't have come.'

'It doesn't bother me.' She smiled, resuming her grooming.

'It was you in the pub that night, wasn't it?' I said after a while.

'That woman we was with, she does recruiting, for women's war work. I want to join up. Do something 'elpful. Find out who I really am. But Dad would kill me if 'e knew. 'E needs me at the garage, see. And Granddad's getting old, and Mum's got the gout. It ain't easy.'

'And that's to be your escape? Volunteering for war work?'

'It's what I want more than everything. I've read all them pamphlets, and been saving up money, under the bed, ready.'

'Good for you, Emily. I really hope it works out.'

'One day, p'raps.' She tucked hair behind her ear. 'What about you, George Duckwell? What do you want more than anything?'

But I had no answer for that one either.

Chapter 3

39 Sqn
Suttons Farm
Hornchurch, Essex
May 12th 1917

Emily old thing,

It is three weeks since we bumped into one another on the dockside at Calais, three weeks since I left France for a new life as a scout pilot, three weeks during which I haven't stopped thinking about you, and all that's happened in the seven months since leaving Shrewsbury. In these three weeks I must have made thirty failed attempts at this letter. This is number thirty-one and little different, except in one respect. I shall post it.

Which brings me straight to the point. I behaved appallingly last autumn, Emily, with my idiotic antics, appallingly and

*thoughtlessly. Then I ran away to the RFC without a word of
apology or explanation. My conduct was inexcusable so all I can
do is offer belated yet heartfelt apologies, and beg forgiveness for
any distress or embarrassment caused. I should like to add that
my feelings for you, though utterly respectful, remain genuinely
fond, and it is my dearest wish we might yet be friends. Truly I
am sorry.*

*I must say it was both a shock and a delight to meet you at
Calais, and I have since spent many hours reflecting on the forces
of destiny that reunited us that night. My friend Mac, who you
also met, had rescued me from what can only be described as a
truly dreadful day, the details of which I shall spare you. Mac is
an outstanding pilot and most loyal friend and I shall always be
grateful to him. (Not for the first time, either!)*

*I have been posted here to Suttons Farm, which is a Home
Defence squadron in Essex. It's a nuisance frankly, as following
my scout training (for which I was assessed 'above average') I
was eager to return to France and have at the Hun once more.
But fate decreed otherwise, and though I fought the posting my
protestations came to nought, so here I am in Essex, which to be
honest is rather dull . . .*

The hallway klaxon sounded at eight, mercilessly dragging
Emily from unconsciousness with its rasping shriek. Her eyes
struggled open, blinking up at the mildew-stained ceiling,
while her limbs ached in protest and her mind fumbled for
explanation. It was morning, she decided, for dust-motes
danced along beams of May sunshine piercing the blackout
curtain. Beyond the window, two storeys below, rush-hour
horse-carts and motor-traffic clattered through the cobbled

streets of Richelieu while raucous French voices cracked coarse jokes and cursed with impatience. Calais had been awake for hours, she realised, its inhabitants cheerfully embracing the new day after the menacing hours of night. Yet she felt no cheer, only exhaustion, sucking at her will like an undertow. Five o'clock was when she had finished the previous night, she reminded herself, and three hours' sleep was not enough. Her eyes fluttered shut. The klaxon was a mistake.

But then it came again. This time she jerked upright, reflexively throwing back the sleeping-bag as she had trained herself. Vehicle inspection, she remembered, nine o'clock sharp and woe betide absentees, sleep or no sleep.

She sat for a moment, rubbing her eyes and taking bleary stock. The room was oppressively stuffy as always, littered with hastily discarded clothing, cold and musty-smelling. As was she. Pushing the sleeping-bag to her waist, she wrinkled her nose at the odour of her own unwashed body. She also found George Duckwell's letter squashed into a fold and pulled it out, guiltily smoothing its pages with her hand. Had she read it? She remembered trying last night, but must have fallen asleep. Dear George. It was touching of him to write after all these months, oddly, and his humble tone sounded genuine. She'd read it again later.

Around the room humped figures were stirring.

'If that infernal woman hoots that hooter just one more time,' a muffled voice warned, 'I shall personally tear it from the wall and ram it down her throat.'

'I can think of a better place,' mumbled a second.

'I thought we were excused reveille today, after finishing so late.'

'Only in your dreams, Phyllis.'

'For God's sake, who's making the tea?'

'I'll do it.'

Eager for air, Emily put George's letter aside and peeled off her bag, idly noting a fresh crop of bites on her ankles. Bedbugs. All the girls suffered; they got worse as the weather warmed, so Hermione said. But they weren't as bad as the body-lice that infested their clothes, or the rats that scampered across their beds as they slept. They were the worst, until Hermione killed them with poisoned chocolate.

She pulled a mackintosh over her pyjamas and padded to the gas-ring by the window. 'We'd better hurry if we want breakfast,' she said, throwing open the blackout. 'Vehicle inspection at nine.'

'Vehicle inspection? I thought I only dreamed that.'

'No, Angel dear, sadly Parker is right.'

'Inhuman, that's what I call it. Monstrous and inhuman.'

Emily lit the gas, wiping dirty mugs with a rag. Slowly the others struggled to life. Six mugs, six cots, six girls, one cramped room. Like a school dormitory, except this dormitory, damp and vermin-ridden, had last been used to house convict labourers. Now it housed B-Watch, of the Richelieu Unit, Calais Division, the First Aid Nursing Yeomanry. Although B-Watch, Emily felt, surveying them bundled in their scarves and overcoats, looked more like six tramps in a squat, with their matted hair, unwashed bodies and filthy clothes stained with oil and blood and worse.

As she watched, one tramp, a wealthy land-owner's daughter called Charlotte, cowering under mounds of bedding topped by a huge fur coat, yawned sleepily into song:

Oh I used to be in society once
I danced and hunted and flirted once
Had fair white hands and complexion once
But now I am a FANY!

A shoe flew in protest, someone blew a raspberry, bleary faces peaked from sleeping-bags, plummy voices joining in tired conversation.

'Charlie, how can you possibly sing when we've been up all night.'

'She isn't singing, it's called caterwauling.'

'Thank you, Miss Clayton-Wells, but I'll have you know I sang for Roedean.'

'Poor Roedean. I say, Parks, is that tea brewed yet?'

'Just coming.' Emily poured, one eye on a motionless hump on one cot. 'Bobby, are you awake?'

'No.' The hump broke into hoarse coughing. 'I'm ill.'

'You're not allowed to be ill. It's against regulations.'

'Maybe she should stay in bed, that cough sounds worse.'

'She can't, Phyll, the Brute wouldn't have it.'

'And don't forget the others. We'd be the laughing stock of the unit.'

'I don't care. I'm not coming.'

'Bobby, dearest.' Phyllis leaned over. 'If you miss another vehicle inspection, the Brute will put you on a charge, and the rest of us on latrine duty for a week. Now you wouldn't want that, would you?'

Half an hour later the six, having quickly breakfasted on stale bread and tinned sardines, joined A- and C-Watches outside in the vehicle compound. Everyone looked tired and morose, and as usual few greetings were exchanged. Emily collected sponge and bucket and joined the queue for water, reflecting upon the sombre mood. They were all doing the same job under identical conditions, yet rivalry abounded, sometimes to the point of spite – a deflated tyre here, pilfered cigarettes there. It was one of the weaknesses of the FANY system, she felt, for surely the job would be easier if everyone pulled together.

Bucket filled, she made for the vehicles, twenty battered Crossley ambulances ranged around the compound like veterans at a parade, khaki-painted, open-cabbed, canvas-topped, with spoked wooden wheels like old wagons. Emily approached hers, number 52, surveying it critically. She'd already cleaned it once the previous night, inside and out, but had inevitably missed a few mud-spots in the darkness. The rear offside tyre had lost pressure, she saw, and the front wheels looked fractionally out of alignment, which would explain the steering anomaly she'd felt. No one would notice these defects, she knew, and she'd attend to both before the evening shift; the critical factor now was cleanliness.

Mopping as she went, she circled to the van's rear, then swung up into its cramped interior, instinctively shutting her mind both to the smell and to what she might find there. But though the stench was ever-present – blood, vomit, rotting flesh, carbolic soap – the scrubbed wooden floor beneath the four stretcher-racks held no unpleasant surprises, save a scrap of bloody bandage which she swiftly removed.

'Stand by your vehicles!' a female voice barked shrilly.

Emily hurried to the front, wiping a final dirt-spot with her sleeve as she went. Two older women had arrived at the centre of the compound: one, short and stocky and holding a clipboard, was the unit's adjutant, Sergeant Collier, the other was her hawk-faced superior, Unit Commandant Evadne Bruton, in full FANY uniform complete with hat, officer's brevets and riding-crop. While Sergeant Collier harried the girls like an irascible terrier, Bruton, known universally as the Brute, paced the compound, eyeing her charges with ill-concealed contempt.

'Hurry up now!' Collier nagged. 'Don't keep the commandant waiting. Stand to attention and stop fidgeting!'

Soon all were paraded, the sergeant saluted and stood back, Bruton stopped pacing and turned to face the assembly.

'Last night was an utter shambles!' she began, her harsh voice echoing round the compound. 'It took nearly six hours to transport three hundred wounded from the rail-head. This is inexcusably slow. Furthermore during that time two of this unit's drivers got lost, two more allowed their vehicles to break down, and one, disgracefully, was discovered at the dockside, asleep at the wheel. They know who they are, they will come forward now.'

Pin-drop silence descended around the compound as eighteen girls looked at one another and waited. After an age, two stepped hesitantly forward, followed a moment later by two more. None was from B-Watch, Emily noted. She glanced at Hermione Clayton-Wells who caught her eye and winked.

'Eyes front!' Bruton snapped angrily. 'And I am still waiting.'

Nobody else moved. Emily stood nervously: the Brute seemed to be glaring right at her, as though in accusation. Still the seconds ticked and no fifth miscreant surrendered.

'Very well. Roberta Waldron will step forward.'

Emily froze. Bobby Waldron, the girl with the cough, the girl standing at the next ambulance to hers. The girl now collapsing into tears.

'I'm sorry!' she wailed. 'I wasn't asleep, I was ill. I have a fever, I needed rest, just for a minute.'

'Be silent this instant!'

'Commandant Bruton?' Emily raised her hand. 'It is true that Driver Waldron has been unwell and—'

'I said silence!'

In the end it was bad, but might have been worse. Everyone suffered, all three watches earning extra chores for the poor performance of the unit as a whole. The two girls who got lost were assigned 'area re-familiarisation' which meant tramping the streets of Calais for hours with a map, the pair with mechanical problems spent the morning stripping gearboxes, and Bobby Waldron was confined to the hostel, docked a month's leave, and put on a charge for gross dereliction of duty. Emily, for having the temerity to speak up for her friend, drew the shortest straw of all: a funeral parade followed by corpse duty.

They called themselves the Vimto Valkyries, she and her friends of B-Watch. One Valkyrie, Phyllis Mason, was related to the Mason of Fortnum & Mason fame, which meant fabulous hampers of food occasionally arrived from her mother, much to everyone's delight. Apart from goose pâté, tinned anchovies, glacé fruit and a host of other delicacies unfamiliar to Emily's palate, these hampers also contained copious quantities of Vimto, a new bottled refreshment Phyllis's mother insisted would protect the girls against contagion. Emily enjoyed the Vimto greatly, despite the protestations of other Valkyries, notably Angela Truscott, who pronounced it undrinkable unless mixed with gin. Angela, whose nickname was Angel, was moody and sharp-tongued, but fiercely loyal to her friends, as was Hermione Clayton-Wells, or CW as everyone called her. CW's father was Sir Richard Clayton-Wells and famous in banking, so apart from being top-drawer, CW was extremely rich, though she wore her grandeur lightly and was never condescending to Emily. It was CW who explained Valkyries to her: formidable Norse goddesses, she said, who carried fallen warriors to Valhalla so they could rise and fight again. Which was more or less what FANYs did and thus, Emily agreed, a most fitting name for their gang.

She'd joined up the previous November, two weeks after the George Duckwell disaster. He'd vanished without a word, leaving her to deal with an enraged father, traumatised mother and a town abuzz with the heady scent of scandal. That Parker girl, neighbours whispered indignantly, and a young gent from the school, in her bedroom, at night, red-handed. Who'd have thought? At first she simply shrugged it off. Nothing happened, she kept insisting, it's all a storm in a teacup. But after a week of police interviews, doctors' examinations, local newspapers implying disgusting goings-on and her own family's tight-lipped reproof, she began to despair. Another week passed and still the furore rumbled, so one morning, following an apocalyptic row with her parents, she packed a bag, collected her savings from beneath the bed, slipped away to the station and bought a third-class ticket to London. One way. Only her grandfather showed support, hobbling down the hill after her waving an envelope of cash.

Her resolve almost crumbled that very first day. London was madness, a mind-numbing chaos of crowded streets filled with stinking rubbish, murderous traffic and unsmiling people in a hurry. Emerging on to the pavement outside the terminus, she stared around in bewildered shock, for the world had turned grey. Grey streets, grey buildings, grey vehicles, grey pigeons, the grey afternoon sky, even the expressions on passing faces seemed to match the city's listless pallor. Fighting a sudden wave of homesickness, she fumbled through her purse. The recruiting woman's pamphlet listed an address in Earls Court. Emily had never travelled further than Worcester; she had no idea where Earls Court was nor how to get there. Buses, she supposed, or trams might take her, and she'd even heard of trains that ran under the ground, but baffled by the maps and timetables, anxious about money and fearful of approaching strangers for help she elected to walk, following vague directions from a policeman. Within minutes she was lost; half an hour more and it began to rain. Eventually, around dusk, drenched and disconsolate, she found herself near Bayswater where a news-seller took pity and pointed her towards a hostel for women. The supervisor there sighed and tutted and said 'another bleedin' bumpkin' before showing her to an open dormitory with iron beds and bare mattresses where she passed a wretched night listening to drunken ranting and old women's snores. Breakfast, like tea, was bread and soup, then she was ejected on to the street where she discovered her savings had been stolen, every penny except the money her grandfather had given her. At that point, weeping bitterly, she conceded defeat and began retracing her steps for home. But within minutes an innate doggedness, a burst of wintry sunshine and the dire prospect of a humiliating return to Shrewsbury rekindled her resolve. Straightening her back, she turned on her heel and set out once more for Earls Court.

'Good gracious me no,' the lady at the FANY office told her, not two hours later. She was grand and imposing and buxom and wore a maroon FANY sash over a floor-length satin gown, with expensively coiffed hair beneath a huge floral hat. Emily thought she looked like Queen Mary.

'Beg pardon, ma'am?'

'I'm afraid you're not for us, my dear.'

'Why's that?'

'Goodness, how can I put this? You see, the First Aid Nursing Yeomanry was established as, well, as a highly selective corps. Our girls all come from a certain social background. All are fittingly brought up and educated, and all are of independent financial means.'

'I'm fittingly brought up, thank you. And I went to school. And I 'ave money, see – well, a little.'

'Yes, of course. Tell me, have you considered the Voluntary Aid Detachment? Or even the Red Cross?'

'No. I read all them pamphlets and want the FANY.'

An awkward pause followed while Queen Mary looked embarrassed and Emily stood her ground, although with growing unease. Then another woman entered, younger than the first and dressed in khaki. Glancing at Emily, she picked up her application.

'Why?' she asked, scrutinising the sheet.

'Beg pardon, ma'am?'

'Why do you want to join the FANY?'

'Because of the 'orses. The pamphlet says the FANY is a mounted order.'

'Which it is, up to a point. Why, do you ride?'

'Better than anyone. That's what Lady Cordingley says.'

Queen Mary stiffened. 'Elizabeth? Countess Cordingley of the Kensington and Shropshire Cordingleys?'

'That's right. I take care of 'er 'unters, see. 'Er address is on the back. For references and so on.'

'How interesting.' The younger woman was still studying Emily's application. 'Tell me, it says here you worked in a garage. Does that mean you know something of vehicle maintenance?'

'You could say that.' Emily smiled. 'In fact, you name it and I've fixed it.'

Matters moved swiftly from then on and by evening, fed, quartered and relieved of her last pound as a joining subscription, Emily was a fully signed-up FANY.

Her appointment, unknown to her, came at a critical time for the organisation which had suffered a crisis of credibility. Precariously financed and suspiciously regarded, the FANY had been formed in 1907, entirely without mandate, by a group of upper-class enthusiasts with the noble if vague aim of 'assisting in times of military emergency'. Elitist from the start, its founders evidently envisaged troupes of smartly uniformed debutantes galloping across battlefields, gallantly gathering wounded into horse-drawn ambulances and ministering to them using the first aid. Strictly a subscription organisation, applicants were selected largely on the basis of breeding, income and equestrian skill, and were not only unpaid but expected to subsidise their travel and living expenses, and buy their own uniforms. Membership unsurprisingly grew only slowly, particularly in comparison to larger competitors like the VAD, Red Cross and newly formed Women's Royal Naval Service, all of which regarded FANYs with scepticism. As did the British military authorities, who couldn't think what to do with them, even when war broke out.

But a FANY is nothing if not tenacious, and as the war spread they gradually secured a toe-hold in France where they developed a reputation among the French and Belgian military as cheerful, courageous and hard-working. Eventually even the British caved in – 'Neither fish, flesh nor fowl, but a damned good red herring,' as one general put it – and at last FANYs were allowed to work alongside their countrymen. But the role they had carved out for themselves by 1917 was not as imagined a decade earlier. While a few FANYs did help run field hospitals and dressing stations, most by far were employed driving ambulances in and around Calais. In short, their job was to collect the thousands of wounded soldiers that arrived nightly from the Front by train and barge and drive them to hospitals in the area, or to the docks to be shipped home. Lorry-loads of often horrifically injured men, in other words, by night, in a blackout, in all weathers, and under bombardment. The ideal would-be FANY of the day therefore was not so much a horse-riding socialite as a steel-nerved lorry-mechanic with a driving licence. Which is why Emily got in.

But not until she'd been to finishing school in Yorkshire.

Corpse duty was an unspeakable business, a task so gruelling it counted as punishment, which is why the Brute allocated it to Emily. Before corpse duty, however, was the funeral parade, seemingly an undemanding assignment that required her only to stand at a graveside while a soldier she'd never met received a decent burial. But many girls, Emily included, found funeral parades upsetting and went to lengths to avoid them – a fact the Brute also exploited to the full.

With her working clothes bundled beneath the seat, she drove her empty ambulance through Calais's southern outskirts until she arrived at Infirmary XV, one of many temporary military hospitals situated around the town. Learning these hospitals by heart was crucial for new FANYs, as locating them, at night, by the glow of a sidelight, with no one but injured soldiers for company, was no trivial matter. Mistakes were inevitable, with girls driving their wounded to the wrong hospital, or in endless lost circles, or worse still up a muddy dead-end. Emily's baptism of fire came during her second week in France when she accidentally drove five soldiers, all suffering new amputations and in agonising pain, to the incorrect clinic for treatment, much to the anger of its staff, and the anguish of the victims. At her insistence she immediately took them to the correct unit and the matter was dropped, but shaken by the experience she slipped from her cot early next morning, set out on a borrowed bicycle and pedalled from one hospital to the next, hour after hour, until by sunset she had them all committed to memory. Absenting herself without permission earned her a week's double-duty, but the Brute never learned the reason, and Emily never got lost again.

Lurching up XV's rutted driveway, she parked to the rear of the hospital, beside the patch of cleared ground serving as a graveyard. She was early and the graveyard was deserted, so she climbed from the cab to stretch her legs, face upturned to the welcome warmth of the sun. Funeral parades required formal dress so she was wearing her full FANY uniform of khaki skirt, blouse and tie, belted khaki jacket, puttees and laced brown boots. On her head she wore the uniform hat, a baggy, beret-like garment with the FANY badge of a Maltese cross in a maroon circle. While straightening it on her head her eyes were drawn to two aeroplanes, no more than tiny glinting specks, circling each other like insects high in the sky. Briefly her thoughts turned to George, and his unread letter. Meeting him on the docks that night had been a shock, but not an unpleasant one. Indeed something of a thrill had surged through her when first she'd seen him striding through the throng towards her. He and his mysterious dark-eyed friend. Called Mac.

Then a door opened and the cortège appeared. It was small, comprising four orderlies carrying the coffin, two French infantrymen, rifles slung, an army doctor to represent the hospital and a Bible-bearing priest in cassock. Returning their polite nods, she fell into step for the short walk to the grave, a familiar disquiet rising within her like a tide. Why the FANY was represented at these melancholy ceremonies she wasn't sure; she only knew a tradition had evolved somewhere and had to be maintained, and that relatives of the dead were always touched by the girls' presence. If there were any relatives. Today there were none, so without ado the priest opened the book and began, speaking in a swift monotone, as though for the thousandth time.

Emily folded her hands, focusing her gaze on a plough-horse

working in a distant field, and waiting tensely for the word. Soon it came, *inconnu*, and her heart sank, for it was this aspect of funeral parades that so affected her. The dreadful anonymity of the dead. This young man, like so many countless others, was going to his grave alone and unknown, a notion she found unbearably sad. He was French, for French soldiers were present, and probably an officer, as he merited a guard of honour; beyond that he was no one, a nameless stranger lost to the world. In all likelihood his shattered remains had been found in French officer's uniform in the corner of a field, and duly gathered, like the last gleanings of the harvest. Now they were hidden for ever beneath the ground, yet somewhere, in a peaceful mountain village perhaps, or busy Atlantic port, or bustling Parisian street, his mother was praying hopefully, or his children laughing at play, or his wife pausing and wondering.

She left as soon as possible, hastening her ambulance away down the track. Weary beyond reason, all she wanted now was to return to Richelieu and the Valkyries, there to sleep in her cot until evening stand-to. But another duty had to be performed, featuring the less spiritual side of the death-by-war business.

She stopped in a lane, ducking behind bushes to change into her work clothes of breeches and smock. As she unrolled them a bottle of Vimto fell out, together with a pack of sandwiches bearing the message *We're with you, Parks! Drive safely & hurry home. Angel*. Munching gratefully, she stowed her folded uniform, climbed into the cab and set off.

Corpse duty involved collecting the identified bodies of dead soldiers from infirmaries and transporting them to a central mortuary for collective burial or onward distribution to relatives. The bodies, often hideously mutilated, often long-dead, bloated and rotting, were stretchered on to the ambulances by orderlies wearing masks. Many had died following unsuccessful surgery so exhibited hastily stitched wounds or badly reattached limbs, like Shelley's monster. Once underway they lolled grotesquely, mouths agape, spilling entrails to the floor, shedding decayed flesh and leaking putrid oil-black fluids. Some even made sounds, sighing with gas or tapping maimed limbs against the ambulance's side as it rocked. Their stench was appalling, putrefying flesh mingled with blood, pus and the sickly-sweet odour of gangrene, and for once the girls were grateful their cabs were in the open. Yet even there the smell could be overpowering, and few FANYs completed their first corpse duty without pulling over to vomit. Once delivered of their loads, the vehicles had to be hand-cleaned using bucket, scrubbing brush and carbolic soap. Even then the smell lingered, sometimes for weeks.

Dealing with corpse duty was an acquired art. Emily learned by disassociation, by detaching her mind from the job and occupying it with diversions such as Charlie's bawdy songs, mental arithmetic or a snatch of poetry CW had taught her. She also learned to separate all emotion from the task. These were not men being carted into the morgue, she told herself, these were carcasses, husks, empty shells, so crying for them was pointless. Save your crying for the living, as Angel would say. Newer girls found this callousness shocking, but after their first few corpse duties soon realised it was the only way to cope.

Punishments concluded, by two Emily was back at

Richelieu, plodding wearily up the stairs to Valkyrie HQ. But a shout from below stopped her halfway.

'Parker! Get down here right now!'

She plodded wearily down again and out into the sunlit compound. At first she could see only the usual assortment of trucks and ambulances, including her own, freshly cleaned and fuelled. But then she noticed another lorry standing discreetly to one side, wreathed in steam like a railway engine in a siding and obscured from view by canvas awnings. She wondered how she could have missed it, especially as FANYs, in various degrees of undress, were standing around it, chatting excitedly.

'Hurry up, Parks!' A grinning Phyllis appeared, clutching a towel to her midriff. 'Quick, we saved you a place!'

Dazed, Emily followed her behind the screens. It was a bathing lorry, she realised, a mobile washing facility, something she'd heard about but never seen. A coal-fired boiler heated a water-tank, then pipes and spigots fed the hot water to bulging canvas baths suspended around the lorry like ripe fruit. Within these water-filled hammocks naked Valkyries frolicked.

'What-ho, Parky!' Charlie sang out. 'Come on in, the water's lovely.'

Emily was speechless. 'But, but, how . . .'

'The VAD sent it over, the darlings! Must have thought we ponged or something. You're just in time, B-Watch got first dibs. And Angel has real Pears soap. Quick, Phyll, help Parky with her togs.'

But she needed no help. Overcome suddenly, fighting tears she hadn't shed in months, she stripped the stinking clothes from her body, mounted steps beside the nearest hammock and plunged gratefully in. And didn't get out until ordered.

The hallway klaxon sounded at eight, rousing them to readiness twelve hours after it had first woken them. Following the surprise luxury of their baths, the Valkyries had slept, eaten, prepared their vehicles, then slept again. Now they waited, talking and smoking, their overcoats, goggles and gloves at the ready. Elsewhere across town, sixty other FANYs in three other units also waited, tense with anticipation. Many would see no respite until dawn, some not even then.

In theory the three-watch system ensured a third were working, a third standing by, and a third resting, but since the Arras offensive began the numbers of injured arriving each night had soared, and often everyone had to turn out just to stem the flood. This put enormous pressure on the girls and their ambulances, and after weeks without leave or let-up both were showing the strain. FANYs were beginning to crack, as were gearboxes and crankshafts; the only question was which would break first. New Napier ambulances to supplement the ageing Crossleys had been promised for months, yet none had arrived. As for replacement FANYs, though they were sent as fast as could be trained, enough never came. Anyway no amount of training, however thorough, could prepare them for the job awaiting them.

Emily's training had taken place in December. Four harsh weeks in the wilds of Yorkshire, under canvas, in mid-winter. The abomination of desolation, recruits dubbed the camp. Finishing school was another popular name, because you either survived it or it finished you. And for some it was indeed too much, local taxi drivers doing steady business ferrying tearful ex-FANYs to the station and a train home to mother. But not many, for once the feeble had removed themselves the remainder knuckled down. Work began at sun-up each morning with tent-tidying followed by prayers followed by physical jerks followed by tending the horses, all before a breakfast of porridge and tea. From then on the day was spent on the FANYs' three main areas of operation: vehicle driving and maintenance, horsemanship, and first aid. The regime was hard, conditions tough, food basic and accommodation spartan.

Emily took to it at once, particularly driving and mechanics at which she excelled. She also developed and refined her equestrian skills, and quickly mastered the basics of first aid. What she found harder to master however was the snobbery of some recruits who mocked her lowly origins and country accent. Money was also a worry, for trainees had to pay for their keep and Emily was essentially penniless. Her tormentors knew this and bullied her into doing their chores in return for twopenny tips. Emily bore these indignities as best she could, particularly as she needed the money, but one evening a brigadier's daughter called Felicity mislaid her purse and turned on Emily, calling her a damned thieving peasant. At that Emily snapped and felled the astonished Felicity with a right hook to the ear. A spirited fight ensued, much to the amusement of onlookers, but before serious harm could be inflicted Emily felt strong hands at her shoulders.

'Not like this, dear,' a kindly voice urged, pulling her away. It was Charlotte Neve, or Charlie as Emily grew to know her, and over the remaining weeks she would not only become Emily's coach and confidante, and a founding Valkyrie, but her first true friend in the FANY.

'It's no use rising to the bait, Parks, old girl,' she would scold, pacing the tent like a lecturer. Charlie was a competition horsewoman whose parents owned a stud farm in Berkshire. Tireless, fearless and hearty, she tended to speak in sporting metaphors. 'You've got to take the bull by the horns, see, and beat these idiots at their own game.'

'Yes, but 'ow 'm I going to do that?'

'By talking like them for a start. And acting like them, eating and walking like them. Everything. And we've got to get you some proper togs, and a decent hairdo.'

'But I 'aven't any money.'

'H-aven't, Parks, h-aven't. And don't worry about money, I've plenty, and anyway there's lots of ways to skin a rabbit. Think you're up to it?'

Emily wasn't sure what she meant, but sensing the outstretched hand of friendship agreed nonetheless. And over the next few days, as she applied herself to Charlie's curriculum, its purpose became clear. Survival. Charlie was teaching her how to fit in, how to stand tall among her peers, how not to be intimidated, in short how to put aside her humble country ways and fake it as a toff. Slowly at first, then more rapidly as her confidence grew, Charlie coached her like a showjumper, with firmness and patience, yet all the while raising the bar. Diction, deportment and erudition were tackled as one: Emily was made to walk the tent with a book balanced on her head, while reading aloud from another, usually Thackeray or Dickens. For conversation and table-etiquette she had to eat porridge with a knife and fork, back straight and elbows tucked, while discussing the weather, or horse-breeding, or the progress of the war. Cultural education consisted of a list of the best shops in London, while personal grooming included scraping the sump-oil from beneath her fingernails each evening, and brushing her hair until her scalp bled. Finance was another vital topic, and Charlie tackled it in characteristic fashion. As FANY training progressed, she noticed many girls having difficulty with the vehicle maintenance test, and several more who still couldn't drive. Exploiting Emily's natural flair for both, she helpfully tipped off these strugglers, who were soon queuing at Emily's tent, money in hand, anxious to learn the mysteries of internal combustion, or how to downshift without crashing gears. As for the bullies, baffled by Emily's rising status and cowed by the formidable Charlie, they soon melted into the snow-covered background.

One freezing morning in January the course commandant called the recruits together and announced that training was over.

'What happens now?' a fur-clad FANY asked.

'You go home, see your families, pack your essentials and be at Charing Cross station by noon on Friday.'

'Then what?'

'Then you go to France.'

The call came an hour after stand-to, the klaxon summoning all three watches with its insistent squawk. Doors slammed, shouts echoed, feet pounded on stairs as eighteen girls sprinted into the darkened compound and scattered for their vehicles. Seventeen, for as Emily reached hers she realised

Bobby Waldron was missing. Coughing Bobby, the smiling bank-clerk's daughter from Croydon, with the weak chest and fragile spirits, always the least confident of the Valkyries, yet loved by them all for her selfless devotion and infectious giggle. But she'd giggled far less lately, and today she'd been wordless since morning, dozing groggily in her cot while the others came and went. Had no one roused her? Had Bobby not heard them leave? Emily swung the starting-handle, listening as number 52 clattered obediently to life. Beside her Bobby's ambulance remained silent and lifeless. Going absent from duty was the gravest of offences, and after the morning's infraction the Brute would punish her mercilessly.

She climbed in and settled behind the wheel, peering anxiously round the compound. Leading ambulances were already moving off, within a minute they'd all be gone, she could do nothing but follow. Then to her relief she spotted Bobby, a lone figure hurrying through the shadows towards her vehicle. She'd be last out, and probably catch it from the Brute, but at least she'd make it, thank heaven. Dropping the clutch, Emily eased the Crossley into gear, released the brake and manoeuvred into the line of traffic snaking through the iron gates to the street.

Driving swiftly through the blacked-out town, the convoy reached the rail-head in minutes. There the drivers were briefed by the duty medical officer. Trains were due from ten o'clock, he told them, and several, so prepare yourselves. Furthermore, he went on, the night is dark and moonless, ideal Gotha weather, so stick to the blackout, sidelights only when driving, and watch out for air-raids.

Then came a lull, thirty minutes of anxious waiting, cupped

cigarettes and muted conversation. Instinctively the Valkyries drew together. Nobody talked of risks, they knew they were overworked women driving worn-out vehicles through blacked-out streets on a moonless night, quickly and without headlights. If that wasn't enough, Gothas, much-feared German bombers, might come and rain high explosives on them from above. Analysing the dangers wouldn't lessen them. Instead they made light, bolstering each other with girls' gossip, black humour and music-hall songs. Bobby Waldron, quiet, pale, still coughing, was especially fussed over. Then came a mournful whistle and the first train hove into view.

You backed your ambulance up close so the orderlies had a short carry. You didn't get out but stayed at the wheel, engine running, in case you had to move quickly, for an air-raid for instance. When you were loaded – four on tiered racks in the back and occasionally a fifth 'walking-wounded' beside you in the cab – the MO gave you a slip with their details and where to take them. Then you set off. Slow out, fast back, that was the rule, slow out, fast back. Slow out because a Crossley gave the harshest of rides and the men in the back were in agony and at the end of their tether. Their journey had begun days earlier, with a bullet in the gut or a shell fragment to the head or a leg blown off or a lungful of mustard-gas. First they staggered or crawled for help, or they lay where they fell, hoping a stretcher-party found them. Then they were carried to an ADS, an advanced dressing station, a simple tent right in the lines where basic first aid was carried out, airways cleared, tourniquets tied, gaping wounds covered. Enough, hopefully, to see them to the FOC or forward operating centre, which was little more than a canvas charnel-house for emergency surgery. Here limbs were hacked off, arteries ligatured, intestines squeezed back, bullets dug out. Then it was more agonising travel, rearward again to the CCS or casualty clearing station, still not a proper hospital but a place of 'triage', a topsy-turvy lottery of assessment for evacuation. Here the most seriously injured, perversely, took lowest priority, for they were doomed anyway; precedence went to those thought most likely to survive. Once triaged, it was another rough ride to the railway, there to wait for hours, sometimes days, until the trains arrived. Then came the painfully slow trip to the coast, followed finally by a bumpy jaunt along cobbled streets in a badly sprung lorry driven by a woman.

So, slow out. But fast back. Once delivered of their loads the race was on, with girls taking competitive pride in the fastest returns to the rail-head. Sound handling and steady nerves were required, for driving a Crossley at speed was a perilous business at best. On icy streets at night without headlights it was suicidal. Yet FANY honour was at stake, not to mention inter-watch rivalry. The Valkyries always scored highly, with fearless Charlie Neve, well known as a breakneck driver, invariably trouncing all comers. Emily and Angel generally came next, then CW and Bobby, followed by Phyllis Mason, who haughtily brushed off all taunts, saying motor-racing was for bookmakers and barrow-boys.

But by two that morning even the Valkyries were slowing. Emily completed her fourth rotation, desperately hoping for a few minutes' break and a reviving mug of tea at the Red Cross van. But pulling into the yard she saw another train had arrived in her absence, ambulances already shuffling into line for loading. Wearily she joined them, inching forward as each departed.

As she drew nearer, she noticed something was different. The normally brisk pace of the orderlies had slowed; they were taking more time and more care unloading the wounded. Doctors had appeared too, supervising matters in low voices. White-clad nurses stood by to assist, their faces strained. Emily saw one turn away, a hand to her mouth. And as she reversed into position she glimpsed the stretchers, blanket-covered figures wrapped top to bottom in bandages, like Egyptian mummies. Then her tail-gate banged down and they were being loaded, which was when she first heard, even above the hiss of steam and rumble of her engine, their tortured cries.

'Burns victims,' the MO said, handing her the slip. 'Some sort of phosphorous bomb. Dozens injured, several died on the train.'

'Infirmary IV, then, I take it,' Emily replied. Infirmary IV specialised in burns.

'That's right. And please go gently, they're in dreadful pain.'

She nodded, gingerly gunning the motor. But scarcely had she set off, coaxing the Crossley across the tracks and out on to the road, than the screams began in earnest.

She'd heard men in pain before, more times than she cared to remember; their cries formed part of her job, a doleful background accompaniment to the Crossley's clatter and squeak. Sometimes they merely hissed through their teeth, or cursed a little, or yelped 'Ouch, steady love!' when she hit a

bump. Some sighed, some moaned, some sobbed, some bellowed. One or two uttered prayers, or cried out for mercy,
and more than a few called for their mothers. She'd heard it
all, or so she thought. She'd never heard anything like the
screams of the four burn victims in her ambulance that night.
Blood-curdling, animal, scarcely beyond assimilating, when
first she heard them she pulled over and stopped, thinking
someone had fallen from a tier, or shut their hand in the tail-
gate. But they hadn't, they were still strapped to their
stretchers, bandaged from the top of their heads to the tips of
their fingers, their arms rigid above their bodies, curved and
trembling as though in spasm. As she stared, the cries subsided, replaced by hoarse, rasping breaths escaping through
gashes in their bandaged mouths. It was the movement, she
realised; any movement and they were in pain beyond human
ability to bear. Yet she had to get them to the infirmary.

'I'm, I'm so sorry,' she said. 'I'll be as careful as I can.'

No answer came, just the rasping breaths. And the moment
she drove on the screams started once more. High-pitched,
piercing, a four-part chorus from hell that went on and on
until her flayed nerves could stand it no more. Stop, she
pleaded, through gritted teeth, can't you please stop. And
then they did, or at least a change came, a dynamic shift in the
pattern, as though for a new arrangement with different par-
ticipants. Something had happened. Pulling in once more she
ran to the back, lifted the flap and saw why. One man had
died, his head turned aside, his rasping gash silent, his bandaged arm swinging limply.

She didn't stop again, even when the pattern of cries from
the back changed once more. She kept driving, urging the

Crossley along the narrow country lanes as smoothly as she could, her gloved hands tight on the wheel, her eyes fixed on the dim black strip ahead. Above her, stars shone through rents in the overcast, to either side crop-fields lay like moody dark oceans.

Infirmary IV was one of the furthest from town. By the time she reached it the first hint of grey was suffusing the eastern horizon. And the ambulance was quiet. She switched off the engine, waiting tensely for the orderlies to come for the men on the stretchers. They're resting, she told herself, or they've fallen into merciful unconsciousness, exhausted by their ordeal. But then a doctor arrived at her side, and his expression said it all.

'What did you bring them here for, you silly clot? They're all dead.'

It was light by the time Mac reached Emily's base. He'd been travelling since midnight, catching the Calais tender from Noyelette after a punishing day on ops. Three times he'd flown, twice with his squadron, once more in the evening, alone. The last was at his request. He'd begun flying solo missions when George left, he found they calmed him, distracted him from earthly anxieties, and helped fill the void left by George's absence. Roaming the air high above enemy lines, watching the dusk draw like a blanket over the earth below, was magical, mystical even, despite the danger. And usually he found the enemy waiting there, ready to test him, a lone Gotha perhaps, or a snooping Junkers. Sometimes these encounters ended in bloodshed, sometimes not. This last evening he'd tangled with a Pfalz scout; they'd circled each other like duelling fencers, probing, lunging, parrying, until eventually fuel ran low and they'd parted with barely a shot fired. When he landed it was dark.

He peered through the iron gates, unsure suddenly. Inside the compound twenty ambulances were parked, but he could see no people. He checked George's watch, wondering for the hundredth time why he had come. It was still early, today was his day off, he should be relaxing in the mess, or horse-riding in the countryside, or sightseeing in some town, Amiens perhaps, or Anvin, or Abbeville. Anywhere. Yet he'd come to Calais. Where the girl was. George's friend. Because he wanted her help contacting George, he'd told himself. But more than that, because he wanted to see her again.

Movement caught his eye, a bundled figure stirring at the wheel of one of the ambulances, its head slumped forward as though in sleep. Cautiously he approached.

'Excuse me.'

The figure jerked. 'I . . . What?'

'Ma'am, I'm sorry.' It was her. The face pale, the expression dazed, but unmistakably her. 'I startled you.'

'Oh . . . I, no, I was just . . .' Flustered, she began to rise, then noticed his gaze. 'Aren't you George's friend?'

'That's right.' He smiled. 'Mac. Here, let me help you down.'

He took her hand and she climbed stiffly from the cab. She was tall, as he remembered, and slender beneath the great-coat, with the warmest brown eyes. Warm but fatigued. 'Bad night?'

'Yes, well, not the best. Long. I only got back a few minutes ago.'

'You should be resting.'

'I will. Um, have you come far?'

'Noyelette. Where I'm based. It's about fifty miles. I caught the midnight tender. It's my day off.' Her hair was black beneath the beret, tiny freckles peppered her nose, and her voice bore the softest trace of a country accent.

'Ah. A day off. That must be nice.'

'Yes.' He shrugged. 'So, I came to see you.'

'Me!' She laughed.

'Yes. If that's OK.'

'Well, yes, I suppose. Only . . .'

'I should have asked first. I'm sorry. I could come back later. Or not . . .'

'No, it's not that, I just need sleep. But let's walk a little, I could do with the air.'

They strolled through empty streets, then came to an open café where they drank bitter coffee from chipped cups while early workers grunted morosely around them.

'Have you heard from George?' she asked.

'Not yet.' He needed to, and soon. Because of the sergeant. The sergeant they'd met that night in the depot near the trenches. Collingwood. I know who you are, Collingwood had written, in a note. Nothing else. 'I'd like to write him, but don't have an address.'

'I do. I had a letter yesterday. He's in Essex.'

'Essex?'

'Yes. Something about a Home Defence squadron. And he mentioned you quite a bit. I could give you his address.'

'Thanks, I'd appreciate it.' Beneath the fatigue and grime of her face, her skin looked alabaster smooth. 'Have you known him long?'

'Not really.' She smiled ruefully. 'We met about seven months ago. In Shropshire. He was still at school, and . . . Well, George can be quite impetuous.'

'He sure can.'

'Do you know him well?'

'He's the best friend I have.'

. . . My mother, incidentally, Emily, a very determined woman, had some scheme to extract me from the RFC and into a staff job, but I was having none of that: my duty is in the air over France, fighting von Richthofen and his chums. (Have you heard of him? He's quite famous, and I believe shot me down on the 21st.) But for now I must put up with Home Defence duties, which involve protecting the Capital from the Zeppelin menace. Important work I suppose, and not without hazard (we fly mainly at night), but nothing compared to being in France. I do hope Mac is safe and sound, I owe him a great deal.

Once again, Emily, please accept my apologies for trouble caused by my thoughtlessness last year. My greatest hope is that we can draw a line beneath the matter and strike up a proper friendship. Should you feel like getting in touch (I'd be most interested to hear of your work with the FANY) my address is as above.

With sincerest best wishes.

Yours,

George.

Chapter 4

I told you it wasn't much of a letter. More a rambling tissue of half-truths. I mean, '*hours reflecting on the forces of destiny that reunited us*' – what was I thinking about? As for the rest, it wasn't a 'nuisance' I got posted to Suttons Farm, it was a hard night's card-playing. Moreover I certainly wasn't hoping to 'have at the Hun once more', and I only graduated from scout training as 'average'; and as for getting shot down by Richthofen, well, actually . . . But that's another story. The only honest part, aside from the expressions of regret, was about forestalling my mother's plan to get me out of the RFC.

Why? Good question. Was it about standing up to my father, escaping my brother's shadow and all that? Partly, but it was more. Joining the RFC was the first remotely useful thing I'd ever undertaken on my own. I was proud of that, and proud of my work with 13 Squadron. Yes I'd been badly scared, and would do anything to avoid repeating the experience – including finagling a transfer to Essex – but that didn't mean I wanted to leave the RFC. On our first morning at scout training we trainees had to stand and give a résumé of our flying experience to date. As I gave mine, talking without embellishment about Bathtub ops in the Arras offensive, I couldn't help noticing the deferential glances of other students, and even the odd knowing nod from an instructor. What I had been through, I realised, was worthy of respect, something I had attracted precious little of up to then. I also realised I didn't want to sit in Whitehall pushing papers around. I wanted to stay in the RFC and become a scout pilot like Mac. I just needed time to recover my nerves first, that's all.

So when scout training finished, which was three weeks or so after Mac rescued me from no-man's land, I got myself posted to Suttons Farm, from where I wrote that letter to Emily. Suttons was a pleasant enough spot not far from Romford in Essex. Later it would become famous as RAF Hornchurch, an important front-line fighter station of the Second World War, but in 1917 it was little more than a few huts in a field. I reported in, was duly billeted above a pub in the village, and settled down to the arduous task of Home Defence. Which wasn't arduous at all, and thus exactly what I needed – a chance to draw breath, gather my wits, and reflect on what had passed.

It was exactly six months since Bertie Wilkins and I had reported to Officer Cadet Training School in Hendon for induction into the RFC. Dear Bertie. It's an odd fact, but some people aren't meant to fly aeroplanes. Maybe it's about hand-eye co-ordination, or being able to pull levers, turn knobs and push pedals at the same time, or maybe it's that impalpable business of fusing an organic being with a mechanical one and making them work. Whatever it is, some folks can't do it, and Bertie, bless him, was one.

But it was weeks until we found out, for becoming a pilot turned out to be a protracted affair, and little to do with aeroplanes. Having sailed through the War Office interview – 'Shrewsbury School you say? That's all right then' – we duly reported to OCTS in Hendon where we and thirty other recruits spent three miserable weeks marching up and down a parade-ground in the freezing rain. Nobody mentioned aeroplanes and the only flying we saw was leaves going sideways past the window. Next we were sent to Oxford for six weeks in a classroom being initiated into the mysteries of 'aeronautics'. This was interminably tedious, furthermore the food was dreadful and the accommodation piteous. It was just like being back at school only without the crumpets, and few days passed without Bertie or I bemoaning our folly. Only three good things happened at Oxford. One, I established a pontoon school which paid for my bar-bill. Two, we were issued with our RFC uniforms, the famous khaki maternity jacket and trousers, and the cap worn rakishly aside the head. Three (and portentously), we were suddenly told midway that tuition was being curtailed, and to report to Brooklands airfield in Surrey for flight training forthwith. How we all cheered.

Had we but known. This was the end of 1916, and the RFC was starting to lose pilots quicker than it could replace them. So the order had gone out to cut training and throw us neophytes into the breach. We of course were oblivious, just delighted things were happening at last. Within two days we were at Brooklands, the next morning our flying clothes were issued and we met our instructors, and that same afternoon we got our first look at an aeroplane, filing into a musty hangar to stare in respectful awe at the flimsy beast of string and fabric crouching on the floor like an insect.

'What on earth is it?' one student asked.

'Bloody museum piece!' quipped another, unwisely.

'That bloody museum piece,' our guide said acidly, 'is the Maurice-Farman Longhorn. And you'd better show it respect because it don't suffer fools, and you're flying it tomorrow.'

And so we did. If the Bathtub was ancient, the Longhorn was positively prehistoric. Known by everyone as the 'Rumpety' it really was a Wright Flyer in all but name; it even had the elevator out front like their first machines. The only difference was you didn't lie on your belly to fly it, you sat in a baby's pram, complete with spindly wheels underneath for undercarriage. I thought it was the bee's knees; my instructor, Captain Graham 'Grumpy' Monahan, was less enthusiastic, cursing it roundly from the back seat while I wrestled it through the exercises. They were an unnerving breed, our instructors. Mad, actually, many of them. For a start they hated instructing, which didn't fill us with confidence, and they particularly hated us, their pupils, referring to us openly as 'The Hun', as though we were the enemy. Twitchy, neurotic and bad-tempered, many were ex-front-line pilots who had been invalided out, some with terrible injuries. Monahan had shrapnel in his head from an Archie burst, which was why he was grumpy, another had a leg missing, a third had horrible burns. Hardly surprising therefore they didn't like to fly, particularly in the hands of clumsy oafs like us.

On my fourth morning at Brooklands my feet finally left the ground. Earlier Grumpy had explained the elaborate series of signals for communicating instructions in a Rumpety. A tap of his hand on my left shoulder meant turn left, on the right turn right, on top of the head meant climb, and one on the neck meant descend. A clout round the ear, I soon learned, meant Duckwell you're a useless bungling imbecile.

That first flight I remember as a dizzying cocktail of raw terror, blank confusion and adrenalin-charged excitement. First, Grumpy led me round the machine to check nothing had fallen off, and to point out the names of key components. These seemed mostly French: 'This mid-section is called the fusel-*age*, see, which is attached to the tail assembly here known as the empenn-*age*, and the whole thing sits on the wheels which are called the undercarri-*age* . . .' Then we clambered into the nacelle, Grumpy in the back where he busied himself with fuel cocks and magneto switches while I sat in front nervously eyeing the control stick and baffling array of (two) instruments. Then a mechanic began pulling on the propeller which clunked over asthmatically before exploding to life in a cloud of smoke. A few more checks and we were bumping out for take-off, then the engine note rose to a roar, we began to accelerate, the grass blurred, the bumps grew more spirited, then with a final bone-jarring crunch everything went smooth. Alarmed, I looked down, expecting smashed wheels and a trail of wreckage, but what I saw was the tiny upturned faces of my fellow students amid a receding sea of green. We were airborne!

For a while I just enjoyed the ride, which was comfortable if unhurried. The engine clattered happily, the wind sang in the rigging and Surrey unfolded below us like a map. Magical, was my first reaction, magical if peculiar. Then came a prod in my back. 'Take over!' Grumpy yelled, and suddenly I was in control. Or not, for the Rumpety's gyrations and my panicked fumblings appeared to have little in common. And the more I tried the worse it got. Convinced the machine could only fly if I forced it to, I expended all my energy trying to wrestle it into submission. I was trying too hard, over-controlling, a common error with first-time students; in due course I would learn the pilot's job is not about brute force but about balance. I pushed and pulled and sweated, the Rumpety careered about the sky like an unruly cow, and eventually Grumpy took over and brought us in to land.

'Seen worse,' he grunted, to my surprise. 'But you'll have to do much better.'

Days passed, slowly I got to grips with the thing. The Rumpety was not an easy aircraft to fly, particularly in any wind. It was just too jittery, and unbelievably slow. I remember taking off one breezy afternoon, flying into wind for twenty minutes, then looking down only to see we were still over the airfield, in fact proceeding slowly backwards across it. I glanced at Grumpy who scowled and pointed down, which meant this is hopeless we might as well land. So I began to turn down-wind and in seconds we were bowling along like litter in a gale. This earned me a monster smack round the ear and Grumpy took over, hurriedly turning us into wind again. Had he not done so, I subsequently realised, we would never have got back.

Christmas came and went, then a morning arrived when he led me across the frosty grass, but when we reached our Rumpety he didn't board it with me.

'Right, Duckwell, pay close attention. You will take off, fly one circuit, and land. Nothing else. Got that?'

'What, you mean alone, sir?'

'Of course alone, you ninny. I'm sending you solo. Try not to cock it up and crash, we need the aeroplane.'

Thursday 28 December 1916, my logbook records, also noting I had accrued a total of two hours and fifty minutes' flying experience, which doesn't seem like much. First solo. It's like losing your virginity: scary, exciting, shambolic and over too fast. And it can only happen once.

Heart pounding, I climbed aboard, started up and trundled off. I didn't feel confident but did feel determined. Part of me wished someone could be there to see it. Actually, I wished my brother Hugh could be there to see it. I checked his watch, turned into wind, opened the throttle and wobbled into the air. Climbing ahead, at three hundred feet I began a careful turn, allowing myself just a few seconds to savour the moment. There I was, alone, in an aeroplane, in sole control. I could do anything, chase clouds, soar with eagles, or set sail for Scotland. But I didn't, I gave a little whoop for joy and flew the circuit, safely if untidily, as instructed. Before I knew it I was turning in to land, blipping the throttle to lose height. Then the grass was rising all around me, I nudged back on the stick, cut the motor and bumped to a halt, alive, intact and triumphant.

That night we celebrated, lurching from pub to pub in an orgy of pubescent carousing. Several of us had 'soloed' that day, much to the jealous admiration of those who hadn't, and we 'aces' made the most of it.

'Nothing to it, chaps!' I bragged pompously. 'Keep the nose up, watch your speed in the turns and Bob's your uncle!'

My audience nodded adoringly. Except Bertie, I noticed, who was standing apart. He hadn't soloed that day, nor, I knew, was his training going well. Elbowing through the throng, I went to his side.

'What's up, Bertie-boy? You've a face like a wet weekend.'

'Nothing.' He forced a smile. 'Well done, George, I knew you'd beat me to it.'

'Pure luck, old thing. Anyway it's not a competition, you'll get there soon enough, tomorrow probably.'

'I doubt it.' He shook his head. 'I just can't seem to get the hang of it.'

'But you will, Bertie, you will.'

'I'm not so sure. My instructor says I'm the worst student he's ever had, and he's going to fail me if I don't pull my socks up.'

'So did mine! That's just their teaching method. Listen, you mustn't worry, it's all just a matter of confidence, trust me.'

He looked at me, his boyish features round with worry. 'That's just it, George. I don't have any confidence.'

It's hard to argue with a statement like that, but how I wish I'd tried. The next day I was sitting in the students' hut, nursing a hangover and reading the papers, when a shout came from outside. I wandered on to the grass to see the fuss. Faces peered skyward, arms pointing. A Rumpety was in trouble, flying in unsteady circles over the field. Who is it?

people shouted, and with a jolt I realised it was Bertie, on his first solo. I started to run, eyes riveted to the aeroplane which even as I watched seemed to shudder in the air, then drop sideways. In a second it was spinning, falling over and over like a dropped toy until with a sickening crump it crashed to the ground. 'Bertie!' I kept running, calling his name, willing him to be unhurt. And as I neared my hopes rose. The impact had looked ludicrously slow, the Rumpety was almost intact and Bertie, I could see, was sitting erect in the cockpit. Behind me I heard the clanging of the fire-tender bell, other runners were converging on the scene, help was coming. 'Hang on, Bertie!' Seconds more and I arrived, clambering through the wreckage towards him. 'Bertie, it's all right, it's me!'

His face was unmarked, his child-like eyes open in surprise. But his skin had a blue-grey pallor, and his expression was slack. As I stared, his head lolled slowly sideways, the neck broken. Yet his eyes still stared at me questioningly, and I can see them even now. 'I told you,' they seemed to say. I climbed into the cockpit, cradled him in my arms and waited for the others to arrive.

I completed my training. Of our class of thirty, only half made it. Seven were dismissed as 'untrainable', four took fright and resigned, two were injured in accidents and one was killed. A sobering introduction to the statistics of war. I took little pleasure in my graduation, even when awarded the coveted RFC 'wings' for my tunic.

On our final morning at Brooklands a notice was pinned up showing our postings. Mine said *Duckwell G. 13 Obs Sqn, Arras*

Sect. Later Grumpy Monahan sought me out. 'You've the makings of a half-decent pilot, Duckwell,' he said, lighting a cigarette. 'But you must focus on being much better, and using your wits and anything else you can think of to stay alive. Do you understand?'

'Yes, sir.'

'Wilkins was your friend, wasn't he.'

'Yes, sir.'

'He should never have applied to the RFC. Quite clueless. But he's gone now and you must forget him.'

'I should have stopped him.'

'You think it was your fault?'

'Something like that.'

Monahan blew smoke. 'Let me give you some advice, Duckwell. If you start blaming yourself for every friend you lose, I guarantee you will shoot yourself within a month. Wilkins didn't die because of you, he died because of the war. He's a casualty statistic, that's all. And if you want to stay alive, you'll forget about friendships and keep that in mind.'

With that he ground his cigarette underfoot and wandered off.

The makings of a half-decent pilot, he'd said – high praise indeed from the man with shrapnel for brains. But not high enough, because he'd passed me only as 'average' so I was destined for a lowly Bathtub squadron and not groomed for stardom in scouts. Which may have been, I have often thought since, exactly the right thing to do.

I went home for a few days' leave. It was not the happiest of reunions, being our first since I'd fled Shrewsbury in disgrace. In fact it was awful. My father, still furious about me not joining the Fusiliers, spent much of it waving sheaves of letters, bills and IOUs from angry Shropshire folk. My mother looked forlorn and wept a lot. I hid in my room, or wandered Greenwich until bedtime, when I lay awake thinking of poor Bertie, and Hugh, whom I hadn't thought about in years, and Emily, whom I had thought about a lot yet had made no attempt to contact. Somehow I'd let them all down, or so it seemed. The days crawled, father fumed, mother cried, then to my relief an envelope dropped through the door with my written orders, and at last I went to war.

I was to report to an RFC aerodrome in Noyelette, a tiny northern French hamlet ten miles west of Arras and about fifty south of Calais, travelling there by troopship and train via Folkestone, Dunkirk and St Omer. My send-off was not as I'd envisaged. At school we'd been shown jerky newsreel films of soldiers going to war. Station platforms packed with cheering crowds, dignitaries making speeches, flag-waving children, and smiling Tommies being kissed by wives, sweethearts and mothers. My mother was too upset to come to the station; she saw me off on the doorstep, clutching at my hand and begging me not to go. My father saw me off from behind the locked door of his study.

Nor did I meet many smiling Tommies. The journey was long and wearisome, featuring a rolling troopship lined with seasick conscripts followed by a series of smoke-filled trains packed with more grim-faced troops returning from leave. All were bound for the trenches, none seemed pleased about it. After two and a half years, evidently, the novelty of war had worn off. As for my feelings, twelve weeks earlier I'd been a carefree schoolboy, now, apparently, I was a warrior.

I'd spent two years blocking the war from consciousness, now I was embracing it, contrary to my every instinct. Yet I cannot deny I was excited. I also felt bewildered at the speed of it all, keyed up, and nervous, not of the risks but of making an idiot of myself. Of my foe, I felt only vague curiosity. As for actually killing him, I felt nothing at all, for the notion was inconceivable.

I reached St Omer after dark then had to wait for the Noyelette tender, so it was past midnight when I reached my destination. Everyone was in bed, and the place closed up; a duty orderly showed me to a damp cot in a side-office and with a muttered 'Good luck, son' left me to it. I lay awake listening to the wind, too nervous for sleep. In the morning, unbelievably, my war would begin. But in the morning, up early to make a start on it, I was surprised to find few people about, a distinct lack of urgency and no instructions for Duckwell. Told only to report to the squadron CO, Major Strickley, at eleven, I was abandoned to my own devices. Bemused, I breakfasted alone, then wrapped myself in scarf and greatcoat and wandered off to discover my new home.

Noyelette aerodrome consisted of sixty acres of hastily requisitioned farmland, much of it still under the plough, which could make for interesting landings. It was also bisected by a road and an avenue of trees which effectively cut one half from the other. All the hangars, huts, tents and so on were in the smaller half, while the bigger half was kept clear for landing aeroplanes. Except that pilots, being lazy show-offs, invariably tried to land on the small half, sometimes with spectacular results. In addition, Noyelette housed not one squadron but two. My own, 13 Squadron with its Bathtubs, lived in huts and tents at the northern end of the field, while at the southern end, occupying a former chateau complete with comfy beds, wine cellar and tennis courts, resided 166 Squadron, a crack scout unit then flying Nieuports. I had been exploring Noyelette less than an hour therefore before I concluded I was in the wrong squadron.

This judgement was confirmed when I met my fellow pilots. Flying had been cancelled for the morning due to low cloud so it was a while before any appeared, venturing out to sniff the air like shy mice, plodding to the latrines, or to the mess where they hunched over mugs of tea. Rarely have I seen a gloomier troupe, their expressions downcast, their demeanour chary, even their movements seemed slow and resigned. None showed the slightest interest in the newest addition to their ranks, and my attempts at conversation were met with either monosyllabic grunts or blank stares. Something, evidently, was amiss with 13 Squadron.

A clue came during my interview with Major Strickley which was equally unsettling. In his forties, stick-thin with grey wispy hair, he spent most of it staring out the window, or muttering about his roses back in Hampshire. He asked no questions, nor did he check my orders or logbook. At one point he stopped talking altogether, then gave a long sigh.

'Sir?' I enquired uneasily.

'It's the weight of them, you see, dear boy,' he murmured, as though in a trance. 'The awful crushing weight.'

'Yes, sir.'

I waited, but he said nothing more. A minute or so later he pulled himself together, clapped me on the back, assured me my stay with 13 Squadron would be a happy one, and shoved me outside.

Lunch was bread and soup in the mess with my cohorts who by then were fractionally more animated, grunting to one another in a clipped shorthand. I was still roundly ignored, until that is I committed the cardinal sin, and mentioned the war.

'Excuse me,' I enquired blithely. 'How many Huns has 13 Squadron shot down?'

Silence fell like a brick, horrified stares circling the table.

'We don't discuss that sort of thing at luncheon,' someone said frostily.

Not many then, I concluded. After 'luncheon' a corporal showed me to my quarters. These consisted of an army cot in a corner of a freezing hut shared with three other pilots. My furniture was a cupboard and a bedside locker, in the centre of the room stood an unlit stove. 'You'll be snug as a bug in here,' the corporal said, blowing on his hands. It was Len Larkin, and the first friendly face I'd met. 'If we ever get coal for the stove, that is. And don't you worry about the other gentlemen, sir, they'll soon warm to you once they get to know you.'

I stared at my cot. 'Was someone else in here before me?'

'He was, sir. Lad by the name of Poppard. At least I think it was Poppard.'

'What happened to him?'

'Bought it, poor chap. But not to worry, he wasn't here long.'

It was unclear why this constituted good news, but Len's cheery reassurances seemed genuine and by now I needed them. He left me with a wink.

I passed ten brooding minutes unpacking my things into Poppard's cupboard, then with nothing else to do wandered outside to continue my tour of the aerodrome. An hour or so later I found myself at the hangars, and took my first close look at a Bathtub.

After the Rumpety it looked huge and daunting and powerful, and with a Lewis gun or two mounted on its nacelle it also looked war-like. Yet there was something superannuated about the design, and these examples appeared especially pensionable. Several had multiple repairs to wings and fuselage, most dripped oil and coolant from their engines, one or two were missing key components, like a propeller or tail-fin. And one, ominously, was just a pile of wreckage swept in the corner.

'A pilot crashed it on landing. Last week, so I believe.'

A dark-haired man was standing behind me. He wore RFC uniform and wings, so he was a pilot, but not one I'd yet met. He looked in his early twenties, tall, guarded, and with penetratingly watchful eyes.

'Was he, you know . . .'

'I'm afraid so. He'd been badly shot up. Died in the ambulance. Observer made it OK though.' The voice was slow and measured, with a North American accent.

'Well, I suppose that's something.'

I couldn't take my eyes off the wreck. War had been done in it, violently: Archie-holes riddled the wings, empty bullet-casings littered the cockpit, and splashed down the side were dark stains of what was unmistakably blood.

'Was it Poppard?'

'Sorry, I don't know, I'm not with this unit. But I guess you're his replacement.'

'You're not with 13 Squadron?'

'No. The other one. 166, across the field.'

'Really?' I studied him anew, a real scout pilot, in the flesh. 'What's it like?'

'It's a fine unit.' He smiled. 'If a little rowdy.'

'This one's dire. And not very friendly.'

'They've been having it rough. You mustn't take it personally.'

'No one's even asked my name.'

'They're just being careful. You'll understand in time.'

'I suppose so.'

'So what is it?'

'Excuse me?'

He was still smiling. 'Your name.'

'Oh, it's George. George Duckwell.'

'How do you do, George. I'm William MacBride.'

And that's how I met Mac.

And so I went to war. 13 Squadron's job in those weeks before the Arras offensive was a mixture of photo-reconnaissance, artillery-spotting and whatever else the army dreamed up for us, including the occasional offensive patrol, under escort of course. With one Lewis machine-gun mounted forward, a second shooting aft and sometimes even a third nailed on for luck, in its day the Balsa Bathtub could put up quite a fight, but by 1917 it was woefully out of date. Too slow, lacking manoeuvrability and no match for the competition, it was really fit only for defensive functions like spotting and photography, which was largely what we did.

My first days were spent doing 'acclimatisation', which

meant learning to fly the Bathtub and familiarising myself with the local topography which was rural, undulatory and wooded with a peppering of pretty villages. To my frustration I was forbidden to engage the enemy, ordered to flee at the first sign of trouble, and banned from venturing near the lines which were ten miles east of Noyelette. On my third day I was assigned a gunner/observer, a battle-wizened sergeant from Northampton called Morris Dixon. Forty, stocky, unflappable, with a florid complexion and commanding voice, Morris was the ideal foil to my schoolboy hot-headedness and he taught me much. We flew a few training sorties together, me slowly mastering the controls, he pointing out landmarks and watching for trouble, then Major Strickley called us in and announced we were ready for the fray. I cheered, Morris looked dubious. The next morning we were assigned to C-Flight and flew our first mission.

Nervous, jittery, excited, yes, all those things, but more importantly at just eighteen and with barely twenty hours in my logbook I was absurdly under-prepared. I could scarcely fly an aeroplane, let alone fight in one, and although that youthful zeal seems endearing now, it was precisely this lack of experience that was killing so many of us. Later on, pilots never went near the lines without at least sixty hours under their belts, often much more, but that was the future; in those first months of 1917 we new boys were lambs to the slaughter, pure and simple. The only thing in our favour was our ignorance: if they'd told me to attack Berlin I'd have happily given it a go, although Morris might have baulked somewhat. God knows how he kept his sanity during those early missions, they were an utter shambles, indeed our first might easily have been our last but for his timely interventions. Barely were we airborne, wobbling along behind the others like the class dunce, when I accidentally turned off the fuel cock. Don't ask why, nervous pilots often do stupid things for no reason. The engine promptly stopped and we began gliding silently earthward, propeller windmilling in the breeze. I froze with shock, literally ceased functioning like a rundown clockwork toy. Morris, however, sitting up front with his arms folded, seemed unperturbed.

'It's gone a bit quiet, sir, wouldn't you say?' he said, after a while.

But my mind was still blank.

'Look!' He pointed. 'I just saw a deer. Fancy that!'

'Sergeant, we're crashing!'

'Shouldn't think so, sir.' Still he waited, hoping I'd work it out myself.

'But the engine's stopped!'

'So it has. And all because . . .'

'I . . . I don't know!'

'Those fuel cocks can be confusing, can't they, sir.'

'Fuel cock! My God, the fuel cock's off!'

Seconds later the engine was clattering away behind us once more and normal service was resumed.

Another twenty minutes and we were nearing the lines, still climbing hard to stay clear of ground fire. Nine thousand feet, ten, eleven, a dizzying height, this was new territory for me. I'd scarcely ventured above a thousand in the Rumpety, and these stratospheric altitudes felt scarily alien. Time and motion seemed to stop, the Bathtub wallowed in my hands, the earth was horribly distant below, the air around us raw and thin. And unbelievably cold. This was January, remember, and we were sitting in an open cockpit in a sixty-mile-an-hour gale at ten degrees below freezing. In no time I'd lost all sensation to my extremities, and my body, unused to the rare air, was becoming weak and lethargic. As was my mind. Gazing numbly down at the stationary landscape far below, my concentration was soon wandering, and I felt an uneasy lassitude taking hold. I was two miles up, I reflected, perched upon a flimsy contraption of wood and canvas, and the only thing keeping me there was my inept fumblings on its controls. Which were getting more inept by the minute. I checked on the other Bathtubs, dangling in space around me as though on threads, but that surreal image only made matters worse, so I returned my gaze to the mist-veiled earth and tried to imagine what falling two miles would feel like with no parachute.

By now, insensitive with cold, panicky, hypoxic and vertiginous, my ability to reason was slipping away, together with my control of the aircraft. A timely juncture for Morris, who was sensing all this through the aeroplane's motions, to step in once more.

'Bracing, no?' he shouted, with a cheery grin. 'Only half an hour more and we're on our way home!'

I recall little of that patrol. The lines were obscured by ground-mist, we met no enemy aircraft, nor were we bothered by Archie. What we did see, eerily, was artillery shells. At first I thought my mind was going again, or my vision playing tricks. I'd be staring gormlessly ahead, trying to think warm thoughts, when out of the corner of an eye I'd glimpse a blob, which instantly vanished. A minute or two later another blob would appear and vanish. I couldn't see them directly, only peripherally, and wasn't sure I'd seen them at all, so fleeting was their presence. Confused, I tapped Morris on the shoulder.

'See that?' I yelled, above the engine.

'Of course!' He nodded. 'Howitzers.'

What we were seeing were some of the thousands of heavy artillery shells fired back and forth across the lines each day. They weren't aimed at us, but at targets on the ground; we just happened to be at the right height to glimpse them at the top of their trajectories. Or the wrong height, depending on your viewpoint. Quite what would happen if we got in the way of one was another matter. Vaporised, we'd be, Morris told me later.

Eventually we headed back to base having spent two hours, in my view, achieving little except frost-nipped cheeks and a blinding headache from the altitude. Not a photograph was taken, not a shot fired, not a single Hun seen. The only consolation was I'd made it round the course without making a complete ass of myself in front of the others.

Then I crashed into a tree on landing which rather spoilt things. The mist we'd noticed earlier had thickened. It didn't look too bad from directly above, but as we angled in for the landing everything went horribly murky. I followed the others down, watching with mounting apprehension as one by one they vanished into the soup like frogs into a pond. Then suddenly we were in it too, descending through an all-enveloping grey cloud, no sky, no ground, nothing. 'Hold her steady!' Morris cautioned, but in seconds I'd lost orientation. The next moment a dark shadow was looming ahead, then came the unmistakable crunch of Bathtub through treetop, then a moment's pregnant pause before we belly-flopped into the bushes like a downed elephant.

Silence descended, together with sundry twigs and leaves. Like autumn.

'Right then.' Morris stepped to the ground, brushing undergrowth from his clothes. 'Lunchtime, I'd say.'

'But what about the aeroplane?'

'Not going anywhere, is it?'

'Well, no, but—'

'I shouldn't worry, sir. Engineers'll have it out in no time.' He strode off into the mist. 'Important thing is we got down in one piece.'

True enough. And after lunch we did it all again.

A routine quickly established itself. Weather permitting, 13 Squadron was expected to mount two or maybe three sorties a day. With its twelve aeroplanes divided into three flights, that meant pilots flew once or twice daily. When not flying I was either at readiness, which meant sitting around reading the newspapers, or at stand-down, which meant sleeping in my bed, or I was duty orderly, which meant wading through the mountains of paperwork dumped on junior officers. The RFC provided for my board and lodging at fifty francs a week, although drinks were extra, and I received one day off a week to pass as I pleased, cycling to nearby Beaufort for a meal of horse advertised as 'boeuf', or catching a tender to Caucourt for a film show. A typical duty day might start at five with the infamous hard-boiled egg and dawn patrol, returning for breakfast and back to bed, then lunch followed by reading, listening to the gramophone, a few hands of solitaire, or simply more bed. (Sleep was always in demand – something to do with open-air flying, the cold, the altitude, adrenalin and stress.) There then might be a second patrol, followed by dinner in the mess and some desultory conversation over a thimble of wine before retiring to bed with a book.

As can be gathered, I soon concluded my fellow pilots of 13 Squadron were a most lacklustre bunch of dullards. Quite why was a mystery, but it seemed to be about low self-regard. We suffered casualties, true, but no more than other observer squadrons, and nothing compared to the carnage to come. Sharing the aerodrome with an elite scout unit might also have invoked feelings of inferiority. Clearly part of the problem lay with Major Strickley who was the epitome of insipidity, partly it was the job, which was thankless and devoid of glamour, partly it was just the ethos of the place. '13 Squadron?' people would say. 'Rather a quiet lot, so I hear.' Which was putting it mildly. I tried to liven things up, playing pranks on my room-mates, doubling the wine order for dinner, showing them card-tricks and so on, but to little avail; at best they smiled politely and went back to their books. I resolved to keep trying. In the meantime I had to find amusement elsewhere.

In the sergeants' mess, for a start, where our observers lived. It's an oddity of the military system, but though we fought and died in the air with these fine men, being non-commissioned meant they weren't allowed to mix with us officers socially, much to their relief. Indeed they had to salute when we passed, and call us 'sir', even though most were much older and infinitely wiser. Another oddity was that this segregation didn't bother them; on the contrary they much preferred living among their own and would have recoiled in horror at suggestions of intermingling. So I was looked upon with some suspicion when I first ventured through their door. In fact the moment it opened everything went from raucous jollity to stony silence in about two seconds. Then Morris spotted me and broke the ice. 'It's only the new boy,' he said, winking at his chums. 'What, you mean the tree-lander?' joked another, and I was soon welcomed into their midst, especially when they learned I played cards. I tried not to impose too often, that would have been improper, but their mess was so much cheerier than ours. They knew how to have fun and relax and make the best of things, swigging beer, singing songs and barracking one another in their sergeant's slang.

'Where's Charlie?'

'Guardroom! On a fizzer for thieving Red Cross twilights. God-botherer went to see him but Charlie thought he was a linseed-lancer and dropped his trousers for short-arm inspection. So now he's got the fizzer *and* three weeks' knee-drill!'

'Silly arse.'

A fizzer was a disciplinary charge, twilights were servicewomen's underwear, the God-botherer the chaplain, linseed-lancer a medical officer, knee-drill was church parade and short-arm inspection – well, you work it out.

My first encounter with death-by-war came during the third week. By then I felt more than ready for action: my flying proficiency was improving, I could hold a neat formation, and I hadn't turned the fuel off nor made a tree-landing in days. Morris said I was coming along 'as expected', which

I think was a compliment. The only problem was I hadn't so much as seen a Hun, let alone attacked one, and was becoming dangerously impatient. Then one morning C-Flight was briefed to photograph German positions near Feuchy, a few miles *behind* enemy lines. This was significant, for the lines represented an enormous psychological barrier. Once crossed, you were entering lethal waters, a devil's lair where death lurked behind every cloud, monstrous guns hurled hell at you from the ground, and neither help nor salvation was at hand should you need it. Venturing there was no trifling matter, so you went across, did what you had to and hurried back, dallying at your peril. At last, I thought. Something to get my teeth into.

The four aircraft of C-Flight took off and climbed to three thousand. This wasn't high enough for anyone's liking, but all we could get because of a thick cloud layer. The weather was sleety and overcast, the wind westerly, and in no time we were crossing no-man's land and heading into the unknown. Minutes later Archie opened up, throwing up its balls of exploding puff. I'd seen some already, at a distance; it had looked harmless, like little bursting clouds of brown wool. But this was much closer. I could smell the cordite, hear the bark of its bursts, and with every near salvo the aeroplane jumped in my hands as though kicked. Then we were nearing the target and Morris turned to me, making 'hold her steady' signals, before bending over his camera. I hung on, wrestling to keep position on the leader's Bathtub. Which then promptly vanished. One second it was there, wings, engine, cockpit, two men, the next it was thousands of tiny pieces in an exploding black cloud. At the same time the controls sprang from my grip, something hit me in the face, the air-craft bucked, and Morris, who was leaning out to operate the camera, disappeared overboard.

It all happened so fast I couldn't take it in. Fumbling frantically, I managed to return the aeroplane to an even keel, although it felt sloppy and unresponsive, nor could I see properly as my goggles seemed fogged with grime, and bits of something else. I wiped them with a glove and everything turned red. I'm shot, I panicked, staring down at myself. Sure enough my leathers glistened with blood and gore. But not mine, I realised sickeningly, it must be from the leader's Bathtub. Or Morris. Only then did I register the empty front seat. He was gone! Thrown out by the blast and now tumbling helplessly to his death. Then I saw a hand, a single gloved hand gripping the edge of the nacelle. Then a second appeared, moving beside it. Morris!

I leaned over and there he was, one leg wrapped around a wheel-strut, the other dangling in space. I reached out and managed to grab his collar but couldn't haul him up, nor could I fly the aeroplane properly. For ten agonised seconds we held on like that, me hanging over the side, him clinging on for dear life, the Bathtub floundering, and Archie still bursting furiously all round. Then he shook himself from my grip and for a horrific moment I thought he was going to jump. But he didn't, he lifted his face and bellowed his one-word instruction: 'Fly!'

So I flew. But first I had to secure him, for I knew he'd never hold on. Undoing the belt of my flying-coat, I slipped the looped buckle over his wrist and wrapped the other end tightly round my own. Then I turned the aeroplane gingerly about and headed for home. I could see no sign of the other two Bathtubs, had only the vaguest notion of our position, or the route back, my aircraft was damaged, my observer hanging over the side, and I was flying one-handed, but apart from that we were in fine shape. Go low, I reasoned, though I don't know why – to get below Archie perhaps, or Morris closer to terra firma, for all the good it would do him. So I dropped down to fifty feet and headed east. Soon Archie did indeed stop, then zigzag lines of trenches appeared and I glimpsed faces upturned in surprise and rifles being brought to shoulders. We took a few hits, holes bursting in the wings with a 'pock' sound, but not many, possibly because we were so low, or possibly because the Huns were too astonished by the sight of a Bathtub with a man dangling from it to shoot properly. Then the shots fell behind, and we were crossing our own lines, safe at last from enemy fire.

But where exactly I had no idea. I fumbled for the map, trying to read it one-handed, but the slipstream tore it from my grip and it vanished through the propeller. I leaned over to check on Morris: he was hanging limply, head down, and looked done-for. I too wondered how much longer I could keep flying and holding the belt, so I made a decision, my first in combat and mercifully a sensible one. Turning into wind I throttled back and landed us in a turnip field. As we bumped to a halt I quickly shut down the motor and jumped out.

'Dixon!'

He was white as a sheet, speechless with shock and cold, but otherwise uninjured save for a sore wrist. I helped him to the ground and propped him against a wheel, pressing a cigarette between his lips. For a while we sat there together, smoking quietly and not speaking. Then came the sound of hooves, and a mounted cavalry officer appeared, all polished boots and twirling moustache.

'Good heavens above!' he roared, handing down a silver hip-flask. 'You RFC chaps have all the fun, what?'

'Rather,' I replied drily.

'Need anything? Medic? Transportation? A driver and what-not?'

'Transportation would be useful, sir,' Morris said, patting my knee. He hauled himself to his feet. 'As for a driver, I have one thanks. A damn fine one he is too.'

C-Flight lost two aircraft that day, and with ours damaged, three-quarters of its strength was down. Four men were dead and but for a miracle Morris would have made five. I'm not going to be hypocritical and say I was grief-stricken at the deaths of the pilots, because I didn't know them well enough. But I was shocked. One, Waters, was in my hut. A softly spoken chap from Ely, the evening before I'd tried to lure him into a game of draughts; he'd declined politely, and now he was gone. The suddenness of that took me aback, and the irrevocability. He'd been alive, then an hour later he wasn't, and that hit home. War, it was dawning, was not about heroes, it was about not getting killed.

We were stood down for the rest of the day. I mooched about the mess while everyone avoided eye contact or sat around reading as though nothing had happened. Desperate to escape this suffocating mood of restraint I considered cycling into the countryside, but the weather had closed in, with dol-lops of snow sliding down the window like sodden bread. I could try the sergeants' mess, but two of their number had also been killed and I sensed they'd rather be left alone. I could go into Beaufort and fraternise with the locals, but somehow horse stew and incomprehensible old men wasn't what I wanted. Then the blessed miracle happened. A polite knock came on the door and Lieutenant William MacBride entered, umbrella in hand.

'George, isn't it?' he enquired. 'A few of our people are taking a tender into Amiens, I wondered if you'd care to tag along.'

Five minutes later I was being hauled unceremoniously into the back of a crowded lorry. Inside were RFC pilots, at first glance much the same as the ones I'd just left, but as different as chalk from cheddar. For a start they spoke, loudly, and laughed and clapped one another on the back and sang bawdy songs, and all the other things 13 Squadron pilots didn't do. They also talked to *me* which was another novelty, quizzing me on my background and training, whistling at my inexperience, congratulating me on my tree-landing and so on. Wine bottles began circulating, and cigarettes. A full-blown party broke out, and by the time we reached Amiens we were all high and hilarious. Except Mac that is, who without distancing himself remained more the watchful onlooker than active participant, smiling and nodding but not saying much. Nor did he drink, I noticed.

In Amiens we disgorged on to icy pavements and set forth in search of amusement and adventure, finding it in a succession of smoky bars and bordellos. Hours passed, champagne flowed, women arrived, sat on knees and departed, sometimes with pilots in tow. I became blissfully drunk, amusing the girls with card-tricks, pounding out music-hall songs on tables and generally being loud and overexcited.

'How the hell,' I pleaded to no one in particular, 'do I get myself out of my squadron and into yours?'

Guffaws of ridicule followed.

'Sing better for a start!'

'Shoot down a few Huns!'

'Slip the CO a fiver!'

'Stop landing in trees!'

'Buy another round!'

Then someone said: 'Ask Mac. He came up the hard way.'

I found him at a corner table, talking to a sleepy-eyed brunette with an ostrich feather in her hair.

'Mind if I join you?'

He pulled out a chair. 'Be my guest.'

'I don't want to interrupt. Is this your girl?'

'Corinne? No, we were discussing Balzac.' He waved a book. 'Or rather I was discussing, but I don't think Corinne here follows my French.'

'You speak French?'

'Not really, nor can I read Balzac, so there you go. Do you have a girl, George?'

Emily's face sprang instantly to mind, then melted in the mist. 'Yes. I . . . Well, no. There was somebody, a few months ago. I was very keen, but I messed things up.'

'Too bad, though maybe it's for the best. You know, war and relationships . . .'

'Maybe.'

'Are you having a good time?'

'Smashing, thanks. But I have a question.'

'Shoot.'

'Why did you invite me today?'

'I heard what you did for your observer this morning. We all did. Holding on to him while you flew him out like that. That takes courage. And loyalty. Worth a trip into town, wouldn't you say?'

'Well, gosh, yes, I suppose.' I hadn't thought of it like that.

'Also, when I met you that day in the hangar you didn't strike me as the usual 13 Squadron type. I figured you could use a change.'

'You can say that again. I'd like to change to a scout squadron like yours. The others said you knew how.'

'Did they.'

'They said you came up the hard way.'

He nodded, his dark eyes surveying the room. Outwardly so composed, I couldn't help noticing his fist opening and closing on the table, and the way his knee jerked beneath it. 'I was in the Canadian infantry. Did a year or so in the trenches. Transferred to the RFC as a gunner in sixteen. Got accepted for pilot training later.'

From hell to the heavens in four short sentences, yet how many volumes were left unsaid? I was drunk, so had to ask. 'Gosh, but, so, what's it like? In the trenches, I mean.'

'It's hard, George.' He smiled. 'Better in the air.'

That concluded my first proper conversation with Mac and was memorable in that I learned he was a serious man who kept himself in check, wanted to better himself with books, recognised worth in others, valued friendship and had somehow marked me out for something. He'd also endured hardship, and was tenser than a turkey at Christmas.

Around midnight befuddled panic broke out. Womenfolk were prised from arms, uniforms reassembled, stray pilots rounded up. We all lurched on to slushy streets in search of the Noyelette tender and soon we were trundling sleepily homeward. I sat beside Mac, staring out at the glistening black countryside unrolling behind us. At some point I must have dozed, for when next I became aware a conversation was going on about Richthofen.

'No, no, Cecil, old chap,' someone was saying. 'The whole circus moves about, you see, by train at night, up and down the lines. That way nobody knows where it's going to pop up next.'

'I heard there's several Jastas all painted in circus colours. So he gets spotted in different places at the same time.'

'And no one knows which is the real Baron, clever bastard. How many kills has he got now?'

'Thirty-something, so I hear.'

I nudged Mac. 'What are they talking about?'

'Richthofen.'

'Who?'

'Baron Manfred von Richthofen. Germany's top-scoring ace. The press call him the Red Baron.'

'Why?'

'Because he flies around in a bright red Albatros. Although not always, in fact.'

'What's the circus?'

'His Jasta – his squadron. All their airplanes are painted different colours.'

'Have you ever seen him?'

'Maybe. Trouble is, someone sees a brightly painted

129

Hun they figure it's him and report a sighting. You can never be sure.'

'Ever fought with him? You know, like in a dogfight?'

'Not that I know of. He is good though, that's for sure. Notching up thirty kills don't come easy.'

'How many kills have you got, Mac?'

But he shook his head. 'It's not about numbers, George. It's about being better than the other man. And if you really want to be a scout pilot you'll keep that in mind.'

'I certainly will. Anything else I can do?'

He smiled his little smile once more. 'Make a name for yourself.'

Chapter 5

I had fought Richthofen. *I just didn't tell George, I didn't know him well enough yet. And somehow these meetings with Manfred were private. It was the previous November, around the time George was having his first flying lessons in England. 166 Squadron was at twenty thousand, providing high cover for 13 Squadron while it photographed Hun positions near Bapaume. Earlier that day Manfred had claimed his eleventh and most famous victim, Major Hawker VC, one of the RFC's finest aces. Then in the afternoon his Jasta took off again. As we drew near to Bapaume a pair of Hun spotter aircraft were seen to the south. Richardson and I were detached to intercept them. But it was a trap. As we closed on the spotters they turned and fled, a moment later four Albatros D2s were racing down on us from the sun. It was the perfect ambush. Two of them latched on to Richardson, two on to me. My trio began circling, round and round, pulling ever tighter to get on one another's tail. The Albatroses were good, but the Nieuport better, and I managed to fire a burst at the* second Hun, who dived away with his engine smoking. That left *Manfred*, whom I identified by his red markings. *Richardson's* trio was lost from sight, elsewhere the sky was empty. *Manfred* stood off, as though calculating; I too circled away to regain lost height. And then, as if by invisible signal, we turned and came at each other. Straight, level, flat out and head-on, we closed at enormous speed so could only fire a few short bursts which looked wide. Then at the last instant, just as collision seemed certain, we both flick-rolled to the left, passing inches apart and in perfect formation like stunt pilots at an airshow. Why we went left I don't know. Until the final moment I'd planned to go right, in which case we would have been killed, but something made me go left instead. *Manfred* too. We zoomed past each other then turned to come in again. But perhaps sensing we'd both been lucky he just gave a little rock of his wings and turned for home. I flew back to base. When I landed I found the main wing-spar had been cracked by a bullet. If we'd kept fighting the wing would certainly have collapsed and I'd have been killed. Like *Richardson*, who never came back.

That was the same day I received the letter saying I was wanted by the Canadian police.

Some two years earlier, in October 1914, two boys were kicking their horses to the top of a forested ridge overlooking the plain of Valcartier ten miles west of the Canadian city of Quebec. The sight that beheld them as they breasted the ridge was almost biblical, and caused them to leap from their mounts and embrace. Spread below was a vast tented camp of ten thousand men. Flags fluttered, sunlight glinted off steel, smoke rose from a hundred fires. A fast-flowing river wound through the camp like a snake; above its boisterous murmur

floated the sounds of blown bugles, shouted orders and whin-
nying horses. The smell of wood-smoke and cooking drifted
on the breeze. The two boys, nineteen, scrawny, poorly
dressed and with barely a possession between them, looked at
each other and grinned.

'Thank the Lord, Mac,' one said. 'It looks like we made it.'

'It sure does, Danny.'

William MacBride and Daniel Warburton had met a week
earlier in Montreal. Although of similar appearance, so much
so that people often mistook them for brothers, they were
unknown to each other until then, MacBride hailing from
the western provinces of Canada and Warburton from the
southern United States. Apart from appearance, the boys had
other traits in common. Both had travelled long and far to
reach Valcartier, both were poor, and both were runaways,
one from an orphanage, the other from an abusive family.
Both were children of the plains, fast on horseback and crack
shots with a rifle, and both had been in trouble. Both finally,
like the thousands of men in the camp, had journeyed to
Quebec in answer to a call.

Canada was raising an army. Following the outbreak of
war in Europe the Canadian government decided immediately to support the Allied cause. 'Our recognition of this war
as ours,' Prime Minister Borden declared, 'determines we
have passed from the status of protected colony to that of
participating nation.' His pronouncement made, Borden
waited nervously. But the response was phenomenal, exceed-
ing all expectations, with thousands applying in the first few
days. Many recruits were already members of the militias, but
many more were civilians, simple farmers and loggers and

shopkeepers and tradesmen who downed tools and set out for Quebec. In no time ten thousand had volunteered. By the time MacBride and Warburton arrived, the Canadian Expeditionary Force, as it was then called, numbered forty thousand.

The signing-on process was chaotic and perfunctory. Overwhelmed by the response, harassed officials struggled to cope. Many volunteers could barely read or write, many had no papers, and many were foreign. Confusion reigned. The two boys had merely to queue all day, sign their names in a ledger, swear allegiance to King George of England, and they were in.

'What you two good at?' the recruiting sergeant asked.

The boys looked at each other. 'Ridin' an' shootin'.'

'Mounted Rifles, then.'

Mac and Danny were enrolled in the Canadian Mounted Rifles, a cavalry unit of the Canadian Expeditionary Force. Billeted in tents along the Jacques Cartier river, the CMR stayed in Valcartier a month. At first equipment was so scarce even horses had to be shared. Training began with recruits taking turns to ride them bareback (and often barefoot), wearing their own clothes and carrying sticks instead of rifles. Slowly kit began to arrive: a consignment of shirts, assorted bags and belts, saddles for the horses. Winter came and temperatures plunged, with ice-floes jostling on the river and canvas tents freezing to board. Little extra clothing was available, the people of Quebec gave what they could, the recruits huddled round their fires, warming themselves with rumours of a departure for Egypt. Then it was Arabia, then Turkey, then somewhere called Mesopotamia. Then came bitter news. Assembling the men one wintry day, the colonel-in-chief announced the division was badly needed in Europe and would ship out in a week. A hearty cheer echoed round the valley, but fell to shocked silence when he added they would be going without the horses which were wanted elsewhere. In a stroke Mac and Danny went from cavalry to infantry, and a week later they marched the ten miles to Quebec and boarded the troop-carrier SS *Hesperian* as part of the 1st Infantry Brigade, Canadian Expeditionary Force.

The crossing was foul, the Atlantic stormy and the *Hesperian* overloaded. The boys, neither of whom had been to sea before, clung to each other in frozen misery, drawing comfort from made-up stories of their homes and childhoods. A week later the convoy reached Portsmouth from where they were transported to Salisbury and sixteen weeks' further training on its famous plain. By late February 1915 their battalion was on the move again, this time by ferry to St Nazaire on the Atlantic coast of France, and thence by convoluted train journey to northern Belgium. By now they were part of the 1st Canadian Division, and drawing near to the Front. Yet more training took place, this time in the new and unnervingly claustrophobic business of trench warfare. And as they trained, manoeuvring through the deeply dug tunnels and troughs, then climbing ladders to charge the unseen enemy, the rumble of heavy artillery could be heard in the distance.

Finally they were delivered to the Front itself and their first taste of real warfare, taking over trenches in Zillebeke, south-east of Ypres. They stayed two weeks, sampling the unpleasant realities of trench life: unseasonably cold March weather, ice and mud, and the occasional mortar-shell lobbed over by the Germans. Four men in their company were killed, several more injured, but activity seemed muted on both sides, like a calm before a storm. Soon they were relieved, pulling back to rest and re-equip before repositioning to St Julien, five miles to the north. There they entrenched once more, settled in and waited. Then came the Battle of Ypres.

'Make a name for yourself' Mac had said in the lorry back from Amiens. *Make a name for yourself*. More irony in those five words, had I but realised it, than in all the foundries in Sheffield. Anyway, determined to get transferred to a scout squadron, and taking his advice to heart, I immediately set to work. My carefully formulated strategy, fully five minutes in the planning, was a three-pronged affair entitled Chaps, Strickley, and Flying, the idea being to make myself popular with my fellow pilots, indispensable to Major Strickley, and brilliant in the air, all within a fortnight.

I began with the toughest of these – courting my colleagues. Choosing my moment with care, one night I suggested we all play pontoon, hastily adding when this met with the usual silence that it was my birthday (a lie) so I was feeling rather homesick (a concept everyone understood) and I had two bottles of fine wine I'd been saving to share with friends (the local farmer's home-brew). Faced with this heart-felt appeal they could hardly refuse, so with much reluctant muttering and scraping of chairs, battle was duly joined.

Now it's an odd thing about gambling. Frowned upon by all and sundry, most people nevertheless love doing it. Forbidden fruit and all that. And I maintain it has valuable social merits. Gambling's a leveller, a breaker-down of barriers, a builder of bonds. It knows no boundaries of race, sex, status, class or creed, it treats everyone just the same. Life's failures can become heroes, the pompous get pulled down a peg, strangers can meet and interact in a unique and intimate way, and to top everything it's excellent fun. Nor do gamblers come in stereotypes. I've met vicars and lawyers and policemen and meek little widows (they're the worst) who were all pillars of society yet inveterate punters. True, I've also seen plenty of victims and destitutes, but in my experience all met their downfall by allowing hubris to get in the way of common-sense, and forgetting the one golden rule: the cards don't care.

Pontoon is the ideal game to break the ice: the rules are simple, any number can play, and you can set stakes as high or low as you like. (Not the preferred game for serious gamblers, incidentally: you play against the bank thus have no human flaws to exploit.) So with about six of my cohorts arranged uneasily around the table I sloshed wine into their glasses, shuffled the pack and settled down to business. Within twenty minutes polite chortling could be heard. Half an hour more and they were positively hilarious. Not all by chance of course: I had generously offered to bank, thus allowing everyone to enjoy the game while I controlled it, surreptitiously ensuring they won and lost in equal measure. I even fostered some gloating.

'Ha! Beat you again, Duckwell! Look, I've got seventeen!'

'What? Drat it, Carruthers, you're just too good for me.'

By evening's end they'd all won about sixpence and were my new best chums. They had also, may I add, engaged positively with one another, thoroughly enjoyed themselves, and gone to bed in better spirits than they had in weeks. Duckwell for class captain, I say. And the next night everyone wanted to join in.

Phase two of the masterplan involved impressing the CO, Major Strickley, for he ultimately was my ticket out of there, and if I wanted a transfer he'd have to approve it. Also, cosying up to him would get me closer to the confidential reports he wrote, the secret orders he received, the pads of blank forms he kept in his desk, and all the other things junior pilots weren't supposed to see. But gaining his confidence was to be no simple matter, for although outwardly sound, within John Strickley lurked a very strange creature indeed. For a start he rarely socialised. Occasionally he'd drift into the mess like a leaf on the breeze, smile awkwardly, mutter 'Carry on, chaps', then drift out again. If you did manage to engage him in conversation he'd invariably lose track and start talking about Chopin or his petunias back in Hampshire. He never flew, nor was he expected to, for majors were not supposed to risk their lives in aeroplanes, so discussing aviation was pointless. As for recreation, his idea of fun was to lock himself in his room and play Paderewski loudly on his gramophone. There were also rumours he suffered from delusions and depression, possibly due to a failed marriage, so apart from being weird and reclusive he was also miserable. Impressing him therefore might have proved ticklish, but in the end I plumped for the obvious – volunteering for things everyone hates, such as paperwork. By becoming super-efficient at admin, I reasoned, and even offering to take on more, I'd be able to gain his approval, plus keep an eye on his in-tray.

Which worked, but not in the way I'd imagined. On my next day as duty orderly I polished up my boots and Sam Browne belt, pressed my uniform, and with cap on head and service revolver on hip began strutting about the place, clipboard in hand, like a headmistress on speech day. First I visited the kitchens and audited the bully-beef and potatoes, then I went to the workshops and made the mechanics list all the spares. Then I did a stock-take of the bar, took inventory of the stationery cupboard, inspected the other ranks' quarters, balanced the petty-cash tin and typed up the week's menu. Amazed by my own efficiency I then presented myself at Major Strickley's for congratulation.

'Oh, hello, it's young, um, Dishforth, isn't it?' he said, vaguely. 'Settling in all right are we?'

'Duckwell, sir, and yes, thanks, although I have been here quite a while now.'

'Have you *really*. Isn't that extraordinary.'

'If you say so, sir. Anyway I've finished the duty orderly's chores, sir, and done a few extras, and was wondering if there was anything else I could help you with.'

'Finished you say? But it's only eleven.'

'Yes, sir. I'm just keen to be as helpful as possible.'

With that a watery glint entered his eye. 'Really?' he said. And before I knew it he was snuffling into a handkerchief. 'Oh, thank you, Duckwell. A little kindness . . . You know, it's such a rare thing these days.'

'Yes, sir. Um, your desk, for instance. Perhaps I could help sorting papers and what-not.'

'Hmm?'

'Your desk, sir?'

'It's the letters you know, dear boy. The awful weight of them, you can't imagine.'

'No, sir.'

He was gazing trance-like through the window, so I sidled up to his desk which looked like a rubbish tip. Centre stage upon it was a thick sheaf of dusty notepaper, an open fountain pen ready on top.

'The awful unbearable weight.'

'Indeed, sir.'

'Duckwell?'

'Yes, sir!'

'Tell me, old chap, have you ever visited the arboretum at Farnborough?'

'No, sir, can't say I have. Although I hear it's quite good.'

'Quite good? My dear boy it's magnificent. You should see it in October. Oh, the colours . . .' And he was off again, waxing poetic about Japanese maples and Canadian sequoias.

I sneaked a look under the fountain pen. January 1917, the top letter was dated – he'd begun it over a week ago yet still it wasn't finished. *Dear Mr & Mrs Cartwright, it is with great sadness that I write to you today of your son, Hector . . .*

Letters of condolence, that's what he was talking about. He couldn't write them, simply couldn't bring himself to. He started them, it turned out, but never finished. They just sat on his desk gathering dust.

He was still at the window, humming to himself. Breath held, I picked up the sheaf.

'Sir. Would you like me to have a go at these?'

'The awful weight . . .'

'Yes, sir. I could do them, get the adjutant to type them

up, then pop them back here for signature. What do you think, sir?'

'Would you do that?' he murmured sadly. 'Would you *really* do that for me?'

That evening after pontoon school I set to work, and though I say so myself did a more than acceptable job. Putting heartfelt sentiments into words has always come naturally (except my own), and in no time a fresh stack of letters sat before me. Then Corporal Larkin wandered by collecting ashtrays and coffee cups.

'Mind if I take a shufti, sir?' he asked, nodding at the pile.

'Not at all.'

Len picked up the top letter and read thoughtfully. 'Very nicely put, sir, if I may say so. Very tasteful.'

The next evening a little delegation presented itself, Len Larkin accompanied by a young mechanic from the hangar.

'This is Harry Reardon, sir,' Len explained. 'From the workshops, you know.'

'Oh yes?'

'Yes, sir. Thing is, young Harry here's been having a spot of bother with the missus back home in Stepney.'

'Oh dear. Sorry to hear that, Reardon.'

Reardon, who had ginger hair and jug-ears, nodded earnestly but said nothing.

'And so he was wondering like, if you'd write him a letter. To his missus, that is.'

'Me?'

'Yes, sir. Seeing as how you did such a nice job on them other letters. I thought maybe you could 'elp him out. In return for the proper consideration of course.'

Proper considerations aside, the next night two more unfortunates visited Doctor Duckwell's, one with marital problems, the other with a nasty dose of something he didn't want his fiancée knowing about, and by the end of the week word of this wonderful new service had spread round the airfield, customers were queuing through the door and the cash was flowing like pub-night on payday.

If only, I mused, totting up the takings, my own letters were so successful.

The ancient Belgian town of Ypres, known for its fine linens and medieval battlements, lies thirty miles south of the Channel coast, and twenty miles north of the French city of Lille. Picturesque, unassuming, with its gothic cathedral and vaulted cloth-hall, Ypres had the misfortune to lie in the path of the German advance sweeping across Belgium at the beginning of the war. The first battle there took place in October 1914 when British forces successfully halted the advance at Passchendaele Ridge, just east of the town. This created a bulge or 'salient' in the German line, much to their frustration, and they soon set about planning a counter-attack, beginning with a ferocious artillery bombardment which reduced much of the town to ruins. The British meanwhile, well entrenched around the area and reinforced by French and Canadian troops, fortified their positions and prepared for battle. Weeks of delay followed, broken only by minor skirmishes and endless artillery exchanges, then finally in April 1915 the winter weather relented and the Germans launched their assault. The Second Battle of Ypres, as it later became known, would last more than a month, and be remembered for two things in particular: firstly the ferocity of the fighting, which was often at close quarters and resulted in a hundred thousand casualties; and secondly, the first ever use on the Western Front of a potent new weapon.

As a prelude to the attack, at tea-time on 22 April German engineers released 168 tons of chlorine gas along a four-mile front. Borne on an easterly breeze, the gas spread like a green veil across no-man's land and into French-held positions. Thousands were immediately affected, many asphyxiating where they sat or stood in their trenches. Those that managed to scramble out were cut down by waiting machine-guns, the rest fled in panic. Within minutes a wide breach had opened in the Allied lines which the Germans rushed to fill. The new weapon had proved a spectacular success.

A few miles to the rear, the 1st Canadian Division, including William MacBride and Daniel Warburton, were in their reserve positions around the village of St Julien, three miles to the east of Ypres. Despite the continuous rumble of artillery, the past few days had been quiet; the Canadians were well back, and no attacks were expected. But as dusk fell and they set to work preparing their evening meal of tinned beef and biscuit, they began to see soldiers materialising from the woods and fields around them like ghosts. Orders were hastily barked, helmets donned and weapons brought to hand, yet no attack followed, and as the soldiers neared the Canadians recognised them as French. Moreover, although none bore visible signs of injury, they seemed to be retreating from battle, staggering as though wounded, doubled over and choking into bloody rags, or tripping blindly to the ground in agony.

'What's the matter with them?' Mac asked anxiously.

'Lord knows. And what's that God-awful smell?'

An hour later, and with the sound of gunfire growing nearer by the minute, word spread that the Germans had taken the French lines and were still moving forward. This meant the Canadian positions, previously miles to the rear, were now the front line. Furthermore they were under orders to hold these positions at all costs, and even counter-attack if possible. Ammunition was circulated, weapons checked, bayonets cleaned, letters hastily written. Orders were issued, only to be countermanded by others, then still more, as the situation developed and changed hour by hour.

Mac and Danny stayed close, peering through the darkness from the step of their dug-out. Soon German star-shells and flares were bursting overhead, bathing their positions in spec-tral light, then came mortars and small artillery rounds fired from the village itself. A detachment was sent out to try and storm it, but was driven back by machine-gun fire. Only half made it to safety, the rest were left where they fell, many screaming in agony. A shocked lull followed, then the boys' platoon was ordered to stand to. A second assault was to be tried on the village, their unit was to provide flanking cover and attack from the side. Leave your packs behind, they were told, carry only your rifle and ammunition, fix bayonets and wait for the signal – a green star-shell.

The thirty men of their platoon assembled at the jumping-off point, a fire-trench with steps cut in the wall. A taut-faced lieutenant with a pistol went from man to man checking weapons and offering encouragement, but his voice sounded shrill, his pistol looked threatening and his hands shook, so no one felt better. Then came another agonising wait, listening to bullets whine overhead and feeling the earth shake from exploding artillery shells. Finally a burst of green overhead, an excited shout from the lieutenant, and they were scrambling up the step into the open. Heads down, the thirty sprinted across a beet field, along a farm track and up a slight rise to their first objective, a disused barn halfway to the village. All made it, gasping breathlessly, pressing their backs to its stone wall in relief. The sound of German gunfire was unnervingly close now, but none was aimed in their direction. It seemed their feint had worked.

The next objective was the graveyard, a walled enclosure to one side of the village itself. At a nod from the lieutenant the platoon peeled off round the barn and set off once more. Halfway to the graveyard the machine-guns concealed within it opened fire. The first Danny Warburton knew was a sparkle of flashes from up ahead, the menacing hum of passing bullets and men falling like nine-pins all around. Instinctively he dived for the ground, a moment later MacBride was scrambling to his side.

'Are you shot, Danny?' he shouted.

'No. What about you?'

'Not me, but we stay here and they'll get us for sure!'

As if to emphasise the point another burst of machine-gun fire tore into the ground around them, kicking earth and stones high into the air. Above the rattling bursts came the crump of mortars, the crash of exploding shells and the beseeching cries of the wounded. Fumbling their rifles forward they loosed off a few rounds, but both knew their shots were useless. And their position dire.

'What do we do?'

'I don't know. Them machine-guns is killin' us. Where's the lieutenant?'

'Up ahead somewhere. I say we make a run for the barn.'

'I say they shoulda left us in the cavalry.'

Just then a pistol-waving figure raised itself from the ground ahead and began running forward; in a second others were rising to follow. Without hesitation Danny and Mac too scrambled to their feet. A hundred yards of hell followed, a mind-numbing chaos of smoke and noise, crashing explosions, flying bullets and tortured screams, all in total darkness one instant and flashbulb brightness the next as a lightning-storm of explosions seared the scene into hellish relief. Lurid images sprang from the darkness like tableaux on a stage: a soldier writhing on his back, another with his head blown away, a third staring at the smoking stump of his leg, and others, everywhere, falling, then rising, then falling again.

Danny reached the graveyard and flung himself over the wall, landing heavily on his back. For a second he lay, gasping for air, blinking up at a stone angel on a gravestone, its hands pressed in prayer. His head was spinning, his chest heaved, his mouth tasted of blood, but he was alive and uninjured. And alone. He'd lost Mac, he realised, scrambling to his knees. 'Mac!' He peered in panic through the drifting smoke. The machine-guns had stopped, but shadowy figures ran through the graveyard, weaving and bobbing as though in macabre dance. Sporadic pistol- and rifle-shots rang out, shouts echoed around the compound, some in strange tongues. Danny picked up his rifle and hurried towards them, yelling for his friend. But barely had he gone ten yards before he collided with someone running the other way. It wasn't Mac. He was older, and shorter, he'd lost his helmet and was holding no weapon, his hair mud-caked and the skin of his cheek black with soot. That meant a machine-gunner. For a moment neither moved, then the German gave a shrug and uttered the word 'bitter' and in a single movement Danny lunged with his rifle, driving the bayonet deep into the man's stomach. The man gave a startled cry then stood, staring at Danny in disbelief. Danny wrenched the bayonet from him and lunged once more; still the man stayed on his feet. A third time Danny thrust, this time into his chest, and at last the surprise began to ebb from the face and his knees to buckle. 'Bitter,' he whispered one final time. Only after the fourth sickening blow did the light die in his eyes and his body fall limply to the ground. Pulling out his bayonet, Danny left the man where he lay and stumbled off in search of his friend.

Days elapsed, their passage merging into a single waking dream. Mac and Danny went forward, they fought, they pulled back, they rested, they went forward again. Their decimated platoon was amalgamated with others, then still more, until faces grew unrecognisable and unit numbers meaningless. They marched in their sleep, they ate where they stood, and they slept where they fell, their minds in suspension, their exhausted bodies stinking and vermin-ridden. After a few days rain began to fall, in torrents, hour after hour, until their skin puckered white and their clothes grew mildew as they slept. And with the rain came the mud. Trenches turned to sucking swamps, an inconvenience at first, quickly a lethal trap. Duckboards laid for walking sank in hours, so did the next layer, and the next, and still the mud rose like an evil tide. Thousands of tramping boots churned tracks and road-ways to rivers of primordial bog, several feet deep, cloying and deadly. Horses foundered, artillery-pieces vanished, dead and injured soldiers sank helplessly from view. Stumbling from the duckboards meant a desperate duel with death, for regaining them was often impossible and only a madman would leave them to help.

Relief from battle came sporadically and without warning. At one point the boys' unit was pulled back and they found themselves camping in the surreal grandeur of a chateau, eating hot food, drinking requisitioned claret and sleeping on a dry cellar floor with the sound of gunfire safely in the distance. Another time they stayed in a fruit barn, feasting on stored apples and watching bats roost in the rafters. In these lulls the boys drew apart from the others, talking in low voices, pooling rations, tending and mending, or squatting on their haunches to pick nits from each other like monkeys in a tree. They'd talk and smoke and tell stories, then sleep for hours, dreaming of wide-open plains and the ranch they planned after the war. A few hours later, or sometimes a few days, harshly shouted orders would summon them to reality, and obediently they'd gather their kit and form up with the others. Hours of marching followed, while the rain drummed on their heads and the thunder of gunfire grew in their ears, then it was down into the mud-filled pits and the sickening wait for the next frenzied attack, or next desperate defence.

'I didn't never imagine war would be like this,' Danny said one night as they huddled beneath a cape for warmth.

'It ain't what I signed up for, that's for sure,' Mac replied.

The next day the rain stopped, and word went round they were going to storm a wooded hill held by the enemy. It was a big operation involving a whole battalion of a thousand men. All morning was spent assembling the force and ponderously manoeuvring it through the trenches into positions to launch the attack. With the passing hours the sky cleared, the west wind dropped, and the sun came out, raising tendrils of vapour from the lines of sodden soldiers waiting in the ground. A while later a British aeroplane flew by, its leather-clad occupants waving heartily.

'You see that, Danny?' Mac pointed. 'That's where we should be. Up there with those boys. That's the cavalry of tomorrow.'

'Flying machines instead of horses, you mean?'

'You bet. Got to beat hiding down here like rats, wouldn't you say?'

Danny nudged his friend. 'Maybe we should ask the sergeant for a transfer.'

'Wouldn't he love that! Say, what are they waving at do you think?'

They were waving at gas. A shallow film, translucent, like molten green glass, was creeping silently across no-man's land towards them, hugging the earth, filling craters and ditches, curling over the lip of the trenches to fall like a curtain.

'Jesus, what is that?'

'Gas!' An alarmed shout echoed up and down the line. 'It's gas, don't breathe it!'

Instantly panic broke out. Although they'd heard about the attack on the French, no Canadians had seen gas, nor dealt with it. No gas-masks existed, nor did any clear instructions on what to do.

'Get low to the ground!' somebody yelled.

'No! You gotta hold your breath till it clears.'

'Scoop it out with your helmet.'

'Piss on a handkerchief and breathe through that.'

Danny and Mac looked on in horror. Further up their trench soldiers were already fighting to get out, scrabbling at muddy walls and falling to the ground clutching their throats. Shouts of alarm were turning to screams of terror. Somebody loosed off a rifle-shot, others threw their weapons aside and started running.

'Danny?' Mac's eyes were wide. 'What we gonna do?'

Just then Danny felt acid in his throat, and a violent burning in his eyes. Instantly he stopped breathing. With his vision dissolving, he glimpsed Mac, face blue, sinking to his knees. In seconds it would be too late for either of them. Grabbing Mac by the collar he hauled him upright and dragged him along the zigzagged trench towards a rear-facing intersection. But before he'd gone twenty yards he found his way barred.

'Where do you think you're going, Private?'

'Out, Sarge,' Danny spluttered. 'There's gas back there.'

'You'll return to your position right now, or face charges for desertion!'

But Danny had had enough and with others pressing behind and even the blurred face of the sergeant looking unnerved he swung a punch with his free fist, pushed past, and half carrying, half dragging his stricken friend, lurched off.

Late that evening he found Mac, together with scores of

others, sitting outside a dressing station. His eyes were bandaged.

'Say, Mac, it's me.'

'Danny!' The boys gripped hands. 'You got me out, the Lord bless you for that.'

'I got me out, you mean! You just tagged along for the ride.' Danny studied his friend. Brown stains seeped through the bandage on his eyes, flecks of white phlegm spotted the front of his tunic. As he watched, Mac doubled over coughing and more froth-like discharge dribbled down his chin. 'You OK, buddy?'

Mac waved his hand. 'Medics say I'll be fine. They put linseed ointment in my eyes and keepin' them covered for precaution. The cough'll wear off in a week or so, they say. You got me out just in time.'

'They sending you back to the hospital?'

'Hell no! I just need a few days off the line to get straight. Then we can be together again, just like old times.'

'Just like old times, sure.'

The boys fell quiet. As Danny watched, stretcher-bearers carried an inert form from the tent and laid it alongside several rows of blanket-covered others.

'It ain't right,' he murmured. 'We lost hundreds, suffocating to death like that, terrible way to die. They shoulda just got everybody out.'

'Yes they should,' Mac agreed. 'What happened to the attack?'

'Cancelled.'

'That's good.' Mac's hand found Danny's knee. 'You know what I've been thinking about, sitting here all day?'

'What's that, buddy.'

'Them airplanes. Like the one we saw.'

'What about them?'

'They're the cavalry of tomorrow. And we belong in them.'

Phase three of my transfer masterplan required me to distinguish myself in the air, although this endeavour was superseded by events somewhat. By now I'd flown several ops, some straightforward, some decidedly not. If anything the tendency was to the latter kind. This was now February, I'd been at Noyelette a month, and developments were afoot. On the ground, troops on both sides were amassing near the Front, trenches were being reinforced, tunnels dug, wires laid, listening-posts manned. And the morning hate began, a pre-dawn artillery barrage that shook the floor and set taut nerves jangling. And we were ten miles away; God knows how it was for the men on the ground. In the air Archie intensified and German scouts began venturing further across our lines to strike at us before we could reach our objectives. A-Flight lost three Bathtubs in a week, B-Flight one, and 166 Squadron, struggling against a numerically and technically superior foe, lost four Nieuports in as many days. Things were getting so perilous I had to shelve plans for quick glory: being a capable pilot now was about getting through missions unscathed. Morris Dixon and I worked on tactics, practising evasive manoeuvres, defensive teamwork and gunmanship. I developed a slew to try to fool Archie, and together we rigged up a third Lewis gun so Morris, now firmly harnessed to the aircraft, could stand and exploit an all-round field of fire.

Then we had our first brush with Hun scouts. We were on an artillery ranging mission for British batteries on the ground. This involved flying along dodging Archie while Morris watched through binoculars to see where artillery shots fell; then we sent corrections to the gunners in Morse code – left a bit, right a bit, that sort of thing – using a new-fangled wireless transmitter. But setting up the wireless was a dreadful to-do: apart from all the knobs and switches, we had to reel out miles of copper wire as an aerial. Unsurprisingly we became distracted, the next thing I knew Morris gave a startled shout, and I looked up to see two scouts diving on us from above.

'Go right and up!' Morris ordered, as practised.

I immediately threw the throttle wide, banking the aeroplane into a steep turn. By now the Hun scouts – Pfalzes I think they were, and no, not brightly painted – had separated, one going behind us, the other squaring up for a head-on attack, but our climbing turn threw them and they had to come in obliquely. Everything then happened very fast. Morris, standing on his seat, legs braced like Nelson on the poop-deck, took aim with the aft-facing Lewis, and I cocked the forward one while turning the Bathtub in to meet the oncoming Hun. Then the whole aircraft shuddered as Morris opened fire. Light-flashes sparkled from my Hun's nose. I too yanked on the trigger and suddenly the air was full of rattling guns and flying bullets. I felt thuds as the Bathtub took hits; a strut snapped with a crack. Instants later the two scouts careered by, one veering left, the other right, then they were gone.

'What happened?' I yelled, searching the empty sky. 'By jove, Sergeant, did we get them?'

'Not a chance.' Morris began reloading the guns.

'Maybe we did though. Shouldn't we claim one as a possible?'

'We can't do that, sir, wouldn't be true. Trust me, we didn't get near 'em. Anyway, look.' He pointed to a cluster of dots approaching from the west. British scouts coming to our rescue. 'That's why they buggered off.'

Somehow I felt cheated. Two against one, yet I'd barely had time to squeeze the trigger before they ran away. How the hell were we supposed to shoot down Huns like that? In black mood I flew the rest of the patrol and returned to base, landing on the short field with scarcely a thought. Walking in, Morris sensed my gloom.

'You did well, sir. All that practice is paying off.'

'If you say so, Sergeant. Although in my view it's no way to fight a war.'

'Hark the conquering hero.' He grinned, clapping me on the back. 'We drove 'em off. That's good enough for me.'

'Well it's not for me! I just want the chance to hit back, actually do some damage for once.'

'But that's not what we're here for, is it.' He nodded towards 166 Squadron's hangars. 'That's for the glory boys over there.'

That evening I stayed at the table after dinner getting sloshed on home-brew. I even turned down offers of cards, so low was my humour. We'd been lucky, I had to acknowledge: a lone Bathtub was no match for two scouts, even a three-gun one. If they'd had time to make another pass we'd be a casualty statistic by now. It was a bitter pill, but I had to accept I was simply in the wrong outfit to become an ace.

And as if to bludgeon the point home, my hero and role-model then walked through the door. And we had a very strange conversation indeed.

'George.'

'Mac.'

'Twenty-one,' he said, lowering himself to a chair.

'Beg pardon?'

His cheeks were grime-ringed and hair dishevelled, as though he'd only just taken off his helmet and goggles. As though he'd only just landed. Yet it was hours after dark.

'You asked how many kills I've got. It's twenty-one.'

'Mac, that's bloody phenomenal!'

'If you say so.'

'Twenty-one, good God, I mean, that puts you right up there with our top scorers, Ball, McCudden and the rest!'

'Hmm.'

'Seriously, Mac, you should be in the newspapers or something, opening church fêtes, kissing babies, all that nonsense.'

'That's just it.'

'What is?'

But he didn't answer, just ground the heels of his palms into his eyes and gazed wearily into space. I sipped wine and waited. Through the door came the sound of pilots having fun with cards, in the distance the banging of hammers drifted from the hangar. Somewhere a gramophone was playing 'If you were the only girl in the world'.

'I was in the infantry once, you know. Came over in fourteen with the Canadian Expeditionary Force.'

'I remember you saying.'

'Been in France ever since.'

'That's a long time. More than two years.'

He nodded slowly. 'Me and a buddy, we joined up together, trained together, did everything together, stuck like glue, people thought we were brothers we were that close. We even applied for transfer to the RFC at the same time.'

'Where is he now?' I asked warily.

'He didn't make it.'

'I'm sorry.'

'Me too.' He paused again, staring abstractedly at his fist as it opened and closed on the table. 'Can I trust you, George?' Suddenly his coal-black eyes were boring into mine.

'Trust me? Well, Mac, of course.'

'I need to trust someone. Someone who's smart with words, writes good letters, knows his way round the system, knows how to fix things.'

'Fix things?'

'Fix things that need fixing, disappear things that need disappearing, make things happen that need to happen. Am I making sense?'

He could have been writing my CV, but a little caution seemed prudent. 'Well, yes, Mac, I think I understand. But, why?'

He hesitated, just for a second, as though weighing me up one final time. Then he came to a decision. 'Because I'm in a heap of trouble, George. And the last thing I need is my name in the newspapers.'

The day after I spoke to George I had my second run-in with Manfred, when his Jasta attacked Noyelette. This was February 1917, about ten weeks after we first tangled over Bapaume. Manfred was now with

Jasta 11 based somewhere near Cambrai and fast becoming famous. I was in the gun-butts with my mechanic, Finlay. The gun-butts were in a far corner of the field, well away from everything so guns could be tested in safety. My Nieuport was up on a tail-jack, engine running; I was in the cockpit while Finlay stood beside me on the wing, adjusting the firing-angle of the Lewis. I wasn't happy with the convergence and decided to fix the gun to fire at a point thirty yards ahead, instead of the usual seventy-five or hundred. This was much shorter than normal and meant I would have to get up real close to the enemy to shoot him down. But it was also more accurate and meant the bullets hit harder, which was what I wanted. The gun was loaded and the engine running so we didn't hear the warning klaxon or the noise of approaching aircraft. The first we knew was the crash of explosions over near the hangars. Looking across the field we saw smoke rising from the bombs, and Hun scouts zooming low over the field, machine-guns rattling. People were running in all directions, and one of 13 Squadron's FE2s was on fire. All I could think of was to get in the air so I shouted to Finlay to jump down and gunned the throttle, driving the Nieuport off the tail-jack and round towards the field. Then I pushed the throttle wide and took to the air. By now Manfred and his boys had finished their attack and were already heading east for home and safety. There were four of them, flying very low, with me giving chase about a mile behind. Until then I had no idea it was Manfred: the scouts they were flying were Halberstadts, because at the time they had development problems with the Albatros D3. At that height the Halberstadt had a top speed of about 100 mph, my Nieuport about 10 mph more, so in a while I began to close the range. But it was a slow business and I wondered if I'd catch them before my fuel gave out. I wished I had the new SE5 we were promised: it had two guns and was a lot faster. Soon we reached the lines. Nobody changed course or height, we just flew all-out across no-man's land and into enemy territory. A few minutes more and the range was down to a quarter mile, but still too far to shoot, and every minute put me another couple of miles deeper into Hunland. Then, just as I was about to give up and turn for home, one Halberstadt peeled off from the rest and zoomed up into a chandelle, which is a tight climbing manoeuvre to reverse direction. I knew then it was Manfred, by his red markings which I saw in the pull-up, by the precision of the manoeuvre, and by his tactic which was to draw me away from his friends. Once again we lined up for head-on attack and raced straight at each other, but this time we pulled away early to get on the other's tail. By now we were over open countryside and still very low, so manoeuvring for advantage was a matter of strong nerve and careful flying. Manfred was not a flashy flyer but he was a precise one. I tried everything to get on his tail and he to get on mine, but the best we got was a few seconds or so before the other wriggled free. We chased each other down forest tracks, between avenues of trees, even along a stream-bed just above tumbling white water. I fired a few shots but the Lewis was still not right; Manfred's shots too went wide, maybe because he wasn't used to the Halberstadt. Then I knew I had to break off as fuel was low and I was far behind enemy lines. Manfred guessed this too, and as I broke off he punched his fist in the air and rocked his wings again like before. As though to him it was all a great game.

Chapter 6

39 Sqn
Suttons Farm
Hornchurch, Essex
May 31st 1917

Dearest Emily,

I have just received your kind letter and though I'm due on 'ops' any minute feel I must pen a quick reply.

What a wonderful surprise! Thank you so much for writing, and thank you also for accepting my apology so generously. I'm relieved no lasting harm was caused by my behaviour, my only wish now is that we can be friends. My feelings for you, it goes without saying, remain genuinely fond. Thank you once more.

It seems ages since the three of us met that night in Calais, can it only be five weeks? And what splendid news about you

and Mac making contact. I had a short note from him a week
ago, but he made no mention of your meeting and sounded
rather strained — I do hope he's all right, he has much to
contend with. I hate having left him, after everything he has
done for me. All goes well here in Essex and I have settled in
comfortably, but my thoughts are with you in France, despite
the horrors there. If only I could come over and visit. Perhaps I
shall look into it.

Your FANY duties sound fascinating — and not a little
dangerous. Wonderful work you are doing there, Emily, tending
to those poor men, and seeing them safely on their way. Your
family must be very proud. The 'Vimto Valkyries' sound most
interesting by the way, I hope to meet them one day.

Emily, I must dash, but wanted to get this off to you now. I
will write more fully later, in the meantime take great care and
thank you again for your letter.

With fondest best wishes,
George.

Emily lowered the page and stared out across the red-tiled roofs of Richelieu. Around her, improperly clad Valkyries disported themselves in the June sun like basking reptiles, dozing, smoking, quietly reading their own letters from home. Over their heads seagulls cruised a cloudless sky, while the street's busy murmur rose from below like song. The sharp tang of salt and seaweed laced the air, together with the oily stench of the docks, where cranes swung ceaselessly to and fro like feeding storks, purposefully disgorging their car-goes of fuel and ammunition. Beyond the port lay the glassy waters of the Channel, with England itself visible as a hazy fringe between sea and sky. Just twenty miles away, Emily reflected, yet another world completely.

She re-read the note, a twinge of unease stirring within her. As fulsome as ever, George seemed bowled over by her letter, which she'd only meant as a polite response to his. That and to let him know, out of correctness, that she'd met Mac. Yet had she implied more? Her feelings for George had become confused. He'd entered her life unbidden, then run off and abandoned her; yet there was no denying she felt flattered by his attentiveness, touched by the sincerity of his affection and impressed by his constancy, which never wavered. Despite all his hot-headed bluster, there was much that was loveable about George.

'All well on the home front, Parks?' CW enquired sleepily.

'Yes, thanks. Or at least, I think so.'

They were all there on the roof, the Valkyries, illicitly enjoying the first true heat of the year. All except the ever-unfortunate Bobby who had earned another corpse duty for keeping an untidy vehicle.

'That doesn't sound too promising,' Charlie said.

'Well, it's not from home, actually. It's from that boy I told you about. The one I had all the bother with back in Shropshire.'

'What, the one who climbed through your window?'

'Yes, him.'

'Gorgeous George!'

'That was *so* romantic,' Angel piped up.

'What's he done now, robbed a bank?'

'Come on, Parks, do tell,' Phyllis urged. 'My letter's as dreary as anything, all petrol shortages and grandmother's rheumatism.'

Emily was still studying the page. 'Well, it's not so much what he's done. It's more what I've done. Possibly.'

They listened as she explained. But the more she explained, the worse it sounded.

'Hold on, Parks. So you're saying reckless-but-adorable George and Mac the mysterious Canadian are good friends?' Phyllis repeated.

'Well, yes. George introduced us when we met that night at the docks.'

'And George doesn't know you're seeing Mac.'

'He does now!' Angel quipped.

'Yes. I mean, no!' Emily felt her cheeks colouring. 'I'm not seeing Mac, not in *that* way. Am I? And anyway, George isn't really a boyfriend. He's just George!'

'Who adores you, and who you care about,' Charlie said.

'Yes. No. Oh, I don't know! I only know he got me into trouble.'

'And out of Shropshire.'

'And into the FANY.'

'And onward to the Vimto Valkyries!'

A chorus of cheers rang round the rooftop, causing Emily, despite herself, to smile ruefully.

A while later clothes and belongings were gathered and the girls descended the attic ladder, returning once more to their underworld existence of night bombings, hospital trains and blood-caked ambulances. All were fatigued beyond reason, some like Bobby even beyond caring. But then so was every girl in every FANY unit across Calais. Despite promises of relief, their workload that spring remained crushing, time off inadequate, spare parts and replacement vehicles illusive, and new recruits too few. To add to their misery, bombing raids on the town occurred almost nightly, making the task of ferrying injured soldiers more hazardous than ever. In the previous two weeks the FANY had recorded its first casualties, one girl badly cut by flying glass and a second losing a foot when her ambulance was hit. Morale was beginning to suffer, with a trickle of girls asking to go home and others defecting to easier billets in less dangerous organisations. And their replacements, if and when they did arrive, frequently failed to stay the course. Shocked by the appalling conditions and harrowing work, several caught the ferry straight back to Dover. Day-trippers, they were known as, by the stalwarts they left behind.

Yet astonishingly most kept going, bolstered by their own fortitude, each other, and their deep seated feelings for the job. Nor were their efforts unappreciated. Tired cheers rose from the trains of injured when the ambulances arrived to collect them. 'Here come the FANY-tastics!' the Tommies would say, explaining to their mates that FANY stood for First ANYwhere. Even top brass were impressed: 'gently bred, indomitably spirited' as one senior general put it.

The Valkyries held together, even if tensions within the group sometimes reached breaking point. A perceived slight, an item borrowed without permission, a petty jealousy – such trivialities could ignite smouldering embers to outright conflagration in seconds, and often it fell to Emily as group peacemaker to douse the ensuing blaze. The spats never lasted however, the girls were too close and too tired to sustain grudges, and protagonists were usually falling tearfully into each other's arms within minutes. In any case there were less tiring ways to relieve the strain than in-fighting. Their rooftop trysts, for example, sitting in a circle drinking smuggled gin, taking it in turns to confess their most intimate secrets. Or fashioning wings from paper and wire and dancing in the moonlight like fairies. Or talking candidly of their hopes and fears for life, womanhood, sexuality, marriage, and their futures after war. And then there were trysts of a different sort. Angel Truscott, always the darkest horse of the pack, went first, beginning a passionate affair with a French colonel. CW and Charlie Neve also embarked upon dalliances, although less full-blooded; Phyllis Mason, who had a fiancé in London, scoffed huffily yet wanted to know every detail; Bobby Waldron had a boy who wrote from the trenches; and Emily had Mac.

She'd seen him just twice, beginning with that first dawn meeting the night of the burn victims. On that occasion after the café they'd walked slowly through the streets of Calais until reaching its wide sandy beach, while around them the morning came to life. They talked little. Emily was too dazed and too fatigued to speak coherently, and Mac seemed content just to sit beside her watching the brackish waves curl lazily to shore. He did speak minimally of the demands of his work, and his need to escape from time to time, and he apologised to Emily for calling on her unannounced. She replied it was nice to meet him again and not to worry. An hour or so later they rose, brushed the sand from their clothes and walked back to Richelieu where they parted with a shake of hands.

A week later he arrived again, this time in the evening. B-Watch was on stand-to, which meant they could be called at any moment. Around ten, an errand-boy clumped up the stairs to Valkyrie HQ bearing a note for a Miss Parker.

'It's him again!' she said in astonishment. 'He's in the bar across the road.'

'Go!' Angel urged.

'But I can't, it's against every rule in the book.'

'Yes you jolly well can!'

Valkyries swarmed around her, pulling CW's fur coat over her work-clothes, brushing her hair up, dabbing her cheeks with powder.

'The Brute's busy in her office.'

'Use the back stairs.'

'If the klaxon goes we'll come and fetch you.'

'Don't forget to flutter your eyelashes.'

Five minutes later she found herself sitting in a darkened corner across from him. This time he did speak, indeed barely had he thanked her for coming before he set off, slowly at first, then more fervently as time went on, as though a great dam was giving way. He talked of a childhood on the North American plains, of a great love of the outdoors and riding. Of his pride and excitement at joining the CEF and travelling overseas. Of the freedom flying gave him, even if the price of that freedom was war. A war he believed in, he said, but feared would never end.

Then suddenly he stopped, breaking off to stare at his coffee as though emptied of words.

'You look exhausted,' she ventured.

'I guess I am a little.' He smiled. 'Sorry. For sounding off like that. Don't know what came over me.'

'No need to apologise.'

'I used to talk about these things with George.'

'Dear George, he's quite a character.' She glanced anxiously at the door. 'Are you two close friends?'

'I believe so. We used to help each other out, it kind of grew from there.' He hesitated. 'You and him . . . I mean, it's none of my business, but I wouldn't want to step on any toes . . .'

'Me and George? Good heavens, we hardly know each other!' She laughed, sensing his relief with uneasy stirrings of her own. But time was too short for stirrings. 'Look, Mac, I'm so touched you came, really, but I'm not supposed to be here and—'

'You like horse-riding.'

'What?'

'George told me. You love to ride. No?'

'Did he? Well, yes, as it happens I do, though it's been months—'

'I'll fix it up. For your next day off. You and me, we'll take off and go riding, out in the country. Take a picnic, maybe. What do you say?'

Urgent rapping came on the window. Phyllis's face appeared, wide-eyed, her hand ringing an invisible bell.

'Lord, I have to go!'

Mac grabbed her arm. 'Say yes!'

'What? Yes, yes, all right, thank you, but I really must go!' She squeezed his hand and fled to the street.

It was the day after that meeting that she'd written to George, as though finally conceding something significant might be happening. And it was four days after receiving his excited reply that her day off finally came round, and with it her rendezvous with providence. All night she lay awake, fretting with uncertainty, excited yet fearful, then at the appointed hour, duly scrubbed and brushed, and wearing the best the Valkyries could muster, she walked determinedly to the railway station and caught a branch-line train to the seaside town of Wimereux.

Mac met her there. As the train slowed and she saw him, dark, tall and smartly dressed in a fresh uniform, her heart unmistakably missed a beat.

'Thank you for coming,' he said, offering his hand at the door.

'I've been looking forward to it,' she replied, accepting it.

True to his word, he had arranged horses. At the stables a cavalry corporal saluted Mac then led two chestnut thoroughbreds from their stalls, both impeccably groomed and saddled.

'I should keep an eye on your young lady, sir,' he murmured to Mac. 'Oscar here can be a handful.'

'I'll be fine, thank you,' Emily replied, mounting the animal in a single smooth movement. Without waiting she then wheeled it around and cantered away.

Mac smiled, watching her go. 'I guess she'll be fine.'

They rode through a wooded rise behind the town, trotting between shafts of sunlight, solid like marble pillars, and ducking to the horses' necks as branches swept low overhead. Then they broke into the open, and a high meadow overlooking the sea. Here they raced, kicking their mounts to a full gallop, flying through the grass like dolphins through an ocean. Eager and energised, Emily felt months of strain and hardship falling away, and with her own laughter ringing in her ears, urged her mount ever higher and faster.

'How do you feel?' Mac called out.

She turned in the saddle. He was close behind, riding one-handed in the American way. 'I feel alive!'

'Me too. See that big oak tree up there?'

'I see it.'

'Last one there's a slowcoach!'

Emily won, or Mac let her, either way felt wonderful. At the tree they paused, watching breathlessly as a convoy of warships steamed up-Channel, like toys on a pond.

'God, it's good to be out here in the open.' She sighed.

'I know what you mean, I hate being shut up indoors.'

'Me too.' She smiled ruefully. 'Actually, I'm afraid of it.'

'And I can't stand nights! What a team! Oh, I nearly forgot.' He produced a small box. 'I got you this. It don't mean nothing, I just thought it was kind of pretty.'

Intrigued, Emily took the box and untied its ribbon.

'Mac, my God!' A brooch lay nestling in tissue paper. Royal Flying Corps wings – not the cloth and braid version Mac wore on his uniform but an exact miniature replica, in blue and gold enamel. Costly to procure and highly prized as talismans, Emily knew such things existed but had never seen one. Sweetheart brooches, they were called. 'Oh, Mac. It's simply beautiful. But I don't know if I can accept it, can I?'

'Only if you want. Like I said, it doesn't mean anything.'

Emily fingered the brooch, her gaze on the English horizon. Of course the brooch meant something, it meant everything, and they both knew it. But George was out there, somewhere, dear impetuous, devoted George. Still she hesitated, her horse stamping and snorting beneath her impatiently.

'Pin it on for me, Mac.'

They rode on in silence a while, gradually descending to the outskirts of Wimereux where they stopped at a sea-front tavern. The bar was busy with uniformed officers, French and Belgian, British and some Canadian. Mac suggested they sit outside. 'It's our day off,' he told her, swiftly surveying the faces. 'Let's try to forget there's a war.' They settled at a table, and soon their waiter brought wine and a dish of almonds.

'Tell me about your family,' she said.

He shook his head. 'You first.'

She'd heard precious little in the months since leaving Shrewsbury. Her mother wrote occasionally, berating Emily for her selfishness one minute, pleading with her to return home the next. Her sister had written once, asking if she could have Emily's room above the garage, now its window was safely barred. And her grandfather sent monthly packets containing clippings from the newspapers together with a ten-shilling note. Her father hadn't written once. When first she began in Calais with the FANY she had tried to write explaining her decision for leaving, and describing her work, but the first sounded trite and the second was inexpressible, so she'd simplified everything to a few lines and left it at that.

'Do you still write?' Mac asked.

'I try. But it feels so pointless. They don't understand, except perhaps my grandfather, nor do they want to. Sometimes it feels as though we've always been strangers.'

'That's kind of sad. It's important to keep contact with family. Otherwise who are we fighting for?'

'You're right.' She smiled. 'I'll try harder. What about you? It can't be easy, being so far from your home.'

'No, it isn't. I think of it often.'

'Are you in touch with family?'

'It's hard.' His eyes flickered. 'You have to find ways.'

They broke off as a party of French officers exited the bar with much back-slapping and bonhomie, loaded themselves into a battered staff-car and careered away in a cloud of smoke.

'Why me, Mac?' she asked, when the dust settled.

He sipped wine, his eyes on a group of children playing in the surf. 'George told me quite a bit about you.'

'I remember you saying.'

'I guess we both know he's sweet on you.'

'Yes, I suppose he is.'

'But the point is, the moment we saw you that night at the dock, I knew who you were. Almost before he did. As though I had a picture of you in my head. Not from what he told me, you understand, but from what I imagined. Does that make sense?'

'I think so.'

'And after that I just had to see you again, to make sure. So I came and found you that morning in the compound.'

'And?'

Trepidation showed in his face suddenly. 'It was the same, Emily. Only stronger. And I knew I wanted to go on. But it didn't feel right.'

'Because of George?' His hand, she noticed, had started opening and closing on the table, like a flower.

'He's been a good friend to me. I wouldn't want to harm that.'

'Of course. Neither would I.'

'But it's not just George. It's me, and my work, and my past. And it's us, Emily. Starting something at a time like this, it's insanity, we both know that.'

'Is it?' She slipped her fingers into his palm, and the clenching stopped. 'We don't know that for certain. And even if it is insanity, what if I don't care? This whole war is insane, yet it has brought us together. And what if I don't care about your past, and what if I understand the risks you take, and choose to accept them?'

'Can you really do that?'

'I can try. We both can.'

'Maybe.' Mac nodded, staring at their linked hands. 'Maybe it could work.'

'Two hearts beat stronger than one.'

'So they say.' He smiled, and for a while they held hands in silence. Then he brightened. 'There's this other saying, you know. In the Flying Corps. Unmarried men make better pilots than married ones, but married ones last longer. The theory is that if you're happily married you're not going to fly and fight as hard as someone with nothing to lose.'

'I suppose that could be true.'

'Sure. Do you know what George says?'

'No.'

'What if you're unhappily married?'

They looked at each other in confusion, then collapsed into laughter.

'See!' She giggled. 'We can laugh, and forget about the war, and have fun. Even if only for a day.'

'True enough.'

'So let's do that, Mac. Let's put the other things aside when we can, be together and enjoy the moment. For as much or as little time as we have. Agreed?'

'Agreed. But there's one more thing you should know before deciding.'

'What's that?' A faint pulse had started, like a rhythmic contraction, gently squeezing her hand every few seconds.

'Time.' He fingered his wristwatch. 'You should know it may not be much.'

She returned to Calais, he to Noyelette. Ten days passed, she drove, he flew, they wrote letters, they saw each other once, an evening rendezvous over dinner in Calais. Organising it was problematical as FANY regulations allowed the girls one day off a month and one evening out a fortnight, assuming no duty commitments, and she had to swap an evening with an unusually irritable Phyllis to meet his schedule. But the rules also stipulated girls could not go on evening engagements alone, only in pairs, so a double-date was hastily arranged with Angel Truscott and her French colonel, with whom, Angel confessed as they waited in the restaurant, matters were coming to a head. What do you mean? Emily asked, but Angel, normally so rock-solid and assured, could only shake her head. I've been so stupid, Parks, she replied, fighting back tears. Before Emily could learn more the colonel walked in and Emily left them for another table. A few minutes later Mac arrived looking wild-eyed and dishevelled, as though he'd run there from Noyelette. But his face softened the instant he saw her, and he embraced her warmly, holding on tight and not letting go, until heads were turning and the breath left her chest.

They'd agreed in their letters not to discuss the war, but with the restaurant packed with uniforms and the news all bad it was hard to discuss anything else. Mac ate sparingly, picking at his plate with one hand while his other clung to Emily's like a lifeline. She too had little appetite, sensing the despair in his nerviness, and in his craving for small-talk. Tell me about your home, he kept asking, and about your grandfather and how he set up Parkers garage. I've already told you, she said. I know, but tell me again. So she told him again, and it seemed to calm him, especially when she recounted the part about George climbing through the window, when he rocked back on his chair and slapped his thigh with delight. That crazy George, he laughed, that crazy George, like an enchanted child. And her heart went out to him and helplessness welled in her like a tide; she wanted to fold him in her arms and protect him from the demons that haunted him so mercilessly. And across the room she could see Angel, her beautiful face drawn and unhappy, and she thought of lovely Phyllis snapping at her, and wordless Bobby Waldron who used to giggle but now hardly spoke, just coughed and muttered and drove her ambulance like a thing possessed, and it occurred to her that the whole world and everything good in it was being poisoned by this wretched war that nobody understood.

All too soon Mac had to leave for his tender. They stood in rain outside the restaurant and embraced once more, this time with lips as well as arms. Stay alive, Mac, she found herself saying, to her shock. But she meant it, and he grinned. I'll do my best, he said, and sprinted away through the puddles. Then she waited beneath the awning, watching the rain fall in silent curtains until Angel appeared, fumbling a cigarette to her lips. It's over, she wept. He's married and I'm finished. Emily hugged her, then took her arm and together they set off through the deluge for Richelieu where the other Valkyries were waiting. You two are nearly late, the Brute scolded when they ran in. My furs will be ruined, CW cried, dragging the coat from Emily's shoulders. And Charlie's drunk again, Phyllis added casually, so how was your evening. But there was so little to tell about her and Mac, except that they'd kissed, and anyway when Angel's news broke they lost all interest, gathering around, questioning and cross-questioning her eagerly, all except Bobby, who sat on the floor hugging her knees, rocking back and forth, watching and coughing and not saying anything.

Then the sirens went and the bombers came and everyone had to troop downstairs and squeeze into the tiny cellar while the Gothas plied their trade. At first no sounds came except the apprehensive breathing of Commandant Bruton, Sergeant Collier, the cook, the maid, and all the FANYs, twenty-four women tightly packed into a windowless box little bigger than a debutante's closet. Emily pressed herself in, feeling the terror rise within her like floodwater. Then the first bombs fell and newer girls began to whimper. Steady there, men, the Brute said, in her dressing-gown and night-cap, and somebody sniggered. Then two big bombs dropped nearby and the walls shook and plaster fell and girls started screaming. Emily's claustrophobia engulfed her. She began pushing for the door, but the press of bodies was too tight and she couldn't move. Our Father, she whispered, like she had as a child, our Father in heaven, please help me. Then a familiar voice broke into song. 'Oh I used to be in society once,' it slurred gaily, 'I danced and hunted and flirted once . . .' Charlie Neve, medal-winning Charlie, who'd saved her from finishing school and now drank to save herself, was saving them all. Emily clenched her teeth. Give us this day, give us this day . . . Then another voice was in her ear, CW's, whispering don't worry about the fur coat, Parks, I'm just glad it went well with Mac. Above the explosions other voices were joining in: 'Had fair white hands and complexion once, but now I am a FANY!' Still bombs fell, further away now, marching towards the docks like giant boots. Grab it, Parks, CW was urging, grab every bit of happiness while you can. And something else was grabbing her, small hands scrabbling at her legs. Emily reached down in panic and found the maid, Adèle, a scrawny girl of twelve, cowering on the floor. Awkwardly she lifted her and clutched her to her breast. 'Je comprends, chérie,' she soothed in Shropshire French. 'Je comprends, je comprends.'

Three nights later they had a double call-out. Having already worked the evening shift from seven to midnight, they crawled back up to Valkyrie HQ and fell into bed, only to be woken within the hour by the klaxon sounding again. 'B-Watch at the double!' the Brute's voice echoed up the stairwell. All six sat up in disbelief.

'It can't be true.'

'She's pulling our leg.'

'Ignore her.'

'Shoot her, you mean.'

'No. We must go. It's our duty.' This last was Bobby

Waldron, already scrambling into clothes. 'Come on, they need us!'

Bemused and bleary the others struggled from bed, re-donned their filthy breeches and followed her downstairs.

'A call's come in from the canal-head,' Bruton explained, reading from a slip. 'A hospital barge has arrived unexpectedly. They need a single watch to take fifty wounded to the port. Six ambulances, two rotations each, you should do it easily in an hour. Off you go.'

'Why us?' Phyllis demanded.

Bobby gasped. At the same moment Angel ran for the door clasping a hand to her mouth. Everyone else froze.

'Because we're the nearest,' Bruton enunciated icily.

'No. I mean, why us in B-Watch. It's always B-Watch. I want to know why.'

'It is not always B-Watch, Driver Mason, and if you know what's good for you you'll stop questioning orders and go to your ambulance this instant.'

'Phyll,' Charlie murmured. 'Come on, it's all right, let's go.'

They turned to leave, but suddenly Phyllis broke free. 'You don't own us, you bloody sadist!'

'What did you call me?'

'You heard!'

'Driver Mason, you are hereby on a charge and will report to me in the morning. Now get out and do your job!'

Bruton turned to her desk and they all left. Except Emily, who stood her ground, the rebuke still ringing in her ears like an alarm.

'Commandant Bruton.'

'What do *you* want?'

'Only to say that Phyllis doesn't mean anything, ma'am. She's just very tired.'

'We're all very tired, Parker. That's no excuse for gross insolence.'

'I know, Commandant. But she's a good driver, one of the best, one of the most dependable. You know that.'

'Don't tell me what I know!'

'No, ma'am. But did you know her fiancé just called off their engagement?'

Bruton hesitated. 'No,' she muttered, her back still to Emily, 'I didn't.'

'Neither did I until today. She's had the letter a week. He said he couldn't marry anyone who put the FANY before their future husband.'

Another pause. 'I see.'

'That's why she's been out of sorts. With everyone.'

'Thank you, Parker, I'll bear it in mind. Now, please go.'

She was last out of the compound. By the time she reached the canal-head the first ambulances were already loaded and preparing to leave. Six battered vehicles, she reflected, joining the queue, and six battered girls whose lives had changed for ever. How would they cope with their mundane pasts when they returned to them? Assuming the war ended and they did return to them. Charlie was first to set off, driving down the line, one hand raised in a 'V' for Valkyrie salute. Emily waved back, and eased number 52 forward behind the others.

Slow out, fast back. She collected her wounded – four stretchers and one sitter – and set off, instinctively driving as smoothly as she could. By now she knew the streets of Calais better than anyone, so chose her route based on comfort rather than distance. Effortlessly she propelled the vehicle through the blacked-out streets, double-clutching on the downshifts, braking minimally on the bends. 'I heard you FANYs was good,' her sitter said, watching beside her, 'but you drive better than my sergeant, and that's saying something.' Reaching the docks, she reversed carefully to the waiting orderlies, barely noticing which other ambulances had been or gone. 'Marry me!' the sitter joked, hobbling off. Emily smiled, checked her watch and let in the clutch.

Fast back. This time she did take the shortest route, pushing number 52 to its limits along echoing cobbled alleyways, and short-cutting through farm tracks and narrow tree-lined avenues. Soon she was alongside the dark strip of the canal, hurtling flat out down the straight road running above it, before braking sharply for the turn down to the water's edge and the waiting barges.

She pulled up for her second load. 'Where are the other girls?' she called to an orderly.

He checked his notes. 'Two ahead of you, three behind.'

Three behind. She'd made up three places on the return journey, despite taking the slower route out. Not bad.

She jumped down from the cab to stretch her legs while they loaded. Just then she heard the roar of an engine and a splintering crash above. Looking up, she saw an ambulance smash through the parapet and soar through the air, caught in perfect silhouette against the starlit sky. Then, as though in slow-motion, it sailed straight over her head, engine racing, and exploded into the black waters of the canal.

For a split second she could only stare in frozen horror as a ring of white foam spread out across the canal. Then the ambulance, half-submerged, nose-down, rolled swiftly on to its back and sank from view.

'Jesus fucking Christ!' the orderly shouted. 'What happened?'

Emily ran to the bank. 'Get help! Get a rope! Hurry!' Bobby. Somehow she knew it was poor burned-out Bobby Waldron. 'Hurry, don't just stand there!' Frantically she threw off gloves and coat, pulled the boots from her feet and waded into the black water.

She tried. She wasn't a swimmer – she'd learned only the basics at school – but she tried, paddling frantically out to the widening ring of white. Soon others were joining her, two orderlies, one of the medics off the barge, all swimming in circles calling for Bobby. But the minutes ticked by and no gasping survivor broke surface. Then a little rowing-boat arrived and someone started duck-diving with a rope. He managed to fasten it round one wheel, then someone else fumbled his way down through the blackness to the cab, but came up spluttering that the roof was crushed and the cab buried in the mud. After that a fatal resignation set in, the urgency ebbed from their efforts and the cold began driving them to shore. Emily pleaded with them to stay, paddling in desperate circles still calling for Bobby. Leave it, they called, no more can be done until morning. No, she screamed, we must keep trying. Soon she was shuddering with cold, numbness filled her legs with lead, and she felt herself slipping under. Still she stayed, struggling and calling. Then another swimmer was beside her, buoying her with strong arms and calm words. Come on, Parks, CW urged, come ashore now or you'll freeze. But Bobby, Emily sobbed. Please, I can't leave Bobby.

'Bobby?' CW stopped in the water. 'It's not Bobby. She's on the bank with Charlie. It's Phyllis. Or it's Angel.'

The four climbed into Charlie's ambulance and hurried back to base, doubling up the stairs to Valkyrie HQ, bursting through the door to find Phyllis sitting on her bed, smoking a cigarette. 'Looks like I beat you all, for once.' She smiled, then saw their expressions, and Emily's soaked clothes, and Bobby's tear-stained cheeks, and the colour drained from her face. 'Where's Angel?'

Bruton was summoned, and listened stone-faced to the facts. 'I'll go there now,' she said simply. 'I must be with her when they find her.'

'We're coming too.'

So they drove back once more to the canal where they waited through the remaining hours of darkness until a lifting-barge could be brought, and a Navy swimmer with a diving suit. While they waited they held hands and prayed, then with quavering voices they sang hymns, and Angel's favourite songs, and wept as they retold her funny stories. Then, inevitably, the talk turned to speculation.

'Was it brakes, do you think?'

'Did she miss the turn in the dark?'

'Going too fast, perhaps. You know Angel.'

'Oh God, I can't believe it's her down there all alone!'

Five girls holding one another in the moonlight. Bruton standing apart.

Then: 'It's my fault,' they heard her say, around dawn.

'What do you mean?' Phyllis asked.

'She was FW.'

FW. Family Way. A state of gracelessness so shameful its name could not be spoken. Angel was pregnant. By her married French colonel, who had used then discarded her. And the Valkyries didn't know. Only Bruton.

'She told me two days ago,' she went on. 'She was distraught, but determined. I asked if she wanted to leave but she said no, she wanted to stay with her friends for as long as possible. But I knew her mind was in hell. And I should have done something. I should have stopped her. Got her help. Anything.'

Then the dreadful truth dawned. Angel hadn't died by accident, she'd chosen her moment – while doing the work she loved – and she'd chosen her method – alone at the wheel of her ambulance, driving in characteristically spectacular fashion. Taking her broken heart and her unborn secret with her to oblivion.

The Richelieu unit was stood down for a week. Leave was given, many girls went home to their families in England, new faces began appearing on the stairs, and lorry-loads of spares arrived for the vehicles. The Valkyries disbanded for a few days, Charlie and CW going home, Bobby and Phyll taking a week's holiday in a *pension* along the coast. Emily stayed, sorting and packing Angel's possessions, helping with the arrangements for the return of her body, writing to Angel's family, and at length to her own. At night she lay alone in the dormitory they'd called home for so long, reliving all that had happened and yearning for Mac, desperate for his masculine solidity and strong comforting arms. On the third morning she began a fervent letter of longing to him, then thought better and wired a telegram to Noyelette instead.

That night she was called to Bruton's office to take a telephone call.

'It's your Canadian pilot friend,' Bruton said brusquely, and left the room.

'I got your wire,' he said over a sea of static. 'What happened?'

Emily gave him the facts, then told him how she ached to see him. 'We're having a service of remembrance on Friday,' she explained. 'Could you come?'

'I'll do everything I can,' he replied. 'Stay strong, Emily, you're an amazing girl.' Then the line was lost and the call ended.

'How did you know?' Emily asked Bruton, when she returned.

'About your pilot? Truscott told me. Angela, that is. Angel. When she told me about the other business. She was worried you might get hurt, like her. She asked me to look out for you.'

'I see.'

'I told her I would, of course. But also said that in my view your judgement was sounder than most, and you'd know what to do, if it came to it.'

'I'm not sure I do know. I only know we need each other.'

'A solid enough basis for a relationship.'

Emily looked up. A wan smile crossed Bruton's face.

'I'm not completely devoid of feeling, you know, Parker.'

'No, ma'am.'

'I shall never forgive myself.'

'It wasn't your fault.'

The two women eyed each other guardedly, then Bruton came to a decision.

'Sit down a minute. There's something I must discuss with you.'

Emily sat, for the first time ever in the commandant's presence. Furthermore, Bruton then pulled two glasses from a drawer and poured a half-inch of brown liquid into each from a small decanter.

'Emily, isn't it?' She passed the glass. 'I was going to wait until this dreadful week was over, but it might as well be now. The thing is, we're sending you to Arras.'

It was a new FANY operation, she explained, one the organisation had been trying to set up for months, a hospital of their own, funded by benefactors in London. Based in a former monastery on the outskirts of Arras, the hospital was for soldiers too badly injured to be evacuated to the ports.

'It's close to the front lines, you see, which will greatly improve their chances, plus it will be properly equipped and staffed by qualified doctors and nurses. Hopefully we'll save hundreds who would otherwise be lost. We can only let you have four ambulances to begin with, and it'll be dangerous fetching casualties so near to hostilities. A senior MO will be in charge of the medical side of things, and a FANY captain in charge of logistics and transport. Think you're up to it?'

'I . . . I think so. Who will be the captain?'

'You, of course. Earls Court asked for names of experienced

drivers with good records, organisational ability and bags of common-sense. I had no hesitation in putting yours forward and they agreed. We want you to head the unit.'

Her glass midway to her lips, Emily could only gape in astonishment.

'And of course' – Bruton shuffled papers – 'Arras is not far from Noyelette.'

The rest of the week passed in a blur of hurried organisation, packing up, endless lists and last-minute letters. Then Friday finally came, the Valkyries returned, and in the afternoon the whole unit assembled in the compound to remember Angel. All the Calais FANY leaders attended, together with dignitaries from the town and senior military representatives, including a Navy captain and a brigadier. An altar was set up using a sheet-draped table with brass cross, and an army chaplain in full robes officiated. Sergeant Collier played the piano for the hymns. The five remaining Valkyries stood together for the last time, straight-backed beneath blustery skies, but when 'Abide With Me' was sung the tears flowed unchecked and they linked arms for support, as they had supported one another from the beginning. Then Bruton gave the address, speaking softly but clearly of Angel's quiet strength, her wry humour, her pride in her work, and her unfailing devotion to the FANY.

Halfway through her speech the compound gate squeaked and Mac slipped in, cap in hand, to stand with the congregation. When Emily saw him, Charlie squeezed her arm, and she felt the life surge in her veins once more like a river in spring.

Afterwards they spoke in a corner of the compound.

'Thank you so much for coming.'

'I'm proud to be here. She sounds quite a girl.'

'She was. Can you stay?'

'Sure. I'm off until noon.'

'Good. I've booked us a room.'

His eyes searched hers. 'Are you sure?'

'Completely.'

Then she led him through the throng to meet the others.

'So this is the famous Phyllis,' he said gallantly. 'And you must be Charlie, a competition horse-rider, I hear.'

She left him in their care to speak to Bruton.

'All packed, Parker?'

'Yes, ma'am, I leave for Arras in the morning.'

'Good. Come and see me before you go.'

'I will. And thank you, Commandant, for Angel's address. It is exactly how I shall remember her.'

Bruton nodded. 'Just so you know, I'm recording her death as an accident. We have no proof otherwise. Nor am I going to mention the other business. As far as I'm concerned, she died bravely in the service of her country and her family should be proud of that. Nothing else matters.'

'I agree. There is just one other thing, ma'am. Bobby Waldron. She can't go on.'

'I know. Everything's already arranged. Earls Court are asking for experienced girls to help with a recruitment drive at home. I feel she'd be ideally suited, don't you?'

'I think she'll love it. Thank you.'

'No, Emily, thank you.' Bruton gazed round the compound. The congregation was dispersing, talking quietly in twos and threes or drifting inside to their rooms. 'Is that your young man, talking with Mason and the others?'

'Yes.'

'He's very handsome.'

'Thank you.'

'Take good care of him, Emily. The best you can.'

The hotel was on the esplanade. Once grand, it now suffered from neglect and the privations of war. An elderly concierge showed them to a second-floor room overlooking the sea and gave them the key, his wrinkled face impassive. The restaurant, he said, was long closed, but there were places to eat in town. And the electricity was off, he added – insufficient customers to settle the bill, evidently – so lighting was by oil lamp. Then he left them. The room, which smelled of wood polish and damp sea air, was small and sparsely furnished with a dark oak *penderie*, a chest of drawers, a single chair and, dominating everything, an ancient wooden bed with candlewick spread. Mac sat on it gingerly, testing the springs which plinked like piano strings.

'Great place.' He grinned, nervously. 'Think we're the only guests?'

'Hope so. That's why I chose it.'

They lay down on their backs next to each other, rigidly, his hands at his sides as though at attention, hers clasped demurely to her midriff. The plasterwork on the ceiling, she noted, was flaking and spotted with mildew. Then his finger touched her thigh and she sat up and kissed him, her dark hair falling over his face. He too raised himself and, lips locked, they began awkwardly to undress, she unbuttoning the front of his maternity jacket, he fumbling with her tunic. Soon her top was bare to her underclothes and he began lightly stroking her nipple through the cotton. A sigh of longing escaped her lips, and her hand slipped through his shirt buttons to the hair of his chest, and on down to the smooth skin of his abdomen.

Then came a brisk rapping on the door.

Chapter 7

Which was me. Bouquet in hand, foolish grin on face, just like in the films.

Why? Because I wanted to tell her how I felt about her. That I adored her, and always had, from the moment I'd first seen her in the Rose and Crown that evening with Bertie. That my schoolboy antics had been crass, but sincerely meant. That running off had been unpardonable, but I'd never stopped thinking about her. That meeting her again on the docks had been a bombshell. And finally, that I'd been trying to express these things since the beginning, but didn't know how. Because I was emotionally incapable.

It was my own fault. Hinting at a visit in my letter was not enough, I should have telegrammed. My only excuse is that after weeks assembling the necessary permits, travel warrants and other pieces of paper needed to get into (and out of) a war zone, everything happened rather suddenly. One night I won a three-day pass off a fellow pilot at cards, so next morning I simply packed a bag and went. And didn't telegram, because I decided to surprise her. Which I certainly did.

The journey was a portent, with the trains in chaos and the ferries backed up because of U-boat alerts in the Channel. So it was late afternoon when I disembarked in Calais and set out for Emily's base. I found it in disarray, with suitcases and crates piled everywhere and everyone in a daze following Angel's funeral. I asked after Emily but no one seemed to know, until finally an adjutant said she'd gone to the Metropole Hotel for the evening. So I set off once more, wilting flowers in hand, located the place on the prom, the concierge gave me the room number and the rest is history.

And here's the sad thing. Part of me was overjoyed to see them. Part of me was even glad they'd found each other. These two people were my closest friends in the world, I loved them both in my awkward hamstrung way, and under normal circumstances would have rejoiced in their new-found happiness.

But the circumstances weren't normal.

'Oh, hello,' I think I said. 'Well, goodbye then.'

And fled for the street, sprinting full tilt along the prom like a madman pursued. Numb I felt, numb, shocked, humiliated and stupid. All I could think of was putting distance between me and them, so I ran, then walked, aimlessly, for hours through the blacked-out streets, until I found myself back at the docks. There I stopped walking and started drinking, lurching through a succession of seamen's bars until my head swam and my cash ran out. Then, since no other options presented themselves, and staying in Calais was clearly pointless, I staggered up a gangplank and caught a troopship home.

Where basically I got on with the job. It seemed the only thing to do, put Emily, Mac, France and everything behind me, draw a line under the whole sorry business and move on. Occupational therapy, they call it now, and it worked, up to a point. Back at Suttons I flew my night patrols, played cards, stared at the ceiling in my room, flew some more, got drunk a bit, went for walks, and pretty soon life, albeit rather an empty and aimless one, was plodding on much as before.

Letters arrived, early on, from both Mac and Emily. Hers were calm and reasoned – *George dearest, I feel terrible about what happened and have nothing but the greatest fondness for you, but we both know there was never any understanding about a relationship* – whereas Mac's had an edge of panic about them: *George, believe me, if only I'd known!* I read and re-read them, pretending I didn't care, gulped down more Scotch and went flying again. Which was my saving grace, and thank God for aeroplanes. I spent much time aloft during that post-Emily phase, particularly at night when flying was magical. And cathartic. Somehow being up there, sailing through the starlit sky all alone with my thoughts while the world slept peacefully below, was immensely comforting. Enemy activity was light; occasionally we were called upon to investigate intruders, but I never saw any. My duties on the ground were undemanding, little was expected of me in the mess, I had time to myself and my billet over the pub, so all in all, I persuaded myself, everything was probably for the best.

I even wrote up my notes on Bloody April.

*

By March 1917 the honeymoon period at Noyelette, if ever there was one, was definitely over. Both sides were gearing up for the Arras offensive, steadily upping the ante in their quest for aerial domination. Pilot losses were mounting accordingly, indeed getting so bad that the War Office, which had blithely decreed an empty chair at supper must be filled by breakfast, was unable to meet its own dictum. Recruitment was stepped up, training cut further, but aircrew kept dying. We in the observation business were particularly hard-hit, with barely a mission passing without a casualty. Flying, once pleasurable, became a dreaded ordeal, something to be endured, survived, avoided even. Pilots on dawn patrol feared sleep lest the morning come sooner, so lay awake praying bad weather might bring a stay of execution. Then came thunder and lightning to the east, heralding not the hoped-for deluges but the artillery-storm of the morning hate. All too soon the corporal's hand was on the shoulder, and with it the awful realisation there would be no reprieve, only the egg wobbling at the bedside, the bleary struggle into flying-clothes, the lonely trudge to the aeroplane, and the day's first dance with the devil.

It was a grim and deeply unnerving existence. Surreal too. Unlike the poor bloody infantry who lived in mud-filled holes, ate tinned mush and were perpetually getting shot at, bombed, shelled, gassed and the rest of it, we lived much of our lives in comfort and safety. We sat at linen-covered tables and ate civilised food with decent cutlery. We drank tolerable wine from proper glasses. We conversed politely, played cards, listened to the gramophone, read books and smoked our pipes, and then we went to bed between clean sheets in a dry hut. But once or twice a day we donned our leathers and Sidcot suits, trooped off to our outlandish machines and flew them into the teeth of an inferno. There some of us met our deaths, often horribly, some of us got wounded, and the rest scurried fearfully home. Then we picked up our magazines where we'd left them and pretended nothing had happened. A few hours later we did it all again. It was like living in a comfortable hotel, then walking out twice a day to face a firing-squad. Only you never knew if it was you they were going to shoot or the man standing beside you. And death by firing-squad is quicker.

Morris Dixon and I kept going, we flew our missions, we took hits, we had two aircraft reduced to scrap while we were flying them, we honed our gunnery skills and fine-tuned our evasion techniques, we did our duty and strove to stay alive. Then on 12 March C-Flight was briefed to attack two German observation balloons, with 166 Squadron providing high cover from above. It was to be the last time Morris and I would fly together.

Before we boarded, he took me aside. 'You've never done sausages before, have you?' he asked wearily. I shook my head.

Sausages was the deceptively innocuous nickname for observation balloons, large hydrogen-filled gas-bags attached by wire to a lorry. Beneath the balloon hung a basket containing two observers. Their job was to report enemy troop movements, direct artillery-fire and generally keep an aerial eye on things. Rather comical-looking, seemingly harmless and vulnerable, sausages were nevertheless useful and effective, able to spy from heights up to a thousand feet, then be winched rapidly down and driven off elsewhere as needed.

They were also aggressively defended by anti-aircraft guns, and apt to explode lethally when attacked. Their observers, incidentally, were the only airmen to be issued with parachutes.

'Disregard everything we were told at the briefing,' Morris warned. His normally unruffled demeanour had become much tenser of late, and more worryingly he wore an air of resignation, as though at forty and with a lifetime of military service behind him he sensed Bathtubs would be the end. 'Once they spot us it's all over,' he went on. 'You have to catch them by surprise, hit them hard, and get the hell out. So don't dive on them, like they said, go in low and shoot them on the up. Believe me it's the only way.'

'But what about the others?'

'Screw the others. And remember one more thing. If this gets messed up today, they'll just send us back tomorrow to do it all again.'

The four Bathtubs of C-Flight crossed the lines at five thousand feet then turned north, dodging Archie and quartering the skies for scouts. The weather was cold and dull, a leaden overcast all but obscuring the watery disc of the sun. High above us five Nieuports of 166 Squadron kept watch, Mac's among them, elsewhere other specks buzzed to and fro in the distance like busy gnats. Our gnats or theirs, it was impossible to tell. I inched my Bathtub nearer our leader's, his white pennant fluttering gaily in his slipstream. Proctor, his name was, newly promoted, keen but inexperienced. Hold formation, he had said at the briefing, hold formation no matter what. Before me sat Morris, hunched pensively into his coat. Then someone waggled their wings, the signal for 'target spotted', and Proctor waved everyone into line-astern for the attack, with us at number three. I too glimpsed the two black blimps far below, then we were nosing over into a dive.

But too shallow, and instantly I realised Morris was right: this was not the way to do it. Four Bathtubs descending in a nice straight line – it was like shooting tin ducks at a fairground. Rivers of incandescent ground-fire poured up at us, together with flaming onion-strings, machine-gun tracer and exploding Archie shells. Within seconds number two in the formation was hit, his aircraft trailing a plume of white petrol vapour which ignited with a flash into a blazing inferno. Reflexively I pulled out to dodge the flames, narrowly avoiding an Archie burst in the process, then he fell out of formation, burning horribly. Still Proctor flew doggedly on, not jinking, not slewing, not even steepening the dive for speed. Another shell burst close by, our Bathtub bucking in protest, then a gun found range on Proctor's machine. I saw pieces flying off his wing and tail, saw smoke coming from his engine, saw his observer slump sideways in his seat, saw poor Morris clutching on like a child in a rowboat, felt another huge kick underneath from exploding Archie. Then I just went.

Yes, I abandoned formation. But the formation was doomed, and staying in it madness. So I rolled away to the right, pointed the nose at the ground and dived for all I was worth. Soon we were clear of the firestorm and heading full tilt for safety, but glancing back a few seconds later I was startled to see the number four in the formation still tucked in close behind us. Its pilot, Cadogan, even waved. He too must have realised the folly of the attack, watched me go and elected to follow. In vindication of our decision, tumbling earthward in the distance behind, like a handful of dropped rubbish, was the shattered remains of Proctor's machine.

So we'd narrowly escaped disaster, and were for the moment clear of ground-fire, but what to do now? Turn and run for home would seem a sensible plan, nor would anyone blame us for it. But half our force was still intact, and I seemed to be leading it, and the sausages were in sight less than a mile ahead, and after the cocked-up attack my blood was up, and I still hadn't a single victory to my credit, which I needed if I was to fly scouts, and Morris had said if we failed today they'd only send us back tomorrow. He turned in his seat then, as though knowing, and shrugged, as if to say it's your call, George, twist or stick. I glanced across at Cadogan. He was a college lecturer from Leicester. He lived in my hut, sang Schubert *lieder* and tried to teach us French. He too was watching me, and holding position, and waiting for a decision.

So in we went. Go in low and shoot them on the up, Morris had said. I opened the throttle wide, easing forward on the stick until the two Bathtubs were going flat out at ground level. Meanwhile Morris and the other observer prepared their weapons, two Lewis guns each. The sausages, ugly fat bloaters, black with a painted white cross, grew rapidly as we closed, their operators unaware our attack was still on, and in no time we'd halved the range without a single shot fired. Then they saw us and flew into action, hurling machine-gun fire at us in long arcing streams that curled slowly up then accelerated, hurtling past with a menacing hum. At the same time their ground-crews threw the winches into gear and began winding the balloons down, fast, but not fast enough for the observers who jumped, trailing brown silk that plopped open like mushrooms.

Then we were upon the sausages, one each, we on the left, Cadogan on the right. Morris stood to fire the upper Lewis, I cocked the lower. Machine-gun bullets filled the air now, shredding wings, snapping struts, tearing chunks off the poor Bathtubs like hounds at two hares. One pass, we would get, I saw, one pass then out. The sausages were half-down and descending quickly. Shoot them on the up, Morris had said, so as the range closed to zero I eased up the nose and we both opened fire in a single long burst. I saw our bullets strike home, the balloon quivering like a jelly, then it was half a second to go under or over, so I went under and as I did so felt a massive concussion from above and the Bathtub staggered and nearly crashed and then we were out and banking away for escape. I risked a glance back and saw both sausages spectacularly enveloped, two vast balls of flame clawing skyward, and as I stared, Cadogan's Bathtub burst through the inferno, spinning like a firework, dived flaming to the ground and exploded.

I'd gone under my balloon, he'd gone over his, and it destroyed him. It could easily have been the other way round. Terrified suddenly, shaking like a leaf, I straightened our bashed-up aeroplane and set course for home. Twenty minutes later we landed, taxied in and shut down. Only then, as I pulled the helmet wearily from my head and leaned forward to pat Morris on the shoulder, did I realise he was hit.

That evening 13 Squadron was supposed to be enjoying a 'gaming night' organised by yours truly as a morale booster, but with C-Flight wiped out nobody felt like a party, least of all me. Even the news that Morris had safely reached hospital failed to raise my spirits; rather it seemed only to emphasise how close we'd both come to disaster. 'I'm sorry, George,' he'd whispered as they lifted him from his seat. As if it was his fault. A decent, brave man, he'd given more than anyone should ask.

Dinner was dismal, despite the well-intentioned efforts of colleagues who sensed my mood and tried to help. But no amount of small-talk could disguise the fact that twelve pilots had eaten together at lunchtime, and by dinner we were nine. A quarter of us had fallen in one swoop, all from my flight, and every day more succumbed, like saplings to the axe. 'Surely things will get better,' somebody ventured. 'Couldn't get much worse,' another replied. 'Someone should do something,' muttered a third darkly. How right he was. I picked at my plate, but could find no appetite, so gave up and excused myself.

I went to Major Strickley's office and let myself in. There in the darkness I sank my head to the desk and surrendered to the day's hideous events. And not for the first time. Over the weeks that shabby little hut had become my refuge and retreat, somewhere I could be alone and think, gather myself, or just give in to my terrors in private. Warmed by a little stove, it was dry and comfortable and undisturbed, for Strickley never used it at night. I felt safe there, insulated somehow from the horror outside by his sketches of flowers, his half-written memos and his rambling reports. Sometimes I spent all night there.

After a while I turned on the lamp. As usual a pile of papers lay waiting for me, each with a spidery note attached: 'George dear, could you reply to this – I don't understand it' or 'Lovely letter, George – thank you' or, simply, 'The usual with this, please, George'. I picked them up and began to read. By now I was practically Strickley's secretary, albeit an invisible one, for our paths rarely crossed. My daylight hours were spent either sleeping or flying, and for some reason he avoided his office at night. 'No admin after sunset, George!' he would cry, hurrying for the door. Too many ghosts, perhaps. Gradually a working relationship evolved, based on chance meetings and a system of scrawled messages. We both gained from it. I helped his office run smoothly, he turned a blind eye to my using it. He stayed on top of his paperwork, I learned how the RFC functioned. I brought order into his life, he brought information into mine.

And information is power. Little now went on at Noyelette I didn't know about. Apart from all the returns and inventories and standing orders and statutory notifications, every Tuesday a mail-bag arrived containing the post for 13 and 166 Squadrons. I sorted and distributed it. If the kitchen needed a new saucepan I requisitioned it, if a consignment of spares arrived I could sign for it, and if 13 Squadron was earmarked for a particular mission I was often the first to learn about it. Gradually my interests widened. I studied situation reports, considered strategic reviews, analysed confidential plans, pondered top secret orders. Sometimes I even commented on them, pencilling little notes to Strickley in the margin: 'This seems a little rash, sir' or 'An interesting idea, don't you think, sir'. And as my understanding of the ins-and-outs of the RFC steadily grew, so too did my creative skills, which soon developed beyond writing letters about dead pilots or mechanics with the clap.

Tonight, however, was new ground. Someone should do something, the pilot had said at dinner, and I would do it. For Morris.

Collecting the latest batch of condolence letters from the adjutant's out-tray, I checked them for typing errors before placing them on Strickley's desk for signature. They were necessarily less fulsome than earlier versions, less individually embroidered and more formulaic, for the sheer weight of them, as he would say, had grown too burdensome for individuality. Anyway he rarely read them, which was what I was counting on. Taking headed stationery from his drawer I wound a sheet into the adjutant's typewriter and set to work.

To Senior Air Officer Commanding, Arras Sector, His Majesty's Royal Flying Corps. From Major John D. Strickley OC 13 Squadron, Noyelette, Arras Sector. March 12th 1917.

Sir, I write to you regarding Observer/Gunner Sergeant Morris Stanley Dixon of this unit. Following an outstanding action this afternoon during which Sergeant Dixon participated in the successful destruction of two enemy observation balloons, Sergeant Dixon was returned to base by his pilot, Lieutenant George Montague Duckwell, suffering a bullet-wound. Sergeant Dixon was transferred to the CCS in nearby Pointbleu where I understand his condition is serious but stable. I am writing firstly to request Sergeant Dixon be recommended for the Distinguished Service Medal for his part in this action which although successful resulted in the loss of three out of four aircraft together with six aircrew, and secondly to recommend he

be transferred to the Air Gunnery School at Aldershot as an
instructor upon his return to active duty. Sergeant Dixon is a
most experienced air gunner and as such a priceless asset.
Putting his experience to use training new gunners . . .

And so on. Well, if it wasn't for Morris I would not have
made it through those early weeks, and that's a fact. I owed
him everything, not least my life. I felt he'd done enough and
deserved to get out.

Nor did I stop there. My campaign for transfer to a scout
squadron was languishing, so dire was the shortage of Bathtub
pilots. Now was the time to revive it, not least because of my
dwindling life expectancy. But to be considered for scout
training you had to distinguish yourself in some way. Make a
name for yourself, as Mac put it. Now at last I had done so.

With commendable aplomb, Lieutenant Duckwell assumed
command of the depleted force, re-grouped it into an effective
unit, and pressed home the attack, with the result that both
balloons were completely destroyed. Although the only surviving
aircraft of the original four, he then flew his damaged FE2 and
injured observer back to base. In my opinion this act of daring
and initiative merits consideration for transfer to a home unit
for scout training forthwith . . .

And words to that effect.

Scarcely believing my effrontery, I typed up neat copies of
both letters and shuffled them carefully into the condolences,
like jokers into a pack. Strickley, I hoped, would sign them
without a glance. Then, before I could change my mind, I

picked up 166 Squadron's mail from the in-tray and went in search of Mac.

We'd already spoken briefly upon my return to Noyelette that afternoon: he'd run over to check I was all right and help with poor Morris.

'Did you see the attack?' I asked him, once Morris was safely with the medics.

'Yes. From the first dive right to when the balloons went up. You did the right thing, George, breaking off like that, I'd have gone sooner. But your roll was a little slow and your run-in to the target too straight.'

He was always doing that, constantly offering tips and advice, as though schooling me for a competition.

'I was going to come down and cover your run-in,' he added, 'but we met a little trouble of our own.'

'Anyone we know?'

'It was him, George, his Jasta. We only tangled for a few seconds, then they disappeared into cloud, but I'm sure it was him.'

Richthofen. I'd wanted to know more, but then wasn't the time.

I found him in the library of the chateau where 166 Squadron lived, pacing up and down with a volume of Molière or Baudelaire or some-such. It was his way of trying to relax, wading through French literature. That and teaching me to fly properly. Waiting on a side-table, as usual, was a stack of paper and pencils.

'George!' He looked up, relief on his face. 'You've brought the mail.'

I hefted the sack. 'Yes. But nothing for you I'm afraid, Mac.'

'Nothing?'

'Next week perhaps.'

'Next week.' His face fell. 'Yes, right.'

'Try not to worry.'

'No. How's Dixon?'

'Hopefully he'll be all right.'

'Thank the Lord. What about you, you look all-in.'

'I feel all-in. It was bad, Mac. Dreadful. C-Flight's gone.'

'I know.' He looked all-in too, distractedly pacing the parquet, clenching and unclenching his fist. 'We should go through it.'

'If you think it will help.'

'Yes.' He went to the table. 'Yes, it will. We'll go through it, step by step.'

So we sat at the table, as we had many times, and I described the mission, and he drew it on paper and pointed out where we'd gone wrong and where we'd gone right. And as he talked his voice grew calmer and his agitation eased, as always when he discussed flying, until in a few minutes he was deeply engrossed, like a maths teacher with a wayward pupil, patiently correcting a geometry paper.

'See here, George,' he explained. 'You did an aileron-roll to escape, which is fine, but it's a slow manoeuvre and describes a wider arc, allowing the Hun to stay on your tail more easily.'

'But there was no Hun on my tail. You made sure of that.'

'Yes, but next time there might be, and I might not be there to get him off. Now, the snap-roll, you see, is a more difficult manoeuvre, but it's fast and will throw him off balance. Here's how you do it.'

Soon the page was heavily illustrated with circles and arrows and pin-men pilots in cross-stitch aeroplanes, and my attention, as usual during lessons, was starting to wander.

'Croft's machine went down like a blow-torch, Mac,' I said at one point.

'I know. I saw. Poor devils.'

'I'm not going like that. I've started carrying my service-pistol. You know, like we talked about.'

He nodded. 'You're not going at all, George, if I have anything to do with it. But that old Webley you Brits carry isn't much of a hand-gun. Maybe I can fix you up with something better.'

'Thanks.'

'Sure. Did you hear from your girl yet?'

'Mac, she's not my girl! I told you, I met her at school, made an idiot of myself, then ran away. That's all!'

'But you did write to her.'

'No! I meant to, I keep meaning to, but what's the point?'

'To make your peace, that's the point. And put things right.'

Before I got killed, perhaps. For some reason, me getting in touch with Emily was important to him, as though he knew we had unfinished business. Which was ironic, considering they'd never met, and what would later transpire between them. And putting things right was also something of a Mac preoccupation, I had learned. One best not to argue with.

'All right.' I sighed. 'All right, I know, and I will write to her, I promise, as soon as I find time. Now can we please talk about something else? Richthofen, for instance. Tell me about Richthofen. Are you sure it was him?'

He sat back. 'Certain. They dropped on us out of the cloud. Suddenly, from nowhere. Six brand-new Albatros D3s, which means they've fixed its problems, I guess. Anyway, one second we were all alone watching you make your attack, the next, airplanes everywhere, all over the place, and all different colours. They could have had us, easily, or some of us; they sure had the advantage of surprise. But then something spooked them, or maybe they were out of fuel or ammunition or something, but suddenly they just pulled up into the cloud and vanished again.'

'Why, do you think?'

'I'm not sure. Maybe Manfred just wanted us to know he had us, but then let us go. Or maybe he wanted to show us his new Albatros.'

'Us?'

'Me, then.'

'Did you get a shot at him?'

'No, nobody did. But boy, he was fast in the turn. That D3 is a quick airplane. Say, George, look, have you heard of the Immelmann? It's a new stunt manoeuvre invented by Max Immelmann, a fine aerobatic Hun pilot . . .'

And he was off again with his circles and arrows and pin-men pilots. Finally he was done teaching and fell into restless thought.

'What time is it?' he asked at length. 'My watch stopped working.'

I checked the Breitling. 'Gone midnight. You should get some sleep.'

'Later, maybe.' He eyed the mail-bag. 'Nothing, you say?'

'Nothing, Mac. But you mustn't give up hope.'

'I guess so. What about the other thing?'

'As far as the other thing goes, no news is definitely good news.'

William MacBride was wanted for horse-theft, a serious matter back in Canada where he'd purloined two animals on his journey cross-country to join the CEF. One horse eventually turned up in a Quebec livery yard, where he'd sold it, unwisely using his own name. From there the authorities traced him to the CEF and on to Europe and the 1st Canadian Division. There matters would probably have rested, except that MacBride had previous records for petty theft back in Vancouver and had also stolen food and clothes while en route across the continent. Complaints had been filed, so letters of enquiry were sent across the Atlantic to the headquarters of the 1st Canadian Division in France, asking for information as to his whereabouts.

All this took time, years in fact, but as is the way with military institutions, the wheels may grind slow but they do grind, and months later a letter found its way to the RFC offices in London asking about a Private William MacBride who may have transferred from the Canadian infantry to the Flying Corps in January 1916. The RFC looked into the matter and discovered the aforementioned recruit had indeed transferred, initially as a gunner/observer, before being accepted for pilot training four months later. They also discovered he had been commissioned to the rank of lieutenant, and was presently attached to 166 Squadron based in Noyelette near Arras, where he was doing very well indeed.

The RFC then made a simple but important blunder: they sent the enquiry letter direct to Mac, assuming it was a personal matter, thus nobody knew about it except him. He received it at the end of 1916, sitting on it in panic until I showed up a month or so later. Taking someone into his confidence required a huge leap of faith, but desperate for help, somehow he decided I could be trusted, and might even know what to do. I can't imagine why.

I'd learned all this in February, on the night he sought me out in 13 Squadron's mess. Hesitantly, he had explained the horse-stealing saga, which I found mildly revelatory, particularly as Mac seemed such an upstanding sort of chap. But it was hardly robbing the crown jewels, and I felt sure a few carefully crafted letters of apology, and possibly a cheque or two in compensation, and the whole business would go away. And I told him so. No, George, he went on anxiously, you're missing the whole point. And then he told me the whole point. My friend Mac, it turned out, was not William MacBride at all. He was Daniel Warburton. And he was wanted for murder.

MacBride had died from the gas. Gradually, over a period of months. At first he seemed to be getting better: the coughing eased, the discharge stopped and colour returned to his cheeks. Within a week he was back in the trenches with his friend. By then it was the summer of 1915 and the Second Battle of Ypres, although far from over, was winding down into familiar stalemate, both sides digging in for the long haul. Attacks were still mounted, positions won and lost, men still died by the hundred each day, but the main offensive was finished, leaving only the abject drudgery of trench warfare to be endured – something no Canadian volunteer had ever imagined. The two boys settled in as best they could, and kept their promise to each other to try for transfers to the RFC. If you could shoot well, they learned, there was a chance you'd get in as a gunner. Once in, you might later try out for pilot training. They filled out the forms on each other's backs, handed them in and got on with the war. But MacBride's health was now in decline, irreparable damage done to his lungs by the chlorine. With the coming of autumn rain and onset of colder weather, his cough returned, and with it bouts of fever. Steadfastly he refused to seek medical help. My health record is A1, Danny, he insisted proudly, and needs to stay that way for the Flying Corps. Anyway, my place is by your side.

Weeks passed, back and forth they rotated through the lines, two weeks front line, two weeks service lines, two weeks to the rear, then forward again, round and round, two tiny husks on the millstone of war. Then late in November the great day finally came. Envelopes from the RFC. Hurriedly they tore them open.

'Danny, I'm in!' MacBride exclaimed, dancing with delight.

'Me too,' Danny replied, quickly pocketing his letter. He'd been turned down. On disciplinary grounds. For striking the sergeant while trying to get his friend out of the trench on the day of the gas.

Danny didn't know how to tell his friend, so he didn't. The letter said the transfer would go through in January, so he decided to tell him nearer the time. Meanwhile he said nothing.

We should get that cough fixed, he kept urging, but MacBride wouldn't hear of it. If I report to the hospital, he said, they'll never let me in the Flying Corps. So he stayed away from the hospital, and soon the ravaged tissue of his lungs was coming up in his cough, and by Christmas he had pneumonia and pleurisy and was delirious when he slept. Danny tended him as best he could. January, MacBride kept mumbling, we've just got to hold on until January. Then on New Year's Eve he asked his friend to hold him, as he was feeling the cold.

'Remember Valcartier?' he whispered. 'That day we rode over the hill and saw the camp spread out over the valley like that?'

'It was quite a day,' Danny agreed. 'And I'm taking you to the hospital in the morning. Like it or not.'

'OK.' He smiled. 'It'll be January then.' Then he found Danny's hand and pressed a crumpled sheet into it. 'You take it, Danny,' he said. 'I know you didn't get in, and that ain't right. So you take mine. You go and fly for us both. Promise me.'

The next morning Danny carried his friend's body back to the dressing station. His name is Daniel Burton, he told them. Here's his identity discs and pay-book. He has no next of kin. He returned to his post wearing his friend's discs and said nothing to anyone. A few days later a message came down the line that MacBride was wanted in the adjutant's station to the rear. His transfer papers had come through. Mac picked up his rifle, set off along the trenches, and never looked back.

I killed my daddy, George. I killed my own father, with my bare hands.

My real name is Daniel John Warburton. I was born in Jackson, North Carolina, which is in the southern United States. Jackson is small-town, simple farming stock, decent folk working the cotton fields and tobacco plantations for the wealthy landowners. We lived in a timber house off the main street in Jackson, next to the Baptist church where my father was the minister. He was a respected leader of our community and folks looked up to him. There were five of us in our family: my father Reverend Tom Warburton, my mother Ella, and me and my two younger sisters, Martha and Rachel. We were not rich but not poor, we had just enough to get by.

I studied hard at school and was good at reading and writing. One day I hoped to leave Jackson and go to college in Raleigh and study for the law, but when I was fourteen I had to leave school and go earn my keep in the fields like all the boys in Jackson. In the evenings I had another job, cleaning up for Doctor Petersen, our town doctor. Doctor Petersen was kind to me and encouraged me to keep on with my studying. In my spare time I liked to go fishing, or hunting with my rifle, or just ride out across the wide Carolina plains and watch the sun go down.

I loved my family, especially Ma, who looked after us, and my sisters, who were good honest girls. But not my father, who beat us, and I hated him for it. I don't know why he beat us, I only knew he'd fly into a rage for no reason and start hitting out. It began when I was young and went on throughout our lives. It always happened at night. Mostly he used his belt for the beatings although sometimes his fists, or a cane he kept on the porch. At first it was mainly me or Ma who caught the beatings; later, as I grew up and learned to take them without crying, he began to beat my sisters more.

One night, just after I turned eighteen, I came home from Doctor Petersen's to find Pa beating Martha. I don't know what she'd done to deserve it, usually nothing, anyway she was on the floor, and he was standing over her, legs astride, hitting her with his belt which was *wrapped round his fist. His face was red with rage and he was panting with the exertion. Ma and Rachel were standing to one side holding each other and watching helpless. 'Get up to your room!' Pa shouted and I duly made for the stair, because I knew the beatings ended sooner if everyone did as he said. Anyway I had one foot on the stair and was starting to go up when suddenly Martha cried out, 'Help me, Danny!' It was the first time in my life anyone said that. Her voice cut through me like a knife and I knew I had to help her. So I came down off the stair and turned to face my father. 'Stop, Pa,' I said, as calm as I could. But he just roared for me to get upstairs and carried on beating Martha. 'Come on, Pa, it's enough now.' With that he threw Martha aside and came striding towards me. 'You gonna dare defy me, boy?' he shouted. His face was purple with rage now, and a vein stood out on his brow pulsing like a worm. 'Just stop please, Pa,' I said a third time, but his hand flew up with the belt to strike me.*

Everything happened fast then, but also real slow, like pictures in a book. As I watched the belt go up I could feel the fingers of my right hand clenching and unclenching in a fist, then in a second the belt was coming down full force. I caught it with my left hand, at the same instant my right came up and hit him under the ribs. Pa kind of coughed, and his eyes bulged out, then he fell to the floor stone dead. At first we didn't realise he was dead, but when he didn't move and didn't breathe no more we knew. Ma came over and took my hand and said it was the Lord's will, and an accident as Pa had the blood pressure. But I knew it was no accident. Even if I didn't mean to kill him, I wanted him dead. The date was May 1914.

Those are the facts, in his own words, nor have I embellished them. He said the words and I wrote them down, like a policeman taking a statement.

It was an accident, clearly, it was self-defence, it happened under extreme provocation and without premeditation, and in a British court today he'd have walked free. But this was small-town America in 1914, and all anyone would say was the Warburton boy had raised his hand against his father – a much-loved leader of the community and respected minister of God – and killed him in anger. Lynch mobs had hanged people for less, and Mac's mother knew it. Desperate for the safety of her son, she bundled food and clothing into a sack and pushed him into the night. I'll tell them he fell, she said. If they believe me, maybe you can come back some day. In the meantime head north and stay away.

So he did. Living rough, jumping trains, foraging for scraps like a hobo, he made his way steadily up the continent. In Virginia he earned a few dollars picking corn, in Pennsylvania he helped with the wheat harvest, in Maine he got a job in a fish factory, netting enough to buy a small pony before moving on. Then in August, while felling trees deep in the forests of Vermont, he heard a rumour. A war was starting in Europe, and across the border in Canada men were signing on in thousands to help their British ally. It was the ideal solution, he realised, a fixed job and a worthy cause; he'd be beyond the reach of US authorities, maybe he could even find a way to send his pay home.

He and his pony crossed the border at Franklin, arriving the following day in the bustling French city of Montreal. There he fell in with a fellow runaway from across Canada called William MacBride. The two pooled resources and set out on the final leg of their journey to Valcartier. Then they signed on, MacBride as MacBride – the adopted name given him in the orphanage back in Vancouver – while Danny gave his place of birth as Montreal and used his own name shortened to Burton.

These, as I say, are the facts. I learned the basics from Mac in Noyelette that winter and spring of 1917, the rest I gleaned later from correspondence with others, notably his sisters. Extracting Mac's memories was a painful business: he was clearly still haunted by his childhood in Jackson, the misery of his home life, and the horror of his father's death, for which he blamed himself entirely. More upsetting was the loss of contact with his mother and sisters, and when talking of them he would often falter with emotion. He also worried about the hardship they must be suffering, but feared sending money in case of discovery. Of his own predicament he seemed less concerned. He presumed he was wanted for patricide and expected one day to return to Jackson and face retribution for his crime, assuming he survived the war.

'It will break Ma's heart,' he said to me sadly. 'And my promise to stay away. But maybe it'd be best for everyone in the end.'

'To get hanged when you're innocent? Mac, you didn't mean to kill him!'

'Didn't I? I wanted him dead. A thousand times I wanted him dead, I even prayed he would die. Then he did. Isn't that the same thing?'

Not in my book, but there was no persuading him.

'So,' I asked, 'what can I do?'

'I don't know. What will happen when they find out, do you think?'

'Find out what? That MacBride is here? Or that you're Warburton?'

But he could only shake his head, poor chap. I too, for the situation was anything but straightforward. I needed time to think, and time to come up with a workable plan. But before I could do that, I needed to get through Bloody April.

Around now, and I make no apologies, the narrative becomes disjointed. These were the days leading up to my final flights with 13 Squadron and that ghastly day in no-man's land with Raymond Gates. It's a period I don't recall clearly, nor was I writing it down. 'Christ get me out of here!' is the last coherent entry in my diary, some time around 12 April, and pretty much says it all. Life for us pilots consisted only of flying and drinking and dying and little else, round and round on the merry-go-round, until time ceased, days fused into an eternal nightmare, and reason fled for the hills. 'I died back in December, you know,' one wild-eyed pilot confided to me one night. 'And this is hell.' Next day he crashed and burned. His replacement lasted four days, the one after, two. Daily they arrived, fresh-faced, chattering ten to the dozen, bursting for the fray. Those that survived their first outing came back wearing 'what the hell was that?' expressions and talking more quietly. Two or three sorties more and the expressions were gaunt and the chit-chat gone. Soon after that they vanished into the void. Meanwhile us older lags grew daily more neurotic, and tried to cope as best we could using guile in the air and booze on the ground.

The one factor in our favour, and we knew it, was the longer we stayed alive the better our odds for survival. A Hun scout could spot a novice Bathtub pilot a mile off, simply by the way he handled the machine, so would always single him out. An experienced Bathtub pilot kept tight formation, knowing the Germans picked on stragglers. He knew never to fly straight and level in Archie, but do everything to throw off their aim. He knew the importance of keeping a good lookout, ceaselessly twisting and turning in his seat until his neck bled on his collar. He practised escape manoeuvres, gunnery, and defence tactics with his observer, and he learned how to throw the aircraft on to its back, or into a dive, or even a spin to escape trouble. Novices simply didn't have time to acquire these habits and skills. Bumbling along with their heads buried in their cockpits, they expended all their energy just keeping their aeroplanes the right way up.

And died in droves doing it. By the beginning of April our losses in 13 Squadron were running at two or three a day. Faces were changing faster than you could learn names – a sure sign things are bad. Stafford and his observer went down together on 3 April, Culshaw leapt to his death on the 4th. Two days later Donaldson had his leg blown off by Archie and bled to death in his cockpit, leaving his observer helpless as their aircraft crashed. Finucane tried to escape the flames of his burning Bathtub by scrambling on to its wing, and even managed to land it from there, thus saving the life of his observer, but losing his own from his burns. Jarrold shot himself behind the hangar, Griffiths accidentally fell from his aeroplane trying to free a jammed gun, and Irving-Jones simply vanished: took off with everyone else, got separated in a mêlée and was never seen again.

I stopped talking to them, for they embodied ill fortune. You said hello in the morning, by tea-time they were dead, and that was intolerable. So I withdrew inward, kept myself to myself, flew my patrols and lived each hour by the minute. Days were spent pacing the floor in panic, nights in a cold sweat on my cot, or staring at the walls of Strickley's office. Desperation took hold. I considered crash-landing behind enemy lines and surrendering, I considered running away to Spain, I considered refusing to fly and facing the consequences. One night I even pointed the Colt at my foot and tried to pull the trigger, but my hand was shaking too much from nerves.

Nerves which were not helped by a succession of useless observers, none of whom was a patch on old Morris. Inexperienced, clumsy, unreliable, erratic, they drove me to despair. Mercifully they never lasted, either removing themselves or being removed by me: 'Sgt. Walker to report to Lt. Stott for further training' I'd scrawl, dashing off Strickley's signature on a memo; 'Assign Lt. Duckwell new observer when available'. One man I remember flew just one mission before leaping briskly from the aircraft and heading back to the trenches; another spent an entire patrol cowering in the bottom of the nacelle; a third sat there staring in disbelief but did nothing else – didn't shoot, didn't observe, didn't navigate, nothing. Useless sack of potatoes, I soon got rid of him. But then his replacement shot our propeller to pieces with the rear-facing Lewis gun, narrowly missing me and procuring yet another crash-landing in the process. 'So sorry,' he said as we clambered from the wreckage. 'I thought there might be a Hun on our tail.' '*Might be?!*' I bellowed, shaking with rage. I dumped him too.

Then one afternoon Major Strickley made a rare visit to the mess.

'Ah, there you are, George,' he murmured dreamily. 'Heard you were short of an observer. Know how you hate to miss a patrol so thought I'd get togged up and step into the breach, so to speak. What do you think, old chap?'

What did I think? I could only gape in horror. He was wearing flying-clothes all right, but not of a sort any RFC unit had ever seen. Boer War cavalry jodhpurs and puttees, ancient rugby boots, an old mackintosh over his uniform, a jaunty woollen scarf round his neck, and to top it off a motoring cap strapped on backwards like racing drivers of old. As if that wasn't enough, swimming goggles dangled from his finger.

'Well, gosh, sir, yes, indeed, thank you, how thoughtful,' I spluttered. 'But do you think it wise? I mean, you are the CO.'

'Am I? Yes, I suppose I am.'

'And regulations, I believe, sir, forbid you to fly nearer than five miles to the lines. For your own safety.' This I knew to be true, having read it somewhere on his desk.

'Pish to regulations, George!' he replied, twirling his goggles. 'Anyway, it'll do me good to see what you chaps get up to all day.'

So I had no choice but to fly the patrol – a patrol I'd earlier got out of by discarding a useless observer. Now I had a melancholic madman dressed as a scarecrow.

We took off into the usual bedlam. The mission was photo-reconnaissance of the lines somewhere around St Pierre, which was doubly worrying because he had to manage a camera as well as everything else. Archie was stiff, and there was an anxious moment when six Pfalzes squared up for an attack, but mercifully changed their minds and went after another patrol instead. All in all it was an average outing, but do you know, he did the job. He sat there taking it all in, cheerfully pointing out landmarks and scribbling on the map, then he leaned over and took the photographs, and when the Pfalzes drew near he even started fiddling with the Lewis gun, although I'm not sure he knew what to do with it. Then we came home for tea.

'Fascinating,' he said, wandering off. 'Most fascinating, George, I thank you.'

He never turned up again, mind you. And the next morning we had to repeat the whole mission because he'd left the lens-cap on the camera.

The days crawled by, somehow I got through them and kept functioning, both in the air and on the ground. In the evenings I plugged away at my campaign to get posted. And also co-opted Strickley on to a few other causes close to my heart: 'Sir, Following my letters of the 4th, 9th and 20th inst, I write once again to urge you to reconsider the RFC's no-parachute policy. Surely it makes better sense to save the life of a pilot so he can fight again, rather than squander it needlessly', or 'Sir, Forgive me, but this business of sending inadequately trained pilots direct to the Front Line is little short of lunacy', or 'Sir, It occurs to me the rate of pay for a Second Lieutenant in the Royal Flying Corps is woefully overdue for review'. Yes, I stuck my neck out (Strickley's neck actually) and probably ruffled a good many feathers, but by then I was past caring.

At the same time as I worked on my problems I also worked on Mac's, which were considerable, yet still he found the time and energy to support me through those last wretched weeks. Without him I wouldn't have survived them, of that I'm certain. His quiet encouragement, steadying logic and patient coaching kept me sane and alive, buoying me up like a life-raft on the sea. Few evenings passed without my going in search of him, like a student to a sage, to hear his softly spoken magic spells. What helped me most was his complete absence of fear in the air. Habitually restless and agitated on the ground, flying seemed to soothe him, no matter how bloody the action. The sky had become his natural element, like the Carolina plains of his youth; he understood and respected it, and in doing so gained both strength and peace of mind. He knew his survival chances were poor but was fatalistic about them in a positive and practical way. The sky is like a desert, George, he would say, or an ocean; if you prepare well and treat it right, there's no need to fear it, even though one day it may claim you. And it was this almost spiritual aspect of our work, I realised, that he was trying to inculcate in me, along with practical tips on how not to get killed. And though much of his wisdom went over my head, talking to him about it did ease my anxieties. A little.

In return I tried to ease his, which seemed to be multiplying. Earlier I'd suggested we simply send back the horse-theft enquiry letter he'd received, returning it to the 1st Canadian Division marked 'Not Known At This Unit' and thumped with one of Strickley's official-looking stamps. This I felt would encourage the Canadians to abandon the RFC line of enquiry and search elsewhere. Mac agreed, we sent it off, and no more was heard. All well and good, but then came a rumour that America was entering the war, which was marvellous news for the Allies but not marvellous for Mac, as any Americans already fighting (and there were many) would have to be identified, sorted, redrafted, re-uniformed and all the rest of it. The odds of him being exposed were not great, I felt, and said so, but it was an unwelcome complication and another source of worry for him.

As was his mother, whom he was desperate to make contact with – without endangering her or giving himself away. For that I eventually decided upon a pseudonymous third party, namely me. Using plain paper, the adjutant's typewriter and a complicated biblical code featuring *Daniel* (of lion's den fame) and a *Father Canard-Puis* (Duck-well) of the fictional town of *Guerrebouton* (Warbutton) I constructed a seemingly innocuous letter to Ella from a distant European clergyman relative, concealed within which was the news that her son was alive and well and living in France. I had absolutely no means of knowing whether she'd understand it, or dismiss it as the work of a crank and throw it on the fire, and inserting a coded return address was particularly ticklish, but in the end and after much tweaking we could only send it off and hope. And Mac was movingly grateful for the attempt. 'What would I do without you, George?' he murmured, prophetically.

Then, if all that wasn't enough, the RFC got in touch with him again. I saw the letter, this time addressed to his CO at 166 Squadron. Mac, it seemed, now with thirty kills to his credit, was making quite an impression with RFC bosses in Whitehall, who having had their attention belatedly drawn to this unknown Canadian ace were minded to groom him for stardom. A publicity campaign in other words, to turn him into a celebrity like Ball, McCudden and the rest, and the very last thing Mac needed. Being Canadian was an added bonus, the RFC enthused, for perhaps Mac's story could be circulated across the Atlantic, thus encouraging our colonial cousins, and boosting recruitment in the bargain.

Mac fell into a trough of despair at the letter. To him it felt as though the whole world was closing in. I too was stumped, for we both knew even the most cursory research would reveal the RFC's new darling was not William MacBride, and not even Canadian, but an illegal combatant from America who had deserted the trenches and killed his own father. All he could do, I suggested, was tell his CO he didn't want to do it. That the glare of publicity would distract him from his mission, which was to help the Allies win the war.

'I just want to fly airplanes, George,' he fretted. 'Just fly airplanes, do my job, then get back to my family. That's all.'

'Don't give up, Mac. We'll think of something.'

But he was shaking his head. 'It's killing me, George. All this. I can feel it.'

'You've got to hang on. We're in this together, you know.'

But I was lying. By now it was mid-April. Two days later, to my astonishment, my transfer campaign finally bore fruit, and orders came through sending me home for scout training. Unbridled celebration followed, then came my day in no-man's land with Raymond Gates. The day after that I was home in Greenwich.

Chapter 8

And he'd trusted and befriended me. And now I was rejecting him because he'd found a kindred spirit in the girl I idolised. They were still over there, I kept thinking as I wandered the skies of Essex in perfect safety. My only two friends, still over there in the thick of all that insanity. On a clear night at ten thousand feet I could see it, artillery flashes from the Western Front, like far-off lightning. And I'd abandoned them to it.

Back on the ground I re-read their letters of apology, and felt guilty and miserable, and drank too much, and became disorderly in the pub, and irritated the locals shooting rabbits in the moonlight with my Colt. Mac's Colt. Pull yourself together, Duckwell, the CO warned. Pull yourself together unless you want to go back there. Yet I did want to go back there, I wanted to go back and see the thing through with my friends. But I couldn't because I was scared. So I stayed in Essex and felt more guilty and miserable than ever.

Then an odd thing happened. I shot down a Zeppelin and became a national hero.

Le Merignac was a former Carthusian monastery situated in a once tranquil vale on the western outskirts of Arras. Normally occupied by a hundred white-robed monks, by 1917 the close proximity of the fighting and the endless noise and shaking from artillery-fire had forced all but a skeleton staff to leave. Through connections in England the FANY had secured permission to use the monastery as a hospital, so in June 1917, while I was shooting rabbits in Essex, Emily arrived there at the head of a convoy of four ambulances laden with supplies and equipment. Accompanying her were five FANY drivers, including Phyllis Mason, who'd begged to join the team, even though Emily was now her superior. The other four were all new, fresh from finishing school in Yorkshire.

Under the baffled gaze of the few remaining monks, the girls set quickly to work, unloading stores, setting up a spares shop, establishing a fuel store in an outhouse, and servicing the vehicles ready for use. By nightfall on the first day they were unpacked, eating hot stew in the refectory, and ready to go into action. Over the following days the hospital staff and equipment began to arrive: army surgeons, Red Cross nurses, bedding, linen and medical supplies. While preparation work continued readying the hospital, Emily made contact with military commanders and reconnoitred routes into and out of Arras. By now the town was a bombed-out hulk, the once proud Grand Place reduced to rubble, its cathedral wrecked, its elegant houses nothing but blackened stumps in cratered streets, like bad teeth in a ravaged mouth. Picking her way round the potholes and fallen masonry, she drove along deserted roads to the rendezvous point, a casualty clearing station in a former school near the cathedral.

'At last.' A Medical Corps major looked up from a desk. 'And about time. How many can you take?'

'None yet, I'm afraid,' Emily replied. 'We're not ready.'

'Not ready?'

'We're a new unit, Major, setting up in the monastery at Le Merignac.'

'Setting up what?' he muttered, returning to his notes. 'Afternoon tea I suppose.'

Emily ignored the jibe, looking around the school-house. Twenty or so stretchered casualties were arranged on desks awaiting evacuation, each with a buff envelope on his chest with his details, while an orderly hovered in attendance, checking pulses and offering weak cheer. 'I expect this isn't all of them,' she said.

'You expect correctly, young lady.' The major tossed his pen aside. 'Come on. You might as well see for yourself.'

He led her outside and across the street to an iron grating set in the cobbled pavement. The grating was hinged and beneath it, to her consternation, she saw stone steps descending into darkness. 'Stay close,' he cautioned. 'Get lost and we'll never find you.'

Cathedral catacombs, and a subterranean network of caves, caverns, cellars and tunnels, spreading out beneath the city like roots from a tree. 'There's miles of it,' the major explained, striding down a tunnel. 'Before the offensive began we had twenty thousand troops hidden down here, unknown to the Hun, waiting for the off. It has its own electricity and water, barracks, dormitories, canteens, arsenal, even a chapel. Now it's where they bring the casualties. Are you squeamish?' He stopped and glared at her suddenly. 'You're as white as a sheet.'

Emily shook her head. 'Injuries don't frighten me, Major.'

'Good, because I've no time for squeamish. Here, this way.'

She followed him along a further series of stone corridors lit by suspended bulbs. Between islands of flickering yellow her shadow slid over algae-stained walls. Here and there soldiers had scrawled names and messages, sketched cartoons and scantily veiled women. As they descended deeper her nose twitched to a familiar odour, blood and disinfectant, and a growing murmur echoed up the tunnel like an approaching crowd. A crowd in pain, sometimes in piercing agony, louder and clearer until rounding an ornate stone doorway they entered the cathedral crypt itself.

Emily stopped in astonishment. The crypt was vast, and injured soldiers filled it completely, tight-packed across the nave floor like sardines in a tin, balanced upon pews in the aisles, tiered two high in side-chapels, even lying atop sarcophagi beside recumbent knights with stone dogs at their feet. Doctors, nurses and medical orderlies moved among them. At one end a screened-off area hid a rudimentary operating theatre. A pall of condensation, mingled with sweat and cigarette smoke, hung in the air like smog.

'They're brought in from the various dressing stations,'

the major said above the babble of moans. He led her among the stretchers. As she picked her way through, men reached up to her in supplication, or pleaded piteously, or even grasped at her ankles. Overhead the lights flickered off, then came on again. 'We get hundreds daily sometimes, depending on front-line activity. We carry out emergency surgery, stabilise them as best we can, then get them out to the railway for evacuation. At least, that's what's supposed to happen.'

Grimly, Emily surveyed the scene. She'd seen suffering men before, but not like this. Buried in an underground charnel-house. Bestial, stinking, acutely claustrophobic, it was a scene straight from her worst nightmare. She wanted only to get out.

'Can we help?' she asked instead.

'You!' The major laughed dryly. 'My dear girl, we're overwhelmed with wounded, there're not enough nurses, transportation's a nightmare, that group upstairs has waited days for a lift to the station, we're hopelessly under-equipped, running out of supplies, and to top it all' – he gestured at the flickering lights – 'the bloody generator's on the blink! What on earth could you possibly do to help?'

'I could take a look, if you like.'

'Excuse me?'

'The generator. It's probably just the governor.'

The major looked baffled. 'The gov . . .'

'Governor. I am a qualified mechanic, you see. I grew up in a garage.'

'You did?'

'Yes. As for your other difficulties, Major, we'll be able to take a hundred of the most seriously injured at Le Merignac the day after tomorrow. I'll have the twenty in the school-house out to the railway by tonight, and I can offer two ambulances with drivers on a daily basis to help with your transportation problems. There's six of us, all first aid trained. I'll send two out this afternoon to give your orderlies a hand, and you can have two a day from then on depending on needs at the monastery.'

'I, well, that is, good heavens, very—'

'Not at all. Is there anything else I can help you with?'

'Well, I, no, not that I can think of, but, thank you, Miss . . .'

'Parker.' She forced a smile. 'The First Aid Nursing Yeomanry. And afternoon tea's at four-thirty by the way, please feel free to join us.'

By week's end Le Merignac was up and running, the monastery filling with patients and the FANYs slipping into a familiar routine transporting injured to and from the cathedral, and to hospital trains at a station outside Porteuil. In addition the girls stood nursing shifts in the crypt, ferried stores and supplies, helped in the monastery kitchens and fulfilled administrative duties including keeping the books and patient records. All day they lived within earshot of gunfire, Arras itself was frequently shelled as they drove through it, and they were woken before dawn to the quaking of walls from a ferocious artillery barrage the soldiers called the morning hate. Emily, determined to learn from her Calais experiences, went to lengths to ensure the girls took no unnecessary risks, and balanced their long working hours with regular time off. You need your wits about you, she told the new recruits, you're no good to anybody exhausted, least of all the patients. To emphasise the point she introduced a strict shift system and insisted everyone stick to it.

Except herself. Ten days in and she'd barely stopped for an hour, constantly fearful something might go wrong, unsure how to delegate. Eventually an exasperated Phyllis had to step in.

'Go, Parks! For God's sake, you're driving us all spare. Go, just for an hour or two. We can manage.'

'Do you think I should?'

Phyllis rolled her eyes. 'Yes! You know you're dying to. And it's only a few miles. Go and see him. It'll do you no end of good.'

So she went, beset by doubts, nervous with anticipation. But as the miles slipped by the doubts subsided and the anticipation grew. Phyllis was right, she realised, she did need a break, and must trust the girls to cope without her. And ignoring her own rules set a bad example. But above all she was dying to see Mac, whom she hadn't heard from since Angel's memorial and the awful night of the hotel two weeks earlier. She hoped to God everything was all right.

But an hour later she knew it wasn't.

I have a horror of sunsets, they're so romantic, so dramatic. Marcel Proust says that in his fine book I've been reading. It's about a man who can't sleep, who lies in his bed at night remembering how he waited for his mother in the mornings. Like I used to wait for Ma. Sunset means the night's coming, and nights are full of horror, so I know what he means. And I know what he means about sunsets being dramatic and romantic. Without doubt it is the best time to fly.

227

When I take off at sunset and fly east across the lines into Hunland, I feel the sun warm and low at my back; it paints the earth in the softest gold, and sends long shadows from the trees, pointing my way like fingers. And dusk is the perfect light for seeking out the enemy. I can see him far away in the distance, glowing like a spark from a campfire. But all he can see is the orange ball of the sun in his eyes. So I'm invisible, and if I plan it right I can draw so near that he never sees me at all, and I can take him down before he even knows it. Sometimes I don't take him down, but get in even closer, stealing in from below and behind until I'm so close I can hear his motor running, smell the castor-oil in his exhaust, see the skin of his machine vibrating in the slipstream like a living thing. I get so close I want to reach up and touch him, press my fingers to his skin and feel his life, like touching the hide of a bull, or the scales of a mighty fish. Then calmness washes over me, and the horrors of the night fall away, and it's like I'm swimming in a cool stream and I feel restored and alive. And I thank him in my mind for giving me his life, then I drop back to thirty yards and end it, quick and painless, like killing a coyote with my rifle.

If I could I'd stay up here for ever, where no one can reach me. Up here I feel at peace, yet also alive and ready for anything. The new SE5 I'm flying is a fine machine, strong and agile and faster than the Nieuport. It's an airplane to equal Manfred's D3 at last. I first flew it the day he shot George down over no-man's land, but it wasn't rigged right and I didn't have the feel of it yet, so Manfred got away. Now Finlay and me have rigged it right, and adjusted the guns to shoot close to, and I've spent many hours up here in its neat cockpit getting the feel of it. So I'm ready for Manfred now, and though I've not seen him since that day, I'm out here most evenings searching for him.

I miss George. I miss Emily. My heart aches for Ma. I guess they're all gone. I hardly sleep at all any more. I do read a lot though.

At first she couldn't find the aerodrome, doubling back along narrow country lanes, reversing up farm tracks, peering at signs in the gathering dusk. Then she rounded a bend and heard the sound of an engine beyond a hedge. A little further and a track led on to a wide grassy field intersected by an avenue of trees. A run-down chateau stood at one end, huts and hangars dotted the perimeter, nearby six khaki biplanes waited in a neat row, one with its engine running. An overalled mechanic was leaning into its cockpit, blipping the throttle. Emily jumped down and waited, until eventually he glanced up.

'Hold on!' he shouted, and shut down the engine. Peace descended, save for a lone skylark singing busily overhead. 'Good heavens, it's the FANY. We don't see many of your lot round these parts. Are you lost?'

'I . . . No . . . At least . . . This is Noyelette aerodrome isn't it?'

'Certainly is, God help us.' The mechanic, wiping his hands, eyed her curiously. 'What brings you here?'

'I, well, a pilot, actually.'

'Who'd of guessed. And what's his name?'

'Mac. Lieutenant MacBride, that is.'

'Ah.' The mechanic's eyes flickered. 'He's flying, miss. On ops.'

'Oh. Right. Of course. Um, will he be long?' Her question sounded haughty, as though she couldn't be kept waiting. 'Not that it matters, I just—'

'Who knows, miss. He's gone off on his own.'

'His own? Is that usual?'

'Usual?' The mechanic took a cigarette from a tin and lit up. 'Listen, love, there ain't nothing usual about this business, even less about Mac. All I know is he flies two or three patrols a day with the squadron, then as if that wasn't enough he goes off on his own last thing. And mostly comes back with his guns empty and his machine full of holes. So's I can spend all night patching it up again.'

'I see.' Emily hesitated. 'You're his mechanic, aren't you. Sergeant Finlay.'

'How d'you know?'

'He spoke to me of you once. On a picnic. Most fondly.'

Finlay's gaze wandered to the horizon. 'Did he indeed.'

They waited together in the failing light, Finlay smoking his cigarettes, Emily wrapped pensively in her coat. As the minutes ticked by, both grew more anxious. 'God help 'im,' Finlay kept muttering. 'God help 'im if he don't turn up soon.'

Then to the east rose the faint hum of an engine. Finlay heard it first, holding up a finger, ear cocked, until he was sure. Then his face broke into a grin. 'That's him!'

Emily exhaled. 'Thank heavens.'

'Right, girl, he's all yours, I'm off for my tea. Tell him I'll look at the damage later.'

A minute later a lone aeroplane arrived overhead, sideslipped neatly towards the ground, touched down and taxied in.

For a moment Mac just stared at her. Lifted the goggles from his eyes, peered through the darkness and stared. Then he was leaping from the cockpit.

'Emily, is it you?'

He ran to her and hugged her, squeezing the breath from her the way she'd missed so badly. And she squeezed him back, clinging to him, burying her face in his neck, her cheek against his, her lips to his throat, and his face, and his mouth.

'Mac, thank God, I was so worried.'

'I thought you'd gone.'

'No, never! It's just, the monastery, setting it up, it's incredibly busy. Mac, I've been desperate, you've no idea.' And she slid her fingers into the hair of his neck, and pulled his mouth to hers, and inhaled the cold leather and engine-oil smells on his skin, and pressed her open lips to his, kissing him deeply and urgently. And she felt him responding, exploring, but slowly and curiously, as though waking from a dream.

Then he pulled back.

'What is it?'

'I can't believe it, that's all. I just need to look at you, and make sure.'

He held her apart and studied her face, closely, as though for the first time, and she studied his, and saw how fatigued he was, how spent, how darkly shadowed his eyes, how deep the creases at the corners, like crow's feet, from hours scouring the sky. And she felt the spareness of his frame beneath his clothes, and the tenseness of his body, and the pulsing tremor in his hand, and it was as if he'd aged ten years in as many days.

Let's walk, she suggested, hiding her concern, and threading her arm through his she led him away from the airfield, along a lane towards the village. He smiled and held her arm tightly and kissed her head as they walked, yet all the while he

231

kept glancing back, as if they were being followed, and when they arrived at the village he stared around as though lost.

'Mac?'

'We came here once. I think. George and me. To that little café.'

'Only once?'

'I . . . I don't know. We ate there. Beef, they said, but George said it was horse.'

'Ugh.' She pulled a face. 'How was it?'

'Not so bad. George made them take money off, for pretending it was beef.'

'Sounds like George.'

'Yes.' He hesitated, fingering his wristwatch, as though struggling to remember something. Then he asked if she'd heard from George, and became thoughtful when she admitted she hadn't. Then, with his tone steadily rising, he told her how much he'd come to depend on his friendship, and how bad he felt to have betrayed it. 'He trusted me, Emily, and look how I repaid him!'

'Shhh, Mac.' She squeezed his arm. 'Try not to fret. I'll write to him again. I'm sure we can sort it out.'

'I don't know, I hope so.' And with growing agitation he spoke darkly of government forces pursuing him, in Canada, and America, even in Britain. Everyone was after him, he said, he felt so hunted and fearful and out of control.

Emily hushed and soothed him as best she could, but in the end had to kiss him into silence. This time he responded, encircling her with his arms, pressing his body against hers.

'God but you're so beautiful,' he breathed. 'That night, Emily, that night in the hotel. I couldn't . . . I couldn't do . . .'

'Mac. We have plenty of time.'

'We do? I want you, so much. I love you.'

'I know. Me too. Perhaps we could, you know, find somewhere, a place, to get away from everything, for a few hours.'

'Away from everything, God, yes, I'd love that.'

'A kind of sanctuary. Of our own. Where there's no war.'

'No war! A place with no war. It would be like heaven.'

In Le Merignac work began in earnest. Specially reserved for the most seriously wounded soldiers, in no time the monastery was filled, and after the filth and chaos of the Front became known as a contrasting haven of order, cleanliness and calm. White sheets covered the beds, white bandages the wounds, nurses in white uniforms moved among the injured, speaking in soft tones. It was a quiet hospital: the men lay in their white-walled cubicles and fought their battles mostly from within. There they either triumphed and travelled on, or they succumbed and did not, and were laid to rest in the monastery graveyard.

Each morning Emily and the senior medical officer, James Ashton, an RAMC captain, met to discuss the day's needs and activities: staff rotas, transport arrangements, stores inventories, vehicle repairs, burial details, new admissions. One of the many logistical problems they encountered was the high demand for beds, and Ashton, a quiet and caring man, was forced to make difficult decisions about discharges and admissions. Another unforeseen issue was the number of injured arriving without identification. Sometimes their whole uniform was gone, including tags and papers, blown from their bodies by explosion, or hurriedly cut away in dressing stations. Nor could many of them speak, so severe were their injuries. Some died without ever regaining consciousness, and went to the graveyard without name or nationality, much to Emily's distress. At least they have graves, Ashton reminded her, unlike the thousands without.

Under her leadership the FANYs settled to an efficient routine. Two spent each day helping in the cathedral crypt while the other three put the ambulances to use, fetching stores, delivering equipment and moving wounded from the crypt to the monastery or the rail-head at Porteuil. They also began the perilous business of collecting injured soldiers from the Front itself, and in doing so unwittingly drove their ambulances into the history books. Emily went first, accompanied by Major Boulter, the officer she'd first met in the schoolhouse.

'Are you quite sure about this?' he asked, handing her a tin helmet.

'Completely,' she replied.

They climbed into her ambulance and set off, he guiding her slowly east from the cathedral, through the bombed-out streets until they neared the town's shattered suburbs. There, at a roadblock guarded by machine-gun emplacements, he signalled her to stop. 'We're on foot from here, so please keep your head down.' She followed in his wake, hurrying at a crouch along a stone wall pocked with bullet-holes. A hundred yards further on they came to a pillbox overlooking the wall. Sandbags fortified the stonework, a few tiny gaps left in between – for shooting through, Emily supposed. With a nod from a sentry, Boulter motioned her to one gap, and handed her a pair of field-glasses. 'Welcome to purgatory,' he said.

A wide plain swam into view. Once a tranquil patchwork of wooded copses, green pasture and manicured crop-fields, now it was nothing but mile after mile of cratered brown wasteland, barren and lifeless, like pictures of the moon she'd once seen, or a troubled ocean, devoid of colour or feature save its own cruel contours. On the nearer shore, zigzag black lines stretched north and south as far as she could see, like waves breaking on to a beach.

'Are those our trenches?' she asked.

'That's it. That's the front line.'

'Why are they shaped like that?'

'Line of fire. You don't want nice straight trenches for your enemy to shoot along, so you put a kink in every ten yards or so. Look across the plain there, and you can see theirs. Which means they can also see us, so we must be careful. The churned-up mess in between is no-man's land.'

She peered through the glasses and duly saw no men, any-where, in no-man's land, in the trenches, on the roads and tracks behind. Smoke drifted here and there, in the distance she heard the occasional crump of a mortar, otherwise all seemed uncannily quiet.

'It's early.' Boulter checked his watch. 'Things sometimes calm down after the morning hate. It can be a good time to get the injured out. See down here' – he gestured towards some farm buildings and Red Cross tents below – 'that's the forward dressing station for this sector, where the wounded are first brought from the fighting. They get basic first aid, then army drivers bring them back to us. But they're hope-lessly short-handed, and don't have enough vehicles. Many wounded have to wait hours for evacuation, days even some-times. A lot die there.'

'What's the route in?' Emily asked.

'Back to the crossroads, and down the hill about a mile. Watch for a sign saying DS6, and a track takes you straight there.'

'We could do it, I'm sure we could.'

'I'd have to check with HQ, they're not keen on letting women this close to the line. But I feel it's safe enough, and could make a big difference to the lads waiting in those tents. Although I expect you'd have to clear it with your superiors.'

'No, Major, I wouldn't.' She handed him the glasses. 'It's what the FANY was created for.'

Two days later the garage-girl from Shropshire and her team began ferrying injured men back from the line, the first women ever to do so on the Western Front. Initially Emily allowed only herself and Phyllis to make these hazardous jour-neys. They were so close to the fighting they could hear shells passing overhead, see the earth erupt skyward from explo-sion, feel the ground quake, even smell the heat of battle. Once or twice a day, with only a painted red cross and tin hat for protection, they drove their ambulances to the war's brink, collected its human debris and drove back again. Despite every precaution, both girls experienced close calls, Phyllis blown from the road by a shell-burst and Emily returning one night with her cab riddled. If the Valkyries could see us now, they grinned ruefully, knowing they'd both been lucky. But it was worth the risk. And it was a way, the only way, she often felt, that Emily could do something to oppose a war she found harder and harder to bear.

Two or three times a week she made the short journey to Noyelette to spend an hour or two with Mac. It was all she and her ambulance could spare, and not nearly enough. Usually he'd be flying when she arrived, so she began timing her visits for dusk when he returned for the night, homing like a swift to the eaves. Waiting for him was torture. Finlay would usually wait too, chain-smoking his cigarettes and muttering gloomily. Together they'd stand in the failing light, tensely scanning the eastern sky for signs. Then they'd hear a distant engine, a speck would appear, grow into an aeroplane, and the waiting and worry would be over for another day.

She learned to accept Mac as she found him – constantly fatigued, increasingly quiet, progressively unhinged. Unpredictable. Yet full of warmth and tenderness, and capable of humour, even surprise. Always he was overjoyed to see her, holding her at arm's length, searching her face with a grateful smile. Thank you, he'd whisper, thank you for coming. Once when he held her, his eyes began to fill. I wish, he stammered fearfully, I wish . . . At times like these she'd press a finger to his lips, and soothe his brow like a troubled child. Then they'd walk, arms linked, slowly round the airfield or into the darkened village to sit by the church. He'd speak in depth about the squadron's losses, or of technical flying matters. Then he'd go quiet, or murmur something unfathomable.

'Do you know what bitter means?' he asked once.

'Bitter?'

'*Bitte*. It means "please" in German.'

'Oh.'

'A man said it to me once. In a graveyard.'

Increasingly he preferred to listen rather than talk, watching her minutely as she recounted her day's news or chatted of life at the monastery.

'You're doing such incredible work, Emily,' he told her late one evening. 'All those hundreds of sick men you help, it's wonderful.'

'Wonderful?' She hadn't thought of it like that. 'Often I just feel it's hopeless.'

'No, never. You bring hope to them. Really, I'm so proud of you.'

'Thank you, Mac.'

'I mean it.' He kissed her forehead. 'Say. Remember what we said the other day? About finding somewhere to get away.'

'I remember.'

'Well, I was wondering . . .' He pulled a crumpled map from his pocket. 'Could you get a little time off, do you think? Sunday afternoon maybe.'

'Sunday? I don't know. Yes, possibly. Why?'

'I saw this place from the air the other day. It's a meadow, by a stream. With trees overhanging. It looks real beautiful. And peaceful. I remembered what you said and thought maybe we could meet there.'

That Sunday Emily drove her ambulance to the location, parked by the meadow and waited. She was wearing a floral summer dress borrowed from Phyllis, her hair was up, her cheeks powdered, her breast bore the sweetheart brooch he'd given her. Of Mac there was no sign, so she strolled to the stream and watched an electric-blue kingfisher pluck minnows from the chuckling water. Thirty minutes later and still Mac hadn't arrived; she began to worry she'd misread the

238

map, or he'd been called away on ops and couldn't make it. Then, as she was about to give up and return to Le Merignac, she heard the now-familiar rumble of an SE5 engine. A moment later Mac's machine zoomed overhead, spiralled steeply earthward and landed neatly on the meadow.

'Mac, my God!' She laughed as he taxied up. 'Does anyone know?'

'Only Finlay, and he won't tell!' he shouted, passing her a sheepskin jacket. 'Put this on, Emily, and step on up. Here, take my hand!'

The aeroplane's engine was still running, its wings shuddering like a nervous bird. His hand was reaching out for hers.

'Mac, what's happening?'

'Don't be afraid. Just put your foot in that step and climb up, like you're mounting a horse.'

The jacket was too big, but she struggled into it, then grasped his hand and hoisted herself up. Suddenly the engine noise was much louder, the slipstream plucked roughly at her clothes, hot oil and exhaust smells filled her head. Guiding her ankles, Mac helped her into the cockpit, which was tiny, much smaller than she'd realised, and very cramped. There was no second seat so she had to sit on his lap, her legs between his.

'Don't worry!' He slipped a reassuring arm around her waist. 'It's a beautiful afternoon and you're in safe hands. All set?'

She nodded, not trusting herself to speak. He kissed her neck, then his left hand reached out, nudging a little lever forward. Immediately the engine note rose to a brassy blare and the aeroplane moved forward, bumping out across the grass.

She had tried to imagine what flying was like many times over the weeks, he talked about it so often and with such passion. But the reality was unlike anything she'd ever dreamed. Take-off was without doubt the most exhilarating and terrifying twenty seconds of her life. They wobbled to the end of the meadow, then turned to face the wind. When he was ready he pushed the throttle all the way forward and the engine note rose to a roar, thundering in her head like the end of the world. Then the aeroplane leapt forward, bucking and bouncing across the grass like a furious bull. Just as she thought it must smash itself to pieces it left the ground and soared skyward, instantly transforming itself into a hawk – graceful, sleek and smooth. Transfixed, she watched Mac's hands move around the cockpit, adjusting knobs, pulling levers, winding little wheels as he settled the aeroplane into a climb. Soon he seemed satisfied.

'OK?' he asked, returning his arm to her waist.

'I had no idea!' She laughed. 'No idea at all!'

And controlling the machine, actually flying it, was also not the great struggle she had imagined. With his feet resting on the rudder-pedals, his hand light yet firm on the stick between her legs, he made it seem effortless, a natural balance of sensitivity and power, like riding a hunter. He began circling so she could watch the broad green swathe of the meadow fall away below. The whole earth seemed to contract, farms, roads and villages shrinking to miniature as they ascended. After a while she stopped looking down, entranced by the turquoise horizon and the deep blue dome above it. And all the while the wind was like surf in her head, the engine a hundred trumpets, the whole aeroplane singing, resonating like a living creature. She felt her insides melting, felt giddy, felt aroused. Up and up they climbed, higher and higher, until the earth dissolved into memory and they were alone in the heavens. There beneath the yellow orb of the sun, Mac's arm at her waist, their cheeks touching, they gently soared and swooped, dancing across the sky like sprites on the wind.

That evening she drove into Arras for her weekly planning meeting with Major Boulter. Rain had begun to fall. Parking her ambulance near the cathedral, she found him at his desk in the school-house.

'Ah, Emily, do come in. Did you have a pleasant afternoon?'

'Yes, thank you, Major,' she replied demurely. Still exhilarated after her flight with Mac, she'd been unable to stop herself telling Phyllis. But no one else would know, she decided. It was a private matter. 'I spent it in the countryside. With a friend.'

'Jolly good. Now, here's the movement list for the week, I hope it's all right. I've rostered two of your girls in for tomorrow and Wednesday afternoon . . .'

They ran through the week's arrangements, then with business over the talk turned to other matters.

'American troops are on the way, did you hear?' Boulter said, sitting back.

'Here? To the Western Front?'

'Apparently. Just a division or so to begin with, but more are promised.'

'Will they be fighting alongside our men?'

'Seemingly not. The Americans don't count as an official ally evidently, but what's called an "Associated Power", which is something quite separate.'

'Do you think they'll make a difference, Major?'

'I dearly hope so, once they get sorted out. Things can't go on like this. The men have had it.' He flicked her a glance. 'We're starting to see SIWs arriving in the crypt.'

'SIWs?'

'Self-inflicted wounds. Soldiers shooting themselves to escape the fighting.'

'God, how dreadful.'

'Indeed. We're supposed to report them.'

'What happens to them?'

'Same as for desertion. They get court-martialled for cowardice and executed by firing-squad. As if that's going to help morale.'

A knock came on the door and an orderly appeared, his shoulders spattered with rain. 'There's been a fall,' he said breathlessly. 'A house round the corner. Can you come?'

Boulter picked up his cap. 'Lead on, Corporal.'

'Thank you, sir.' The corporal nodded at Emily. 'But it's her we need.'

He led them through black streets gurgling with rain until they reached the building, a four-storey house in a terrace. The sight that met them was incongruous, but not uncommon: a row of identical houses, all apparently intact, between them a rubble-filled gap where another had stood, as if a giant fist had smashed it to the ground.

'Good God. What happened?'

'It just fell down.' The corporal shrugged. 'Foundations

couldn't take any more, I suppose. Family of seven was in it. We got them out. Two dead, the grandparents, two adolescents and the father injured but alive.'

'It's incredible anyone survived.'

They surveyed the wreckage. Hastily strung lights lit the scene like a stage, curtained by silvery rain.

'Yes, sir. We got them all down the cathedral. All except one, that is. Up there.' He pointed to a small group amid the ruins.

'Is that a woman?' Emily asked.

'The mother, and she's in a bad way. Can you come, miss, and mind your step, nothing's safe.'

Emily and Major Boulter followed him through the debris towards the group – two firemen in brass helmets, a policeman in a cape, and another soldier. As they drew near, cautiously surmounting mounds of slippery masonry and loose rubble, Emily saw the woman, a heavy-set figure in black, her head swathed in a blood-soaked bandage. She was bending to the ground, whimpering beseechingly.

Emily went to her side. 'Can't we get her out? On a stretcher or something?'

'That's just it, miss. She won't go. Not without her baby.'

Emily felt a chill. 'What baby?'

'The one down there. Under that lot.'

As if on cue the group parted to reveal a roughly cleared crevice in the debris. Immediately the injured woman struggled towards it, bloody hands outstretched. Strong arms pulled her back.

'It's eight or nine feet down, miss, in a bassinet or something which probably saved it. We heard it crying a while ago. We managed to clear a little tunnel down part-ways, but it's too small. Too tight for any of us, that is. Then someone suggested a girl might make it, being smaller and that. So I thought, maybe the FANY . . .'

Emily stared at the hole. 'You want me to go down there.'

'Might be its only chance, miss.'

'You want me to go down there.'

'No.' Boulter struggled up. 'I absolutely forbid it.'

'But Major—'

'But nothing, Emily, it's too dangerous. The whole lot could collapse any second. We'll wait for heavy lifting equipment to arrive.'

'That won't be 'til daylight, sir,' the corporal said. 'Maybe twelve hours or more.'

'I don't care, the risks don't—'

Just then they heard it, the faintest cry, like a mewling kitten, deep within the debris. Everyone froze, except the mother, who shrieked and lunged forward again. This time Emily stopped her.

'I'll go.' She gripped the woman's arm. 'Tell her it's all right, I'll go.'

'Parker, I'm ordering you—'

Emily was already unbuttoning her jacket. 'You can't order me, Major, unfortunately. I'm not in the army.'

Two minutes later, stripped to blouse and breeches, she was inching her way into the crack, a bicycle-lamp clutched in her outstretched hand. The surface beneath her was rough and angular, broken bricks, twisted metal and shattered glass lay everywhere, rivulets of gritty water dripped from above, dust filled her eyes and nose. The tunnel was barely a foot

244

high in places so the only way to move was to crawl on her belly. And the only way to get out, she realised, was back-wards. She struggled forward, dread rising with every foot. Here and there her lamp picked out a forlorn personal item — a worn shoe, a framed photograph, a baby's doll. She reached a trembling hand for the doll, and something snagged her arm. Struggling to free it, her blouse tore and a sharp pain pierced her shoulder. She dropped the lamp and cried out.

'All right, miss?' the corporal shouted from behind.

'I . . . I can't . . .' she whispered. 'I can't . . .'

'It goes down, see, and to the left about six feet or so. Then there's a roof-timber to get under, which is as far as we got. Can you see it?'

'No!' Blood trickled down her arm, something was pierc-ing her thigh. Waves of suffocating panic began to engulf her, smothering her like a dog drowning in a sack. 'Our Father, our Father, which art . . .'

She fumbled for the lamp, aiming its feeble beam through the fog of dust. The passageway stretched ahead, blocked at the end by the roof-timber, with only a narrow gap beneath. Beyond that she glimpsed a larger cavity, beyond that a solid wall of bricks and rubble. I'll look under that wooden beam, she told herself, I'll look under it, and if there's nothing I'll go back.

She managed to reach the timber. She even managed to squeeze beneath it, partly, first pushing an arm under, then her head and one shoulder. But then she became wedged. She struggled on to her back but her shoulder jammed on the timber, so she tried to turn back again, frantically, but only became more tightly stuck. Petrified, she pushed upward with all her strength, and the timber moved, then the rubble shifted, and cascades of dirt and grit fell on her, and a faint shout of warning came from far behind. Then the earth fell in.

She was at home, in the garage at Shrewsbury. Lying in an inspection pit her father had dug in the ground, so they could work on the undersides of vehicles. The pit was about a foot deep and six feet long, like a shallow grave. She was on her back in it preparing to drain oil from the sump of a coal lorry. The lorry was up on jacks, wheels off, so her father could replace the tyres. While he was struggling to remove a wheel-nut the jacks collapsed and the lorry crashed to the ground. Emily was pinned in the pit, unhurt but unable to move, with five tons of coal-lorry an inch above her face. It was two hours before they managed to jack the lorry up and let her out. Afterwards her father just laughed. That was the day she resolved to leave the garage.

Time passed. Tears dried on her grime-caked cheeks. Her throat was coated in dust, her chest struggled for breath, pain lanced through her shoulders and back. She was going to die, she knew, suffocate to death, alone, trapped in a filthy hole, just as she'd always feared. Yet the fear was gone, all she felt now was regret. She thought of her bedroom above the garage, and the hours she passed at its window, staring at Shropshire's rolling hills. She thought of Lady Cordingley's hunters, and riding at a break-neck gallop along the ridge above Uffington. She thought of her ambulance, of sitting in its open cab with the wind in her hair, rushing through the moonlit streets of Calais. She thought of the wondrous joy of her flight with Mac that very afternoon. Carefree, unfettered, no wonder he loved it so much. Then she thought of her friends. Of dear loyal Phyllis, and the other Valkyries, Bobby, CW and Charlie. Of poor lost Angel, alone in the cold waters of the canal. She thought of George with his irrepressible humour and boyish charm, and how sad it was things had gone so wrong between them. And she thought of Mac again, so troubled, yet so loving and gentle. The war was destroying him by degrees. How would he manage without her?

Sounds disturbed her reverie – a brick moving, dripping water, distant murmurs, her own hoarse breaths. She was growing weaker, she realised. And numbness was spreading, particularly up her arm, which was pinned painfully above her head. Teeth clenched, she strained to move it to a more comfortable position. And in doing so her fingertips brushed something. Something soft and warm. Like a tiny foot. And as she touched it the noise came again, the cat-like mewling, from very close, from just beyond the baulk of timber. She groped for the lamp, twisting her head upward in an effort to see. At the same moment vice-like fists closed round her ankles and she felt herself being dragged painfully backwards.

'Wait!' she screamed. 'Wait, for God's sake, wait! I think I've found her!'

Collingwood came today, as I knew he would. If not today then some day, and if not him then someone else. But in the end it was Jack Collingwood, the sergeant George and me met the day George crashed in no-man's land. He was waiting when I landed after my flight with Emily. We'd had the most perfect time together, Emily so brave and beautiful, so determined not to show nervousness. Soon she was

247

laughing with joy. I understand now, Mac, she laughed, her eyes wide with delight, I understand why you love this so much. I was filled with pride for her, it was the happiest I can remember being for years. Then Collingwood came and everything turned to dust. I dropped Emily at the meadow and flew back to Noyelette and there he was. I knew it was him, even as I circled to land, from the 1st Division uniform, and the way he stood, hands on hips looking up at me. I knew it was him and knew it meant the end. You're Burton, aren't you, he said, straightaways. You're Private Dan Burton of D-Company the 1st Canadian Infantry. No, I said, I'm Lieutenant William MacBride of 166 Squadron the Royal Flying Corps. That's horseshit, he said, MacBride's dead, you killed him and stole his transfer papers, then you deserted. No, I said, that's not right. Yes, he said, and do you know why? Because Colonel Peck came to me a few months ago. Say, Jack, he asks, did we have a Daniel Warburton, or some name like it, attached to this unit back in fifteen? Well, colonel, I reply, we had a Dan Burton, but he died of pneumonia. Oh, says the colonel, because Division HQ are asking about him, apparently he's wanted for questioning about the death of his father, but if he's dead of pneumonia then I guess that's that. And Colonel Peck dropped the matter, but I didn't drop it, I got to thinking, and I remembered that skinny MacBride kid, and how sick he got, and I remembered how you weren't never sick, but did get put on a charge for striking a sergeant in that gas attack. Something ain't right here, I figured, then I saw you that day in April and everything fell right into place. And now I've found you, just like I said I would.

Yes, I said, you've found me. And what is it you want?

Everything, you son of a bitch, he said. I want everything you got. And we'll start with that fancy wristwatch of yours.

After that I couldn't think straight, even in the air. I turned on my *heel and went back to my airplane, started her up and headed east. All I could think of was fighting and killing. I had to find a fight and get in it, and the bloodier the better, so I flew on and on, deeper and deeper behind enemy lines in search. Ten miles I must have gone, twelve even, but when I did finally find the enemy he was harmless, just a two-seat Junkers out on a recon flight. He was three thousand feet below me, flying slow and straight with both pilot and observer totally unawares. I should of realised then and gone in search of something else, but I wasn't thinking straight so I just squared up, rolled over and dived on him from the vertical, dropping straight down and raking him with a nil deflection burst that tore him to pieces like a dog at a rooster. He went down so fast he never knew what hit him, he never even fired a shot in return. Then as I watched him go, turning over and over, I realised why he didn't shoot back. It wasn't a recon flight. It was a training flight.*

That was when my heart went out of the war for good.

Chapter 9

Though we didn't know it, that evening of 5 July 1917 was a turning-point for all three of us. For Emily, it was the date she scrambled from the rubble of Arras holding a baby and knew she was a changed person. For Mac, it was the date Jack Collingwood caught up with him and his fragile world began to implode. And for me, it was the date I shot down a Zeppelin and learned the meaning of selflessness.

Here's how.

Suttons Farm at that time was equipped with a useless contraption called the BE2c. The 'BE' stood for Blériot Experimental which gives you some idea of its provenance and vintage. The great ace Albert Ball, a master of understatement, once described the BE2c as 'a bloody awful aeroplane', while the British press, ever helpful, dubbed it 'Fokker fodder'. The Germans, rather chillingly, called it *Kaltesfleisch*, which means 'cold meat'. We pilots, meanwhile, simply knew it as the 'Quirk'. Universally reviled, except by the Hun, I rather liked it. Slow, heavy, underpowered and inadequately armed, the Quirk was no aircraft in which to do serious battle, which is why it was relegated to Home Defence duties before going to the scrap-heap. It had a big old engine out front which was probably better suited to agricultural than aeronautical uses, the single cockpit was snug yet roomy, and if you let go the controls to light your pipe or sip from a hip-flask the thing virtually flew itself. Comfortable, stable and easy to fly, it was the ideal conveyance for a pleasant evening's jolly. Going to war in it was another matter.

I was sitting in the bar of the Hornchurch pub playing cards that evening when a 69 Squadron junior pilot burst through the door.

'A Zeppelin's been spotted over Sheppey!' he spluttered. 'It's heading this way!'

'Is that so,' I replied, collecting a knave. 'Must be the fourth time this month. One day those coastal spotter chaps will learn the difference between a Zeppelin and a passing cloud. Now run along, Watson, there's a good fellow.'

'But George, this one's for real, they've got three confirmed sightings, all from different stations!'

'They always do. Yet it's still clouds, or a flock of birds, or smut on the binoculars. Anyway, I'm off duty. And by the way, Watson, it's Lieutenant Duckwell to you.'

'But George, I mean Lieutenant Duckwell, don't you want to have a go?'

'*Have a go?* Why would I want to *have a go?*'

'For the thousand-pound prize! From the *Daily Sketch*. Didn't you know?'

Now I'd had a few drinks, I don't mind admitting, I was also holding three aces against a pair of jacks with a fiver in the pot, but a thousand pounds was an enormous sum and could make a glum fellow feel a lot happier. Also I was bored, fed up and hadn't fired a shot in anger for weeks, except at rabbits. Furthermore an expectant hush had descended on the pub, with everyone on tenterhooks to see if the great Duckwell would don his spurs and take on the beast. Crying off might not look good.

'Oh, very well,' I sighed, and followed him outside.

The night-ops system at Suttons required that two pilots were always on stand-by to fly. This meant they were either already aloft or waiting on the ground ready to go. But if anyone else felt like a jaunt, and an aircraft was free, there was nothing in the rules to stop him, he was just considered gung-ho and a jolly good sport. Feeling neither of the above, I collected flying kit, strapped the Colt to my hip and headed for my Quirk, closely followed by the ever-eager Watson, yapping at my heels like an excitable puppy.

'Phillips and Stobbart are already up, George,' he reported. 'Phillips went north towards Chigwell, Stobbie's heading for the river.'

'Hmm.'

'Which way will you go?'

'Haven't a clue. Upward for a start.'

'What about ammunition! You'll need Buckingham, and lots of it.'

Good point. Buckingham bullets were special incendiary

rounds they loaded into drums of standard Lewis-gun ammunition. They allowed you to see where your bullets went and were supposed to ignite the gas inside a Zeppelin. 'Oh, all right, run and fetch me a couple of drums, would you? Better make it three.' Ten minutes later, and with no fewer than six drums of ammunition jammed into the cockpit by the irrepressible Watson, I cranked the Quirk to life and trundled into the night.

Much feared by the public, more for their size and stealth than the damage they inflicted, Zeppelins were great growling monsters of the air. Over six hundred feet long, with a crew of twenty and a bomb-load in excess of a ton, these gas-filled, cigar-shaped leviathans (precursors of airships like *Hindenburg* and *Graf Zeppelin*) were for the most part slow, ponderous and poorly armed machines. Yet also damned difficult to locate and attack on a dark night. Their big advantage was their fuel endurance: they could take off from Germany at sunset, sneak towards their target by deviously circuitous routes, drop their bombs unseen, sneak out again by different and equally circuitous routes, and arrive back at base the following dawn. These were the days long before radar, remember, all we had were spotters on the ground and occasional brief glimpses by searchlight if we were lucky, so finding one at night was like blind-man's buff – a matter of intuition, feel and luck. Despite the difficulties, a few Zeppelins had been bagged, and if you could set one on fire the results were spectacular indeed. As were the plaudits. The first chap to bring one down, Reginald Warnford, was awarded a Victoria Cross and fêted as a national hero, as was the second, William Leefe Robinson. By the summer of 1917 however Zeppelin incursions had dwindled, nobody had seen one in months, and a blood-thirsty public was getting restless. The *Daily Sketch* cash prize was clever publicity, and probably sold lots of newspapers, but I doubt they ever seriously expected to pay out.

I took off and climbed to nine thousand, heading vaguely west. The Zeppelin's target, if indeed there was a Zeppelin, I guessed as London, probably east London and the docks, the city's industrial heartland and a favoured Hun objective. The night was dark and moonless, with a layer of broken cloud at three thousand which I climbed above, and another solid layer at ten which I stayed just below.

Nothing happened, nor did I expect it to. Half an hour went by, an hour. I stooged around, fired up my pipe, hummed tunelessly to myself and pondered the meaning of life. After ninety minutes, with feet numb and fuel getting low, I gave up and began a slow gliding descent for Suttons and bed. Then I saw something, just for a second, a huge shadow, like a whale glimpsed below the surface of the sea, then it was gone. It was so fleeting, so ephemeral, I was unsure I'd seen it at all, but with breath held and eyes riveted to the spot I reversed course, still gliding, and waited, willing it to reappear.

Ten seconds later it did, more solidly, and this time I didn't hesitate. Stuffing the Quirk's nose down I slammed on full power and plunged towards the thing, simultaneously fumbling for the Lewis which was mounted on a slide above my head. Wrong tactic. Before I knew it the Zeppelin was huge in my sights and I was swerving to avoid collision, barrelling past it without a single shot fired. Now I was in full view of the beast, and its gunners quickly spotted me. In seconds bright dots of machine-gun fire began curling outward from its gondolas, at the same time the huge snout rose and it started climbing for the clouds and safety.

Ignoring the gunfire I banked round for a second, head-on attack. This time I managed to rattle off a few rounds before careening down its side like a gull down a cliff. It was vast, like a flying ocean-liner. I could sense its huge animal power, see the pulsing fabric of its skin and skeleton of girders beneath, see figures moving in a control-room, see its six propellers turning, its huge cruciform tail. Then I was past and clear and hauling round once again for attack.

I made five passes, head-on, side-on, from above and behind, all to no avail. Sometimes a few bullets appeared to strike home, without effect, sometimes they missed by miles. Twice the Lewis jammed on Buckingham bullets and no shots were fired at all. It was most absurdly frustrating. A gas-filled target the size of Euston station and I couldn't hit the bloody thing, or if I hit it nothing happened. The main problem was the difference in relative speeds. It was like hurtling down a hill on a bicycle trying to hit a parked van with a pea-shooter. You got one go and it was gone. Then indeed it was gone. Banking round for yet another attempt, I looked up in time to see it sliding into cloud like a snake into a lake, and in seconds it had completely vanished. Heart pounding, furious and dis-believing, I could only stare at the empty sky in exasperation. I'd found it, I'd attacked it, and it had brushed me off as though I was a fly. I hung around a little longer, but unsure of my location, low on ammunition and horribly low on fuel I had little choice but to abandon the hunt and make for home.

Then it gave me one more chance. It was in cloud but not far enough in. I glimpsed a faint blue light, the exhaust-stub of one of its engines, glowing like a tiny beacon in the mist. Slow down, George, I urged myself. Throttle back, get the Quirk down to stalling speed, creep up on the thing from below and have one last go. Slotting the final drum of Buckingham into the Lewis, I lined up on the blue light, timed my moment, guessed the rest and squeezed the trigger, giving it one long raking burst. For once the gun didn't jam, all hundred rounds vanished into the murk, the blue glow moved steadily onward, and that was all. For about ten seconds. Then another glow appeared in the fog, orange this time. It flickered, dimmed, then suddenly burst to life in a huge ball of yellow. A few seconds more and the beast itself appeared, sinking from the cloud like a torpedoed tanker, its entire mid-section furiously ablaze. It was so bright it hurt the eye; I could feel the heat, hear the grumble of its burning. Quickly the fire spread until in seconds the Zeppelin was enveloped from end to end. It hung there in the sky for a moment, a monstrous suspended firestorm, then began the long dive to oblivion.

It is September 1914. I am fifteen years old. It is the end of the summer holidays and I am at home packing my trunk ready for school. It has been a fine holiday, the days long and sunny, I have enjoyed an exciting time and been afforded unusual freedom by my parents, who seem refreshingly cheerful. As does everyone, for in July war broke out and the whole country went mad with patriotism, cheering and celebrating like it was all a glorious party. One day I went into town with Bertie and we stood on the pavement in the Strand with thousands of others, waving flags on sticks while soldiers marched past in a river of khaki. 'Our brave lads' everyone called them proudly. I was so close I could see them smiling at the fuss and smell the camphor on their new uniforms. Apart from celebrating the war and discovering the forbidden delights of London with Bertie, I have passed the holidays with school-friends, lounging on a beach in Dorset, and learning to sail a small boat on a river in Norfolk. But now it is time to return to Shrewsbury and start the new school year. Just as I am putting the final touches to the contents of my trunk, the front doorbell tinkles down in the hall. I think nothing of it and carry on packing, but a few minutes later am aware of low voices on the stairs. At the same time something flutters inside me, like the pages of a book left by a window, and I know something has happened. My parents enter my room, side by side, faces solemn yet proud, as though a great honour has been conferred on them. Your brother has been called to God in the glorious service of his King, my mother says. I don't understand at first but it turns out Hugh has been killed in a place called Mons which is in Belgium. He only joined up a matter of weeks before, travelling to France with the British Expeditionary Force in July. Now he's dead and we're all meant to feel grateful about that. But I don't. In fact I am so shocked I don't know what to feel. Later that day I am put in a taxi to the station as though nothing has happened, and by evening I am in my dormitory at Shrewsbury. Lying there while the others chat excitedly of their holidays, I stare through the window at the moonlit playing-fields and try to analyse my feelings. Hugh is nine years older than me, we are altogether different. He is serious, studious, logical and given to introspection. I am none of these. Nor are we interested in the same things, nor do we wrestle, or build models or play games together, he being so much older. But he does talk to me like a friend, and takes an interest in my childish doings, and one summer when I was eleven he spent weeks teaching me to hit a cricket ball properly. We are strangers, yet I adore him completely, much more than my parents, idolising him as only a younger brother can idolise a much older one. And I am heartbroken he is dead, yet am not allowed to feel it, only gladness and thankfulness that he has given his life so nobly. I don't understand this so I bury it deep inside like a guilty secret. And soon I don't feel anything any more. And I stop taking school seriously. And the gambling begins.

When I went to visit Ann Gates that time in April, just after I got back from France, I gave her the letters Raymond had been carrying in his pocket. All except one. It was little different from the others in tone and content but to me was the most perfect expression of love and longing I had ever read, and carrying it with me was a reminder of something I yearned for but had lost. I know it was wrong to keep it, but I simply couldn't bear to part with it.

Raymond love,

How are you getting on, handsome man? I hope they're treating you right in your new billet. I'm so happy now your out the trenches, and I'm glad the food's better and that, but can't help worry a bit about this flying lark. Mrs Speight at no 23 says you royal flying corpse lads are dropping like flies but then she do go on. Just make sure you take good care of yourself and don't take no stupid chances.

Thanks for your last letter it was lovely. Jimmy and me are getting along fine you mustnt worry so. Your Mum drops by and lends a hand and the rent collectors all paid up and the coal has held out well. Now the weathers warming up a bit things is looking up. Jimmys out all hours playing in the yard and his chest is better and he's talking proper words and sentences all the time. Every day he points to your photo on the mantle and says my Dadda then starts looking for you behind the chairs like your hiding.

He looks behind chairs Raymond love, I look for you in my dreams. I lie there feeling the new baby we made growing inside and I can feel your arms closing tight round me and feel your wide manly chest and the hardness of your back and the force of your manhood in our lovemaking. Then I cry out for you in my dreams and wake up with tears on the pillow and aching in my loin.

I love you so bad it hurts see. And it hurts more to know your out there in so much danger. But though it hurts I know our love is our strength and that you <u>will</u> come back to me and the four of us will be together a family for ever.

Look for me in your dreams, handsome man. Im there waiting with open arms.

Will write again soon.

Your loving Ann.

I couldn't feel love, you see. Didn't know it, couldn't comprehend it. Hugh's death did that to me. It robbed me of my capacity to respond emotionally, except on the most superficial level. That's why I made such a hash of things with Emily, why I couldn't 'empathise' with my mother, as they say these days, or relate to my father, and why I felt only numbness when Bertie got killed. Emotionally crippled, that's the phrase. Yet I longed to feel these things, longed to know love and be accepted into its mysteries, gain membership of it, like it was some exclusive club. I wanted it so much I envied those who had it. Like Ann Gates. She had membership all right, I must have read that letter a hundred times, marvelling at its simple beauty, searching its lines for clues. So did Emily. She had love with her Valkyries, and in her work with the FANY, and with Mac, who loved his mother and sisters, and loved his friend who died in the trenches, and loved Emily. I didn't love Emily, not really, I know that now. I was infatuated with her, which isn't the same thing. I was in love with the *idea* of being in love with her. She knew this, and rightly chose Mac. Because theirs was the real thing.

He came to see me, Hugh did, just before he shipped out for Belgium. That's when he gave me his watch. He took the train down to Shrewsbury for the day specifically to see me and say goodbye. As if he sensed we might never meet again. We sat on the grass and watched a school cricket match, me in my Sunday blazer, he in his new uniform. What's this war about, Hughie, I asked, after he told me where he was going. So he explained about the Austro-Hungarian archduke getting assassinated, and about overlapping defence agreements, and the 1839 Treaty of London, and something called the Triple Entente, but little of it made sense to a fifteen-year-old schoolboy watching cricket. Isn't it just about right and wrong, I asked, chewing on a grass stem. Not exactly old chap, he smiled, if only things were that simple. Then he gave me his watch. Keep this for me, he said, strapping it on my wrist. Keep it safe until I come back. But Hughie it's your Breitling, I replied, scarcely believing my luck, father gave it to you for your twenty-first. I know, George, it's precious, for lots of reasons, that's why I want you to keep it. You can give it back when I come home. And then he left and I never saw him again.

And I did keep the watch, even though he never did come home. And gradually I learned its value had nothing to do with cash, but was about friendship, and love, and longing, and loss. I kept it until the day I gave it to Mac, when his need was greater. The day I shot Raymond Gates. The day I finally began to feel something akin to real emotions again.

Thousands saw my Zeppelin go down. You couldn't miss it — the brightest thing in the sky for forty miles around, the papers said next day. The *Daily Sketch* printed a stunning photo captured by an onlooker. The huge Zeppelin is plunging earthward in flames, while caught in perfect silhouette against it is the tiny outline of my Quirk. 'George Slays Dragon!' trumpets the headline. Below it is a smaller photo of G. Duckwell holding his cheque for a thousand pounds. 'To the Victor the Spoils' the caption reads, rather less enthusiastically.

Instant fame, not to mention riches, is the headiest of all cocktails, and I drank it greedily. By noon next day I was literally a household name, with letters and telegrams arriving by the sackful, including one telegram from Prime Minister

Lloyd George and another from the King, which I still have: 'Congratulations Capt. Dickwell on heroic achievement. The nation thanks you. Gratefully George R.' Grateful the King was, note, although not enough to spell my name correctly. Note also what must be the fastest promotion in history. Another typing mistake probably, but if the King says captain, then captain it is, and in due course the paperwork (and pay-rise) followed from the War Office. As did a medal – not the VC sadly, but the Distinguished Service Order, and most dashing it looked too stitched on to my tunic beneath my manly breast.

Days of dizzying celebration followed. Apart from champagne in the mess and endless free drinks at the pub, the War Office publicity-machine ground quickly into gear. A car was sent to Suttons, with my own driver to chauffeur me hither and thither. Breakfast with Lord Trenchard, boss of the RFC ('parachutes, my lord, pilots must have parachutes'), lunch with cheque-book-waving publishers, tea at the Commons with the War Cabinet, then dinner in a West End restaurant surrounded by fawning bigwigs and glamorous girls pestering me for autographs. I received presents: a cut-glass decanter from the MP for Essex, gold cufflinks from Lady Trenchard, a painting depicting my exploits by the artist John Sillitoe, and my personal favourite, a silver cigarette case engraved with a Zeppelin, enticingly sent by an anonymous admirer. I received cards, letters and telegrams from all over the country, some with money enclosed, others with photographs, and several containing offers of marriage. One lady from Gloucester sent me hand-embroidered pyjamas, while a vicar from Dorset sent me his treasured Bible, 'in grateful thanks for our deliverance'. People's enthusiasm grew out of all proportion, as though celebrating their need to celebrate was the thing, not the deed itself. Which was precisely the aim of the exercise, and well the Government knew it.

As did I, for drunk on fame though I was, I retained enough sense to know I was playing a role on their behalf. This won't last, George, I told myself, so make the most of it. And so I did, delighting in all the gifts, handshakes, speeches and parties, not to mention the endless photo sessions – me shaking hands with Trenchard, me taking tea with Queen Mary, me surrounded by cheering schoolchildren, me sitting in my aeroplane. Me even artfully re-enacting the deed on a stage, complete with inflatable Zeppelin and cardboard Quirk.

Me at the crash site. That one brought me up short. It must have been three or four days afterwards, and a most melancholy scene it was too. The Zeppelin had come down near Barking, fortunately in fields well away from any housing, and the *Daily Sketch* was insistent I be pictured next to it. But all that remained of that phenomenal machine and its twenty-man crew was an acre of smoke-blackened girders and a few ominous stains in the grass. It was a sad and sobering sight and I took no pleasure in it. This is the reality of air warfare, I wanted to say to the reporters, burning to death while trapped in a doomed aircraft, and believe me it's nothing to cheer about. Then there was the matter of statistics. Up to that point my tally of 'kills' accrued in the service of my country had amounted to precisely one, and he was an Englishman. Suddenly I'd created twenty more grieving widows, twenty heartbroken mothers and countless fatherless children. Nor did it make me proud. Indeed standing there surrounded by all that death and destruction felt shameful, the carry-on hollow and distasteful. I posed dutifully for the pictures, hurried back to Suttons and waited for it all to finish.

Because do you know what? Exciting though it was to have all that attention, in the end it didn't mean a thing. Because I'd no one to share it with. No one who really counted, that is. My parents were pleased of course, particularly when we were entertained to dinner by an air vice marshal, but though I'd rehabilitated myself in their eyes I took no real pleasure in the achievement, no self-respect, no *pride*, because for those things, I was learning, you need people you really care about, and who care about you, to share them with. People like Bertie, and Emily, and Mac. And Hugh.

'What happened to him?' I asked my father late one evening. We were alone in the library at Greenwich, smoking cigars and swirling brandies following a rare family dinner. He'd been more civil to me than in years, now I was newly respectable, he'd even asked a few fumbling questions about flying. But at my mention of Hugh he harrumphed and fidgeted and avoided my eye, until in the end I had to press him. 'Father. He was my brother. Surely I have a right to know.'

Eventually he grumbled into submission. 'Your brother was an academic,' he began. 'A thinker. They make poor soldiers, in my experience.'

The corollary being that fools like me do very well. I ignored the slur and waited.

'His company sergeant wrote to me a month afterwards, you know, in strictest confidence, giving me the facts. The real ones that is, as opposed to the official ones.'

'That was kind of him.'

'Yes.' He shot me a warning glance. 'I've never told your mother.'

'I understand.'

Hugh was covering a withdrawal, he explained. A railway bridge leading out of Mons. The fighting had been heavy all day, the Germans were counter-attacking over the bridge, orders came to pull everyone back. Hugh was told to dig his men in around the bridge and cover their retreat, holding the enemy 'by any means possible'.

'What does that mean?' I asked.

'George, do you want to hear this or not!'

He glared at me again, and suddenly I saw how hard this was for him.

'I'm sorry, please go on.'

'The Germans started across the bridge, but Hugh had deployed his men well and they managed to hold them. For about an hour, when they ran low on ammunition.'

He paused again, his old soldier's eyes on the carpet, picturing the scene. From outside came the tolling of the church bell; upstairs my mother moved quietly; all else was silent.

'At that point he should have left it. Fallen back and rejoined the column. But he didn't. He sent his men back, then put down his weapon, tied a handkerchief on a stick and walked on to the bridge.'

My mouth had gone dry. 'You mean he surrendered?'

'That's what everyone thought. But a white flag does not mean surrender, it means parlay. He went to talk to them. That's what he told his sergeant. He said he was going to buy time by talking to the Germans. By persuading them they should go back, to avoid further unnecessary bloodshed.'

'Jesus.'

'They didn't believe him of course. They listened for a minute then shot him out of hand. Even though he was unarmed. Then they took the bridge.'

Any means possible. That didn't just mean guns and bullets for Hugh, it meant logic, and reasoning, and initiative. God bless him.

'Officially he was killed in action,' my father went on sadly. 'Maybe it would have been better that way. The officer who ordered the withdrawal called it cowardice, stupidity and a direct contravention of orders.'

'Because of the white flag?'

'I suppose so.'

'What did Hugh's sergeant say?'

'He said it was the bravest thing he'd ever seen.'

'It was, father. It was selfless and brave and logical, and absolutely in keeping with his character. We should all be very proud of him.'

The next day I was picked up by my driver and taken off for another round of handshaking, magazine interviews and photos with dignitaries. But the fuss was at last beginning to wind down. Then one day it ended, as swiftly as it had begun, packing up and moving on like a circus in the night. I strolled out from breakfast to find my car gone and no journalists waiting to buttonhole me on the pavement. The job was done, the public appetite satisfied, the Hun humiliated, so now it was back to the grindstone and on with the war.

Gentle rain fell. I lit my pipe, turned up my collar and

wandered off towards Suttons. Arriving there the adjutant advised me with a wink that I was back on the duty-roster and due to fly that night. Then he handed me two slips of paper. One was a message from the RFC in Whitehall telling me to attend for interview that afternoon. The other was a telegram.

'Mac needs you. Please come. Emily.'

I stood there in the drizzle and read it. And re-read it. And instinctively understood. And my mind flew unbidden to Noyelette, and a half-forgotten afternoon spent with Mac. An afternoon of emergent friendship, of intimacy, warmth and rare humour. An afternoon that came to define the nature of our bond. And with its recollection came the certainty I would comply with the telegram.

It was February 1917, just a few weeks after I arrived at Noyelette. Morris Dixon had to go to the RAMC dentist in Pointbleu to have a troublesome molar removed. C-Flight was due on patrol but Morris didn't make it back in time, so they went without us. Feeling slightly miffed (this was weeks before Bloody April), I watched them go, then wandered back to the mess to await their return. A while later Mac walked in wearing flying gear.

'I hear your observer didn't make it back yet,' he said.

'No, worse luck.'

'I'll spot for you if you like.'

'I beg your pardon?'

'I'll fly as your observer.'

'But, Mac, they're long gone, we'll never catch them.'

A mischievous glint crossed his eye. 'Doesn't mean we can't do anything useful.'

'What sort of anything?'

'A little training maybe.' He tossed me my goggles. 'We'll stay our side of the lines and practise a few manoeuvres. Come on, I'll show you.'

I kitted up and we walked out to my aircraft. Now, bear in mind Mac had just landed from one sortie with his own squadron, his second of the day as it happened, and here he was *volunteering* for a third, with me, a ham-fisted novice from a completely different squadron, flying in a clapped-out old rattletrap to boot. Why was he doing this? For fun, apparently.

'How many hours have you got on Bathtubs?' I asked him, as we drew near.

'A hundred or so.'

'A hundred! Jesus, that's phenomenal. Where?'

'The Somme mostly. Last summer. Before I got accepted for scout training.'

It was his first posting after leaving the trenches, I learned later. Straight into Bathtubs as a gunner, flying in the bloodiest battle in the history of warfare. Then he was accepted for pilot training where he astounded instructors with his natural flair and skill. Back on ops as a pilot, within two months he'd notched up five kills.

'You fought at the Somme.' I shook my head. 'In Bathtubs.'

'Yes, I did.' He touched my arm. 'But do you know, George, this machine's called a Royal Aircraft Factory FE2b, and back then it was a pretty fine aeroplane. I don't like to think of it as a bathtub, it deserves better.'

Lesson one. Respect your aeroplane no matter how antiquated. Look for its strengths and exploit them, for even dinosaurs have teeth. Lesson two came swiftly after.

'The FE2 climbs quite good if you let it!' he yelled as we taxied out. He was lounging up front in Morris's seat, half turned to me and munching on a sandwich, like we were in the stalls at the cinema.

'Really?'

'Sure. Low stalling speed. Here, keep the rudder straight and I'll show you.'

With that he tossed his sandwich aside, reached back into my cockpit, opened the throttle and off we went, bounding across the grass like a startled hare. In seconds we were airborne, but instead of pulling up into a normal climb he held the aeroplane low and let the speed build up. Which it did very quickly. Barely two feet off the ground, in effect he was flying the thing backwards, kneeling on his seat, one hand on my control-stick, head twisted round to see where we were going, which was straight at Major Strickley's hut. I could only watch in horror as the hut raced towards us, but at the last second he pushed the stick back, stood the Bathtub on its tail and the thing blasted skyward like a cork from a champagne bottle.

'Get my drift?' he asked, handing me the controls.

I nodded dumbly. And what followed was a flying lesson unlike any in history. First we warmed up with a few steep turns, loops, and a stall or two. Then it was time for my first spin. Spinning was banned in many aircraft at that time, including Bathtubs, because recovery was so difficult. Many pilots had tried the stunt, many had died in the attempt. I had long decided to steer well clear of spinning, but Mac assured me all would be well.

'Nothing to be afraid of!' he explained. 'It's all to do with centre of gravity.'

'If you say so,' I replied nervously, and against my every instinct we reduced power and slowed the Bathtub right down and kept raising the nose higher and higher until the thing was teetering on the brink of oblivion like a drunk on a cliff.

'Kick left now!' he yelled, so I did, and in an instant we were whirling madly earthward.

'Jesus, Mac!'

'Good spin, George!' he shouted. 'Now, power off.'

'Power off!' I closed the throttle. Still the earth whirled.

'Kick full right rudder.'

'Full right rudder, yes!'

'Stick full forward.'

'Yes, yes, the stick's full forward!' But we were still spinning, faster if anything.

'Now move!'

With that he threw himself to the front of his nacelle. I did the same, and lo and behold with a stomach-churning lurch the spin stopped.

'Remember that, George,' he said afterwards. 'Centre of gravity. Mighty useful.'

I assured him I would.

More followed, much of it terrifying. But gradually I began to feel more confidence, both in the machine, which seemed to relish the abuse, and also in my ability to fly it, to control it, to *use* it as a tool for a job. Most of all I felt confidence in Mac, who was calm and patient and utterly fearless, something he never was on the ground. He was in his element, I realised, like a fish returned to water.

'Say, George, swap places a minute,' he said at one point, and began clambering back into my cockpit.

'Mac, for God's sake, what are you doing!'

'Just hop in front. I want to show you something.'

An unbelievably dangerous palaver then took place, with me scrambling under him while he climbed over me to take my seat. Either of us could have slipped and plunged to our deaths any second, and as for who was actually flying the machine I have no idea. Anyway we survived and Mac installed himself, and a moment later was diving us steeply groundward, towards a long straight road lined with trees.

'Do you know how far apart they planted those trees, George?'

'Haven't a clue. Fifty feet?'

'Fifteen metres. That's the metric system. And what's the wingspan of our FE2?'

'Ah, forty-seven feet. Or is it fifty-one? I can never remember.'

'No, George, in the metric system!'

'Metric? Christ, how should I know?' The road was fast approaching, the two lines of trees looked horribly close together, regardless of the measurement. 'Um, divide by thirty-nine and, ah, take away a sixth . . .'

'It's fourteen and a half metres, George. You gotta know these things. You get a Hun on your tail that won't quit, this might just persuade him. So how much clearance do we have from the wingtips down that road?'

Practically none. Our wingspan was fourteen and a half metres, the gap between the lines of trees fifteen, but only low down, at trunk level; above that the canopy closed overhead like an arch. 'I, ah, half a, half a . . . Christ, Mac, look out!'

Pulling out of the dive, he nudged the Bathtub down to

271

ground level, straightened up, then plunged us into a tunnel of green. Suddenly everything went dark and blurry and thunderously loud. Half a metre. Our wingtip clearance was half a metre – less than two feet. Far ahead a semi-circle of light marked the end of the tunnel. I clung on, scarcely daring to breathe, while trees flashed past to either side, wildlife scattered and leaves flew in our wake like a cloud.

Then, inevitably, a car appeared. At the far end. An open car, painted in khaki, with military people on board. Coming straight towards us.

'Oops.' I heard Mac say. There was nothing we could do. Pull up into the canopy and we'd be smashed to smithereens, nor could we veer left or right; all we could do was carry straight on, inches from the road, and hope the car saw our plight and took action.

It did, but only at the last second, careering aside to skid ignominiously into a tree. I glimpsed furious faces, shaking fists, army uniforms with flashes of red. Staff officers, that meant. Bigwigs. Important people. 'Oops,' Mac said again, but he never flinched from his course, and a moment later we were hurtling out into daylight, and zooming for the heavens.

Peace descended. Mac throttled back, levelled the aeroplane and set course for home as if nothing had happened. Unamused, I waited, eyes closed, for my blood pressure to fall before turning in my seat to confront the mad bugger. But when I did he was wearing an expression of such complete innocence, like a schoolboy caught scrumping apples, that I found it hard not to smile.

'Do you think they saw us?' he asked, in all seriousness.

'Possibly, Mac, yes.'

And at that point I started laughing. I couldn't help it. Tension perhaps, or relief, or Mac's wide-eyed sheepishness, I don't know, but laughter was all I could manage. All the way back to Noyelette.

The Gates house was as I remembered it – the cluttered pavement, the little front garden, the threadbare hedge, the same front door. The woman who opened it, too, was the same, only a little older somehow, more tired, and noticeably more pregnant.

'Mrs Gates, good evening, it's George Duckwell. Raymond's, um, associate.'

'Oh.' The messenger of misfortune. 'You.'

'Yes. I hope . . . Is this a convenient time?'

For what? her eyes said, then she glanced away. 'Suppose. Jimmy's in bed.'

We stood on the step in silence a few moments, the widow and the man in uniform. Curtains twitched in the twilight, a man cycled by watching curiously, the cat made an appearance.

'Was there something you wanted?' she asked eventually.

'Well, there is actually, yes. I wonder, may I come in?'

'If you want. I ain't got nothing though, and the place is a tip.'

'That's all right. I'll only be a minute or two.'

It wasn't a tip, it was just different. A little less tidy perhaps, and the atmosphere had changed, the feel of the place. The preparedness had gone, the sense of anticipation. We sat at the same two chairs, in the same little parlour, eyeing each other in the gloom.

'Saving on the electric,' she explained. 'Don't use it unless I 'ave to.'

273

'Good idea.'

I glanced at the mantel. Raymond's photo was still there, but tied with a black ribbon. The clock had stopped too, as though monitoring the time was now pointless.

'Saw your picture in the papers and that,' she said, by way of conversation.

'Undeservedly, I assure you. A big fuss about nothing.'

She nodded, shifting her weight on the chair with a wince.

Small-talk over, I commenced my preamble. 'So, Ann. How are you keeping?'

'Money's tight.' She shrugged. 'We'll have to move, can't afford the rent.'

'Where will you go?'

'His mum's p'raps, for a bit. Don't know. We'll cope somehow.'

'And the, um, the little one?' I nodded at her stomach. 'Everything going well?'

'S'all right, thank you.'

'What about young Jimmy? His chest and so on.'

'Jimmy's fine.' She shot me a glance. 'How do you know about 'is chest?'

'Raymond mentioned, I believe, something. A weak chest, was it? Anyway—'

'I thought you said you didn't hardly know him.'

'No, I, well, that is true.' This was not going as planned. I was supposed to be allaying doubts, not arousing them. 'Only, he did talk of his family. Of you particularly.'

'Look, I don't mean to be rude and that, but what exactly is it you want?'

Good question. The same good question Lord Trenchard's

274

aide had put to me not three hours earlier, during my RFC interview. Well, now, Duckwell, he'd said. And what ideally do you want? I wasn't sure I followed, but it emerged I was being offered my choice of postings. You're a clever sort of chap, he said, good at making speeches, talking to newspapers and that. We could send you to Canada, or even America now they're joining the war, do a sort of publicity tour to boost recruitment. Or you could stay at Suttons if you prefer, we'll make you a flight leader; better yet we're setting up a new Home Defence unit at Joyce Green, equipped with Sopwith Pups, we could make you squadron leader perhaps. Or you could become an instructor and put all that talent and experience to use teaching new pilots. Or there's this aircraft testing centre up on the Suffolk coast, interesting job there for a good pilot, comfortable billet too. Anything, he said, anything I liked. It was to be my reward, for being a hero and deflecting public attention from the drudgery of the war. Comfort, security, and immunity from death. Just what I'd always wanted. Wasn't it? He leaned forward across his desk and filled my glass with Scotch.

Then everything became clear. Like a veil lifting from a picture, suddenly I could see every detail. Hugh, the last time I'd seen him that afternoon at Shrewsbury. Don't do anything stupid, I'd joked, half seriously, as he rose to leave. Don't do anything stupid like getting killed. Jucundi acti laboris, he'd replied, patting my head – betterment through service to others. And Emily. Why do you want to join the FANY, I'd asked her all those months ago at the stables. To do something helpful, she'd replied, so I can find out who I am. And Mac. Honest, loyal Mac, struggling against the world for wanting only to do right. *Mac needs you*, Emily said in her telegram. *Mac needs you. Please come.* And I would come, because he'd given of himself when I needed him. Selflessness, that's what it was about. To know love, you need to act selflessly. Nothing else.

Thank you, sir, I replied to Trenchard's aide. Thank you, but there is only one posting I want. And I'm afraid nothing else will do.

'Excuse me.' Ann Gates was still waiting.

'Oh, I'm so sorry.' I pulled out an envelope. 'I came here to give you this.'

'What is it?'

'A thousand pounds.'

'Pardon?'

'For you. And Jimmy. And the baby of course.'

'A thousand pounds?'

'Yes.'

'Are you mad? I don't want your money!'

'But you must. And it's not mine. It's from the, um, fund.'

'What fund?'

'*The* fund.' I hurried through my lines. 'The 13 Squadron Family Benevolent Fund. Society. Mutual. Thing. Have you not heard of it?'

'No.'

'Well it has most certainly heard of you, Ann. Everyone in the squadron, you see, from the CO right down to the most junior mechanic, contributes a little of their pay each month into the fund. In case anyone gets killed. In case anything untoward happens, that is, to someone. Then, if it does, the fund pays out to their family.'

'But, a thousand pounds! I mean, it's a fortune. How much were they paying in for God's sake?'

'It's a lot, I know. But they're exceptionally generous fellows, 13 Squadron, you know, generous, close-knit, and surprisingly well off. You should meet the CO, Major Strickley, life and soul of the party he is, loved by everyone, jolly wealthy too, he paid in tons. Anyway, the point is, you must accept it, otherwise great offence would be taken. Also they wouldn't want any fuss, no letters of thanks or anything, just take the money and put it to good use. Those are the rules.'

'But a thousand . . . My God, I can't believe . . . How . . .'

'Ann.' I looked at her sternly. 'It's what Raymond would want, now, isn't it?' She nodded blankly. 'Good, then it's all settled. Oh, and by the way, I also found this, while, um, tidying at home. It's one of your letters, must have slipped from the others when I . . . anyway, sorry.'

She took the letter, adding it to the bundle of cash. Then her eyes were searching mine, half questioning, half disbelieving, then the shoulders were slumping, the head falling and the tears starting in hot floods on her cheeks. I too felt an unaccustomed lump in my throat, and went quickly to her side. There I took her awkwardly in my arms, and rocked her a little, while her tears flowed down my neck and the last of the light died around us.

Chapter 10

I climbed down from the Noyelette tender one hot afternoon a week later, precisely twelve weeks after departing the place vowing never to return. Instantly a nightmare torrent of unstopped memories came rushing back, and I nearly climbed right back in again. But running away was not in the plan, my new CO was striding across the field to greet me, mechanics watched curiously from the hangars, and anyway I was there of my own volition so had no choice but to brazen it out.

I sniffed the sultry air, surveying the familiar landscape like a wary dog. The grass had lost its spring viridescence, and the leaves rustled more dryly in the trees; apart from that Noyelette in high summer appeared much the same as the winter version. A few tatty clouds hung in the sky, the wind-sock drooped limply, crows paced about like black-cloaked undertakers, and across the field rose the unmistakable clatter of a Bathtub engine, as though a summons. Involuntarily I shivered, despite the heat.

'Captain Duckwell? You made it, how marvellous!' 166 Squadron's CO pumped my hand. 'I'm Fothergill, do call me Charles, and may I say how delighted we are to have you with us, the famous Zeppelin ace and a DSO to boot, simply marvellous. Have you had a good journey? Here, let me take your bag.'

We set off for the chateau, Fothergill chatting eagerly. I didn't know him. In his thirties, short, sprightly, he'd only been in post a few weeks, his predecessor having been shot down. As had, it emerged, many of the old guard.

'Johnny Kingston's still with us, of course,' he said. 'As is Cecil Pargeter, though he's down with this influenza thing. Tim Clough's here too, did you know him?' I shook my head. 'Ah, well, it has been a dreadful year.'

I noticed he didn't mention Mac, though he was uppermost in my mind.

We passed a hangar with eight SE5s parked outside, which meant one flight was probably aloft. The aircraft looked businesslike if careworn. Inside the hangar lurked a Quirk and a couple of Pups, the Nieuports having by now all gone.

'What about 13 Squadron, Major?' I couldn't help asking. 'How are they getting on?'

'Dreadfully, so I hear. Down on pilot numbers and half of those sick, pitifully short of serviceable machines too, they're barely operating sometimes. There's talk of amalgamating them with another squadron and pulling back to Frévant for a rest and refit. Best thing in my view. Particularly as they have no CO at the moment.'

'Really? Where's Strickley?'

'Gone, didn't you hear? Damn peculiar business. Apparently he'd been firing off hundreds of letters demanding better conditions for aircrew – you know, parachutes, more training, improved weaponry and so on. Trenchard's chaps got fed up with it and had him posted off to some desk job in Scotland.'

'How odd.'

'Indeed, especially as he claimed he couldn't remember writing the letters. He's having a splendid time now though. Sent us a postcard, says he's become expert at bird-watching.'

As a captain, a DSO and Zeppelin ace I warranted a bedroom to myself in the chateau. Fothergill showed me to a handsome second-floor one with ornate if crumbly cornicing and tall shuttered windows overlooking the airfield.

'I've put you in A-Flight, if that's all right,' he said. 'There's an SE5 for you to familiarise yourself on, let me know when you feel ready to start ops. In the meantime, relax. Drinks are at seven in the drawing room, dinner at eight. If there's anything else . . .' He turned to go.

'Yes, there is one thing, Major.'

'Oh?'

'Lieutenant MacBride.' I had to know. Now. 'Can you tell me about him?'

'Ah.' Fothergill looked uncomfortable. 'Of course, I forgot you knew him before. Well, how can I put this? Mac is still flying, a great deal actually, and still shooting down Huns at a terrific rate, and still very much a part of this unit. But he's in a bit of a state.'

'What sort of state?'

'Exhaustion, I'd call it. Mental as well as physical, almost to the point of collapse. Furthermore he won't accept medical help and won't take leave. Nor can we force him, not unless he fails to do his job, and there's no sign of that. Frankly, he's the best pilot we've got.'

'I see. Has anyone tried talking to him?'

'Of course. I have, as did the CO before me, and the medical officer, he's tried countless times. But that's just the point.'

'What is?'

'Mac doesn't talk back. To anyone. Barely a word.'

'What about friends?'

Fothergill shrugged. 'Not many left. And all the new faces seem only to make him more anxious. He spends most of his time in his room when not flying. Except when his young lady visits.'

'Pretty, dark-haired girl? In the FANY?'

'That's her. They go off for long walks in the evenings. Mind you I haven't seen her in a week or so.'

Mac was flying, Fothergill added, on patrol with A-Flight and not due back for an hour. Then he left me to it. So with little else to do I unpacked my belongings into an elegant mahogany *armoire*, then lay down on my four-poster bed to rest. Before long I was slipping into uneasy slumber.

When I awoke Mac was sitting on the bed beside me. The last time I'd seen him was three months earlier, on the day he rescued me from no-man's land, the day of Raymond Gates and my final patrol with 13 Squadron. No it wasn't, it was that dreadful five seconds in the Metropole Hotel in Calais, but I don't count that. He looked bad, there was no getting away from it. Older, was my first reaction, much older, and wilder somehow, scabrous and scruffy like a cat gone feral. He was still in flying-clothes – it looked like he lived in them – and his face was deeply weathered, and unshaven beneath layers of grime. His thick black hair was long and unkempt; occasionally he raked it back from his forehead with oil-stained fingers. Within the pale circles left by his goggles his eyes still gleamed blackly, but they seemed to have sunk in his brow, as though from insupportable weight, and they switched rapidly from side to side as they studied mine. His nose sported deep red welts from his goggles, and his chin was thickly stubbled. He was twenty-two, yet he looked forty. Only his lips and mouth seemed youthful, curled into a child-like smile.

'You came back,' he whispered.

'Hello, Mac. How are you?'

'You came back.'

'Yes, I've been posted here.'

'You came back.' His right arm shook, I saw, trembled as though in spasm.

'That's right. 166 Squadron, to fly SE5s, with you. Once I've worked out how to fly them, that is.'

'You've not flown an SE5?'

'Not as yet. But it shouldn't be too diff—'

'Let's go.'

'Mac, wait!' But he was already going, and before I knew it I was chasing him down the chateau's grand staircase and out into the evening heat. 'Mac, look, hang on, don't you think we should have a briefing or something? Anyway I haven't the right togs on, and Fothergill said . . . Mac, wait!

Oh hell.' He tramped off towards the parked aeroplanes, me trailing behind, muttering protests.

As we drew near the leading SE5 he stopped and turned to me. 'Stay close and do what I do. Everything will be fine.'

'But Mac, I don't even have goggles!'

He lifted his own from his neck. 'Take mine, I don't need them.'

Five minutes later I was bounding across the field in an aeroplane I'd never flown before, clad in my best uniform and borrowed goggles, clutching on for dear life and praying to God nobody was watching, which of course they were. There goes that mad so-and-so MacBride again, I could hear them saying, but who's the nincompoop trailing in his wake? The power of the machine was phenomenal. When I opened the throttle the torque veered me towards the trees and I had to stamp the rudder to compensate, but I overdid it and veered the other way. At the same time the tail came up, so I banged it down again, then up once more to stop the thing leaping skyward. In no time I was hopping across the grass, careering left and right like a panicking rabbit. Somehow Mac stayed beside me, but he was soon airborne and climbing hard, so with options a-few and fast running out of airfield all I could do was yank back on the stick, wrench the machine from the ground and climb after him.

Fortunately for me the Scout Experimental 5, as well as being strong and fast, was also a wonderfully forgiving aeroplane. Too much so, some people said, complaining that its inherent stability robbed it of agility compared, say, to the Camel, which was devilish to control but could turn on a sixpence. But comparing the two was pointless, like later arguments about the Spitfire and Hurricane: both were excellent aircraft in their own way, just different, yet equally potent in the fight against the Hun. The SE5 was better, that's all. And within twenty minutes or so I had the measure of the thing. Its single cockpit was compact and well laid out, visibility was good, the water-cooled Hispano-Suiza engine purred lustily up front, and gentle pressure on stick or rudder produced the smoothest of responses. With Mac at my side and a deliciously mild breeze in my face I was soon handling it with confidence.

After a few gentle warm-up exercises Mac began to lead me through a series of increasingly complex manoeuvres – steep turns, chandelles, slow rolls – and suddenly all those hours in the library, those sketches and diagrams, those lectures on thrust and drag, poise and control, began to fall into place. Try the Immelmann, George, I could hear him saying. That's good, but more rudder. Now we'll loop together, with a stall-turn off the vertical. That's it. Now the barrel-roll, smooth and balanced, like wiping round the inside of a saucepan. Soon we were gambolling about the evening sky like dancers on a floor, entering a deeper form of communication, he leading, me following, not effortlessly but with growing understanding and assuredness. The key, as he'd said so often, was to think of the machine as an extension of the self. Like a horse and rider, to work best they must combine into a single entity – the horse-man. Mac, I realised, as we glided home together beneath the setting sun, had achieved the same with his aircraft, a higher state, altered, hybridised, unified. Aeroplane-man.

The problem was, aeroplane-man could no longer function on the ground.

Emily hadn't seen him in a week. With Le Merignac full, the cathedral crypt overflowing and demand for front-line evacuations never-ending, she simply hadn't had time. Nor could she spare the ambulance: one of hers had broken a drive-shaft, obtaining a spare was problematic, so she was forced to manage on three. Other logistical difficulties were mounting. Just keeping the monastery provisioned with food and medical supplies required use of one vehicle, which left just two to fulfil other duties. Then a flu outbreak descended, affecting staff and patients alike, then the trains stopped running because of bomb damage, and suddenly the monastery's corridors were filling with casualties, and the refectory, the chapel and the outbuildings, until Le Merignac seemed carpeted with wounded soldiers. Nerves became frayed, tempers flared, patients cried out in frustration, and staff in despair. The medical officer, Captain Ashton, exhausted beyond reason, came to Emily's office one night and broke down in tears. I can't do this, he wept, it isn't human. She gave him brandy, and asked Phyllis, intuitively, to talk to him until he calmed. The next morning she part-solved the transportation crisis by drafting the monastery's horse-cart into service. By nightfall she had two more, lent by sympathetic villagers, and her FANY contingent returned to its roots, fetching and carrying on horseback. The day after that the railway reopened, and patients could be moved out once more, but the monastery well ran dry, a horse went lame, and one of her girls went down with the fever. And that night the morning hate began at midnight.

The war was spiralling out of control, she felt, driven by its own unstoppable momentum, sucking the world into a vortex of death and desecration. For the first time she began to feel anger at those who continued to wage it, those with the power to stop it. Why, she found herself asking, why is this war still happening? To what possible gain or end? A generation of young men was being erased from existence, tens of thousands more condemned to a life of pain and mutilation, even those untouched by bullets would be forever scarred by their experiences. Countless thousands of families were suffering the anguish of a killed or injured father, or son, or brother, and for what? No one could give an adequate explanation. Logic was fleeing in the face of obstinacy, she realised, the war nourishing itself on a failure of reason.

Nor was she alone in this realisation. Voices were rising in protest, mutinies were starting to happen, and desertions, with soldiers on both sides laying down their weapons and melting into the countryside like outlaws. More and more casualties were arriving at field stations with self-inflicted wounds, some of them deep and dangerous. Major Boulter told her of two French deserters hiding in the cathedral catacombs, one with a wound to the neck from a bullet fired by his friend. If he reported them they'd be shot, he said; in earlier days he wouldn't have hesitated, but now he wasn't so sure. I've been a soldier all my life, he said, yet can no longer understand this war.

One morning she drove her ambulance to the front line to collect wounded. By now the journey through the shattered town, past the roadblock crossroads and down the hill to the dressing station, had become almost routine. If falling bombs, flying shrapnel and the howl of heavy artillery could ever be routine.

'One for the cathedral, ma'am,' the orderly said as she pulled up. They used to call her miss, or dearie, or even love, now they called her ma'am. Out of respect, Major Boulter said. Because you've earned it.

'Only one?'

'We've more due later, but they can hang on. This one can't, he's in a bad way.'

The stretcher duly appeared, the ghostly white face of a young boy showing above the blanket, in repose like a sleeping child.

Emily sighed. 'God, he looks so young.'

'In a dreadful state, poor lad. Shrapnel wounds to the guts. No ID neither, at least nothing that matches.'

'Matches?'

'Over there.' The orderly gestured to a cardboard box on a table. 'We don't just get men without IDs, you know. We also get IDs without men.'

Emily approached the box and lifted the lid. Identity tags and discs filled it, hundreds of them, French, Belgian, British and Canadian, some even German.

'They get handed in all the time,' the orderly went on. 'They find 'em in the mud. Some are years old, all corroded to buggery, some buckled by explosion or with bullet-holes.'

Emily dug her fingers into the box and grasped, lifting a score of unknown men's lives in her fist, slipping them through her fingers like precious jewels. To her the box summed up the awful poignancy of the war, all its waste and wretchedness. Come and see this, she wanted to say to the generals, and the politicians, and the warmongers, come and dip your fingers in here, and feel what you made.

'What happens to them?' she asked.

The orderly shrugged. 'We make a note of those we can read. Check 'em against lists of dead and injured passing through. Occasionally we get a match. Mostly we don't.'

She drove the injured soldier back through the town to the cathedral, parking adjacent to the crypt entrance. Major Boulter appeared and made a swift assessment.

'He's done for, Emily,' he said, stepping down from the ambulance. 'Intestinal tract all but blown away. We can keep him here if you like, until it's over. Free up your ambulance for something else.'

'Thank you, Major, but I'll take him back to the monastery. We have a few beds spare now, and it'll be more peaceful there, at the end.'

'I understand. It shouldn't take long.'

But it took hours. And in those hours Emily found she couldn't bear to leave him. In case he awoke, in case he talked, in case he died, alone, in a strange place, and unknown. Eventually, unable to concentrate on routine matters, she asked Phyllis to take over, carried a chair to the boy's room and stationed herself at his side, reading psalms to him in French from a book left by the monks. Occasionally he would stir, his face creased in pain, and she would stop reading to smooth his brow, and murmur softly in his ear, like a mother to a fretful child. You can go now, John, she found herself saying. It's all right, John dearest, Mother's here, don't be afraid, you can go if you like.

Darkness fell and still the boy lingered. Emily refused food, refused relief, refused to be moved. To her, nothing of importance existed beyond the room's walls, and as she sat, and watched, and comforted her white-faced child, she felt the world contract around her, and her own centre of momentum shifting, realigning, like a ship altering course on an ocean. As it had when she'd pulled the baby from the rubble. As though everything was changing. At some point someone slipped a blanket round her shoulders, a little later a candle appeared on the table beside her. Then she dozed. When she awoke, somebody else was in the room, standing in shadow by the door.

'Hello, Emily.'

'George?'

'Yes. May I wait with you?'

'Of course.'

They waited, the room silent save for the doleful hoots of an owl in the woods.

'When did you arrive?' she asked after an interval.

'A few days ago.'

'Thank you for coming. Back to France. It can't have been easy for you.'

'Easier than you'd imagine. I'm just glad we're all together. You, me and Mac, that is, not just, you know . . .'

'I know, George. I'm glad too.'

Another silence fell, broken only by the boy's faint breathing.

'He looks so young.'

'Yes.'

'Do you know his name?'

'His name's John.'

The boy died around midnight. I stayed with Emily until it was over. We didn't talk much, not then, it wasn't the time. Anyway we were both wrapped up in the boy and his final hours. Uncannily so. Neither of us knew him, both of us had seen death countless times, yet this youth's sad passing touched us deeply. Emily especially. After he died, she leaned over his bed, lowered her head on to her arms and wept, inconsolably, as though she'd lost everything. Which in a way she had. Her anguish was profound, and in overdue need of expression I sensed, so I let her cry, watching the moon through the window and thinking of a beautiful dark-haired girl grooming a horse in Uffington, so sure, so single-minded, so determined to fulfil her dream. It's what I want more than everything, she'd said proudly. And she'd given everything, more than anyone could ask. Now she was spent.

Eventually I could bear her suffering no longer, and raising her from the bed, turned her to me. She pressed her head to my chest and cried on for a while. I stroked her hair. Finally she fell still.

'He couldn't have asked for more,' I said. 'You were his family.'

'I suppose so.' I felt her nod. 'I hate this war, George,' she went on. 'I hate what it's done to everyone.'

'Things certainly haven't gone as expected.'

'Are you not angry with me? For what happened in Calais?'

'No. I was angry, but then I realised I had no right to be.'

'I'm sorry it didn't work out for us. I would have liked it to.'

'Much better this way. You and Mac, it's wonderful, I'm so pleased for you both.'

'Thank you. For understanding.' She hesitated. 'How is he?'

'Bad. You were right to send that telegram.'

Her hand squeezed mine. 'We have to save him, George. Not for my sake but for his. And for the sake of this boy here, and the sake of all the others.'

'I know. And we will. Somehow.'

Easier said than done. We talked for an hour or so, I promised Emily I'd think of something, then I headed back to the airfield.

Later that morning Fothergill called me into his office to talk about Mac. I know you're his friend, he began uneasily, so thought you'd want to know.

Know what? I wondered, but said nothing.

'I've only been with 166 a short while,' he went on, 'so I know practically nothing about Mac. Or his past.'

'Yes, sir.'

'Nor am I sure I want to.'

'No, sir.'

He flicked me a glance. 'Did you know an infantry corporal from the Surreys was executed last week for forging transfer papers to the RFC?'

'No, sir, I didn't. But what has that to do with Mac?'

'I don't know. Nothing at all, I hope.' He slid two envelopes across the desk. 'You'd better see these.'

I picked up the envelopes. The first, to my astonishment,

was the same dog-eared letter Mac had received from the 1st Canadian Division all those months previously, the horse-theft one enquiring about a MacBride who transferred to the RFC in 1916. It was even in its original envelope, the one I'd sent back rubber-stamped by Strickley. Now, months later, they were following it up. Sealed with it inside a fresh envelope, also addressed to Strickley, was a second letter of enquiry. And a photograph. Grainy, poorly reproduced, almost indecipherable, it was a picture of a tousle-haired youth holding a numbered board. The real William MacBride, I guessed, taken presumably at a police station back in Vancouver. Even through the graininess the face was clearly not Mac's.

'Has Mac seen this, Major?' I asked. 'Or anyone?'

Fothergill shook his head. 'Nobody. Since Strickley's gone it came straight to me. What do you think it means?'

'I'm not sure. A case of mistaken identity possibly?'

'I should ask him about it.'

'Perhaps not just now, sir. Seeing how he is.'

Fothergill grunted, studying the photo. Meanwhile I turned to the other envelope.

It was a memo from the publicity office of the RFC in London, the same publicity office that handled the puff over my Zeppelin exploits. Lieutenant William MacBride, the memo said, was now the top-scoring Canadian pilot in the entire Corps, and the RFC meant to make the most of it. A huge publicity campaign was planned at home, in Canada, and in the USA. And to set things in motion two journalists and a photographer were being sent to Noyelette to interview the hero. Arriving, according to the date, in the next three days.

'You can't let them do it,' I said immediately.

'I can't very well stop them, George.'

'But sir, you've seen him, he can't cope with publicity, or interviews, or anything like that.'

'I appreciate that, but what do you propose? This memo isn't an invitation to tea, you know. Trenchard takes this sort of propaganda very seriously, he's desperate to recruit more colonial pilots.' He picked up the memo. 'This is a direct order, right from the top. I can't just ignore it.'

Three days, we had, at most, until Mac's cover was blown, less if Fothergill started probing. I left him in brooding mood. There was nothing I could do, and anyway A-Flight was due to fly, so I togged up and trudged out to the aeroplanes.

Mac was already aboard his. As I neared he looked up and smiled. He looked dreadful, a shadow of the man I once knew. I tried to smile back. This was an important patrol, my first on active service with 166 Squadron, and I needed to stay sharp and put up a good show. Which was just as well, because it was also to be my second encounter with Baron von Richthofen.

We took off in pairs, the flight leader, Clough, with his number two, and me tucked in beside Mac. By now I'd accumulated twenty hours or so in the SE5, and so long as Mac was at hand I felt reasonably ready for the fray. Beneath a high milky overcast the four of us set course east and began the long climb to twenty thousand. As we went I busied myself around the cockpit and made ready my guns. The model we were flying was the SE5a which had the more powerful 200hp engine and two machine-guns, a Vickers synchronised to fire through the propeller and a Lewis mounted on the upper wing. The Vickers was fixed in front of the cockpit, the Lewis on a slide over my head, so it could be angled to shoot forward or upward. Together they amounted to some impressive firepower, assuming you could manage it all and still fly the aeroplane.

Though the sky was cloudless the visibility was hazy, and we crossed into enemy territory without seeing anyone, nor being bothered by Archie. Our patrol route was to the north and east of Arras: German aircraft were reportedly active in the area, our job was to deter them, or better yet blow them from the sky. But after twenty minutes we still hadn't spotted so much as a seagull. Then Mac gave a tiny rock of the wings and gestured down. Far below, a flight of three aircraft slid across the landscape, heading west. Bathtubs, I recognised, and thought how vulnerable they looked. Then came another wing-rock, this time to point out two fast-moving specks off to our right. They vanished into the haze before we could identify them. Then some Archie started up, but far to the south, and aimed at some other unfortunates, not us.

The next thing I knew Mac was gone. Just a quick wing-rock, a glimpse of his wheels and he'd vanished. Half-roll and dive, that meant, the fastest way to reverse direction, so without thinking I threw the stick over, flicked the aeroplane upside down and pulled back. A moment later I was vertical, diving flat out, slipstream screaming, and there he was, directly ahead, but already coming out of the dive and into a steep twisting climb. I too pulled to catch up, harder, feeling the airframe strain and the sagging crush of gravity, then it was on with full power and climb like mad. I glanced left, Clough's pair was there but way behind. A few seconds more and I was level with Mac, who was still climbing, still turning, striving for height and position, to meet the six German Fokkers tumbling down the sky towards us. It was Richthofen's Jasta all right, triple-winged DR1s all brightly coloured and flying like I'd never seen in my life, twisting and twirling like acrobats in a circus, zigzagging in and out of one another then separating suddenly for attack.

Everything then happened very fast. With a closing speed of three hundred miles an hour I had time only to fumble for my guns and note my attacker was blue before he was gone and past and I'd never fired a shot. Instantly Mac was after them, hauling us round in a vertical turn, and after that everything went to mayhem, a full-blown dogfight, the sky full of madly duelling aeroplanes, tracer bullets, the howl of tortured engines and chattering guns. In seconds we'd separated and it was every man for himself. Spotting a yellow Fokker above, I stood the SE5 on its tail and roared upward in pursuit, then something green flashed across my sights so I kicked left to get on it. For four seconds he ducked and weaved in and out of range while I clung to his tail and squeezed triggers, but my shots looked wide and then he was gone, replaced by a clattering of guns from behind, and a loud bang as a wing-strut snapped. I flick-rolled and veered right just as a flame-red triplane raced by, jinking madly, followed a second later by Mac's SE5. I fired, the triplane fired, Mac was firing. I tried to follow but their flying was insane, wild and furious, like two mad dogs, and in seconds I lost them, so I broke away, climbing and turning to regain the fight.

Manfred and me had finally found each other. He'd changed aeroplanes again, this time for the three-winged DR1 specially designed for him by Herr Fokker. It was wonderfully agile, fleet as a fox, and at first I had trouble staying with him. I believe he let me, I believe he sought me out and led me away from the others so we could be alone and finish it.

We began where we'd left off before, circling each other, checking our machines, loading weapons and making sure we were alone. Then he waved his fist and peeled off for the first attack, which was head-on. Once again we closed at full speed then flick-rolled as we passed, veering away like horse-riders in a jousting contest. I managed a burst with the Vickers, he fired too, but we were going too fast and missed. After that we worked the old game of getting on the other's tail. The DR1 was amazingly tight in the turn but the SE5 more powerful in the climb, so I flew for vertical gain while Manfred sought advantage in the horizontal. He was always good at this. Manfred grew up hunting on horseback and won many prizes for gymnastics at school, and I could see his mastery of these skills in his flying, with his manoeuvres quick and neat, and every move designed to bring his guns to bear, like a true huntsman. This was most impressive to see, and after a while my SE5 began to take hits as he learned its limitations. But hunters get used to always being the aggressor and sometimes he made defensive errors. On one pass he rolled out from a tight turn and fired a fine burst that tore my wingtip to pieces. But as he broke away he showed me the DR1's belly so I got in a good burst behind his engine. This seemed to anger him and I began to notice harshness creep into Manfred's flying, like I'd seen before. It was like he had no patience for his machine's weaker points, one of which was slowness in left turns due to engine torque. I began to work on this, all the while watching and waiting for my moment, even if that meant allowing Manfred to hit the SE5 a few times more. But I waited too long and a bullet went through my radiator which began to stream coolant. *Manfred was behind me and could see I was trailing vapour. We were turning right and he was shooting hard to try to finish it. This gave me my chance, and after one burst I flicked up into a vertical roll, as though my controls were smashed, then kicked hard to bring me in behind him, and suddenly there he was, in my sights, breaking left to escape. But left was slower; he'd made a mistake and he knew it. I fired a full deflection burst which I saw hitting all around his cockpit. Then his head jerked and I knew he was hit. Straightway he went out of control and into a spin, falling down and down until he vanished into cloud far below.*

I didn't follow him. I knew he was hit, but also knew he was alive, because his spin was neat and controlled, not the spin of a dead man. But my engine was shot and my controls ruined so I had to head home. I wondered if we'd ever meet again, feeling somehow a sense of completion between Manfred and me. I turned the SE5 to the west but felt so tired all of a sudden I could barely hold the controls. Blackness came over me like a blanket; I felt my hands and feet go heavy and my head fill with darkness. I didn't want to go back to Noyelette. I had no strength left for the evil searching for me there. I didn't want to fight any more. I wanted to fly home to Ma. And lie in the sun, and not think about anything ever again.

In the meantime my own dogfight had gone. Vanished. Not a single aeroplane in sight. I couldn't believe it. Circling round the empty sky, my torn wing flapping, the Vickers pinging with heat and my heart still banging madly, not a soul was to be seen. It didn't seem possible. One moment we'd been ten aeroplanes chasing round the sky like gnats in a jar, the next none. One, rather, which was me. And then Archie opened up so I went home.

Clough's wingman was already safely down, although his oil-tank had been holed. Clough was gone, he said, crashed in flames; as for Mac he had no idea, nor did he know about Germans, although he thought he'd hit one. I waited, pacing the grass anxiously. Dogfights, Mac had said in the library. They're about height and position, they happen very fast, and they're over before you know it. To win them you must react, not think. Think and you're dead. I thought of the last moment I'd seen him, locked in mortal combat with the most feared aerial killer in the world. Had they been thinking? Or only reacting?

Five minutes dragged by, ten. Finally I heard the splutter of an engine, and a moment later he appeared over the trees, trailing smoke. He landed heavily, swerving to a halt in the middle of the field. I set off at a run, and when I reached him his head was back, his eyes staring skyward. 'Mac!' His engine was still ticking over. I leaned in and switched it off. 'Mac, are you hurt?' But he just stared up at the clouds as though in a trance. Behind I heard the tinkle of the fire-tender bell, and suddenly I was back at Brooklands, holding Bertie's broken body. 'Mac, for God's sake, can you hear me!'

'Let them come, George,' he murmured. 'I can't fight no more, let them come.'

'Mac, are you hit?'

He shook his head. 'Tired.'

I saw him safely back to dispersal and up to his room. There he stood, swaying, staring at the bed as if seeing it for the first time; then he crawled on to it, fully clothed, and hunched up against the wall, clutching his shaking arm. I talked, but he was beyond conversation, so I pulled off his boots and crept to the door.

'Your watch,' he whispered.

'I'm sorry?'

'Lost. So beautiful.'

'Not to worry now, Mac, we'll look for it later. Try and get some sleep.'

I closed the door. Downstairs Fothergill was waiting.

'How is he?'

'Resting, sir.'

'Thank heavens. I hear it was Richthofen's mob.'

'Yes, sir. I think we got one of them.'

'Good. Clean up, then come and have a drink. I expect you could do with it.'

'Yes, sir, I could.'

'Very well. By the way, do you know any Americans?'

'I'm sorry?' A chill ran through me.

He flapped a sheet of paper. 'Directive from the War Office. All American nationals serving with the Allies must identify themselves immediately.'

'Why?'

'Something to do with being officially reclassified, now America's in the war. The directive says they've fourteen days to come forward, after that they'll be considered illegal combatants and face the consequences. Shot at dawn, I suppose that means.'

'I see.' I hoped he was joking.

'I know of a few Americans in other units, and there's that whole squadron serving with the French, but I've not heard of any round here, have you?'

'No, sir. Not that I can think of.'

'Good-oh. Thought I'd better check. I'll circulate the memo just in case.'

'Right.'

'It's all my fault,' he went on, eyeing the stairs. 'Mac. I should have grounded him, you know. Should have ordered him to stop flying.'

'Flying is all he has, sir. All he is.'

'That's not what I mean. Those journalists. Trenchard's publicity campaign. I've had a telegram. They're coming early. They'll be here tomorrow night.'

'Christ.'

'Indeed. What if we'd lost him today?'

There'd be no publicity campaign, that's what. They'd have to find someone else to be their hero.

I headed outside, feeling dazed and dizzy. Half an hour ago I'd been fighting for my life, now journalists were coming, Americans being identified, Canadians closing in, everything was happening so fast. I needed time to think, time to review possible options, time to come up with a plan. But there was no time and no plan. In twenty-four hours Mac would be exposed and handed to the authorities to face desertion charges, or worse. I had to get him out before they arrived. But how? And where? A hospital perhaps, but Fothergill would have to know, and the authorities would soon trace him. Smuggle him out then, in Emily's ambulance perhaps, to Calais and a hospital ship for England. But without clearances? Without paperwork? And then what? Where would he go? What about a hide-out, a temporary bolt-hole until something better could be arranged? Rumours abounded of infantry deserters living rough in the woods. But how to make contact with them? And would Mac cope? Would he even agree to go? Let them come, George, he'd said. Let them come, I can't fight no more.

I sat on the step and watched a breakdown truck tow his aeroplane away. 'How is it?' I asked the driver, as it passed.

'Buggered,' he replied. 'A total write-off. It's a wonder he made it home at all.'

'What will happen to it?'

The mechanic shrugged. 'We'll strip it for spares, then strike it from the register, and that's that.' He looked at me curiously. 'Aren't you his friend? The one from 13 Squadron, back in the winter?'

'That's right. George Duckwell. You look familiar too.'

'Arthur Finlay. His mechanic.'

'I remember.'

'He's in a bad way, isn't he. End of his tether.'

'I'm afraid so.'

'Poor bastard. I've seen it before. In the trenches.'

We studied the wreck. Battered and broken beyond hope, it seemed perfectly to embody Mac's own condition.

'So that's that, you say,' I said. 'The aeroplane. Once it's written off.'

'Totally. Once it's off the register, it don't exist.'

I got Finlay to drop me over at Le Merignac where I spent the evening with Emily and her friends. It was a still, airless night, but an oddly peaceful one. A calm before the storm. All the FANYs and medical staff dined together around a big table in the refectory. The fare was simple but wholesome, the mood companionable. Everyone was tired, but morale was strong – clearly Emily and Captain Ashton had moulded an efficient and close-knit team. Afterwards everyone dispersed

301

to their various duties. Emily and I wandered out into the sultry air, heavy with the scent of jasmine, and sat on a bench in the garden watching swallows scythe through the night.

'Hear that?' she said.

'No guns.' I nodded. 'An hour or two of peace perhaps?'

'That would be nice.'

'You're doing incredible work here, you know. All of you. It's astonishing.'

'We could do with a break. I'm desperate to get over to Noyelette.'

'He's had it, Emily. Mac has. He's finished. And they're coming tomorrow.'

'Then we must act now. Right away.'

'Yes. I suppose so.' A dull buzz was starting in my head.

'What about help? Phyllis will do anything. James Ashton, too, probably, if I ask.'

'Finlay's a good man, too, we can count on him. But not Fothergill. He's a stickler for the rules.'

We stayed outside on the bench together, talking, planning, pondering in silence. At one point she rested her head on my shoulder and we dozed, like pensioners in a park. Then we awoke and talked on. By dawn we knew what had to be done.

She drove me back to Noyelette in her ambulance, expertly propelling it through sleeping villages and country lanes overhanging with trees. Calm now, composed, wearing her FANY uniform and gauntlets, she looked wonderfully serene, fully in control, every inch the unit commander.

'What will you do?' I asked her. 'Afterwards.'

'Stop all this. Find somewhere quiet. In the countryside. You?'

'God knows.' I rubbed my throbbing neck. 'Depends what happens I suppose.'

She glanced across. 'Are you sure about this, George? About what we're doing.'

'No. But we're doing it anyway.' I forced a grin. 'It is one hell of a gamble.'

'Something you're rather good at, as I remember.'

'Lucky at cards, as they say . . .'

'You mustn't think like that. I chose him because he needed me more. We needed each other more.'

'You don't have to explain.'

'Yes, I do. Because you're a good man, and I'd have been proud to be with you.'

She dropped me behind the chateau. I climbed the stairs to my room, pausing to look in on Mac. He was as I'd left him, curled on the bed in his clothes. His breathing was rapid, his eyes like slits. I whispered his name but he gave no response, so I peeled off his jacket and covered him with a blanket. Back in my room I drank water and lay down to doze, my whole body hot and aching. Then at nine I rose, dressed in full uniform, Sam Browne belt and side-arm, and began my preparations.

Beginning with Finlay. Once it's off the register, he'd said, it ceases to exist. From his words Emily and I had formed our plan. I found him in the hangar, sweating over a dismembered SE5 engine.

He glanced up. 'Morning, Captain. Looks like another sticky one.'

'Yes, it does.' I checked we were alone. 'I need a Bathtub, Sergeant. Tonight.'

'Beg pardon?'

'An FE2. One of 13 Squadron's. I shall need it left outside their hangar, fuelled, oiled and ready to go. Around sunset.'

'Should be all right, sir.' He tossed his spanner in a tray. 'With the proper authorisation of course. I'll speak to their engineer.'

'That won't be possible. It's a hush-hush job you see. No one must know. And no paperwork.'

'No paperwork? I never heard of such a thing.'

'You have now. Nor will I be bringing the aeroplane back.'

'Now hold on just a minute—'

'You'll have no responsibility, nor will you be implicated in any way. You simply arrange to leave it outside when they lock up. The rest is down to me.'

He stared incredulously, lips working, then shook his head. 'No, sir. Sorry. Can't do it. They'd have my guts.'

The air in the hangar was stiflingly close, my shirt already wet on my back.

Finlay took a cigarette from his tin and lit up, watching me closely. 'Are you all right, Captain? You don't look too well.'

'It's nothing. Just a headache. Listen, Sergeant—'

'This is to do with Mac, isn't it?'

'Yes. Yes it is.' And because I had no choice, and because I had no time, I told him, pretty much everything. He listened and smoked and spat on the floor, and when I was finished he said nothing, just stared at his feet, head shaking.

'You're asking a lot, Captain,' he murmured at last. 'I mean, it's stealing a bloody aeroplane. If I get caught . . .'

'I know, Arthur.'

'I can't,' he said after another pause. 'At least I can't promise anything. All I can say is, if it can be done, if there's an aeroplane outside the hangar at sunset, then it's on. If it isn't then it isn't. That's the best I can do.'

Afterwards I wandered into the daylight, feeling light-headed and feverish. The air seemed insufferably humid and oppressive, and heavy with the threat of thunderstorms. By now I knew I was ill, probably with the flu-bug everyone was down with, but there was no going back. In just hours flash-bulbs would be popping in Mac's face, together with impossible questions posed by journalists. Tell me, Lieutenant, where in Canada were you born? What about family life, what does your father do? Is it true you fought at Ypres with the Canadian infantry? Which unit exactly? He wouldn't last five minutes, and as if to emphasise the point the final straw was waiting for me at the chateau. A-Flight was grounded for the day, having effectively lost both Clough and Mac, which was just as well, for flying was the last thing I needed.

I stepped into the cool of the hall, making for the stairs and bed. As I crossed the threshold an infantry sergeant pushed past going the other way.

'Excuse me!' I snapped tetchily.

'Sorry, sir, didn't see you.' Canadian voice, vaguely familiar.

'Just a minute. Don't I know you?'

'Shouldn't think so, sir.'

'What are you doing here?'

'Came to see someone. One of the pilots. But he's asleep, kind of, out cold. Anyway, must dash, sir, got a tender waiting.'

He stepped back and threw up a hasty salute. And as he did so I saw it, clear as day, shining like a beacon, right there on his wrist. Hugh's Breitling. And suddenly I remembered standing in a vehicle compound in the moonlight with Mac, and a quartermaster sergeant approaching from the shadows. Dan Burton, is that you, he'd said. And then everything fell into place, and calmness came over me like a breeze, like when the stakes suddenly double at the table, and everyone goes quiet, and you know it's all just a matter of nerve.

I wanted to kill him. I wanted to draw the Colt from my hip and empty it into his head. But I didn't.

'Goodness, Sergeant,' I said, as amiably as I could, 'that certainly is a fine watch. Where on earth did you get it?'

'This? I bought it. Off a friend.'

'Bought it, you say? Perhaps you might consider selling it again, then?'

'Well, sir, not really . . .'

'I have thirty.'

'Thirty quid? Not likely!'

'In cash. And this fine silver cigarette case, with a Zeppelin on it, see? Aspreys of London. The best.'

He stepped nearer, peering at the case. 'Very nice too, but—'

'It certainly is. And have you ever seen one of these?' I produced the Colt. 'It's American, a Colt, the finest side-arm in the world.'

He fingered the gun lovingly. 'Handsome it is too, sir, no doubt about it. Still—'

'I'll cut you for it.' It was my final trump. The irresistible lure of a punt.

'Eh?'

'The watch. There's a pack of cards right here in the lounge. I'll cut you, straight cut, highest wins. If I win I get the watch, and you get the cash, the case and the Colt. If I lose, you still get everything, and I get nothing.'

'Well . . .'

'And I won't report you for blackmailing an officer. You have my word.'

I shuffled, we cut, he lost, I made sure. But he knew he had the better deal, and departed without fuss. I couldn't have cared less. I had my watch, the rest was trinkets, and in a few hours what he knew, or thought he knew, would be irrelevant.

I strapped the Breitling to my wrist and set its chronometer. The clock was running. Like a bomb. Then I climbed the stairs and collapsed wearily on to my bed. But sleep wouldn't come, just a nightmare kaleidoscope of dreams and illusions endlessly circling my fevered mind like a film-loop. Pilots jumping in flames from their aeroplanes, Bertie's limp body, Raymond's plea – 'the missus' – Emily sobbing over the bed, Hugh holding a white flag on a stick, Ann's wide-eyed shock, Mac, head back, staring into space like a corpse. And all the while the air grew thicker, and thunder grumbled in the distance, and the sweat poured from my body in hot rivulets.

Around six I forced myself to rise and shave, penned one note to my parents and another to Fothergill, and dressed in full flying gear. The hall downstairs was deserted, outside the air weighed heavy, solid and unmoving, and the airfield was silent, all flying cancelled for the approaching storm. I went to stores and signed out for a can of petrol and a Webley pistol to replace the Colt. As I returned I could see 13 Squadron's hangars were locked shut, but a lone Bathtub stood outside. Finlay had come through. Another rumble of thunder came, louder this time, and lightning flickered. A wave of dizziness engulfed me then passed. Fothergill and the journalists were due any minute. It was time.

Mac was still on his bed, but awake seemingly, on his back, staring at the ceiling.

'Mac?' I sat down beside him. 'Mac, come on, we're going.'

A blink. Nothing more. No response, no recognition, just a blink.

'You see, Mac, we have a mission to fly together, just you and me. A very special mission, top secret. But we have to hurry, or else we'll miss it.'

Still he showed no reaction, and from outside came a louder thunderclap, followed by the unmistakable crunch of wheels on gravel.

I bent to his ear. 'Danny! You have to come right now. Mother's waiting.'

We took off as the first raindrops were falling. Within minutes we were flying through a deluge, the sky thick and dark, churning with turbulence, and lightning bursting all around. The poor Bathtub was tossed about like a leaf; it was all I could manage to hold the thing upright. Flying it again felt eerie, especially in my fevered state: I became convinced I was still with 13 Squadron, and the last few months had all been a dream. With each lightning flash the hunched figure of Mac kept changing into Morris or Raymond or a host of other observers, and ghostly images of Pfalzes and Fokkers rushed at me from the boiling clouds. Navigating was practically impossible. I had Emily's map but it was useless, soaked in seconds. I could see nothing in the rain, all I could do was hang on, keep low and follow instinct, and the occasionally glimpsed landmark.

We pressed on, the sky went from brown to black, water poured at us as though from a hose. My head was spinning, my throat raw, my hands felt like balloons on the controls, my feet like lead. Another flash came, blindingly close. Trees and fields seared on to my eyes. I glimpsed a road, a meadow, a stream overhanging with trees. This was it, I'd found the place. Mac recognised it too. He turned to me, his face glistening with rain, his expression questioning.

'What are we doing?' he yelled above the tumult.

'Getting you out! Getting you to safety!'

'No!' And he launched himself at me, fighting furiously for the controls.

Chaos ensued. In seconds the Bathtub was on its side. Mac slipped and nearly fell. I grabbed at him, scrabbling for his collar while his legs hung in space, but I couldn't hold him and fly as well, and suddenly I only wanted to hold him, so I let go the controls and clasped his arms. And he grasped mine and our eyes met, and he smiled, and mouthed my name, and the Bathtub rolled over and dived for the ground.

Chapter 11

To Senior Air Officer Commanding, Arras Sector, His Majesty's
Royal Flying Corps. From Major Charles E. Fothergill OC 166
Squadron, Noyelette, Arras Sector. September 19th 1917.

Sir, I write regarding your request for further information
concerning the loss of Flight Lieutenant William MacBride of
this unit. I apologise for the delay in replying, obtaining the
necessary statements and affidavits from those involved has
proved a protracted matter, further complicated by sickness and
redeployment issues. I am however now satisfied all the
available facts are to hand.

In summary these are as follows:

At approximately 1900 hours on July 30th, Flight
Lieutenant William MacBride, accompanied by Captain
George M. Duckwell DSO, also of this unit, took off from
Noyelette airfield in an FE2b observation aircraft. The weather

conditions were unsuitable, with low cloud, heavy rain and intense thunderstorm activity. Lt. MacBride was piloting the aircraft with Capt. Duckwell as passenger/observer. At approximately 1930 hours the aircraft crashed and caught fire in the St Pol vicinity, four miles south-west of Arras. Capt. Duckwell suffered some burns and injuries, Lt. MacBride unfortunately was killed. Both the aircraft and his remains were virtually destroyed by fire, thus the exact cause of the crash is impossible to determine, but is assumed to be lightning-strike to the airframe, compounded by the particularly unsuitable flying conditions.

Following my enquiries, the following additional information has come to light:

The FE2b aircraft in question (serial number D1876) was assigned to 13 Squadron, which is also based at this airfield. 13 Squadron, as you know, is currently operating without an Officer Commanding, and with a reduced staff owing to operational losses and the influenza epidemic. Having interviewed the Adjutant and Duty Officer however, I am satisfied that none of 13 Squadron's personnel were aware of Lt. MacBride's use of the aircraft. In short, he appears to have taken it alone and without permission. This assumption is corroborated by Capt. Duckwell's statement (attached) which attests that he observed Lt. MacBride taxiing the aircraft, while watching the thunderstorm from his bedroom window. As Capt. Duckwell and Lt. MacBride were close associates, Capt. Duckwell then ran out to remonstrate with Lt. MacBride, but was unable to dissuade him from taking off. He then elected to board the aircraft with Lt. MacBride, rather than let him fly alone, an act of commendable fortitude in my view.

Why Lt. MacBride took the aircraft remains a mystery. He left no note or explanation, nor was Capt. Duckwell able to ascertain his reasons. However the following factors may have relevance:

1) It was not unusual for Lt. MacBride to fly solo missions in the evenings.

2) Despite his operational successes, Lt. MacBride had been under much strain in the period leading up to his loss.

3) Capt. Duckwell in his statement (para 7) reports that Lt. MacBride had been speaking and acting irrationally in the days prior to his loss.

4) Lt. MacBride was of a shy and retiring nature and exhibited particular anxiety when told of the RFC publicity campaign being organised on his behalf.

In conclusion it is my view that Lt. MacBride took the aircraft whilst the equilibrium of his mind was disturbed by over-work and anxiety. The possibility he crashed it deliberately cannot be ruled out. I appreciate that as an important component of the RFC's recruitment effort, a top-scoring 'ace', and a future public luminary, this explanation will not be acceptable to the RFC, nor the wider public. (I note German newspapers claim he was shot down by Richthofen's circus.) I humbly suggest therefore that his death be recorded as 'killed in action whilst on a secret mission' or somesuch similar, and also that he be accorded every honour befitting a pilot of his stature and record. A low-key approach might also be appropriate.

My apologies once again for the delay compiling this report.
Respectfully,
Maj. Charles E. Fothergill OC 166 Squadron.

*P.S. Notifying his next of kin is not proving straightforward.
Lt. MacBride transferred from the Canadian Infantry to the
RFC in early 1916. I have written to them asking for contact
information but as yet have received no reply.*

No, I didn't write Fothergill's report. He did. I just filled in
a few gaps.

I sent him my statement from a hospital bed in Gravelines,
a few miles up the coast from Calais. The burns and bruises
I'd received in the crash were indeed trivial, however the ill-
ness I had contracted most certainly wasn't, and laid me low
for nearly three months. It turned out to be the precursor of
the infamous Spanish influenza pandemic that would sweep
the world over the next year or two, ultimately killing an
estimated forty million people, and going down as the worst
plague in history. All I knew was I spent weeks moving from
hospital to hospital in a delirious daze, before finally coming
to my senses in Gravelines.

Of that last night with Mac I remember only fragments, a
surreal series of snapshot images and sounds. An appalling
crash in a field. Staggering from the wreck, blood pouring
from a gashed brow. Rain drumming on my head like thunder.
Screaming frantically for Mac. Sitting on the waterlogged
ground, holding him, our blood mingling with the rain. The
ambulance finally arriving, Emily and Phyllis lifting his body
on to a stretcher, then carrying a blanket-wrapped bundle to
the wreckage. Me sloshing petrol everywhere, and trying to
light it with a soaked rag, the muffled thump of explosion,
and orange flames leaping skyward through the deluge. Then
I too was on a stretcher in the ambulance. My last image is of

Mac lying motionless beside me, while I tried desperately to reach across the void to touch him. Then everything went black.

Time passed, the flu spread like wildfire, we the infected had quickly to be isolated for fear of passing the contagion to the troops. I was moved from pillar to post, occasionally surfacing from delirium to find myself in a new bed, in a different hospital, in yet another town. Each time I awoke, terrible fear would clutch at me and I'd cry out in terror, yet not know why. I sensed something dreadful had happened which was my fault, and began to associate my condition with failure and powerlessness. More time passed, I kept being moved, no one knew where I was, no messages or mail found me, no word came from anyone. I was a log adrift on a river.

Then I arrived at the Gravelines infirmary and began at last to recover. Word came I was to be repatriated, which felt like both good and bad news, but another week passed and nothing happened. Then one morning I received a visitor, a tall, striking young woman in FANY uniform, introducing herself as Hermione Clayton-Wells. She was deputy commandant of the Calais Richelieu unit, she said, and a close friend and former associate of Emily's. She had news for me, received in a letter. Emily and Phyllis were both well, she said, our mutual friend however was still poorly, and improving only slowly. Nothing else. I wasn't sure what this meant, but after Hermione left I spent the rest of the day searching the clogged corridors of my mind for clues. Slowly some surfaced, and by dusk I had pieced most of them together.

That night I lay awake listening to the waves breaking on the beach outside, and weeping like a baby. I couldn't stop and didn't try, much to the consternation of my fellow room-mates. I wept for Hugh my lost brother, and Bertie my fallen friend. I wept for Raymond Gates, his widow Ann and their children. I wept for the scores of faceless unknowns I'd met at Noyelette, I wept for the poor bloody infantry still dying in droves in the trenches. I wept for my mother, I even wept a little for my father. I wept buckets for poor old George and everything he'd been through. And I wept for Mac and Emily whose plight I felt most acutely of all. I loved them both, I finally admitted, and at last understood what that really meant. But by dawn I was done weeping and felt able to approach the new day with hope and clarity. I don't want to be repatriated, I told the medics, I want to recuperate here in France, then return to active service somewhere, although not Noyelette. Flight testing perhaps, or even instructing.

A week later I was sitting bundled up on the veranda, busily filling in my report to Fothergill, when Hermione visited again, this time with a longer letter from Emily. Still carefully encoded, still cautious and circumspect, I was at last able to learn the full story.

Mac had received a bad head-wound in the crash. This was certainly not in the plan, but ultimately played into our hands. Originally Emily and I intended only to remove him from Noyelette, under sedation if necessary, and take him to a place of safety until something better could be worked out. In the meantime we would fake his death. In this way his pursuers would be thwarted, and he could safely disappear.

Emily showed me a place on the map where she and Mac had once spent an afternoon. I was to fly him there in the Bathtub, and she and Phyllis would take him away in the ambulance.

That's more or less what happened. Having tended to his wounds, they removed his uniform, discs and papers right there at the crash-site, placing them with the body of the unknown boy we'd sat with two nights previously. Then the petrol was poured and ignited. By the time the burned-out Bathtub was discovered next day, little was left of his cremated remains but scorched discs and a few scraps of uniform, sufficient only to identify him as Mac. In due course he would be buried with full military honours, as per Fothergill's suggestion.

Mac and I meanwhile were in a side-room at the monastery. Apart from the head-wound, he'd also broken an arm and cracked several ribs; I was less seriously injured but in fantasy-land with the fever. The day after the crash Major Boulter visited and filled in the necessary paperwork: me for immediate transfer to an isolation unit, Mac just one more unidentified soldier with a head-injury. He remained there a week, during which time he showed no sign of regaining consciousness, then as I began my tour of Picardy's flu hospitals Emily went to work on her part of the plan, meticulously obliterating him from existence.

Anonymous soldiers were her passion and speciality. She'd mourned hundreds, now she was creating one, moving Mac from place to place, constructing identities then changing them, swapping discs and files, removing documents, obfuscating, confusing and erasing, until he vanished in the multitude like a snowflake in a blizzard. From the monastery he went to the crypt, from the crypt to a French military infirmary outside Basseux, from Basseux it was back to the monastery, then a convalescent home in Duisans. For a while his identity settled there as Daniel Friett and he wore the damaged discs of an Alsatian foot-soldier found in the box at the dressing station. His eyes opened and he began taking nourishment, but he uttered no words. Then discharge papers released him on medical grounds and he became Daniel De-Fries the immigrant farmer, injured by falling masonry in Arras, and living in a home for the infirm in nearby Simencourt. Emily visited daily. After a month he was on his feet, slowly walking the grounds with her, but still showing no recognition and still not talking. Major Boulter visited together with a neurologist from Paris; they said mental breakdown was probably the cause of his condition, not the injury, and that only time and patience could eventually bring recovery. It was then that Emily wrote to FANY headquarters in London and gave her notice, saying she wanted to devote her energies to campaigning to end the war, and spend time with a friend who needed care. The FANY, she said, had been the best thing to happen her, adding that Phyllis Mason should be given charge of the monastery. A fortnight later she left Le Merignac, collected Mac from the infirmary and moved into a cottage on a neighbouring farm.

That was in late September. I received her letter a week later, together with a bundle of mail that had been chasing me round France for weeks. Included among the bar-bills and chatty epistles from my mother were three items of

317

particular interest. Yes, three. The first was a newspaper clipping from *The Times*, sent by my father. Anonymous sources in Germany, it said, had discovered that Manfred von Richthofen, the so-called Red Baron, scourge of the skies, with sixty Allied kills to his credit, had some weeks earlier suffered a head-injury during a dogfight with a British scout. The clipping went on to say that despite German assurances to the contrary the injury was sufficiently serious to require several weeks' hospitalisation, and the Baron was only now returning to limited duty.

I re-read the clipping with casual interest, then my eye caught the date. The date of the action in which he was injured. It was the same date 166 Squadron had tangled with his Jasta. The day Mac and him had locked horns. The day of our final mission together. I sat back in astonishment. Mac had got him, I realised. He'd winged the master-warrior, driven him from the field of battle. It couldn't be anyone else. Richthofen was too good, he'd said after their first encounter, he was too good, and he got away. But he was wrong. Mac was better. I gazed out to sea, replaying those frantic minutes in my head. I too had squirted my guns in Richthofen's direction, I remembered, as he and Mac had raced by. It was even tanta-lisingly possible I'd fired the shot that got him, and what a delicious notion that was for a sickly chap.

The second item of interest was a letter from Ann Gates. Its contents were private and I'm not going to recount them. Suffice it to say she'd guessed there was more to my story about Raymond's death than I'd let on. And about the money I'd given her. But I wasn't to worry about it, she said, she knew a good man when she saw one. Her letter meant a great deal. It also set in motion a friendship that continued for years.

The third item was a letter from America.

Dear Reverend Canard-Puis,

I am most highly grateful for your letter bearing such welcome tidings of our distant relative in France. I can't tell you what a happy relief it is to know he is alive.

Your letter reached us at a most relevant time. Our mother was took sick with the melancholy more than a year ago, and my sister and me have been caring for her. At times we feared greatly for her life, so low was her spirits, but following delivery of your kind letter her spirits have been greatly revived and she is on the road to recovery, thank the Lord. She reads your letter aloud every day.

With regard to our situation, these is not easy times. Our father died suddenly more than three years ago and our brother had to leave home to find work to support us. At first the coroner was troubled by our father's death, but Doctor Petersen made inquiries and it lately come to light that our father had a heart condition from childhood and so the matter can finally be laid to rest. Doctor Petersen has been a wonderful support to our family in its troubles.

Although the matter is now closed, these are troubled times in our community so our brother must know he can't return to Jackson to find work but should maybe settle somewhere else and write us from there. It is my sisters and mine most heartfelt desire that we move our mother away from Jackson and begin our lives again. Reuniting with our brother some day is our greatest hope of all.

Please give our relative in France our dear wishes. Tell him
not to worry, we are managing just fine, and dearly hope to
meet him one day.

I trust this letter finds you well, Reverend, God bless you for
all your help.

Sincerely,

Martha Warburton.

A couple of weeks later, fed up with hospitals and feeling
well enough to travel, I donned my uniform and tottered off
to the railway station. Covering the fifty miles to Arras took
all day, much patience and not a little cash, but by evening a
taxi was finally dropping me at Le Merignac. I stood at the
monastery gate a minute, catching my breath and relishing
the autumn stillness. No guns could be heard, only the soft
hiss of drizzle, and my feet rustling the leaves.

'What wonderful timing,' Phyllis said at the door.
'Everyone's here.'

'Everyone?'

'Yes. Major Boulter popped over to see James – Ashton
that is, our medical officer. And Emily's here, with Daniel.
And now you, just in time for tea.'

Daniel, she said. His real name. Emily had found him his
real name.

We took tea in an orangery behind the monastery. It was
disused and overgrown, its glass cracked from months of
bombardment, but nobody minded, it was just wonderful to
be there and see everyone looking so well and happy. Mac, or
Daniel as I learned quickly to think of him, had lost weight,
and a scar still showed above his ear from the crash, but he

looked more tranquil and composed than I had ever seen him. Nor did his arm shake, I noted. And the strength of his bond with Emily was obvious: side by side they sat, she tightly holding his hand in her lap while he looked on in admiration. She was radiant, quite the Emily of old, chatting gaily of the Vimto Valkyries and the rustic realities of life in their cottage. Even her accent slipped a little, back into the warm Shropshire burr I loved so much. To my horror she insisted on recounting, yet again, the story of our meeting, and my drunken entry through her window. Everyone duly fell about laughing, Captain Ashton and Phyllis, also clearly a twosome, exchanging smiles and knowing looks while Major Boulter guffawed like a genial uncle. Even Daniel chuckled.

He didn't speak much, but he did smile curiously in my direction from time to time. He didn't know who I was, I realised, and perhaps it was best that way. Earlier I'd given Emily the letter from his sister, saying I'd leave it to her when to show it to him. Thank you, she'd said, kissing me on the cheek. Thank you for saving him. I could only blush like a schoolboy, and thank her back.

They left France four months later, travelling by sea to America under their new (and final) married name of Daniel and Emily Frith. We stayed in contact by letter. They settled in Pennsylvania, joined in due course by his mother and sisters, who both married locally. Daniel recovered fully, became a successful farmer, then entered politics, eventually being elected to the Senate where he championed the cause of America's rural poor. Emily too campaigned, firstly to end the war, then for women's suffrage, then racial equality, sexual equality, workers' rights, you name it. They had two children, a girl named Ella after his mother and a boy called George.

I stayed in the Corps and went into flight testing, firstly at Orford Ness in Suffolk, then later at Martlesham, near Ipswich. I never flew in combat again, at least not in that conflict, preferring to devote my energies to improving aircraft for our crews. Stronger airframes, more reliable engines, better protection and armament, higher performance – these were the things I campaigned for. And parachutes, of course, I kept bashing away at that, and in the end finally won, albeit within weeks of the war's end in 1918. After the war I became a civilian test pilot working on the development of many famous aircraft including the Spitfire. I also started writing, becoming aviation correspondent for a number of newspapers and magazines, giving talks and penning books on the history of flight. When the next war came I rejoined what was by then the Royal Air Force, and saw action enough. But that's another story.

Daniel never spoke of his time in the Royal Flying Corps, Emily once said in a letter. Nor in fact of the three-year period from his father's death to us crashing by the stream that night. Effectively it was gone, safely buried deep within him somewhere, or better yet erased altogether. Emily told him who I was, in general terms, and that we'd once helped each other, but that was all, and though I missed the closeness of his friendship, and his unique insight into the world of flight, I was glad for him. God knows there's plenty I'd like to forget of that period. She asked me not to speak or write about him in his lifetime, and I readily agreed. Daniel Warburton had died in the trenches, William MacBride was a Canadian orphan who never existed, it was better to leave things that way. Meanwhile a man from Ontario called Billy Bishop was credited as Canada's top ace, and an Irishman named Mannock ended the war as Britain's.

Germany's, of course, was Manfred von Richthofen.

Postscript

One morning the following April, six months after we'd all had tea at Le Merignac, I was on my way by car to Sailly-le-Sec, an airfield on the Somme about fifteen miles east of Amiens. The purpose of my visit was to fly a captured German scout called a Halberstadt, a powerful little two-seater that had fallen into our hands following a forced landing. I was looking forward to this job, as opportunities to fly enemy aircraft were rare, and the Halberstadt particularly so.

Anyway, driving along, puffing my pipe and enjoying the spring sunshine, I stopped to ask directions at a checkpoint manned by an Australian machine-gun crew. Suddenly there was a whoosh and a Sopwith Camel thundered overhead, closely followed by a red Fokker Triplane. I could scarcely believe my eyes. It was him, Richthofen, without any doubt, on his own, miles from his lines, and flying very low in pursuit of his quarry. We stood watching in fascination as they careered away and vanished over a ridge, then to our astonishment they banked steeply round and started back, the Camel bobbing and weaving in desperation as Richthofen steadily closed in.

'Shoot at the bastard!' I yelled at the gawping gun crew. 'Don't just stand there, shoot!' But the gunners seemed rooted to the ground, mesmerised by the spectacle.

I was standing beside their gun, a Vickers .303 as fitted to the SE5, so I grabbed hold of the thing, swung it round and let rip with a burst. Nothing happened of course, and in seconds the two aircraft were lost from sight. But later in the day I learned it had been Richthofen we'd seen, and furthermore he'd been shot down and killed less than a mile from the spot. A Canadian pilot ironically had done the deed, one Captain Roy Brown of 209 Squadron in another Camel. Manfred managed to land, but died in his seat.

It was twelve months to the day since he'd shot me down over no-man's land.

That was the end of the Red Baron, and I thought little of the matter for more than forty years. But the 1960s brought renewed interest in his life and career, and particularly in his demise, which became a matter of hot debate. Roy Brown, enthusiasts argued, could not have shot him down, for postmortem results showed Richthofen was killed by a single bullet fired from below. Months of further argument followed, with experts pacing the site with slide-rules and theodolites trying to triangulate the spot from where the shot, which was confirmed as a .303 round, was actually fired. Finally a consensus was reached.

Guess what.